ADVANCE PRAISE FOR DOWNWINDERS: AN A

D0000761

"At its best, fiction reveals truths. In *Downwinders*, those lessons resonate to the next generation of Westerners who are struggling to keep the atomic era from coming full circle with the shipping of poisonous wastes to their desert homelands."
—Chip Ward, Author of *Canaries on the Rim: Living Downwind in the West*

"The authors skillfully weave carefully researched chapters on the background of atomic testing with a fictional plot that makes this compelling book not only a hell of a good read, but an incredibly important chronicle of the real toll of nuclear testing and a powerful reminder that we should be very skeptical of anyone who assures us of absolute safety. Frankly, there were so many chapters that got me in a big way, I had to keep putting the book down to bawl."
—Mary Dickson, journalist, creative director of KUED Public Television, and native Utahn diagnosed with thyroid cancer at age 29

downwinders

downwinders
AN ATOMIC TALE

CURTIS OBERHANSLY
DIANNE NELSON OBERHANSLY

BLACK LEDGE PRESS
2001

Published by Black Ledge Press, Salt Lake City, Utah:

All inquiries should be addressed to:
Black Ledge Press
P.O. Box 58009
Salt Lake City, Utah 84158 USA
www.blackledgepress.com

Publisher's Cataloging-in-Publication
(Provided by Quality Books, Inc.)

Oberhansly, Curtis.
    Downwinders : an atomic tale / by Curtis Oberhansly
and Dianne Nelson Oberhansly. -- 1st ed.
    p.cm.
    LCCN: 2001087177
    ISBN: 0-9707965-9-5

    1. Nuclear weapons--Testing--Nevada--Fiction.
2. Nevada--History--Fiction. I. Oberhansly, Dianne
Nelson. II. Title.

PS3565.B45D69 2001   813'.6
                QBI01-700142

Cover and book design: Victoria Hindley
Typeset in Sabon

Printed in the United States of America

FOR DOWNWINDERS EVERYWHERE

past, present, future

CONTENTS

DALLAS PARKER DID NOT ARRIVE WITH THE INTENT OF KILLING the old man, but it happened—not in slow motion like the movies would have it, but quickly, surely. The knife in, levered sideways and then out. Nothing technical about it. The windpipe cut, then a brief gurgling.

Afterwards, sitting there in that strange, darkened bedroom, Dallas tried to get used to the idea. He'd had no choice, he told himself, everything in this big house narrowing and narrowing until finally he'd picked up the knife and introduced this rough and clammy silence.

It was midnight or after. Pale light fell through a nearby window, enough for Dallas to see more than he wanted. Even the soft, blue netting of Jack Daniels diffused through his brain did nothing to dull the facts: an old man in a silk robe collapsed on the bed, one chalky leg stretched out from beneath the covers, and a bare foot sticking up, as unreal as a wax museum piece. The yellow, manicured toenails squared and buffed.

"Jesus Christ, mister. Why couldn't . . ." But all of his reproaches fell quickly away. Normally, Dallas didn't mull the unnegotiable past, much less talk with the dead. He was fifty-nine years old. A rancher, a horse trainer, a bachelor—a hard-boned realist—still strong and muscled. Tonight, however, he was dizzy, his knees soft as oatmeal. He needed to get up, get going, but he stayed sitting. Like some leaky faucet, the question kept repeating: What now?

Minutes stretched, then ebbed. Dallas reached into his shirt pocket and pulled out papers and tobacco, something he'd been doing since he was sixteen and never once tried to quit. He opened the pouch, tried to run a precise furrow down the paper crease, but his hands were trembling. He licked and closed the cigarette, finally struck a match, inhaled deeply, then again, calming.

If smoke had the power to soothe, it did not, however, have the power to hide that awful smell. Blood, raw and almost sour, mixing with Vicks VapoRub?

He tapped his ashes into his left hand and briefly considered their weightlessness. Made a few stark connections with his own life, then, wanting to avoid self-pity or the undertow of regret, he stood up, forced himself to move. It was an expansive master suite, full of art and crystal, typical of these country club homes near St. George, Utah.

He moved tentatively, circled the room to the walk-in closet, where he found a leather suitcase, solid cowhide, soft, rich, and worn. An old-fashioned satchel type, but it was the beginning of a plan, mostly scattered thoughts linked by urgency and fear. He picked up the suitcase, carried it into the room, and pulled the zipper open.

A heavy crystal dish glimmered on the dresser and Dallas reached for it, then reconsidered. The absurdity washed over him again, the whole idea of a robbery. Nothing else had come to him, though, and there were still a few things he had to protect, had to salvage from this night. He picked up an expensive-looking watch and a wallet, instead of the crystal, and dropped them into the suitcase.

He peered through an open archway into an adjoining study, dark except for the solitary eye of a glowing computer, a squadron of brightly colored, winged toasters flapping silently across its screen. He picked up the suitcase and moved toward it.

Turning the study lamp on to low, he searched the polished mahogany desktop next to the computer, but found nothing much—a fountain pen, a single letter. The drawers were neatly organized, even paper clips linked in a chain. On a wall behind the desk, the old man's ordered life hung silently in pictures, diplomas, and plaques. Dr. Franklin Rudd, M.S., University of Chicago; Ph.D., Massachusetts Institute of Technology. In the middle of the wall, printed on a scroll of aged paper edged with gold, a certificate of gratitude from the Nevada Test Site for all the years he'd served as manager. Here and there, black-and-white photos: men in lab coats, men with hard hats, everyone smiling. Grainy pictures of atomic explosions with hand-printed names below: Badger, Harry, Diablo, Grable. There was a host of other mementos and awards, but Dallas could see them for what they were—scraps of an old man's ego and power and selective memory.

He didn't know Rudd personally, only by reputation and various newspaper articles. Once, back in the fifties, he'd seen him give a speech. And then, earlier tonight . . .

Dallas sat down in the swivel chair facing the desk, those goddamned toasters still flapping endlessly. He was confused, discouraged. He slid his hand down his cheek and across his chin in a reflexive gesture that usually helped him to think, but all he felt was his wiry mustache and day-old beard. The dead—he'd heard that their beards keep growing; their finger-nails, too. Christ almighty, at this rate he'd be here to watch and find out.

He opened a couple of drawers in the mahogany desk, found nothing of value, and slammed them shut. The keyboard jumped, the toasters suddenly disappeared off the computer screen, and in their place a letter emerged. The first words he saw were centered in boldface type: PERSONAL AND CONFI-DENTIAL. He paused. It was from Dr. Franklin Rudd to a Mr. Frederick Manzelle, Verill Literary Agency, London, England. He hurried down the page, then went back and read it a second time, slowly.

Dear Mr. Manzelle:

Per our last conversation, I am now prepared to show you my manuscript. I will be in England in a few weeks and will have my attorney draft the appropriate agreements of confidentiality. As I explained, my autobiography, my inside story as manager of the Nevada Test Site during the 1950s and early 1960s, will blow the lid off the U. S. atomic testing program. It will finally tell the true story about the Atomic Energy Commission, what we knew about the fallout from these atomic test blasts, and when we knew it.

If your agency and I reach an agreement, you will be allowed access to the manuscript in a controlled environment of my choosing and given enough time to look at it and make your decision. For obvious reasons, I am dealing only with agents and publishers outside this country. I look forward to hearing from you.

Sincerely,

Dr. Franklin T. Rudd

What the hell did that mean, "blow the lid off" atomic testing? But Dallas had lived on the Utah-Nevada border all his life and had a feeling he knew exactly what that meant.

He rose, moved to a matching mahogany credenza, urging himself along now. Squatting down, he examined the lower doors, pushed one, and watched it spring open. Within, he saw the faint dials of a combination lock set in a small safe. He stood, looked at the pictures on the wall, scanned the area for any sign of numbers oddly out of place. Nothing. He reopened the desk drawers, a bit less tidy now after being slammed so hard, rifled through the contents, and closed them again. Then, in a small burst of inspiration, he retrieved Rudd's wallet from the suitcase and flipped it open: credit cards, driver's license, money, Red Rocks Club membership, and underneath them all, a card marked SureLock Safes, with explicit instructions, including the clearly hand-printed rights and lefts. Dallas returned to the safe and, on his third try, opened it. Inside was an assortment of jewelry, diamond rings, some keys, a packet of computer disks, and savings passbooks. And a three-inch thick, bound manuscript.

He sat down in the chair again and began going through the

manuscript, pausing over copies of photos, internal memos and documents all boldly stamped TOP SECRET and CLASSIFIED at the top and bottom. Without taking his eyes off the pages, he rolled another cigarette, more steadily this time.

Very quickly, the bits and pieces of the manuscript came together and a clear picture emerged. Finally, he slapped the pages closed and tamped his cigarette out on the expensive finish of the desk, scattering small embers, then dropped the manuscript into the suitcase. Going down on one knee, he scooped everything else from the safe and added it to his stash.

Standing up, he pulled the desk drawers open again and scattered their contents. With one swipe, he cleared much of the desk top, sending everything flying. He gazed at the computer screen for a moment and then gave it a solid right hook, a body shot, the same hard stroke he used on opponents years ago as a young man in the ten dollar smokers. There was a loud pop as the vacuum tube exploded inward. A small puff of smoke and a dark hole remained. Dallas peered into the smoldering cavity and was surprised at how empty it looked, at the lack of substance behind all that bustling imagery. Bright sequins of blood appeared on two of his knuckles. He had to admit this small bit of vandalism felt good and fit his new image as a robber. He knocked the monitor out of the way, jerked the hard drive off the desk and slammed it to the floor. It felt strangely comforting to be heading toward some kind of exit now. He turned off the desk lamp, hesitated, then grabbed it by the neck and threw it against the trophy wall, another bang and clatter in the dark followed by an airless silence. It occurred to him that his fingerprints were all over the place and, for the first time in several hours, he nodded with some degree of satisfaction.

Dallas walked out of the study and back into the bedroom, suitcase in hand. Any urge to talk to the dead was gone, completely gone. His only concern now was for the living. As he passed the bed, he paused one last time, grabbed a corner of the thick comforter, and pulled it up over the old man's head. At least whoever found the bastard wouldn't have to see everything all at once.

IT HAD TAKEN LONGER THAN EXPECTED TO DRESS THE PIGS. There were sixteen of them, Poland Chinas and Chester Whites, bristly haired and squealing, strong yearlings at 250 pounds each. Orders were to put them in uniform and get them transported.

The truck was a converted pea-green deuce-and-a-half on loan from the Army, a stiff and rumbling leftover from the last world war. The pigs were herded up a stock chute and onto the slippery metal bed, then the tailgate was dropped into place. Finally, just before one a.m., Jersey Alton, the driver, turned the truck north onto Mercury Highway, white smoke billowing as he accelerated, and headed toward Yucca Flat. They were running late and he was nervous, his palms clammy against the metal steering wheel.

The temperature had topped 118 degrees during the day and even now the heat continued to rise off the parched desert floor. There was no moon out and high cloud cover had stolen most of the stars, so that both ground and sky seemed composed of the same weightless blue-black. The truck's headlights poked two weak holes in the dark. A VIP sedan surprised Jersey as it quickly came up from behind, then whispered past without slowing and disappeared over a small rise. The truck gradually picked up speed, metal churning against metal as the cranky transmission labored through the gears.

"Hey, grind out another pound," said Nash, sitting in the middle of the cab. McVea, the big, irritable redhead who had recently transferred over from the road crew, was slumped against the passenger door, already trying to get some sleep.

At forty-five miles an hour the front wheels began to shake furiously and Jersey had to fight the steering wheel, yet he couldn't afford to slow down. Both cab windows were open, but Jersey still risked one quick hand off the shimmying wheel to pry back the window wing, twisting it all the way around to scoop in more fresh air.

Windows or not, the fetid sour of pig shit was planted there in the cab, smeared all over these three young civilians with low seniority who had been assigned the detail. For almost four hours they had wrestled pigs, forcing them one by one into custom-made army uniforms, trying to get each animal's powerful hind legs through short, boxy trousers. They had worked while Lard Ass Dumas, their boss, shouted futile instructions: "Tie those front legs down!" and "Get that spotted sonofabitch next." The pants were followed by jackets and, because pigs have no real necks, the collars slipped over their mouths, making them shake their heads crazily. As soon as they were dressed, the pigs began chewing the fabric—a bitter, green synthetic that the Army was testing for its durability under the most intense conditions—but as long as the damn jackets stayed on, more or less, the three exhausted pig dressers didn't care. And doping the pigs, Lard Ass had said, was out of the question because "the boys in science want these ani-mules alert" when the countdown reached zero.

Jersey pushed his foot harder into the stiff accelerator, tightening both hands on the steering, struggling against the heavy front tires that vibrated with a fanatic, high-pitched hum. A lone truck and trailer going back toward Camp Mercury blew heavily by as Jersey hugged his side of the road. He leaned forward to gulp more of the incoming air.

"Jesus, hang on, Jersey," Nash said. "Keep this double-clutchin', mudder-fuggin' truck on the road." He let out a war-whoop that woke McVea, who shifted his burly form, trying to find a comfortable position.

Jersey hadn't dared ask Lard Ass if they could wash up before getting on the road. They were running almost two hours late with the pigs and the last thing Lard Ass had said was, "Step on it. Get those bastards out there and unloaded." He loomed over Jersey—his gut alone weighed more than the skinny kid—and put his big puss right in Jersey's face. "And make damn sure you get the right pig in the right pen. Got your list? Screw this one up, kid, and you just as well stay out there with 'em."

Not that Jersey was known as any kind of screwup. In fact, it was his first time running a load just before a big test like this, and he'd discovered that it wasn't any privilege, especially with the clock ticking anxiously away. Shot Huey was scheduled for 5:30 a.m. Strobing green lights set high on poles around Camp Mercury and the outlying compounds indicated that everything was a go, that the countdown was on.

Jersey wanted to know why he had such rotten luck, got all the worst jobs. First it was the dogs, and now the pigs. "Lard Ass don't like me," he said. "Gives me every shit detail comes along." His voice quivered uncontrollably as he wrestled the wheel.

"Lard Ass don't like nobody," said Nash, "but hey, try singin' right now, you sound like one a them opera guys."

"Try bitin' my wire," Jersey said, and then backed off the accelerator until the front tires rolled out a little smoother. To hell with it, he wasn't going to shake his fillings loose for this lousy job.

"Butt me," he said, holding two fingers up to Nash for a cigarette.

Nash shook a couple loose and bent forward below the rush of hot air to light them with a flaming Zippo.

Pigs were only a small part of the daily routine for these three laborers assigned to the ranch compound. Other animal subjects were housed there as well: dogs, cows, cats, monkeys, birds, mice, sheep, burros. The one that usually interested visitors most was a live Holstein cow with a big hole in its side. A round, plastic-covered opening the size of a dinner plate served as a bay window into its guts, so anyone could peer in and watch the cow digest radioactive hay—just turn out the lights and spot glowing particles as they inched through the translucent intestines. It had the makings of a freak show, but for the guys living in Quonset huts at Camp Mercury, feeding and cleaning up after a bevy of animals was boring.

It was important work, they were told. They were helping to advance science. But when Lard Ass had temporarily assigned Jersey to the dog kennels, Jersey couldn't see advancement of any kind. Day after day, the dogs whined chronically, some of them dragging themselves back and forth across their cages in dazed, neurotic paths. They persistently scratched at the concrete floor and the corrugated wire pens, trying to dig themselves free, and Jersey worried that he'd never get that infernal rasping out of his head.

The place was called Block 33, a well-lighted, well-ventilated area where the postexposure dogs were housed for observation. The scientists and their lab technicians bustled back and forth making notations on clipboards. Jersey quietly changed the dogs' food and water and hosed out their cages twice a day. He tried going about his chores without looking at the dogs, but it was impossible. Some moved anciently with swollen joints while others' teeth fell out right in their feed bowls. Open sores erupted and most of them lost their fur, which came out in big clumps and lay in the bottom of the cages. Before it was washed away, the dogs would roll in it, as if they understood how naked and sad they looked, as if they were trying to get some of it back. By then, all aggression and instinct faded, and the dogs merely crept to and from their bowls, fleshy and pink as new mice.

The testing, he learned just in overhearing the lab assistants talk, was painfully simple. Like the other animals, the dogs were driven out and placed at predetermined distances from ground zero, left there in pens to be wild, barking spectators when the bombs went off. Afterwards, if they returned at all, they were monitored for various injuries and illnesses. In another set of complicated experiments, some of the dogs had been taught specific tricks—roll over, bark, shake hands. After the blast, they were tested to see what they remembered, but most of them had little desire left for parlor games. All this to see how soldiers would ultimately fare in a nuclear war.

At first when no one was looking, Jersey's reaction was to bend over and put his open hand out and talk soothingly to the dogs, "Hey, it's okay." But they didn't respond, just looked at him with watery eyes, and there wasn't much he could do for them, though he'd found that a black Lab, subject D-4-12, enjoyed his cigarette smoke. It would walk stiffly to the wire enclosure when it saw him, stick its muzzle forward, and wait for Jersey to sit down and light up, the feathery, white smoke floating like a ghostly breath between them.

The truck was rolling along quietly now, and Jersey took a long drag off his cigarette and held it. They crested a small rise and the lights of Gate 200 suddenly came into view, bright and seeming just within reach, but night or day, this desert was deceptive. Over thirteen hundred square miles of sand and rock, sage and saltbrush composed the test site, and under a bleached-out sun or floating in the liquid black of night, these expanses became soft and foreshortened.

"Boy, you two are a crack-up and a half tonight," said Nash, who yawned, then flipped his glowing cigarette butt hard out the window, over McVea's reclining head, sending a small shower of sparks cartwheeling into the dark. "A little ripe in here, ain't it?" Nash asked, laughing. "And let me tell you something, Jersey boy, Lard Ass don't treat you no different than the rest of us. Last week he damn near kicked Sid's ass clear up around his ears. You're just too sensitive for your own good, Jer-seeey."

Jersey looked at Nash and wished for the hundredth time that he'd disappear. The dials in the tin dashboard cast a sickly greenish light throughout the cab so that he could see the brown smears of pig shit on Nash's shirt and streaked down his arms. Jersey adjusted the window wing again, the heat and smells conspiring against his gag reflex.

McVea was still slumped in silence. In the back, the pigs were sliding and banging around, trying to get purchase on the slippery bed. Squeals and high-pitched wails resounded each time the truck took a dip or curve.

"Listen to them crazy sons-a-bitches," Nash said, leaning forward and stretching.

As if he'd received a sudden jolt, McVea sat up, turned to his two fellow workers, and bent toward the center of the cab. "Those pigs know what's in store for them," he said. "They're not stupid."

Jersey didn't care if pigs had brains or not. All he knew was that if he never saw one of these stinking animals again, it would be way too soon. They were belligerent, filthy beasts, though they were reputed to be smart. Even a skinny greaser kid from the East like himself knew one thing: these damn pigs were not going to be trained the way the scientists hoped. The original idea was not only to dress them in uniforms, but also to have them stand up, simulating men in combat, just as the countdown reached zero.

Nash kept grinning over at McVea, then slowly, snidely said, "Sid fed them used Kotex and they ate them. Fought over them, regular tug-a-wars. Some real smart animals, huh?"

It was mindless conversations like this that sent Jersey on a bus to Las Vegas two nights a week to attend dealer's school, though he had washed out the first time around because he couldn't add up his numbers quickly enough.

Gate 200 loomed dead ahead now. Jersey figured that once he passed through that gate, drove over the saddle, and started down toward Frenchman and then on to Yucca Flat, there would probably be a swarm of lights and activity around ground zero that would really get Nash lathered. Then the three of them would have the privilege of wading among the stinking pigs again, finding their ear-tag numbers and matching them to pens, cutting them out from the rest in pairs, and herding them down the chute into their own personal barbecue, as Nash put it. Some older guy would be out there waiting for them, pissed off and worried because they were late, cussing and giving them orders like Lard Ass, without lifting a finger to help. Hell with it. If all the pigs didn't get put out, they could fire him.

Finally Jersey slid the big truck into Gate 200, air brakes hissing, and cut the motor on a hand signal from a stocky Marine sergeant striding their way. The engine reluctantly died in a clatter of loose pistons. Except for the grunts of strapped and girdled pigs, an eerie hush shrouded the checkpoint—not the normal stillness of the desert at night, but something else, something imposed by guards and fences and technology. The sergeant approached the driver's side of the truck. His hard jaw alone seemed to maintain the silence. A hand-crank field telephone in the guard shack gave off a hollow burp of static.

"Step down," the sergeant said. "State your codes and present your ID."

Jersey and the other two men stepped out onto the truck's high running boards and swung to the ground. They stood hatless and squinting under the intense spotlights surrounding the gate, illuminating the truck and its contents, cutting a sharp circle into the black night. Nash took one last, long drag off his cigarette and dropped it, twisting the butt under his shoe. Jersey tried to pat his oily black hair, a swooping greaser cut, back into place, but it was too far gone. He was embarrassed to see his filthy Levi's and T-shirt in the white light.

The sergeant stepped back a couple of paces. "Jeesus. You boys are rather odorous tonight."

Jersey just kept looking at the ground, expecting Nash to come back with something smart, but he didn't.

The sergeant motioned four MPs forward and they swarmed around the truck, shining flashlights underneath, into the cab, and finally down into the bed. The pigs, black marble eyes glistening beneath the brims of green utility hats which had been jerry-rigged with straps and halters, looked up at them.

"Holy shit!" said a Marine perched on the slats of the truck.

Another broke out laughing to the excited murmurs of his comrades. "Wow, it's Porky and his pals go to war."

A young boar halfheartedly mounted a sow in pants who turned and shook him off.

"Hey, makin' bacon!" laughed one MP, while another encouraged, "Petunia, get it while you can."

"At ease up there," the sergeant snapped. Turning to Jersey, he said, "State your project code."

Jersey, by now more tired than embarrassed, glanced around and sighed, "Porcine Chorus Line." The various project scientists rarely missed an opportunity to amuse themselves, their Ph.D.'s and serious research barely transporting them, it seemed, beyond their boyhood decoder rings.

The sergeant pointed at the radio operator, who called in a clearance. A static-ladened "Affirmative" could be heard over guffawing from the command center. The sergeant walked around to the side of the truck and peered through the slats, trying to smother a grin of his own. "Is this vehicle secure?"

"Vehicle's secure, Sarge."

Muffled voices from MPs on the far side of the truck said, "These look like commies to you?" and "Amazing who they let in the Army these days," to another round of chuckles.

"Knock off the grab-ass," the sergeant finally barked.

McVea was now sitting on the running board with his big, bowling-ball head in his hands.

Jersey kept looking at his watch, trying to retain any shred of dignity. Their coworkers would already be showered and back at the commissary, which stayed open all night when there was a shot. A festive mood erupted in an otherwise serious Camp Mercury as people celebrated through the night, waiting for the grand-slam fireworks. This particular shot was rumored to be big, perhaps the biggest yet, and no one wanted to miss that. Jersey's buddies were no doubt sitting this very moment at a long, linoleum-topped table, drinking beer and placing bets on which pigs might survive. None of them would be covered with pig shit or pulling any kind of duty.

The Marine guards climbed down off the sides of the truck and walked back to their security posts.

"Reboard your vehicle, gentlemen," the sergeant said, checking his watch. "And, at this point, I would advise that you proceed with all due haste in dispatching your mission."

CHAPTER ONE

CHRISTINE PARKER HAD NO IDEA WHERE SHE WAS. SHE COULD tell you what the signs said and point to a spot on the map, but discounting these and gauging by her heart and mind, Christine was lost. The long night had passed, and in the bruised first light of dawn, she had finally run to ground in the only place open—Big Red's Cafe, St. George, Utah—where worry, lack of sleep, and caffeine had combined to make her half-crazy. The waitress, a talkative old heater in a stained white uniform and ruffled apron, walked over to Christine, rubbing the small of her back with one hand and carrying a coffee pot in the other. She was tiny, probably not quite five feet tall, and her hair, a platinum bun with bangs bubbled forward, looked like it had fallen and been resuscitated several times with hairspray. Across the knuckles of her left hand, in crude blue script, the letters L-O-V-E were tattooed.

"Honey," she said, "I don't know who the bastard is, but he better be worth plenty to be worth all this."

Christine looked up from the counter where she was sitting, a mile of chipped beige Formica punctuated by ketchup bottles. She was the only customer in this full-time coffee shop, part-time bus stop, and it was the waitress's third attempt at being friendly. "I'm sorry," Christine said. "It's really not . . ." and her eyes teared. She pinched a napkin from the stainless steel holder. "Excuse me, I'm not usually like this," she struggled to speak through the watery knot in her throat. And it was true—

she wasn't usually like this—but tonight more than a year of rotten luck piled up around her.

"Men," the waitress said, shaking her head, oblivious to what Christine had tried to say. "They're just about a no-win proposition. I should know." She cupped her free hand to the side of her mouth. "I've had three husbands, I'm dating a possible fourth, and still I'm trying to learn my lesson. Codependent as hell," she said. "Probably have a sex addiction, too. So whatever you're in the middle of, honey, it won't shock me."

Christine, momentarily stunned out of her own troubles, couldn't think of a reply, couldn't even quite understand what the woman was telling her. She felt like the satellite featured in the news recently that had been receiving signals from another galaxy. These might be intelligent messages or not.

The waitress grabbed a clean cup from under the counter and set it in front of Christine. "Here, let's can that old stuff. I just brewed a fresh pot." She glanced toward the kitchen and whispered, "Doubled up on the grounds. That watered-down bus stop junk is hardly worth the effort." She winked as she poured a new cup and carried the pot back to its hot plate. Normally, the thick, brisk smell of coffee was one of the small joys in Christine's life, but this morning there was not an ounce of pleasure in the first cup or any of the refills. She lifted the heavy porcelain mug to her mouth.

What she needed was Dallas, her uncle, not more coffee, not more aimless searching. She was worried sick about him, about the mess she had created. She couldn't just sit still. She had gone to his ranch well after midnight; Dallas wasn't there, and after a short wait, she left a rambling note and drove the thirty-five miles back to St. George, twenty of them over teeth-rattling county gravel.

In town, she cruised the broad, silent avenues, squinting through the pinkish glow of street lamps for Dallas's battered white pickup, nervously watching for patrol cars that might be scouting for drunks or burglars. There was no law against her driving at night, she thought defensively, but she watched the speed limit, nonetheless, and stopped fully at each sign. She was unfamiliar with anything other than the town's commercial strip, but no matter where Christine drove, there was always the St. George Temple towering as a landmark, a huge, spired beacon that rose unabashedly near the center of town. Against the night, it looked excessively white, lit up like some sixteenth century mosque where the work inside never stopped. Maybe they were baptizing the dead tonight. If the Mormons couldn't convert you during life, they sought you at random after death, cleaned your soul up, took you as one of their own. But even daredevil theology didn't hold much interest or amusement for her tonight.

All streets eventually led out to the edge of town and into the blackened desert. She knew the world was round, of course, but felt tonight that if she drove out into that long, ebbing darkness, she might drop off the edge. Turning back, braking occasionally to let a jackrabbit clear her headlights, she varied her route so as to be less conspicuous. She stopped at several outdoor pay phones, quickly got stiffed out of her only quarters by faulty return levers, and then had to call the ranch collect, and convince cranky operators sitting in Denver or L.A. to let the phone keep ringing. And ringing. She forced herself to periodically swing past the sheriff's office, searching for Dallas's truck or any sign of excited activity. Finally, she had to chance it, had to drive south of town to Vermillion Hills, through the clubby golf and tennis development where Dr. Rudd lived.

Even in shadowy moonlight, the yards there were huge and manicured, some decorated with the earnest lawn sculpture—plaster of paris deer, terra-cotta ducks—of retirees who couldn't quite afford Palm Springs. The streets were absolutely deserted. She crouched lower in her seat, feeling as if her obscure little silver Honda was ablaze in neon. She avoided Rudd's house, circling and doubling back on other streets named from some cruise brochure—Dominica, Bonaire, San Juan—until at last she found herself on Nassau.

Slowly, she drove past Rudd's walled stucco fortress in suburbia, not daring to look, but unable to avoid it. Nothing, absolutely nothing. No lights, no people walking around, no sheriff's cars nosed in at disorderly angles, no yellow police tape drawing a crowd to its boundaries. And no white pickup. Christine sped up and did not feel herself breathe again until Vermillion Hills fit into her rearview mirror and then disappeared.

Under the bright fluorescents of Big Red's Cafe, surrounded by the smell of ancient bacon grease mounding in hidden crevices, Christine tried to coax some logic back into her life. She had looked everywhere she knew to. What next? There were rules for solving an equation, steps to take in applying first aid. Even the waitress had retrieved the salt and pepper shakers from the tables, lined them up on the counter, unscrewed the lids, and was methodically filling them—salt, salt, salt, pepper, pepper, pepper. She kept her eyes on her work, but stayed close enough to Christine to continue her conversation.

"Tell you what the problem is. We're always thinking about them."

Christine surfaced out of her own thoughts. She watched the waitress stop pouring pepper for a moment, turn her head into her shoulder, and sneeze hard twice.

"Always thinking what men want, what makes men happy, whether men care about this or that." She screwed a lid onto a glass shaker, and walked toward Christine and looked earnestly into her face. "Know what you need to do?" she asked. "Take some time to feel *you*, honey. It's like a simplicity thing. Kind of Buddhist. Who are *you*? What do *you* want?"

Ordinarily those questions from a stranger would have made Christine squirm, but she understood that the waitress was not waiting for answers, was, in fact, just caught up in the goofy, self-help TV talk that had infiltrated even grocery checkout lines and hardware stores. Christine shook her head and smiled vaguely. "Thanks," she said. She stood up and smoothed the thighs of her jeans. "Save my place for me. Okay?"

The waitress made a show of looking around the empty cafe. "You bet," she said, and winked.

The pay phone was back in the musty hallway near the restrooms and Christine resumed her frequent calling. She waited for at least twenty rings, each one becoming more tinny and desperate than the one before, then hung up and simply stood there dazed, as if she were waiting for someone to call and tell her what to do, what to think, where to turn.

Dallas had been her saving grace for more than a month now. On leave from her teaching job in Phoenix, she had come to stay at the ranch with him, to talk and laugh and have good company. And to get away from home. She was only thirty-seven, too young, everyone said, to have the cancer she had been diagnosed with, and though the doctors talked optimistically now, she was tired of the fishbowl, of her family and their questions and their good intentions, their concern each time she coughed or had a headache.

Dallas, on the other hand, just let her be. He always seemed to sense exactly what she needed. In a way, she was the child he never had, the oldest of his brother's three children and the only one to be born out on the ranch. She had been two when her parents, Warren and Audrey, moved their little family to an easier life in Phoenix, but that shared beginning had connected uncle and niece in ways that negated time and distance. Each summer, growing up, she had returned to the ranch for a month-long visit, and each year she was taller—a permanent record laddered up the kitchen doorjamb where Dallas made her stand in her stockings with her shoulders squared, then etched another line and the year with his pocketknife. Each year she had made new friends, talked differently, saw the world composed of entirely new colors, but come July, the same old Dallas was always there, laughing and full of tricks, telling her that the two of them were made from the same stuff—stardust and bullshit.

When Christine returned from the phone, the waitress's back was to her. She was reaching into the pie case and shifting things around, humming something vaguely familiar. For a moment, Christine considered moving to a booth, just parking herself in some quiet blank space, but she didn't want to hurt the woman's feelings. Besides, what was she doing here but passing time, waiting for Dallas to show up somewhere, or for the police? She sat back down on the stool. She wasn't ready to imagine the possibilities.

"How about a piece of pie?" the waitress called over to her. "Sometimes a little sugar makes the world look a whole lot better."

"No. Thanks," she said. "Just coffee is fine." She only wished that a wedge of pie or a drippy glazed doughnut could turn this night around.

The waitress set a full pie down on the counter and began to blast away at it with a spray can of Reddi-wip. She stepped back, viewing the achievement, licked her fingers, then looked up and saw that Christine was watching.

Christine attempted a weak smile, and the waitress walked over and patted her hand. "Now don't you sweat it, honey, there'll be others. Moving on means letting go." She grinned saucily. "Hellfire, hon. I had your age and looks, I wouldn't be pulling graveyard shift, hustling quarters in a dump like this."

Her age and looks! Lord! Christine wondered if the woman could actually be talking about her, because since the surgery and chemo last year, she had felt so tired and ancient. She was getting stronger now, was thinner, and her finger-length hair was growing back in a burnished chestnut. Only her eyes seemed the same to her, green and deep set.

The waitress suddenly peered over Christine's head. "Oh shit, the bus is here!" She spun and headed toward the kitchen. "Billy Boy! Quit jerkin' off back there and crank up the griddle. We got a load comin' in." She disappeared through the swinging doors.

Christine pulled a five from her wallet and dropped it on the counter. A Greyhound bus, with its sleek and ironic logo, rolled slowly into view and stopped, filling all the front windows. She knew that she had to get out of here, that she simply couldn't handle a crowd right then.

The restroom was dim and foul, a combination of Pine Sol and urine. Christine used the toilet without sitting on it, then splashed water on her face at the sink and rubbed her sore temples. She couldn't drive back out to the ranch and sit there by the phone, waiting and waiting, or wander around town anymore. She needed a plan. Think, she said to herself, you need to think.

Back in the narrow hallway, she halted at the phone again and dropped in another quarter. Expecting little else, she listened to the hollow ringing at the far end of the line, envisioning the heavy black dial phone clanging out there in the isolation of the old ranch cabin. Her eyes ached, and the thick, electrical waves of a major headache began settling just above her brows.

"Excuse me."

Christine twisted around, the receiver frozen in midair. A placid Indian woman stood in the hallway holding a baby, trails of mucus waxing its tiny nostrils. Christine stared at the woman, then looked down into the baby's sweet, grubby face as if they were messengers, somehow bearing an answer.

The woman pointed. "The bathroom. Can I get past?"

Christine exhaled rapidly, her body deflating. "Oh, I'm sorry. I'm—" She hung up the phone and backed against the wall. Others were filing through the front door: wrinkled shirts, flattened hair, yawns. A lanky young man with sharp body odor slipped past her to the men's room, giving her a look as he pushed open the door. It swung back in place with a swoosh, and in the webbed and contorted way that memory comes to people, it reminded her of something. She grabbed the small Washington County phone book hanging in tatters from a dirty piece of butcher's string. It was barely a footnote compared to the thick Phoenix directory, but these scant Yellow Pages might hold her last hope.

Dallas had talked about a man a few days ago, a lawyer named Harding who had helped him prove up on some water rights. Dallas had the cash to pay, but this man Harding had his eye on a good horse Dallas was training and he preferred to trade. The horse was worth five hundred dollars more than the legal bill. Harding had offered to pay the difference, but Dallas laughed, said you couldn't hold a bake sale anymore without a lawyer on retainer. Fair enough, goods and services rendered, taxes avoided. Dallas seemed to get a kick out of the whole business—a lawyer who had no burning desire for cash, one with a soft spot for a surefooted buckskin. Moreover, a lawyer that Dallas had actually spoken highly of, even seemed to trust. And Christine knew that Dallas trusted a psychotic bronc or a rattlesnake more than most men, said he never met a hypocritical horse, or a snake that tried to conceal its nature.

Christine flipped through the Yellow Pages to "lawyers" and found no listings. A high school English teacher for ten years, she thought she should manage indexing better than this. Some of the pages were torn in half or missing; dabs of sticky syrup made handling them something more than irritating. She swore silently. Damn it, how were they listed? Then she recalled the haze of legal correspondence preceding her divorce almost five years ago and envisioned the letterhead. Attorney at Law—that was it. She quickly turned to the beginning and scanned in the bad light: artificial limbs—asphalt—attorneys. And there it was, Harting with a t, Layne Harting, address given in the town of Saraville, Utah. The place sounded only vaguely familiar, but of course she had her well-worn map out on the car seat to help her fill in the blanks.

Then Christine Parker did something totally out of character. The former Maricopa County Teacher of the Year, the woman who believed in good citizenship and Earth Day and the sanctity of printed words, looked carefully over her shoulder, then ripped yet another page from the hapless phone book.

Layne Harting stood in front of his house on the gravel shoulder of Fillmore Street, giant cottonwoods lining either side, and, with as much tact and humor as he could manage this early in the morning, refused John Culley's load of White Holland turkeys. They were loud and obnoxious, primal garglers that did nothing to enhance the mood of his sleepy, rural neighborhood. Jean Allred, Layne's closest neighbor across the way, had twice walked to her big front porch and curiously peered over at the noise. Layne's shaggy golden retriever, Limbo, came bounding up, fresh from some morning adventure down by the river where Fillmore dead-ended, to add his bark to the hubbub. When Layne hushed him, Limbo backed away and settled for merely peeing on the front tire of Culley's stock truck.

"Go ahead. Take a look at 'em," Culley said over Layne's laughing protest.

Like a man politely obligated to consider life insurance, Layne moved hesitantly, bending his lanky frame to peer between the high, slatted sides of the truck. He knew that, unlike their canny cousins in the wild, domestic turkeys were some of the dumbest creatures drawing breath, all the brains having been bred out of them somewhere between Pilgrims and pantyhose. They eyed him suspiciously and shifted from side to side in a single wave of feathers and fleshy throat wattles, stretching their necks and gobbling at him.

"Well, they look like the real thing," Layne said, straightening up and suppressing a grin, "but I just can't take them, John." He waved his arm behind him, "My little pasture and its three-wire fence. It wouldn't hold those birds for ten minutes."

There was no real acknowledgment on Culley's part. His arms were stolidly folded over the bib of his coveralls and he stared into the distance, as if he hadn't heard. Layne had learned how silence was as important to these rural conversations as any vocabulary, and so he didn't worry that he had offended. He liked Culley well enough—knew him to be a cagey man who worked fewer acres better than most—and he was amused by the offer of turkeys. There was something in the barter system that suited the retrofitted life he was in the process of shaping here, but he had to draw the line somewhere. Still, he didn't fault Culley for trying. If you couldn't wrangle a slight edge or exchange out here, you weren't crafty. And if you weren't crafty, you couldn't make it off the land anymore.

Besides, Culley could afford the small legal fee. And to be honest, Layne had found him a fairly difficult client. Three months ago, Layne had negotiated a settlement over a disputed property line for the Culleys. Come to find out, it wasn't the fence or the few inches it encroached that bothered Culley and his wife; it was the new neighbors themselves and the design of their geodesic-dome house sitting on a grassy knoll in the Culleys' plain view. Compared to St. George's rampaging growth of condos and subdivisions and golf courses, change was coming slowly to this town of 1,753. But it was still change, it was still coming, and Layne understood exactly. When he had first arrived, he was part of that shift, but after three years now as Saraville's part-time city attorney, he'd been pretty well accepted, had even become a prime liaison between the old townsfolk and the newly arrived hippies and yuppies.

Layne wrote a mild letter to the dome folks and ended up with an invitation for wine and cheese. Chad and Linda Peterson, desktop publishers from Boulder, Colorado, were in touch with the entire globe on their fancy computers and modems. They produced a national newsletter called *Skids* for children with disabilities. They had three kids—two healthy and one in pain—a shaggy dog that looked like Limbo, and an intriguing collection of antique wheelchairs. People didn't come any more normal.

He finally settled the Culleys' concerns by simply introducing them to the Petersons over the troublesome fence—Mrs. Culley, a grandmother of ten, couldn't speak at the sight of little Lucinda Peterson, her bright eyes and twisted limbs—and by drafting a simple agreement barring any adverse possession. Layne almost didn't even send Culley a bill, but he knew that would be a bad precedent. So here he was, declining a load of turkeys instead.

John Culley, none the worse for trying to do a little business, extended his hand and gave Layne's a firm shake. "Well, okay," he said, "stay out of trouble," then drove off.

"You, too, John." Layne stood in his wake, a blizzard of turkey feathers spinning in the air, slowly flecking the roadside white. He returned to his front yard, amused and relieved. He already had one large bird on the property and that was enough. Two years ago, an old domestic goose had wandered into his pasture and just stayed. No one had shown up to claim the hissy-mean creature, and it was still out there eating his grass and cleaning up grain after the horses, rarely missing an opportunity to make a big show out of rank independence. Layne didn't consider it his goose—that crazy bird owned itself—but he'd heard that geese live a very long time, forty years or more, and every morning that it was still out there trying to boss his two horses around had come to feel like a good omen.

He strolled through the open gate of his wrought iron fence, circa 1910. A small yard surrounded the old Saraville two-room schoolhouse that Layne had so painstakingly renovated into a combination office and home. The lawn was mowed and trimmed and the flower beds well edged. Tall lilac bushes marked the corners of the yard and oozed their sticky fragrance. Help with the gardening was another barterable skill, and Layne had grown to depend on Hazel Roosevelt with her bags of strange and magical compost. He paused for a moment on the walkway up to the house and reveled in the pure, glassy energy of spring. Sweet Jesus, what a day!

He mounted the steps and crossed his porch, then reached out to a small brass plate imbedded in the stone next to the front door which read, *Layne Harting, Attorney at Law*, and gave it a quick rub for luck. He had a few superstitions, a few irresistible knocks-on-wood. And he certainly hoped the nameplate was lucky. Considering all he'd given up, it ought to have been made of fourteen-karat gold.

Layne stepped through the open front door of his schoolhouse. Faye, his secretary, had her back to him and she jumped at the sound of his shoes on the hardwood, dropping the file in her hands.

"Quit sneaking up on me," she said, picking up the file from the floor. "I already had to dodge that damn goose this morning. I don't need any more excitement." Everyone knew how Faye felt about the goose's antics. Most mornings, to pick up and deliver work, she walked over to Layne's through his back pasture, hissing and flapping her arms in defiance at the charging goose, threatening it aloud: *Mess with Faye and you're pâté.*

Layne glanced at his watch: 7:45. "You're a little early, aren't you?"

"Hey, I was hoping to catch you coming out of the shower."

"Right," said Layne. "You were hoping for a cup of coffee. I know your story, lady."

Faye Barlow worked half-time for him, which is how he wanted to keep it, because as long as she was part-time, so was he. Faye and her husband, Roger the silent sheetrocker, and their six kids lived on the next block, directly behind Layne. Other than picking up and delivering work for him, she was self-contained at home. Layne had called in a favor from the phone serviceman, who ran a special cable through the barnyard so that Faye could answer his phone, have an intercom and be networked into his computer, all part of the increasing rural irony of satellite dishes fifty feet from hog-scalding tubs. And with six kids, all under the age of fourteen, she didn't take many vacations and rarely needed the answering machine he bought for her.

Faye was shaped like a three-way lightbulb topped with a two-hundred-watt smile. She managed a family of faithful Mormons and coffee was just one in a litany of proscribed sins, so Faye couldn't brew it at home or drink it in front of her kids. But there were times when she couldn't hold back and just had to sneak over to Layne's to indulge herself in a big cup of the stuff—lots of cream and three dollops of honey—and to talk to an adult. Faye was a lot smarter than most things around here.

"Well," Layne said, "I do have some fresh-ground ninety-octane Kenyan laced with Bavarian Hazelnut brewing."

"Oh, be still my heart." Faye rolled her eyes, faked a swoon.

"But, hey," he said, "I don't know if I like helping a lady down the road to hell."

Faye turned with the agility of a large woman who was constantly snatching toddlers from the brink and said, "That's not what I hear," then smiling, switching on the dental lights, "dear."

The smile fell from Layne's face. He pointed toward the coffee pot, but she said she'd left young ones at home and the restraints might be working loose. "I'll come back in a little while, when I can savor every swallow," she told him, and hurried out the back door.

Walking over to the large pine table that served as his desk, he exhaled noisily, then retrieved his coffee cup. Faye had no idea she'd hit such a nerve. Layne never discussed his romantic life with her, or anyone else for that matter, but not much went unnoticed or untalked about in these small towns.

Layne's love life had begun its downward spiral years ago, as soon as he married The Turk. After their divorce, and after leaving the big firm and moving to southern Utah, Layne staggered through a few relationships, but they all felt like interchangeable parts. Then, less than a year ago, he met a young girl, just turned eighteen and barely street legal, the daughter of a St. George Mormon bishop. Kathy Lee. She had the body, the face, and the innocence. With her silky blonde hair and peachy complexion, she was someone Pat Boone would sing to at the fair.

Here's how it started: with Layne, turning forty, same age as her father, meeting Kathy Lee in her car, in his car, on a rock in the desert . . . anywhere clandestine so others wouldn't see. And every new door that Layne opened, Kathy Lee seemed to walk through, with just enough hesitation to keep the illusion of naivete alive.

And here's how it ended: four months ago, just last winter, with Layne returning to their expensive Las Vegas hotel room, complete with a big hot tub in its center. It was three in the afternoon and the meeting with his client had been cut short. As he keyed the lock and opened the door, managing an armful of flowers, he saw Kathy Lee nested in the tub like a baby bird, noisily moaning and groaning and thrusting about with some bodyguard they had met earlier in the bar who called himself Mau Mau.

Kathy Lee immediately moved to Las Vegas, and Layne immediately moved to celibacy. Even now, he only vaguely understood that it was Kathy Lee's eyes that had invited Mau Mau over to their table, her body language that had kept him there. It didn't matter; Layne blamed himself.

In any event, the real winner was Josh, Layne's big, raw-boned buckskin, who loved to be saddled and run the mountains. But even on horseback, with the ground flowing beneath him and the sky blazing a deep, unforgettable blue, he wondered how guilt and lust could tangle in such an ugly knot. And what the hell kind of name was Mau Mau, anyway?

The dashlights of her trusty Honda—one of the few dependable things in her life over the past five years—glowed steadily, the gauges reassuring her that she had plenty of gas and all functions were normal, that she wouldn't be stranded in the middle of nowhere, finally broken by some mechanical last straw. The mere act of leaving St. George, exiting Interstate 15 and heading due east on State Route 9, made Christine feel slightly better because she had at least picked a direction and was trying to do something.

The morning light grew brighter, accentuating the odd shapes—flat tops, mounds, spires—leading into the sandstone wonders of Zion National Park. Saraville looked to be about thirty-five miles east, judging from the map, about seven miles this side of the Zion Park entrance. She drove slowly over the deserted highway. She had no appointment. What time did lawyers get to work? Would this Harting even be in town? Just finding the name, grasping that simple fragment of hope, had been enough to propel her out of Big Red's and away from St. George. But what if he wanted nothing to do with her, claimed some other legal specialty and ushered her straight to the door? Other troublesome questions began to crop up and now she felt ridiculous—just what did she think she was doing?

If she were a smoker, she would have lit a cigarette now, Christine thought—the slow, hypnotic match flare and then the long, pleasing inhalation—but she had never smoked, and in fact, for over a year now she had been nauseatingly good. It still shocked her how quickly her life had taken on the straight and narrow shape of a crusade. Three square meals a day, exercise, and good sleep. And that included almost zero booze—until last night, that is, until that crazy drinking bout with Dallas in the Ancestor Bar, downing round after round of Jack Daniels and soda. Her uncle, always a good listener and sometimes full of folksy wisdom, had joined in wholeheartedly—laughing, joking, recalling family stories. Letting off some steam. It was something she'd been working up to—they both had—and it was great therapy while it lasted.

The stinging counterpoint of last night's ease and laughter compared to this morning's distress hit her squarely, and she resorted to her one occasional vice: swearing. Unlike most people, who curse when they're angry, Christine sometimes swore when she was scared and alone, when she felt the world bounding away from her grasp. It was a habit she had taken up long ago. She had been a good and obedient kid, no trouble except when it came to her mouth. It had been washed out repeatedly by her mother with both soap and Tabasco for using bad words, the only effect being that she hated the taste of Tabasco. Thankfully, with age, the language police had lost their control. She rolled down her window now and cut loose with a stream. "Dammit all to shit, piss, hell." The words opened a well and brought back images from last night of her thickly reasoned actions, actions that had spread outward into a sticky, uncontrollable net catching others, maybe holding those she loved. Then she leaned her head out the window and yelled into the rush of air, "Christine Parker, how could you have been so fucking stupid?"

The strong wind in her face soon cooled her dramatics, and

she pulled her head back in. The bout of profanity had been cathartic. It was something she should have done all last year, she thought—bay at the moon, release the bad energy—but she had been the ever-brave and composed girl, through the initial bad news and through all the rest.

During that gruesome period of hospitals and clinics, it had been all the questions, oddly enough, that had bothered Christine the most: "*How are you?*" (either the *how* or the *are* drawn out into a nasal tone of melancholy, often by people she hardly knew). "*Does it hurt?*" (because almost one hundred percent of the time it did—long, lightning-edged needles slipping into her veins; tattered stitches festering along a red incision; IV bottles draining like fog into her). "*Is there anything I can do?*" (kiss me, hold me, reupholster my sofa, get the hell out of here). Or the best of all, "*Have you found Jesus?*"

It was the hospital's roving, non-denominational minister who had asked Christine the latter. She was flat on her back, just two days out of surgery, a tube with yellow stuff draining from the too-intimate incision in her chest. The old man scuttled up to her bed with a Bible in his hand, sat close by her side, and it was in that groggy moment that Christine fully understood the phrase *captive audience*. He sat quietly in his black jacket with the white collar—a kind of tux for the Lord. His eyes were closed tight and his head half-bowed. Thick plastic glasses slipped down to the end of his nose. A dull white forest of hair sprouted from his ears; dander from his shoulders predicted an early winter. The TV, mounted high on the far wall, brightly vaulted a lucky someone buying a vowel off the Wheel of Fortune into the room.

The generous doses of Percocet they had given Christine created a cool, subterranean cave where she could not even feel her toes, but from which she could see the Reverend What's-His-Name as if through a giant magnifying glass. His chin trembled. Saliva gathered with a quiet force in the corners of his mouth. Finally, he opened his eyes and reached out, touching the sheet on the bed, connecting them in a nervous, dry-as-dust way, and asked: "My dear, have you found Jesus?"

Christine attributed her reply to the fact that she was doped to the gills. "Yes," she said in a hoarse voice, sounding like someone else, "I think I spotted him in the rec room, but his crew cut nearly threw me."

Maybe she only imagined herself saying that, and maybe the reverend only imagined himself hearing it, for each remained in a separate dream. The reverend merely eased himself deeper into the chair and, hitting the remote control, summoned up Donahue, all bug-eyed and sympathetic and working another group of whiners, while Christine drifted to and fro on milky waves of consciousness.

For months and months after the operation, Christine's mother, Audrey, had not been able to say it—the C word; cancer, breast cancer. She called it "Christine's illness," as if it were no more than childhood chicken pox or mumps, the early trials she had already seen her daughter through. Back then, she had carted coloring books and popsicles to Christine, read to her endlessly, and even paid her dimes so she wouldn't scratch the scabby pox, though Christine still ended up with two small, star-shaped scars on her chin.

Postsurgical and halfway through the exhausting rigors of chemotherapy, carrying a stout vision of the future, Christine had finally interrupted her mother during an evasive conversation one afternoon in Audrey's kitchen. "Cancer, Mom. You can say it. It's not like anything will change, will get worse if we say the word."

Her mother's back was to her. Christine watched Audrey reach out to the pie dough she was kneading on the kitchen counter and squeeze the floury paste so hard her hands turned white, and in that moment, Christine saw with absolute clarity how a mother's pain must be tenfold and bottomless. She moved toward her mother, reached her arms around her from behind, and held her tight and long.

Most of the time, or at least to the outer world, Christine marched forward, believing in her own future, educating herself about treatments, enduring the worst with either a hard silence or irreverent humor. At first she unnerved, then later entertained, the doctors and nurses with round after round of medical jokes: "What do you call a hundred IRS agents with cancer? The good news." It was only when her hair fell out—a daily ritual of dark brown, shoulder-length strands gathering on the floor of her shower—that she fully realized how her own body was betraying her. For almost six months, she wore scarves and floppy hats and one particular baseball cap, custom embroidered across the front: HAIR JORDAN.

That was a little over a year ago, and now, driving the desert toward Saraville, Christine looked more like herself again. Though the cancer had certainly taken something away from her, it had also left something new—a rough seasoning carved in higher cheekbones, a fatalism that widened her light eyes, a recognition of life as a gift and not a right.

The wind blew in through the open window and ruffled her hair, felt fresh and cool on her face. The sensations took her by surprise. To feel the wind, to have hair, to still be alive: these were the kind of everyday events that crept up on her regularly and stopped her heart.

The good feeling was short-lived, however. Her overriding concern for Dallas crowded its way back; the pit in her stomach returned. She had covered some twenty miles through the bleak lava hills east of St. George and as she topped a long rise, the sun hit the windshield full on. The glass hadn't seemed that dusty or bug splattered before, but now, with the brilliance and reflection, she could barely see. She glanced out her side window, hoping for a place where she might pull over, and saw a brand new RV/trailer park cropping up here in the middle of nowhere, the soulless housing of Americans seeking sun on a budget. There were some aluminum-sided double-wides, but the new facility was still mostly empty concrete pads and hundreds of staked saplings. Christine pulled into the expansive parking lot, thinking she might find a way to clean the windshield.

It was too early for activity. The lot was empty; the trailer park, lifeless. At the back of the lot, Christine saw an immense metal building, across its front, in nine-foot letters, Lava Lanes

Bowling. She got out of her car and took in the panoramic view. She was on a small plateau and there was nothing else in any direction.

From the garbage sack on the car floor she salvaged a fistful of stiff Kleenexes—she was out of new ones; these had seen her through the night—and began rubbing the windshield. The dust cleared a little, but the bugs held fast. She spit on the glass and smeared the bugs into a dark, binding gruel. She laughed, a little too high pitched, a little too easily, and then saw tears splatter on the dirty hood. She threw down the tissue and kicked the tire. To hell with this. She was turning around, driving straight back to St. George, to the sheriff's office, and then, no matter what Dallas had instructed, she was spilling her guts to the first official she met.

A mild breeze picked the tissues up from around her feet and rolled them in pieces across the parking lot. "Oh, shit," she said and chased each one down, gathering them up before anyone saw the litter. She jumped back into her car, drove to the parking lot entrance, and came to a complete stop. Dallas had been adamant—*Don't do anything until you talk to me. Nothing.* At her core, she trusted Dallas, trusted his seasoned authority and judgment far beyond her own, but doing nothing simply felt impossible to her.

She was at a crossroads—literally. Turn left or turn right? Nothing swam down through her, strong and icy in its certainty. For a moment, she pictured herself driving back onto St. George's main boulevard, McDonald's golden arches glaring and the Sands Motel sign boasting free HBO and king-size beds, all of it useless to this weary traveler. Besides, she'd come this far now, so what difference were a couple of hours going to make?

She knew her logic was thin, but turned east toward Saraville and continued through the strange, blue hyperspace of rural Utah.

Just an hour ago Layne had been standing in his yard singing hosannas to spring air, and now he was sitting at his desk fighting off something of a funk. He wished Faye hadn't made that crack about his love life earlier. Here he was, turning forty, headlong into middle age, and feeling clueless about love, sex, family, commitment.

He scanned his credenza, noted a couple of photos taken while hiking and river running, great trips with friends from his old firm, Raleigh, Rudge and Humber.

Certain names have a rhythmic, almost musical quality to them, and, at first, the law firm that had employed Layne for twelve years in Salt Lake City struck just such a silvery note in him. He had always worked hard, graduated in the top quarter of his class from Stanford Law School, then shunned the prestigious West Coast offers because he disliked California and wanted to return home to Salt Lake. The Stanford experience seemed to dictate that he go with the most powerful firm, run with the biggest dogs in town. He chose Raleigh, Rudge and Humber because, with over one hundred and fifty lawyers, they represented or sued every major corporation doing any kind of business in the West.

During this period of his life—in retrospect, it felt like a chain of dominoes falling—he married the Turk. They were two high-octane attorneys practicing in Salt Lake City with different firms. After they married, he came to understand that the Turk was wild about predatory sex, but bored with the legitimate variety. No matter. They both quickly learned that their best orgasms came from lifting megabucks out of any deep pocket. She specialized in contracts and the commercial code, in making "deals," and together they bought BMWs, subscribed to the *Wine Spectator*, sipped merlots, and discussed mergers or the countless exceptions to hearsay rule. All in the two hours they had together at night before dropping into hard, dreamless sleep. Saturdays were always worked and even Sundays if a trial or big deal was brewing. Layne and the Turk strode arm in arm through the competitive world of young associates trying to out-produce all the others—bring in new business, bill more hours, demand larger retainers, slam dunk bigger verdicts—striving to impress the seniors by plowing the straightest furrow toward that coveted partnership.

But after ten years of childless marriage, powerhouse litigation, seventy-hour work weeks, easily achieving the partnership and the recognition as a rising star, Layne had been forced to stop and take inventory. He and the Turk were well off, but politely washed up as a couple. The senior partners, those over fifty who had earned a little rest, were working harder than ever. They started dropping dead, their vital organs shot through with stress. The clients were becoming more demanding, the stakes ever higher. And any hope for the loftier goals of the practice—compromise, conciliation or simple problem solving—was buried deep under spiraling overhead and increased competition and pure greed. He and his colleagues joked in the hallways about their modern gunslinger's creed: sue first and ask questions for a fee. Plainly, the environment of high-powered litigation had become unnatural—jousting for hungry warlords who made millions off your thinning blood, while you turned dry and albino under fluorescent lights.

Then, the most esteemed partner died, a brilliant lawyer of fifty-eight, Layne's friend and mentor within the firm. On a gloomy November evening at Harkin's Mortuary, the man's viewing turned into a heated parking lot argument over who would get his large corner office. Layne, overhearing all this from the shadows at the lot's edge, realized then that perspective had become the most important casualty in this unending war of attrition. And that's when he chucked it all—the firm, the Turk, city life—in one, fell swoop.

It was a thread waiting to break, but one that might have held, had he not been sitting alone at the end of Saraville's Fillmore Street near the north bank of the Virgin River four years ago. He'd been backpacking that weekend and was dreading his return to Salt Lake and work. He was bleakly tossing pebbles and posing Siddhartha-like questions into the spring runoff when he heard a fateful hammering. Turning around, he saw a real estate woman from St. George nailing a sign to a giant cottonwood.

He walked up the road to the old, abandoned schoolhouse just going up for sale and made a few inquiries about the listing. She whipped out her card: *Cindy Wells, Sells the Desert Quickly!* Its message was delivered in three colors, including a studio photograph revealing no trace of irony or self-consciousness. He asked her if the newspaper article he'd recently read was really true, that Saraville was being taken over by new artists and old hippies, that it was only half Mormon now. She wore tight Levi's and boots, hiked one foot up on her bumper, lit a cigarette, and said, "You can be the swing vote, partner."

After a brief tour of the property—a wrecked building full of pigeon shit and broken glass, a five-acre pasture overgrown with thistle and a dying orchard—he signed an Earnest Money Agreement on the hood of her fire-engine-red Grand Jeep Cherokee and bought the place for cash, for next to nothing.

Layne's former colleagues in Salt Lake kidded him that, like so many men humping their load into middle age, the grass always looked greener. They had good-naturedly given him the brass nameplate for his schoolhouse, though they believed this little rural romance would soon be over and he'd be back at their door. Even his Salt Lake accountant had sat and patiently tried to convey Layne's present and future net worth to him when he'd announced his resignation from the firm, but Layne had done a deeper accounting of his life and knew intimately what he was giving up—cars and condos, a hefty pension and chic respectability—and what he nervously hoped to gain.

Now, after plenty of sweat and a lot more cash, just about everything Layne owned was vested, debt free, in or around the old Saraville schoolhouse. He had thrown himself into the renovation, sandblasting the walls until swirling veins of red, pink, and yellow reappeared in the old sandstone blocks. He was especially fond of the tall, arched, and latticed French pane windows on either side of the front door.

The two rooms of the original school were spacious and equal in size. The front half of the building became his combined office and living room. Some comfortable furniture, a few rugs over the restored hardwood, some local art on the walls and it generally surprised people by its warmth and hominess. The back room of the schoolhouse was divided up to accommodate his country kitchen, master bedroom, and bath.

"Excuse me."

At first Layne wasn't sure that he had heard anything. His front door was wide open and a gentle tide of morning sunlight washed over the threshold and across the floor.

"Mr. Harting?"

A figure stood in the doorway, an outline that was difficult to see backlit by the morning sun. He rose from his chair and crossed the room. "Oh, yes," he said, squinting. "Can I help you?" It was a woman, someone he didn't recognize.

She looked frazzled. Sunglasses skewed on top of her head. A wrinkled white blouse. There were plenty of tourists who came to town, looking for hiking trails or convenience stores on their final leg toward scenic Zion Park. Maybe this one only needed directions. He could see that she had a pretty face, nice eyes. Tired, but nice.

"Yes. I'm sorry to barge in unannounced," she said. "Are you Layne Harting? The lawyer?"

"That's me," he said. "Come in, come in."

"I don't have an appointment," she adjusted the shoulder strap of her large purse, "well, of course you know that. But I really needed to talk to you."

"Well, a . . . of course." Although he had scheduled no appointments for the day, had only planned to work a couple of case files, once the woman was inside, Layne immediately began kicking himself. He thought he had learned his lesson about drop-ins, about screening potential clients who didn't have appointments. He stood there awkwardly, not sure now whether to offer her a chair.

"Actually," she said, "I really need to use a restroom if you have one."

Not wanting to be rude, he nodded slowly. "Oh, well that's. . . yeah," he said, feeling ever more awkward. He piloted her back through the kitchen into his bedroom and to the only bathroom, then returned to the front room and sat down behind his desk.

Damn! What was he doing? A complete stranger in that part of his house. His experience of several months ago came glaring back at him. A young man had showed up on his doorstep and Layne cordially asked him in. The guy turned out to be deeply disturbed and unstable, convinced that the county sheriff had wired a chip into his brain and was controlling him with radio signals. He wanted to sue everyone in sight. Layne spent a miserable hour getting nowhere with the guy, who began ranting about vengeance and who wouldn't leave. Layne finally had to slip into the bedroom and call the cops to swing by his office.

He tried to smooth things over for himself now: Don't overreact, it's probably just some distraught wife from somewhere out in the county who caught her husband face down in Bimboville last night.

Layne impulsively grabbed the phone, hit the intercom button, and Faye picked up. In a low voice, eyes trained on the kitchen doorway, he told her to call him back in exactly fifteen minutes. "And if I tell you to get me the Gardner file" — that was the name of the crazy guy a few months ago — "then please get over here, pronto."

"Got you," Faye said. "Another crazy in tow, huh?"

"We'll see. Thanks." He hung up and relaxed a little. If this turned out to be just some babbling woman, Faye would be able to talk her down, massage her bent ego back into place.

He nervously pushed a few things around on his desk, then leaned back and stared out the windows. Sunlight shimmered down through the tall cottonwoods so that the street looked shrouded in a golden aura. Aura? He couldn't believe he had even thought of that word. Last time he'd heard it was from Bill Ginsberg, an accountant transplanted from Atlanta to Saraville, a good guy whose life was also under a new phase of construction out here in the West. Just last week Layne had been over on the Rockville Bench breaking perspiration with the Ginsbergs, Bill and Mary, in their new willow sweat lodge.

The blistering rocks were hissing and Bill was telling Layne that Mary's aura was turning red, that they needed to sweat it back to blue. Or was it blue to red? Layne was drinking Cuervo Gold straight from the bottle, occasionally dumping a shot on the steaming rocks for nasal hits, so he couldn't quite remember the color thing. Now, almost unconsciously, he was using their New Age lingo. Christ!

He drummed his fingers on the desk, then got up and walked toward the kitchen, stood there and listened. The sound of running water came from the bathroom. He wondered if he should call out to the woman, ask if everything was alright, but thought better of it. He returned to his desk and buzzed Faye again.

"Make that five minutes," he told her.

Just then, the woman emerged. Layne stood to greet her and could see that she had straightened herself up, combed her hair, put lipstick on. Her blouse had been smoothed and tucked tight into her jeans. In an automatic response, he straightened the rolled-up sleeves of his cotton shirt.

She attempted a weak smile. "I'm sorry for that entrance," she said.

"That's okay. Can I offer you something? Coffee or — "

"No, that's alright. Thanks," she said.

He pointed at one of the client chairs across the desk and they both sat down. "I'm Christine Parker," she said, "Dallas Parker's niece." She spoke the words with finality, as if they would explain every mystery of the morning.

"Well, sure, Dallas. Best horseman in the county." Layne relaxed in his chair. Dallas Parker's niece? Why hadn't she just said so? Dallas was a friend, someone Layne admired, a hardworking rancher and an entertaining cowboy. He gestured toward the window, indicating his pasture. "That mare, the one out there with the buckskin that Dallas and I traded for, is ready to foal anytime. I've been hoping Dallas would work with the colt," he said. "When it's ready, of course."

"Mr. Harting, excuse me, but maybe I should get right to the point." She crossed her legs and moved forward, perching on the edge of the old wooden chair. "I have a serious problem, and my uncle has mentioned your name as someone he's done business with, someone he trusts."

Layne nodded slowly, taken aback by this sudden shift to getting right down to business. The time she'd taken to freshen up was well spent, had done wonders—her lips were full, her eyes wide and deep green. There was color in her high cheeks, a resemblance to Dallas in her jawline. Of course he would listen, see if he could help.

"You see, I," she paused, "where to begin?"

The phone interrupted. It was Faye. "Yes, yes, everything is fine, right on schedule," he told her, chuckling. "Tell Widow Lumplear that the insurance company is replacing her carpet and even paying the vet bills for her cat."

Faye asked him what the heck was going on over there. "Does someone have a gun to your head? Remember our code—the Gardner file? Just whisper it, Layne, and I'll have the police there faster than you can say Jell-o mold."

"No, no," he said, laughing, feeling good again. "Really. Everything is just fine. Call you in awhile."

He nodded at Christine and laughed softly again, mostly for her benefit, trying to draw her into all this joviality. "Sorry about that. Now where were we?"

A full beat passed during which they looked straight at each other. Then, in a quiet voice, sounding as if the words were hauled up from some difficult, ravaged place deep inside her, Christine said, "Last night, I . . . I think I killed a man."

Mill Drill

EXACTLY TWO MILES FROM GROUND ZERO, A NEW REINFORCED slit trench had been backhoed into the desert floor. The forty Marines assigned to First Platoon, Bravo Company had been trucked out to the trench shortly after midnight for a field exercise, a "problem," as it was known. Dosimeters were taped inside their pants cuffs, shirt pockets, and helmets. Waiting around for almost five hours now, they sat together in small groups or stretched out on the ground alone under the moonless sky with only their thoughts. The temperature had finally dropped below ninety, but that was the only good news. The Marines were alternately nervous, joking, or trying to sleep. One group, the platoon rowdies drawn together, recounted and embellished stories about their recent leaves into Vegas and the "show girls" they had met, each one trying to top the other's story with a tall, scenic wonder of his own—all blondeness, boobs, and wishful thinking.

The platoon sergeant, known as Porkchop to his friends and Sergeant to his men, stood alone in the dark, listening, recalling some youthful excesses of his own when he was their age, before the Big War II. These kids were ground-pounders who had packed it through the swamps of Lejeune or the sands of Pendleton, who were lucky to be sent to Nevada instead of Korea. And they were doing what all Marines do. When they weren't mounting assaults on imaginary enemies or spit-shining buckles and shoes, they were bullshitting, waiting for new orders.

But tonight, Porkchop thought, the orders were weird. This was some kind of a hurry-up-and-wait mill drill with fireworks tacked onto the end. His unit had seen a few atomic blasts go up, but that was back at base camp, over the mountain, way in the distance. This was their first time actually taking part in a blast, engaging in maneuvers out here, and Porkchop was uneasy about it.

"Hey, Romeo, this's your big chance, man," one of the voices in the dark said. "I heard the bomb lights you up. You can maybe see your own balls."

"Well, maybe you better look at mine then," came the retort, "cause I don't think you got any."

"Oh, yeah? I got a knuckle sandwich over here says different."

"Knock it off," Porkchop said sharply. "You girls can stand formation if you're that bored." Tempers were frayed from the heat and waiting, lack of sleep, anxiety over the unknown.

Porkchop's doubts about this whole thing began two months ago when he arrived at Camp Desert Rock, home to all the troops stationed at the Nevada Test Site. The camp had the look and feel of temporary quarters, of a wartime emplacement. Row upon row of heavy, green canvas tents quartered the men.

Porkchop had arrived at Desert Rock alone, not as part of a unit. His orders were strictly Temporary Duty. The thirty-nine Marines under him came in the same way, from various bases, all strangers to each other. First Platoon, Bravo Company, was formed, but it soon became clear that it would be disbanded sometime later, that the men would be scattered far and wide to different duty stations. Even more unusual, there were units from the Army, the Air Force, the Navy—troops from all four services had been taking part in the tests.

If Porkchop had harbored doubts as he arrived, the rumor mill at The Rock quieted none of them. Everyone had heard by now about other troops being positioned in some relative proximity to a blast, performing senseless maneuvers out there. Some soldiers got sick, according to the scuttlebutt, and were sent away, never heard from again. Accurate information was impossible for the average Marine to come by.

Porkchop was only a few months out of Korea. Over there, stories about disappearing GIs were frivolous, fueling many happy hours at the NCO clubs. Everyone's favorite involved some exotic and incurable venereal disease contracted in the alleys of Manila or Okinawa, focused on boys disappearing deep within isolation wards where they watched their balls swell to the size of watermelons and then rot on the vine.

But somehow this was different, and no one was laughing.

The minute Porkchop arrived at this new duty station, he was informed that all talk, discussion or gossip regarding the subject of atomic testing and any related maneuvers was strictly forbidden. A big sign at the entry to the camp put it in explicit terms: "What you see here, what you hear here, and what is said here, leave it here!"

Porkchop couldn't be sure, but scuttlebutt also had it that his unit was, if not privileged, rather unique. These Marines would supposedly be closer to ground zero than any in previous maneuvers—a mere two miles from the largest blast to date. There were a lot of variables in a shot and no one knew for sure how close to an atomic blast field troops could survive and then mount a counteroffensive. First Platoon, Bravo Company was about to find out.

The men had grown silent after he barked at them, but now conversation was starting up again in muted tones. Countdown to zero was only twenty minutes away and he was awaiting the order to climb into the trench and proceed with the maneuver. He was ready to get it over with, feeling just as irritable as they were.

The previous afternoon the temperature had reached almost 120 degrees, and trying to catch some sleep in anticipation of tonight's assignment had been nearly impossible. It had been even hotter inside the canvas tents back at the Meltin' Hilton— as it was called—and a hot wind had blown fine, bleached dust through the open flaps, smothering their ears and heads, blanketing their sweating bodies. They had lain around in skivvies, their hair dusty white, handkerchiefs tied over their noses and mouths so that they resembled a gang of ghostly bandits who were terminally irritated with each other and the constant barrage of sand fleas.

When the sun had finally dropped from sight, they were rousted for showers and chow. Sharply at twenty-two hundred hours, Porkchop moved his men in formation to the outdoor theater just beyond the tented area. A young information officer, an Army lieutenant holding a microphone, stood before them, beaming with enthusiasm, well scrubbed, and full of pious intentions. Porkchop stood in the back, behind his Marines seated on rows of makeshift benches. He disliked the Army in general and, after two wars, their punk lieutenants in particular.

"Welcome, gentlemen. You men have been selected to participate in Shot Huey tomorrow morning," the lieutenant smiled his congratulations. "I quote Commanding General Storke in saying that 'you can hereafter remember with a sense of pleasure and accomplishment that you were one of those troops, a real pioneer in experimentation.'"

The microphone squealed loudly and the lieutenant held it away from his face. A technician jumped up to fiddle with the controls. The young officer continued, explaining how to man the trenches, what to wear—normal combat field dress—what not to wear—watches, chains, dogtags, or any jewelry.

"Keep your head down, stay low in the trench, and cover your eyes with your forearm." Then he called an assistant, an Army private, to the stage, who assumed a position down on one knee, while the officer walked around him and adjusted his pose like a stage director, pointing out all the particulars.

"Remember, men," he said, excusing the kneeling private with a touch on the shoulder, "the desert sun, not the bomb, is your worst enemy out here." This drew scattered applause and an anonymous "No shit, sir" from the darkened crowd.

"That's right, Marine," the officer nodded. "And in closing, I quote from the *Infantry School Quarterly*. 'Radioactivity does not affect sexual potency. Men exposed to radiation can have normal children. Radiation sufficient to produce permanent sterility or impotency would also be lethal.' Are there any questions?" He looked around earnestly.

Some of the Marines elbowed each other, wiped their brows, or rubbed their crotches in a show of young, masculine burlesque. There were many questions, of course, but not a single hand went up. It was too late for questions. They were Marines, they were here, and they had their marching orders. Besides, they had been promised a show—a grand spectacular display of force and energy that would reshape the future. In preparation for this event, they had posed for individual pictures in front of an artificial desert scene with sand and rocks and yucca painted in the background—as if there were a shortage of the real thing a few feet away—and those pictures had been sent to their hometown newspapers, the captions boasting of their local son's participation in the Nevada atomic tests. The press releases were carefully prepared and the men were warned not to elaborate.

"Well, okay then," the instructor said, "and don't forget your cotton." He paused and chuckled into the microphone. "We don't want a bunch of Marines over in sick bay tomorrow because they got some bomb dust blown into their ears."

Now, after a long night of waiting, the first purplish hint of dawn began spreading out across the desert floor. Porkchop and the men of First Platoon could dimly see the landscape taking shape in front of them. Exactly two miles across the dead-flat terrain of Yucca Flat, the cross-members of the huge, spot-lighted tower, like a latticework skyscraper, seemed to grow from the desolate ground. The tanks and trucks and buildings scattered around the Flat emerged as dark silhouettes that sharpened as the light swelled.

"What the is all . . ." one Marine said to his buddy as they stared out at the vast, sandy laboratory, the night slipping away faster, more forms and shapes coming into focus. A disembodied voice over a tinny loudspeaker interrupted him.

"H minus ten minutes," it reported. "Proceed immediately to your trenches."

Before Porkchop could say a word, could yell for everybody to get up, the Marines were scrambling to their feet, tightening helmet straps and slinging arms.

"Alright, alright," Porkchop barked, his back to the trench. "Two squads on line. Here, form up on me."

The Marines fell in with boot camp speed, the kind of hustle only adrenaline brings.

"Listen up," he bellowed, augmenting the orders with hand and arm signals. "Right squad, right end of the trench. Left squad, left end."

The five-foot-deep trench had been ramped at either end for easy access. The two columns broke in opposite directions and filed quickly downwards.

"Move it. Move it. Get down in them trenches. Now!" Porkchop kept yelling with drill sergeant reflexiveness to ease his own tension. "Stop bunching up, keep it moving," he said, unaware of any contradiction.

Finally they were all standing in the trench, Porkchop following the last one down. The sun was looming just below the far horizon, so what they saw of the world was opaque and new. All of it appeared strange, even chilling, as their eyes peered over the edge of the trench, but none more so, during those last moments before kneeling down and assuming the position, than a female mannequin standing only fifty yards away. A forlorn figure on the outskirts of Doomtown, wearing, of all things, a fur coat, her spring-loaded arm waving in the warm breeze, back and forth, back and forth.

CHAPTER TWO

"YOU THINK YOU KILLED A MAN?" LAYNE ASKED HER. "YOU mean you don't know?"

Like most everything else about her so far, Christine's reply was cryptic. "Dallas will know. We have to find Dallas."

Layne rose from his chair and walked around the room as if his feet moving over the aged hardwood created a better conductor for thinking.

"I, uh, tell me, have you been arrested for this?" he said, addressing the back of her head. "Or talked to the police at all?"

"No," she said simply, without turning around.

"Did it happen around here?" He was swimming hard, trying to recall how to interview a defendant in a murder case. The only thing he could remember was *never* ask point-blank if they did it.

"No. Over in St. George," she said, twisting slowly in her chair and facing him. And then, in a sudden rush, "I'm so worried about Dallas. He—"

"I have to tell you that this really isn't my area. I do normal cases." He paused. "What I mean is that I don't specialize in that. I've never done a serious criminal case, let alone a murder."

"I'm not even sure if I want a lawyer," Christine said. "I just don't know where to turn. Like I said, Dallas had mentioned your name and I don't know anybody else in Utah."

"You're not from Utah?" he asked reflexively.

"No, I'm just visiting Dallas."

Layne came around his desk again and sat down. "Where is your uncle?" he asked.

"I don't know," she said sharply and put her face in her hands. She sat like that for a moment, as if behind her hands she could change something, make it all go away. She stood suddenly and excused herself, said she needed a minute of fresh air and walked outside onto the front porch.

Layne picked up a pencil and tapped it on his desk, then checked his Rolodex and dialed the Washington County Sheriff's Office.

He recognized the voice on the other end. "Good morning, Betty," he said. "It's Layne Harting. Thought I'd better call and see if that good-for-nothing husband of yours is still making his alimony payments."

He listened and then laughed. "Oh, I appreciate that," he said, "but I'll need to take a raincheck." Betty McKee was the dispatcher for the Sheriff's Office. She lived a few blocks away from him in Saraville, commuted the thirty-odd miles to work and enjoyed passing on the "news" to Layne from the great metropolis of St. George. Last year, when Betty had found herself in a sticky divorce in which she was threatened with assuming her soon-to-be-ex's debts, Layne had been her lawyer, got her the divorce, and stuck it back to the husband so Betty didn't have to file for bankruptcy. Afterwards, Layne had gracefully handled her overtures to go out on a date or to fix him dinner, and even though her fantasies never materialized, she considered the two of them buddies, frequently flirting with him.

"Come on," she said to him, "don't dance around me. I know exactly why you called, and it isn't about me or my lousy ex-husband."

"Oh? What is it then?"

"Well, I'll say this much." Betty's voice had a happy rhythm to it, as if she might just as easily sing as speak to you. "You've sure got an interesting case this time, counselor."

"Which one are you talking about now?" he asked her.

"Dallas Parker. He claims you're his lawyer. The geniuses still have him down in interrogation, but all he says is, 'Call my lawyer.' Has he called you yet?"

"Haven't heard a word," he said, his stomach tightening as if she were about to describe a serious operation or a mangled car wreck. "What's the charge?" he asked. Layne could imagine Betty—a big-boned blonde who seemed to be all chest and curly hairdo—leaning back in her chair, injecting all the drama she could into her voice.

"Well, let me break it to you gently, Mr. Harting," she teased. "We've got him in here on first-degree murder. Victim is Franklin Rudd, *the* Dr. Franklin Rudd, our local Einstein—you know, the guy who was just given the Citizen of the Year award from the Chamber of Commerce. Didn't get to enjoy it long, though. He's stiff as a board. There's word of an excavation 'in and around the throat,' as they say." She lowered her voice. "This one might even make the tabloids. You're going to be all over the news, counselor."

Layne was momentarily speechless. These days his clients were more likely to be accused of leaving the headgate in the irrigation ditch open fifteen minutes longer than their share. With the notable exception of Kathy Lee, his life had settled into monotones, the highs and lows reserved for others.

"Well," she said finally, "things are popping over here. I guess you'll soon be motoring in this direction."

Layne pieced together a rattled good-bye and slowly hung up the phone. The charge against Dallas was too farfetched—my God, a cut throat? From the first time he'd met him, Dallas had impressed Layne as a smart, good-hearted rancher and a wisecracking humorist. In spite of the occasional stories over at Dick's Coffee Shop in St. George about Dallas's early days as a boxer, as a young man with stamina, speed, and power, Layne had never seen anything approaching meanness or bad instincts. Layne had watched the cowboy train horses, had observed him in the arena displaying mountains of patience. What could possibly lead to a killing?

The last time he'd seen Dallas was two or three months ago, out at his small ranch near Motoqua, a remote area about ten miles from the Nevada border. Layne had driven out and tagged along with Dallas for an afternoon, watched as he kicked turds and trained some young horses. The "X factor": Layne had only read about it until that day, when he had actually seen it in Dallas—the ability to communicate on a deep, instinctual level with the animal. He watched Dallas gently sacking a wild mustang, talking quietly in reassuring tones, while the animal's rolling eyes and shivering skin conveyed its state of mind. It wasn't the sort of horse Dallas usually trained. Some wealthy Bloomington doctor had acquired it for his spoiled kid from the Bureau of Land Management's Adopt-a-Wild-Horse Program, and too much money finally hit the table for Dallas to refuse the job. After sunset, Layne and Dallas sat by the fire pit in Dallas's front yard and told stories in low tones, laughed easily, and drank whiskey and watched, small and earthbound, as the brilliant night sky slowly assembled itself.

When Christine walked back into his office from the front porch, Layne tried to pare all the information down to the simplest facts for her: Dallas had been arrested. He was in the St. George jail. Her uncle wanted to see him and he needed to get over there. Right now.

She listened with a new, icy poise, then immediately responded. "My uncle is not going to take the blame for something I did. I'm going to St. George to straighten this out."

Layne was out of his chair, unconsciously moving toward the door, putting himself between her and her leaving. He instantly recognized this as a bad idea—using his body to try to convince a woman of anything. He had once seen the famed psychic Uri Geller perform in a college auditorium and that's the expression Christine wore now—a wrinkled forehead, a burning gaze powerful enough to bend spoons and make keys jump off the table. He stayed blocking the door anyway.

"Let me talk to Dallas first. Can you wait here until I talk to him?" he asked her, but she was already pulling that big purse of hers onto her shoulder, which was answer enough.

"No way," she said and took a few steps forward.

"Okay," he said. "Then come with me. But don't do anything rash until I talk to Dallas. Promise?"

Christine just looked at him—or maybe it was right through him—and headed toward the door.

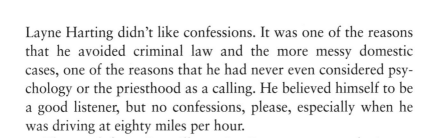

Layne Harting didn't like confessions. It was one of the reasons that he avoided criminal law and the more messy domestic cases, one of the reasons that he had never even considered psychology or the priesthood as a calling. He believed himself to be a good listener, but no confessions, please, especially when he was driving at eighty miles per hour.

The road from Saraville to St. George was mostly innocuous, widened and newly paved, but now Layne was dropping off a plateau and onto the last unremodeled stretch of the old road, down Dead Man's Wash and into the precarious curves along the river that had claimed the lives of several drunks and behind-the-wheel sleepers. A faded white roadside cross and plastic flowers marked one of the spots.

Layne decelerated as he came up behind a clunker of a station wagon, liver-colored and slung low to the ground. It was full of women and children and balloons, and it wasn't so much steering as banking through the tight curves, the front end mushing around as though it were pulling a water-skier. Layne rode the tail of the wagon and watched impatiently for a clear stretch where he could pass. A kid suddenly crowded his way through all the balloons in the car, opened his mouth wide, and smashed his potato-like face against the back window.

Sitting in the passenger seat of Layne's old Land Cruiser, Christine Parker was trying to add her voice to the confusion. She wanted to talk. She wanted to start at the beginning with him, wanted to tell him the truth, with a capital T.

"Wait a minute," he said to her as one of the balloons from the station wagon twisted out a window, caught smooth air, and sailed away. "I'm sorry, but I think I need to stop you again. I don't want to hear . . . first I have to see Dallas and know what I'm dealing with."

"That's ridiculous," Christine said. "Why did I come to see a lawyer if I can't talk to him?"

Regardless of how diplomatic he was, Layne just couldn't find the right thing to say to this woman. Starting with that moment in his office less than half an hour ago when she had somberly told him that she thought she'd killed a man, things had only become more mixed up, more puzzling and convoluted. To be sure, Layne had heard things from clients before that had taken him off guard, had come way out of left field, but Christine's statement was a first, a grainy black-and-white scene almost laughably out of "Perry Mason."

Layne hit the controls on his door that rolled down the back windows—fresh air, his prescription for anything that was going badly.

"Look, I may not be able to represent both you and Dallas," he told her. "That may involve a conflict, a conflict of interest or something like that. I just need to sort out a couple of things." He took his eyes off the road and looked her way. "I don't even practice criminal law."

"Yeah, you mentioned that already," she said without trying to conceal her sarcasm.

Layne thought about a retort, but they were in an enclosed space and he didn't need to toss any gas on the fire. He proceeded more cautiously. "Just let me see Dallas and talk to him before I hear your side of the story. It's that simple. Okay?" Maybe all that was BS, but it felt safe as he was saying it. He had a friend in Salt Lake, one of the best criminal lawyers in the state, and he'd call him later, get dialed in on capital crimes, client confessions, and potential conflicts. The kid in the station wagon still had his face against the glass, doing a respectable imitation of a slug with his tongue.

"No, it's not okay," she said. "There is no my side of the story or Dallas's side of the story. There's just the story, just the truth." Her voice was seamless, but an octave too high. She folded her arms across her waist and sank lower in the seat.

The truth? Lord, what he could tell this woman about the truth. It wasn't that he had any reason to doubt her intentions or honesty, but fifteen years of practicing law had convinced him that people's notion of the truth was about as subjective as their choice of underwear.

Christine gazed out the passenger window, watching the quiet rise and fall of the sun-scoured hills, and thought to herself that he drove too fast. She had sensed his impatience as they trailed close behind the weird party-on-wheels station wagon, and when he'd finally found his chance to pass, he had gunned the accelerator. Normally, she would have suggested in a pleasant voice that they slow down, but there simply wasn't any normal left.

She was in the middle of "The Twilight Zone"—her uncle was in jail and her worst fear had come true: Rudd was dead. No, not just dead. *Murdered.* That was the charge. And now some speed-demon lawyer was chauffeuring her back across the desert, telling her not to talk about last night. She wanted to wake up from this dream, start the last twenty-four hours over—hit the rewind button—but didn't know how and was slowly beginning to grasp the idea that it wasn't going to be possible.

"So," Layne broke in, Christine's thoughts having traveled far enough away that her hands jumped when he spoke, "you're from Phoenix, huh? Interesting place. What do you do there?"

Christine glanced over at him. He was younger than she had imagined, nice looking and well kept, not one of Dallas's typical cronies. Christ, she thought, has it been so long that, even in the midst of bad circumstances, I'm sizing up this man? "Look, Mr. Harting," she said, more snappishly than she'd intended.

"Layne," he told her.

She sighed. "Alright, Layne. I've been up all night. There's a man who's dead. My uncle is in jail. And I'm at fault. So excuse me if I'm having trouble making polite conversation."

He stared at the road ahead. "I'm sorry," he said. "We don't need to talk if it bothers you, Ms. Parker."

"Christine," she corrected him.

He nodded. "Okay, Christine."

She sat up in her seat and unfolded her arms and put them uncomfortably at her sides. "Look, I want to talk. But chatting about the weather and ignoring my situation just won't cut it. How do you make a conflict of interest simply out of listening to me?" She leaned her head against the headrest and felt tears gathering in her eyes again and tried to will them away. She understood that by any standard she was not behaving well, but she couldn't help herself. All she wanted to do was make the facts clear to him from the beginning.

She sat up, unzipped her purse, and began digging toward the bottom for Kleenexes, then remembered that she'd used them on her windshield on the drive to Saraville. She glanced over at Layne, who was stoically glaring straight ahead, then reached up and pulled down the overhead visor. In the little attached mirror, she got a narrow glance at herself. She used her fingers to wipe around her eyes and silently said to hell with the rest, then flipped the visor back up with a resounding snap.

Maybe the problem was simply men: these strong, silent semi-Neanderthals patronizing the much-talked-about communication gap. That gap had certainly existed between herself and her ex-husband, T. C. Falco, a jazz saxophonist who had forever been struggling for that elusive break into the big time. At first, he had seemed so eager to share all his ideas and dreams, but slowly he had traded in love and companionship for long hours clamped between stereo headphones, studying the riffs and runs of all the greats before him. He called it "art and discipline," though she came to see it as "zoning out."

"I understand that you're having a hard time with all of this," Layne said, without looking over at her. "Please be patient. Just let me talk to Dallas first." He swung into the right lane of Interstate 15 and took the first exit for St. George.

"Okay," she sighed, "let's do it your way for awhile. But I want to know exactly what Dallas thinks he's doing in there."

"Good," he said with no trace of enthusiasm, as he moved up the ramp to a stoplight. He turned into the instant flow of traffic. "Welcome to St. George Boulevard. The Chamber of Commerce has an annual prize for whoever puts up the biggest and tackiest new sign."

She had to admire his tenacity. He had a plan—become the king of daytime small talk—and he was sticking to it. "Well," Christine said, "it looks like any street in Phoenix to me."

"My point precisely." He glanced over at her. "Ah, don't mind me. Picking on The George is a local sport among us gentiles."

"And now you're expanding it to Phoenix," she said, a little more good naturedly.

There were frequent stoplights down the wide street leading to the middle of town. As Layne slowed for a right turn, Christine saw a handful of people carrying placards and pacing the sidewalk—mostly women, a few kids, and one man—near the curb, politely waving as they passed. OUR GOVERNMENT NUKES KIDS. BAN THE TEST SITE. DON'T GET DOWNWIND OF UNCLE SAM.

Layne looked in the rearview mirror and then left over his shoulder. "People around these parts got plastered with fallout for two generations. They say there's only two kinds of cancer around here. The kind you've got or the kind you're going to get. Anyway, they may finally have a chance for vindication with this big downwinder radiation case going on in federal court in Las Vegas right now."

Christine spoke in clipped tones. "You mean vindication against Dr. Son-of-a-Bitch Rudd and his kind? I thought you didn't want to talk about any of that."

If Layne heard her, he didn't, for even a second, show it.

Any courage and fight she had mustered immediately evaporated as a cluster of press vans came into view. As they drove closer, she could clearly see the swarm of microphones and cameras ready at the entrance to the sheriff's office. A news helicopter with smart graphics down its side suddenly banked over the building.

Christine began tentatively, "Is that—"

"I'm afraid so," he said. "This whole mess—situation—has already hit the news." Layne abruptly turned away from the scene, drove half a block down a quiet residential street, and parked under a big shade tree. "Okay, I promise you that as soon as I talk to Dallas, I'll tell you what he says, what the situation looks like in there, and try to advise you as best I can. Deal?"

Christine didn't answer. She felt cold and shaky, as if her heart were trying to leap to the other side of her chest.

"Just let me talk to your uncle. Then it's your call. I swear. Is that fair enough?" he asked.

Worn through with waiting, she snapped at him, "Don't patronize me, Mr. Harting. It's my call any time I want it to be." She quickly looked away from him at someone watering flowers in a nearby yard—huge purple blooms on wavering stems. In a moment, she heard him walk away, steady as clockwork.

Shoes. Dallas sat and stared at his shoes. They looked and felt as odd as everything else in this new world. They were worn, black canvas slip-ons, gym shoes with no laces because you could hang yourself, he presumed, or someone else. Laces as weapons. And it didn't end with the dumb shoes. He'd been ordered to strip off his street clothes, then stand inspection for weapons or contraband. Afterwards, they'd given him an orange jumpsuit to wear, a goofy outfit more suited to retired men in their RVs. What did he expect, though? He'd been arrested for murder this morning and every single aspect of his life had changed.

At the end of his narrow bunk lay two crisply folded sheets and a blanket. Not that Dallas was worried about the accommodations here; he was simply taking a dazed inventory of everything around him: the concrete floor, the pea-green cinderblock walls, the stainless steel toilet poised shamelessly in the corner.

His cell was the last one down a long corridor. When the guards had escorted him onto the block about an hour ago, the first thing he had seen was a dayroom full of inmates, apparently free to wander, and then, further on, other prisoners lounging in their open cells away from the commotion and chatter. The guards marched him all the way down the hall through this new world of concrete and metal bars to a dead end before locking him up. He was completely alone, the adjoining cells closed and empty.

As he sat there feeling dreary and stupefied, one question kept coming back and circling the inside of his skull like an angry wasp. Where was Christine? Somehow, in all the chaos late last night, they had missed each other out at the ranch. He needed to talk to her, to bring her up to date, to make sure she stayed calm and did nothing—just went along with the program.

Dallas pulled himself from his trance, sat up, and shook his legs, trying to relieve the radiating pain, the fiery knot, dead center between them. He walked over to the toilet, unzipped, knew this wasn't going to be easy. He gripped the vent pipe behind the toilet until his knuckles stood like marbles and his bladder finally let go. A couple of months ago, he'd had to endure a catheter, consult science just to take a piss, and he was about done with all that nonsense.

Finished, he turned around to find someone standing at the bars watching him.

"Hey. Welcome, Pops." It was a young man with obvious muscles and long, stringy hair. "What you in for? They got you down here alone?"

Dallas gazed at the spacy inmate like someone confronting an abstract painting.

"Egan! That area's offlimits," a guard bellowed down the hall. Egan shrugged and sauntered off.

That's right, keep them away, Dallas thought. He was a big-time criminal, sequestered down here by himself, surrounded by empty cells, segregated from all the others who were probably petty thieves and drunk drivers and child support wimps. He was . . . what? A murderer, that's what.

The word, the whole concept, was slowly and irrevocably starting to sink in. If last night embodied the sensations of a dream—actions and reactions, events spinning out of control, surprises at each turn—this morning was the polar opposite: concrete and absolute and measuring exactly eight by ten. And, perhaps worst of all, this reality was completely controlled by others. For fifty-nine years he had lived and roamed without walls or women or weather stopping him. It was simply a fact, taken for granted. He understood on some level that he was very fortunate, had never punched a clock, never picked up his orders from any kind of boss. Even when he contracted for outside work, training someone else's horse or guiding a group of deer hunters, he did it on his own terms, answerable only to an occasional payday and some rough, intermittent voice inside himself.

But then, he guessed no matter who you were, nothing prepared you for this.

After leaving Rudd's house last night, Dallas had driven out to his ranch at Motoqua. With the stolen suitcase next to him on the front seat, his mind was racing. He wasn't exactly sure yet how this manuscript fit in, but it was the only thing he might have working on his side. He was surprised to find that Christine wasn't at the ranch, but he couldn't second-guess her right then, couldn't let his mind wander. He read the note she'd left, then wrote one to her, simply saying to stay put until he got back. He tested a large flashlight and carefully wrapped Rudd's book and the computer discs in plastic. He knew exactly where he was headed.

The moon was half-hidden behind marbled clouds as he hurried toward the corrals. In a strange darkness that seemed to spread from another world, Wasco, his six-year-old, raw-boned gelding, appeared at the far end of the corral. Dallas gathered his tack from the shed. Each piece—the blanket, saddle, and bridle—felt cool and intricate in his hands. He worked slowly, as if savoring the texture of each object for the first time or perhaps for the last, allowing himself to feel all the welling sentiments of an old fool. The horse reflexively huffed against the cinch, shook out the sleep, and rattled the gear, then blew hard and relaxed as Dallas tightened it down. The smell of hay, grain, saddle leather, sweat in the pads overwhelmed him. His two dogs, an old Aussie and a young heeler, were lying in the cool night dirt, heads up, watching him. As he swung into the saddle, Wasco stepped out briskly. The dogs were already moving ahead.

Finding hole-in-the-rock—about three miles up on a high ridge—was a little tougher in the dark than he would have thought. After some time circling, shining his light and picking up his own tracks, then narrowing onto a couple of landmarks, he finally honed in on a truck-sized block of sandstone. He tied off the horse and walked around to the back of the boulder.

His light discovered what he was looking for: a porthole in the side of the rock covered by a thin, flat piece of sandstone that had been shaped to fit the opening. Carved by the Anasazi, these ancient ones roamed the entire Colorado Plateau and Basin, then mysteriously disappeared over a thousand years ago. He removed the rock lid and set it to the side. Shining his light into the hole, only an arm's length in depth, he could see the ancient cache: pottery shards, arrowheads, rocks.

Dallas had shared hole-in-the-rock with Christine when she was a girl and tonight those memories washed over him. It had been their special secret. He told her that it was bad luck to remove anything from the ridge, but that the spirits wouldn't mind if she selected one perfect arrowhead as a special good luck piece, so long as she was careful and carried it with reverence. Christine had taken him very seriously, didn't select her one piece until she was thirteen, and then had it fitted for a necklace and wore it only on special occasions for the promised luck.

She had reminded Dallas of that conversation just a couple of weeks ago in a fit of laughter at sundown over Jack and water. She said that he must have gotten the story wrong, that the spirits were actually pissed off because she had removed the arrowhead. They had sent her T. C. Falco as a husband and then consigned her to the one-breasted clan for good measure.

Dallas shook his head, unsure how much to laugh, and mumbled something dumb about luck never being a straight line leading anywhere.

She agreed completely and said that she was now looking for a rich, one-armed man who was smart enough to know that anything over a handful was wasted. Dallas finally laughed hard until his eyes watered, thankful for the lifelong bond with this woman whose sense of humor hadn't been fazed one bit by a bad marriage, chemotherapy, or scalpels.

Now, as he peered into the cache at all her collectibles, something in him ached over all this new trouble—not for himself, but for her. He tied the heavy flashlight to a juniper branch and sat down with his back against the boulder to read the manuscript. The night breeze topping the ridge gently rocked his circle of light. He flipped through the pages, going back and forth at random, stopping to read certain sections, and scanning through the headings, looking for the things that jumped off the page at him. It was thick, over four hundred pages, including perhaps a hundred separate exhibits.

It had been a long—a very long—night. Dallas finally rode back to the house in the first hint of dawn, tied up some loose ends there, then drove back into St. George. The police spotted his truck and pulled him over at 7:58 a.m., apparently thanks to one of Rudd's neighbors who had flipped on his lights and come to the front door last night as Dallas sat noisily revving up his truck before leaving the scene. He had actually convinced himself that he was mentally ready for his arrest and felt some sense of relief when it happened, partly because he was tired of being so obvious and partly because he was running out of gas.

The arrest had gone about the way he had imagined it. After the short, handcuffed ride to the sheriff's office, he had been led to the booking area. The jailers were all straight faced and silent except to give him instructions—"Look straight ahead" and "Turn right"—but Dallas could tell that the whole place was buzzing over the crime and his arrest.

At one point, he had looked up and recognized a tall, sandy-haired officer as Wallace Mooney's son. Wallace, a guy he'd known forever, ran a road grader for the county and tried in vain to keep the tops of the washboards knocked off the back-country gravel roads. Without thinking, Dallas had almost lifted a hand and waved, but some part of him instantly knew better. Anyway, Mooney's kid had been quicker and glanced away.

Dallas was then taken to a room and questioned for well over an hour. They brought in the suitcase full of Rudd's valuables—wallet, watch, jewelry, passbook savings, stock certificates—that had been conveniently discovered behind the seat of his truck. He answered all of their questions about himself and his background and none of their questions about the previous night.

Herm Zitting, the sheriff, came in and personally took charge of the interrogation. Dallas knew the man by reputation only, a typical St. George Mormon, a pasty-faced politician in love with pot roast and heavy cream dishes. He kept rocking his considerable weight over his small, well-polished shoes and repeating himself, as if he couldn't think of anything new to say. "Mister, looks like we got you dead to rights," he said. "May as well confess."

Dallas calmly replied, "Talk to my lawyer," or "You already seem to know all about that one."

Eventually, Jim Bidwell, the county attorney and a first cousin to the sheriff, came into the room, red-faced and in a huff. He called the sheriff out for a short conference. The two men, obviously at odds and waving their arms, stood almost belly to belly as Dallas and the others watched through the open door. Finally they came back in and the sheriff grudgingly picked up a telephone from the corner, set it in front of Dallas, and told him to call his lawyer.

Dallas stared for a long moment down at the beige telephone. "I don't know the number," he said.

The sheriff opened the door. "Phone book," he growled in the direction of Deputy Betty. "Need a phone book."

The dispatcher, topped by that mound of blonde hair, walked slowly toward him, picked up the small directory sitting on a desk about three feet from the sheriff, and offered it to him. "And how about room service? Root beer or Sprite?" she said. "Us girls aim to please. Sir."

The sheriff waved her off impatiently and closed the door.

Dallas took his time finding the number and dialing. Layne's secretary answered the phone and informed him that Mr. Harting wasn't in, that he had just left not two minutes ago for St. George. Dallas didn't leave his name. He simply thanked her and hung up.

"Not in," he said stoically. He could have told them that Layne was on his way to St. George, but he didn't. He figured Layne would probably hear about all this when he got to town and would most likely come over to the jail anyway. That's the way Dallas saw it and that was good enough. He didn't need a lawyer to deal with these guys.

"Not in," he said again.

They looked at each other, a little puzzled, a little frustrated. "Ooh, fuzz," the sheriff said, "we already have plenty to convict this guy." He glanced at the county attorney for assurances. "And I'll bet his fingerprints are all over that house. And the knife." They all nodded assent.

Open and shut. That was precisely what Dallas wanted them to think.

Dallas stared at his new companion, the small, open-top stainless toilet in the corner of his cell. He'd never been in jail before, but looking down at this metal device, he understood at least part of the psychology: confine a person and remove even this last bit of privacy. It was like taking off the top layer of skin, making you feel that much less human.

The heavy thud of boots on concrete made Dallas turn around. Two guards appeared at the bars. "Parker. Your lawyer's here." They refastened the restraints to his wrists and ankles and led him through the small jail complex to an interview room only about twice the size of his cell. Layne Harting was already there, leaning against a metal table, looking preoccupied and unamused. The jailers backed out without saying a word and closed the steel door behind them. One remained just outside, clearly visible through a heavy glass window embedded with wire mesh. Three matching metal chairs were placed at random around the paint-chipped table. Like the rest of the place, no excess of taxpayers' dollars had been poured into the furnishings.

"Well, good morning, counselor," Dallas said, trying his best to fake a good-old-boy smile and coffee shop airs. "Now that's the mark of a true professional," he said. "Arrives before the client has even phoned him for help. How'd you find . . .?"

"The stars must have pointed in your direction," Layne interrupted. "And the sheriff's office was only too happy to connect the dots." He had straightened a paper clip and was aimlessly re-bending it. "So, are you interested in cutting through the good-fellowship routine and telling me what's going on here?"

Dallas shrugged casually. "I did it," he said. "Everything they say is true. I killed the old boy." Dallas knew he had to level with Layne if he wanted him to help out here, and admitting to the murder seemed like a good start, but he also appreciated just how strange and jarring it must sound—no rationalization, no explanation.

"Just like that?"

"Just like that." Dallas could hear how off-the-cuff it

seemed, even confrontational. And Layne wasn't the enemy here.

"Well, sort of just like that," Dallas said and dropped his head a little. "It's been a long night, and it's a long story. Why don't we sit down?" Dallas short-hobbled it over to the table and, using his manacled hands, pulled out one of the chairs. He had expected Layne to show up but was still surprised by how quickly he'd come. He remembered when Layne was new in the country and was still trying to adjust. He had followed some part of his heart down to southern Utah, and now was anxious to learn all about horses, talking to ranchers, subscribing to magazines, and reading the books. Dallas had worked a gelding around the paddock the day Layne came out to see him, and he could tell that the young lawyer was intrigued, admired both him and the horse.

Dallas understood that an old cowboy sitting pretty on top of a young quarter horse, putting it through its moves—spinning it right and then left using only his knees, roping a training log and having the horse pull it backwards across the yard, sliding it to an abrupt stop, and crow-hopping quickly side to side—must have been an irresistible sight to someone like Layne, with his lingering romantic notions of the Old West. The funny thing was, Dallas saw more and more people who, like this lawyer, were leaving the cities in search of something they had misplaced, but he usually couldn't get past their giant king-cab pickups and shiny horse trailers, and their thinking that new Butler buildings were the same thing as old barns. Layne, however, had turned out to be quietly different.

The horse they ended up trading for legal work was uncommonly smart, and, for a novice, Layne had done very well with it. After that, Layne came back out to the ranch every few weeks, making no secret of his desire to watch Dallas work with the horses, to drink a little whiskey and bullshit about it all. And in a way that he could not have even put into words, Dallas came to enjoy these visits. Layne was quick and comic, every once in a while throwing in a personal little barb about his ex-wife, the law practice or a client, or the way middle age was staking its claim on him. Dallas was humored and liked these brief, dizzying glimpses into the lawyer's life, but for his end of things, he stuck to the topics of horses, weather, irrigation—anything but himself. No touchy-feely for this old cowboy.

The interview room smelled vaguely of stale . . . something. Layne dragged a chair, noisily across the concrete and sat down across from Dallas. "Just like that," Layne repeated only half-aloud, seeming more puzzled than irritated now. "No shit? You killed this guy?" He tossed the paper clip onto the table.

"Yes, sir." Dallas watched Layne's expression. "So I guess I'll need to retain your services." The lawyer's face was still a billboard of doubt. Dallas was puzzled. Why didn't Layne believe him?

"Well, you've certainly got my attention," Layne said. "And, according to the reports, you then robbed the guy?" Layne leaned toward Dallas with his hands on the table. "Or was it the other way around? Burglary first?"

"What's the difference?" Dallas said, trying to keep his voice casual.

Layne's eyes narrowed and Dallas could see that the lawyer's bullshit detector was on red alert. He felt bad stringing Layne along like this, but he wasn't completely sure how to proceed, when and how much to tell him about stolen property, distraught relatives, or classified government documents. He hadn't seen Layne for several months, and didn't feel good about renewing their acquaintance like this, but his nerves were shot. Layne was his only hope, and there was Christine to think about.

"The difference," Layne interrupted his thoughts, "is that I don't believe you. Not for an instant. You slit some guy's throat for his credit cards and a watch?" Layne shook his head.

Dallas was suddenly irritated. "Well, I'm not wearing this monkey suit and bracelets because I mowed his lawn the wrong way."

"Why do you need me then?" Layne snapped. "If you're that cavalier about it all, why not just confess to the authorities, save everyone a lot of time?"

"Don't worry, I intend to, eventually, counselor," Dallas shot back.

Then he sighed and slumped back in his chair, feeling bad that he was letting things get crossways with Layne. "But they'll assign me some damn freebie lawyer from around here," Dallas said, trying to lighten things up a little, "some mojo in polyester whom I won't be able to tolerate." He faked a grin, "And at least I know you won't screw up my guilty plea."

"Don't be too sure," Layne said. Dallas noticed Layne's eyes, a multicolored hazel, deceptively sleepy-looking when he was casually appraising or amused, much more intent when he was focused. Right now they were drilling holes in him.

"But at least you got something right," Layne continued. "The court will require you to have a lawyer. Even for a guilty plea." Then he slid his chair back and gazed up at the ceiling. "I have to say that this has been quite a morning, Dallas. And you know something? You're not the only person I've met in the last two hours who's champing at the bit to confess."

The fog around Dallas cleared instantly; the fatigue evaporate as well, replaced by fear. There was a ringing in his ears, a bad backtaste when he swallowed. He struggled to keep his face blank.

"I have someone out in the car," Layne said, "who claims to be a relative of yours. Says she thinks she killed this Dr. Rudd fellow. Maybe you guys could get together, figure out one story."

Dallas nervously reached up to thumb his mustache, but was jerked short by the cuffs. He attempted to settle his hands smoothly back in his lap. "Chrissy?" he asked. His voice was giving everything away. "You're with Chrissy? Is she okay?"

"On a scale of what to what?" Layne asked.

Dallas's shoulders dropped. "Oh Christ," he said. "I've been going crazy in here, so worried about her." The air went out of him and his head hung down. "You've got to believe this," Dallas said. "She's not guilty of anything here."

"Well, you better tell her that. She's been threatening all morning to confess to anybody wearing a uniform. She's probably out there talking to the mailman right now."

"Has she really talked to anyone else?" Dallas knew his voice sounded urgent and he didn't care anymore. If she was with Layne, then that was as good as he could hope for. But he had to convince Layne to watch out for her, and to go along with his agenda.

Layne shook his head. "No, I don't think so, Dallas. Just me," he said more softly. "I'm pretty sure she's only talked to me about it. So far."

"Jesus. What a mess," Dallas said. "Hell, you've met her. Does she look like someone who could kill a man?"

Layne drummed his fingers on the tabletop. "Cut somebody's throat?" Layne shook his head again. "No. But then neither does her uncle."

"Well," Dallas said, "in your business, you must get a lot of surprises."

"I'm not convinced. I don't believe you did this. Not the murder. Not the robbery," Layne said. "It'd be the surprise of my career, alright. Not unless there was one hell of a compelling reason."

Dallas thought for a moment. They were on a path to nowhere. "Look, what's done is done. And I think that soon you'll better understand the reasons. But right now I don't have time to go into it all. I need you to get back out to Christine. Don't let her do anything stupid."

Layne stared at him as if he were reciting riddles.

"I need your help on something. Don't worry about my case right now. I'll be fine." Dallas paused, realizing that he could really use a cold glass of water. "There's no place else I can turn, Layne. I don't like asking for help, I don't like involving you in this, but I don't have a choice on this one." It was a matter of pride and independence, not asking for help throughout most of his lifetime, but if pride was going to bring the roof down, well . . .

Dallas looked up at the light fixture and cocked his head. "Is this place bugged?"

Layne followed Dallas's eyes upward. "Bug this jail? I assume that'd be an ACLU dream case, but I'm new at this jail-house stuff. What do I know, so keep your voice low."

"Okay, now look," Dallas whispered, glancing over at the window. The jailer out in the hall had his back to them, appeared to be talking to someone they couldn't see. Dallas motioned Layne in closer. "After I left Rudd's place, I went back out to the ranch. I left something out there. You and Chrissy have to go take a look at it."

"What is it?" Layne asked.

"Seems to be a book or something this Rudd guy was getting ready to publish." Dallas lowered his voice even more and motioned Layne to move in closer. "He's written all about his years as general manager out at the Nevada Test Site, back in the fifties and sixties. He's got all kinds of government documents attached, Top Secret and Classified stamped all over the damn thing. Could blow the lid off some stuff around these parts."

"What—?"

"You heard me right," Dallas said, straightening up a little.

Layne bowed his head and rubbed at his temples. "Good hell, Dallas," he said. "How many more surprises are down this road?"

Dallas smiled vaguely. "One thing you learn being around horses all your life. Surprise is what it's all about. You just hope it doesn't come on the steepest part of the trail."

"Yeah? And what part of the trail are we on right now, Dallas?" Layne shifted in his seat. "I don't know. This—"

"Yeah, you do know," he said, because at rock bottom, Layne could be counted on. They both knew it without hanging any words on it. "This is damn important. Trust me. At least take a look, then come back and talk to me."

Layne was abstractly shaking his head, but Dallas wasn't

about to let him off the hook. "I need a big favor," he said. "Go out to the ranch tomorrow and feed the stock. Tomorrow morning is soon enough. Chrissy's probably been up all night."

Layne nodded. "She looks pretty wrung out."

"Well, I fed and watered early this morning," Dallas said, "so they're good for the day. You guys just feed tomorrow and don't forget the dogs. Then ask Hollis, my neighbor on the east, to take over the place, if you will. He knows what to do until I get back."

Dallas's own words rang in his ears. *Until I get back.* The phrase was so full of nostalgia and fear for him that all he could do was rush headlong away from it, try to crack some egghead joke. "Come on," he said. "You're always looking for a day of vacation."

"Some vacation," Layne sighed. "So I'm sitting here in the middle of this and you're not going to tell me the full story?"

"We don't have time right now. You need to get back out to Chrissy. We can talk tomorrow, after you see that book." Dallas sighed, "Besides, what's to tell? The facts don't lie. The cops have this one down cold."

Layne picked up his pen—a blue-and-gold promo from the Saraville High Chargers—and tapped it against the table a couple of times. "Then I guess I'm going to have to rely on your niece to tell me."

Dallas shook his head. "Go easy there, friend."

Layne started to get up.

"One more minute," Dallas said. "I need to give you some directions."

"Yeah, right," Layne said. "I was kind of hoping you'd forgo them."

Dallas awkwardly reached over to Layne's legal pad laying on the table. "Do you mind?" Layne nodded and handed him the pen as Dallas pulled the tablet into his lap, opened it to a blank page in the middle, and began writing, managing the cuffs in the process. "This is a note to Chrissy. See that she grabs a good night's sleep someplace, then you guys head out to the ranch early tomorrow. I owe you big on this one, Layne."

He looked up and stopped writing. "They can't take this pad away from you, can they?"

"No," Layne said quietly, "my files, including that pad, are privileged."

"Good. Show this to Chrissy and tell her to mind it. And make damn sure she does." Dallas looked at Layne. "Okay? Make sure of that."

"Make sure she minds? Are we talking about the same niece?" Layne said. "Dallas, I'm having a hard enough time just keeping her calmed down. She thinks you're taking the rap for her."

"She's headstrong and always has been," Dallas said. "You just show her my note and tell her not to do anything at all until she discusses it with me personally. And make that emphatic. Talks to me personally." Dallas closed the pad and slid it back over to Layne. "You got to keep a lid on this for me, Layne. You're all I have to help me here."

"No commitments yet, Dallas," Layne said. "But I'll take one look. I suppose the Feds would allow me a quick peek to see if you're hallucinating or what." Layne rose from his chair. "But that's it. Then we talk again, tomorrow, no promises. And I can tell you that your niece may not go along with all this. When I left her, she wasn't too happy with me."

"Well, it's not you," he said. "That poor girl's had a hard time finding anything to be happy about the last year. She's been through hell. She was diagnosed with cancer a year or so ago. Breast cancer. They pumped her so full of different shit that she couldn't see straight. Lost all her hair. It's just now growing back. She's doing better, but sometimes she has a hard time thinking right. Help her out here, will you?"

Dallas could see that he'd set Layne back with this news, left him in the territory of no wisecracks. He stood up and extended his right hand across the table toward Layne while trailing the left.

"Cancer? Jesus," Layne said, absently grasping and shaking the outstretched hand. Then mumbling to himself, "Goddammit, me and my big mouth."

His birth certificate read Daniel Benito Briggs—a name haphazardly chosen for a first son by a thirteen-year-old mother—but on the fiery summer streets of East L.A. where he grew up, he had quickly become Manos. Now, years later, it was the only name he answered to.

He didn't give a shit about the past or how anything came to be called what it was. Numbers were what mattered right now. He had just turned forty—the big 4-0. Plus, he was always trying to gain weight, reach 160 pounds, put more bulk on his small, well-muscled frame. His handicapping efforts at the track were in a slump, and his last stint in the Nevada State Penitentiary had lasted four years and forty-four days. But it was twenty-five-thousand that really had his attention. That's what Samuel Cope owed him on a meth deal—which meant that Sammy Boy was cutting into Manos's working capital and that chunk-face's personal number was up if it wasn't paid. And soon.

Manos's ten-year-old, beautifully reconditioned black Jaguar wound down from its quick 120-mile freeway sprint from Las Vegas to St. George, Utah. It was almost ten in the morning and he figured his timing was about right, except for one thing—it was Monday, and he should have taken care of this little job on Friday. But hey, blame Sammy Boy. He'd disappeared on a rather quick and irresponsible note, and Manos had been chasing the piece of shit around Vegas all weekend.

The remainder of a half-pound bag of pistachios lay on the sleek leather seat next to Manos. He brushed salt off his pant legs and watched for the Vermillion Hills Country Club exit, which was supposedly on the southern edge of town. An enormous billboard came into view: WELCOME TO WASHINGTON COUNTY—GREATEST EARTH ON SHOW. Manos was in no mood to appreciate such cuteness. He lived in Las Vegas, where desert was desert and rocks were rocks and D-9 cats made both tolerable. He pointed his trigger finger at the billboard as he passed.

"And you sophomoric small-town hicks need to look up 'trite' in the fuckin' dictionary," he said aloud as he fired an imaginary bullet.

Manos himself had more than a nodding acquaintance with *Webster's*, having read the *College Edition*, cover to cover, three times on different trips to the joint. Even back as a juvenile inmate, he had quickly discovered that he was smarter than most cons. Reading smart books was just another way to prove it. Back when the social workers had tried to ply a young Manos with hope by telling him how perceptive he was, by telling him that the standard IQ tests couldn't begin to measure the raw intelligence of this fifth-grade dropout. But hope was subjective, his version quite different from the do-gooders trying to save him.

His freeway exit appeared and he consulted a handwritten map for the various rights and lefts that were to guide him to the designated house. Manos would case the area and set his plan during the day, then go back tonight and have a forthright conversation with the man in question, one Dr. Franklin T. Rudd. Together, they'd decide that it would be best for everyone concerned if Manos took possession of the old guy's files, his floppies and computer, anything that looked vaguely connected to a book-in-progress. He would tell the old boy some bullshit story about being a CIA affiliate, a contractor, a special agent of sorts, and that if this book idea continued, they'd find him in pieces in his dishwasher one morning. Get the manuscript, scare the guy, don't hurt him; that was his "assignment." Manos had nodded and told Hiney that he'd leave the guy crapping down both legs in a little cesspool of his own private making. Intimidation had always been the least of Manos's problems.

He followed the crisp green-and-white signs standing perfectly erect and unmolested on the corners of broad streets, the pavement smooth as black ribbon. The only graffiti he'd seen in the last fifty miles was on a big painted rock marking the outskirts of town. It said GO MUSTANGS. As he drove slowly through the tidy neighborhood, he appreciated all the generous windows and country club manners, the tea parties and bridge clubs and aperitifs. Neighborhoods like this one had certainly been generous to him—he would go in alone after Mr. and Mrs. Success had left for the opera, fill the wife's new Range Rover full of electronic equipment and jewelry, then drive the whole load over to one-stop fencing, a guy who just happened to be a longtime acquaintance, who knew Manos well enough to prefer prison to fingering him. It wasn't a difficult conclusion—you didn't have to know the specifics of Manos's reputation, his background, or his psychosociopathic profile to understand that you didn't want to fuck with a Las Vegas maniac like this, a sunbaked crazy with a permanent sizzle in his brainpan.

It was just like he had told Sammy Boy—as if he really had to say anything: Don't cross me; have the money by Friday or the serious fun begins.

Sammy's welfare-case brother had stood in his apartment doorway and blinked drunkenly into the bleached midday wall of light in Henderson, Nevada. Manos had shoved him back inside and down onto a cheap coffee table that splintered to the floor.

"He's not here," yelled the brother, who looked sick, white, and puffy, a tick ready to ooze.

"No duh. I can see that." Manos kicked him on the left ear.

A woman, tattooed roses wandering down one arm, ran into the room and screamed. Toward the kitchen, a baby in a high chair began crying and flinging little handfuls of refried beans, momentarily disturbing the flies.

"You tell Samuel exactly this," Manos said. "Get the money. Get it to me post-fucking-haste. If it don't happen by tomorrow, I'll take down the whole family, one generation at a time." Manos straightened up. "Starting with you guys."

Tonight, he'd scare this old-shit scientist alright, scare him to death if the guy so much as gave him a minute's worth of trouble. And since Sammy had dented his cash flow projections, Manos hoped the old buzzard had some liquid assets he could snag, a little unanticipated bonus to make the trip worthwhile—a Rolex, some guns, a rare coin collection.

He consulted his directions again, watched the street signs, and turned left. Suddenly he was facing a gaggle of cop cars parked half-assed into the street like they owned it all. They were in front of a house cordoned off by yellow police tape. Presumptuous dickheads, he thought, driving by and checking the address. Shit, this was the place he was looking for. What was going on? Had Hiney forgot to tell him something? Maybe there was some competition around snagging this book.

Manos had known Deputy R. C. Hiney, a grunt dead-ended in the United States Marshall's Office in Las Vegas, for several years. They had exchanged a few "unofficial" favors, so it was not totally off base that R. C. had called him and set up an afternoon meeting last Friday at the Bingo-Bango-Bongo, a topless bar in North Las Vegas.

"What do you mean, break into the guy's house?" Manos had asked. "Since when are you guys into burglary?"

R. C. acted deaf, kept watching a tall nineteen-year-old with Kansas farm tits dance for the next table. Manos could smell her perfume ten feet away. She put her head down and mimed a blow job in the air over a dusty construction worker's crotch, rubbing the top of her head on his stained Levi's and bumping against his dick. Then she stood up and tossed a rangy leg over his shoulder, the back of her knee resting on the guy's collarbone, and began gyrating her crotch, covered only by a narrow strip of cloth, a few inches from his face. When the guy was a little too slow in snapping another dollar bill under her garter belt, she grabbed her G-string and pulled it to the side, giving the guy a quick shot of the motherland so he'd ante up. The music ended and she offered her artistic services to the next table.

Fickle bitch, thought Manos. "So what do you want burgled?" he asked.

R. C. looked away from the girl. "A book," he said.

Manos and R. C. had a sort of reciprocal thing going. A little information for me, a little dirty work for you—it all evened out. And Hiney was pals with Manos's current parole officer, which didn't hurt. But most of all, Manos loved the idea of getting in close on a cop, even if he was just a guy who served summonses and guarded judges, because he nonetheless had access to information and influence with adult probation. If you can't afford to buy the judge, then get to his driver. Besides, he enjoyed being invited by the law to break into a civilian's house and, more than that, he relished in particular having something to hold over dear old Deputy Hiney. A chit he could call in.

"What's the book?" Manos asked. "Does this particular tome have a title?" The girl was headed toward them, but Manos turned her away with his eyes. Hiney had put on some weight since he'd last seen him, looked kind of bloated and stressed out, like he was drinking too much. He needed to get his fat ass off the couch and run it around the block. Manos worked out like a fiend when he was in prison, and outside his regimen was almost as tough.

"It's not published," R. C. looked at him, "yet. And won't be. You need to get his files, his computer, his backup disks. Everything. Ask him nicely to cooperate, but let him know that he should stick with golf, that writing this book ain't a healthy retirement activity." R. C. swallowed down the last inch of his beer, then set the glass on the outer edge of the table, crumpled the cocktail napkin, and dropped it inside the glass.

"Sure." Manos said, "Where do I go?"

Here in Rudd's fancy Vermillion Hills subdivision, Manos was heading toward a 220-pound, baby-faced cop with a blond crew cut standing by the hood of his patrol car, arms folded across his chest, nodding occasionally to a talkative older couple who looked like Dr. Rudd's neighbors. Manos, having parked on the next street over, was momentarily tempted to head straight back to Vegas and keep after Sammy, not mess around with cops and crime scenes. But he hadn't broken any laws in Utah, not that he could recall anyway, and so he might as well at least check it out, see if there were any pickings left. Maybe things were just getting good.

He walked up to the young officer as the old couple backed away then meandered down the street.

"Morning," said Manos.

The officer turned his head slightly, examining Manos from behind his mirrored aviator sunglasses. The officer looked barely off the high school football team and seemed to be compensating for it, his uniform fitted and pressed severely, the creases so sharp that you wouldn't want him to hold a baby. His posture was all weight lifter, with upper arms that looked like hams wrapped in khaki. Manos had the guy figured in three seconds; he'd met all of his cousins, on either side of the bars. The only thing more boring than a prisoner is a prisoner's guard.

"Morning," said the deputy.

"Yes, and a glorious morning it is, sir," Manos said. "Looks like this is all the excitement. Or was."

The cop eyed him suspiciously. Manos knew he had been trained to observe strangers closely, but the kid didn't quite have it down yet. "Can I help you?" the officer asked.

"Oh, just doing a job, you know. I'm a stringer for UPS, out of Las Vegas." Manos pulled a pen and notebook from the inside pocket of his sleeves-up black Italian-waiter's jacket. Combined with the tiny gold hoop in his left ear and the pressed sand-washed jeans, the rigorously manicured fingernails and bleached ultrawhite teeth, it all suggested he might actually be an L.A. dealmaker scouting locations for a new movie or beer commercial. Not that the officer would know the difference.

"Well, this must be the residence of the esteemed Dr. Rudd, I presume."

"It was. Till last night." The cop remained planted, feet apart, arms still folded, as though his chest really needed help looking bigger. Manos loved it when big dumb cons towered over him like this in the joint; it left their guts wide open.

"Ah, the ominousness of past tense." Manos turned toward the house and cupped a hand over his eyes against the bright sun. The garage door and the front door, all the doors, were wide open. Through a large bay window, he could see shadows moving inside. "What happened here?"

The officer said without turning, "Don't even think about it. No one's allowed in the crime scene."

"Of course not. That's standard procedure, we see it everywhere." Manos shrugged his compliance. "Maybe you could give me a little help though. I've got a deadline to meet and, well, truthfully, I'm covering for an associate back at the newsroom. His wife went into premature labor about three hours ago. I hope she's okay; we all do. But I need to meet this deadline for him. Could you kindly bring me up to speed here?"

The officer stared at him like he had babbled some archaic language.

"Just the basics, sir. The old who, what, when, where," Manos paused and gave the cop a smile full of proud teeth, "and, hopefully, a little of the why and how." Manos tilted his head to the side and slumped his posture like a young dog admitting dominance. "Just as a favor to that new dad in Vegas?"

Doomtown

NEAR THE CENTER OF YUCCA FLAT—A DRY ANCIENT LAKE BED which was talcumy white in the daytime and silvery gray at night—lay ground zero. There, lit by glaring searchlights, stood a steel tower five hundred feet high, and at the top, a small room accessible by elevator. Inside that room sat a round metal canister the size of a washing machine, and inside the canister—everything held within something else, like Chinese nesting boxes—waited an atomic device code named Huey. It was designed to produce seventy-eight kilotons of energy, the largest atmospheric bomb ever tested over the continental United States and five times bigger than the one at Hiroshima. The canister holding Huey had every conceivable kind of wire and cable running up to, surrounding, and hooked into it—the red ones for detonation, the blue ones for blast monitoring and measurement, and a variety of other colors for lighting, sound, tracking, and all the other wonders technology could produce.

For weeks, scientists, engineers, test site employees, and news people had been talking about Huey with excitement. It was the seventh shot in the Green Angel series of nuclear test bombs, though almost no one used that word—*bomb*. It was referred to like all the others, as a *shot*—Shot Huey—the word recalling not just the act of exploding or discharging, but vaguely suggesting an injection as well, something that would make this country stronger, healthier. Huey's purpose was twofold: to test explosive forces and, surreptitiously, to provide information on fallout.

Clem Wheeler, the volunteer head of the Civil Defense Network in Evanston, Wyoming, waited at an observation point about twelve miles from ground zero. He and almost fifty of his counterparts from the Rocky Mountain states had been invited to witness Huey. They were dressed in heavy-duty blue jumpsuits designed to block radiation and had been given hats with earflaps and special welder's goggles. They looked as if they were dressed for some invisible blizzard, though the night temperature had barely dipped to a hundred. Warm and sweaty, they were about to watch one of the most dramatic events of their lives. Large thermoses of coffee were being passed around, though many of the men wished for iced tea. They held paper cups, chatted, and looked upward. It was five a.m. and the sky was barraged with fading stars.

They were all tired from a full day of lectures and touring and then being up all night, but no one was really sleepy. They had been brought to the test site, like other VIPs, to be pumped with enthusiasm and—now that the Russians were squarely into the nuclear arms race—frankly, to have the bejesus scared out of them. Mission accomplished, even without the blast, for Clem Wheeler.

The previous afternoon, the visiting civil defense volunteers had boarded a tour bus and headed for Yucca Flat, where they had been shown various buildings and test objects fanned out over the sands at prescribed distances from ground zero. White dust trailed the slow-moving bus as they passed trucks and tanks and automobiles, each containing mannequins dressed as soldiers or civilians, and listened intently to the canned discourse of their tour director. They viewed a man-made pine forest—about fifty blue spruce and Douglas firs planted in concrete blocks, looking like the most forlorn Christmas tree lot.

"Well, it's not exactly Yosemite, fellas, but it's going to tell us a whole lot about bombs and forests," the director said from the front of the bus, his dark blue uniform mottled with sweat.

Clem's group stopped for a good look out the bus windows at several railroad cars that had been craned onto a two-hundred-foot section of elevated trestle which oddly dead-ended midair. A thousand yards from ground zero, a specially designed bank vault housed a table and chair, safe deposit boxes, and paper money, which, the men were told, would supply valuable data to the Federal Reserve Bank. Close by, a multifaceted communications system composed of a network of black boxes and cables and surrounded by thick, steel walls would be relaying steady signals back to the control center. As civil defense coordinators, they would appreciate testing the reliability of this essential flow of information—words over airwaves and wires—in the event of a national emergency. The group nodded gravely, fanning themselves with the complimentary maps they'd been given.

There were lighter moments. The men had been amused by "motel row," a hollow movie-prop series of rooms situated facing the blast, each constructed from a different material—brick, block, concrete, wood frame, steel, plaster, aluminum. Wagers, they were told, had been placed on the most durable materials, and a crew of bricklayers from Las Vegas, who had confidently pooled a hundred dollars against the test site engineers, had stacked their odds by backing their motel wall with two feet of reinforced concrete. The tour director chuckled as he let them in on the little secret, let them know that it wasn't always *that* serious out here.

After motel row, they had toured the streets of Doomtown, USA, a mock community about a mile and a half from the tower, built to test the effects of nuclear warfare on civilian populations. "Meet the Darling family," the director said as the bus inched up alongside what appeared to be a typically furnished two-story frame house. Clem felt the bus list to the right as his fellow passengers, pressing for a better view, crowded the windows closest to the Darling house, and spied on them through the open front door and the big picture windows.

There they were—Annette and Bill, Bill Jr. and Jenny—seated around their kitchen table, frozen in erect, happy poses.

Bowls of oranges and apples, canned and packaged goods were set out on the table as part of an experiment regarding blasts, radiation, and food. Bill Darling's stiff mannequin arm gestured toward the kids, whose heads were tilted attentively, as if they were being complimented on their clean rooms or good grades.

The bus tour was indeed fascinating. A South Dakota volunteer sitting next to Clem had clapped and whistled and sucked on Necco Wafers as if he were at a matinee, but Clem himself had been disturbed, particularly by the Darling family. Tanks and trucks and trains were one thing, but the mere thought of blowing up families at the breakfast table seemed unnecessarily bizarre, felt too much like toying with a self-fulfilling prophecy. It didn't take a genius to figure out what would happen if a nuclear blast went off nearby when the kids were pulling their socks on for school.

Back home in Evanston, Clem had already felt the discomfort of knowing more than the other citizens. He had dutifully passed out the ominous literature from the National Civil Defense Network, tried to be a good patriot. With the hearty okay of the school board, he conducted lectures around the county on what constituted a safe shelter and supervised civil defense drills—had kids climbing under their desks as he yelled, "duck and cover," or filing into the gym, closing their eyes tight, and putting their heads between their legs. Standing behind temperamental, outdated film projectors, hoping he wouldn't have to splice the film yet another time, he showed the instructional movie *A Is for Atom, B Is for Bomb* and waited to take questions and comments afterwards. He learned to answer questions like "Why?" from the elementary school kids by recalling for them the fable of the big bad wolf, huffing and puffing to blow their house down.

He fielded questions for the local newspaper about the right kind of dried food supplies, the best water containers to store in the basement. He even disbursed, upon request, a simple design for a backyard bomb shelter. That frightening reality came to quick life when Stuart Lyon, his neighbor across the back fence, dug a massive hole in the backyard, lined it with foul-smelling railroad ties, and covered the top with a huge mound of dirt—steel trapdoor and air pipes with crazy-looking filters protruding from the top—all the while making a show of the fact that the new shelter was well armed. When the Ruskies popped the big one, the neighbors had better not even try to come near his family shelter with its stores of food and water or the bullets would be flying.

"Hey, no problem, Stu," Clem had told him, knowing that neither he nor any of his neighbors would want to face months in an enclosed space with Stu and ValDene Lyon and their mouthy brood of kids.

In addition to his part-time civil defense work, Clem was irresistibly drawn into the legions of weekend uranium prospectors scouring the hills of Wyoming, Nevada, and Utah trying to change their luck and lives. They hiked and watched and listened to the clicking gauges on Geiger counters sold to them with hopeful names such as Lucky Strike, Vic Tic, Snooper, and Babble. Clem had practiced with his new Geiger counter around his own yard and found that some days he was getting a fairly significant reading off his front lawn and from the idle water in the backyard ditch. He wasn't sure what this meant, had been told that incidental radiation from fallout wasn't harmful—some radiation was even good; we get it every day right from the sun. But he finally became genuinely alarmed during one of his elementary school demonstrations where, showing off his new geiger counter in the school lunchroom, he obtained a moderately high reading from the glistening milk mustache on a little girl's upper lip.

He was uneasy about such occurrences and had decided to ask some questions when he visited the test site. But in the midst of the barren Nevada desert, and between tours and drinks, free steak dinners and patriotic camaraderie, he lost his nerve, kept quiet and listened, feeling some degree of shared inevitability with the Darling family.

Now, milling around the observation point and their bus, drinking more coffee than they should in the predawn, Clem and his new friends kept a watchful eye on Yucca Flat with only half an hour to go. Though educated and entertained, they of course were not privy to the classified aspects of the testing. Among other things, they had not seen or heard about the experiments set in place after dark. The pigs were finally all out there, still biting and kicking at their uniforms. At other sites— in open pens and in underground bunkers—there were dogs, burros, and monkeys tethered, strapped, and even hung from bunker ceilings in experiments that made sense only to the Green Angel team zoologists. Restless soldiers were out there as well, dressed in utilities and steel helmets—many wishing for a cigarette—waiting to complete their assigned maneuvers.

Farther out, near the gravel pit at the north end of the Flat, two unofficial subjects—a scruffy gray coyote and her pup— stood still on the distant rise and watched the last vehicle start up and drive slowly away from the tower. A stiff morning breeze ruffled their fur. The mother bent, licked her pup's ear, then shortly both of them trotted away, retracing their steps back into darkness and sagebrush.

CHAPTER THREE

MACK SAYLES, SOON TO BE RETIRED FROM THE FBI, SAT ON the low flagstone retaining wall that bordered the driveway up to the Washington County Sheriff's Office and watched all the commotion with amusement. Mack was a career observer, and as long as he was going to sit out here, he might as well enjoy the sideshow. Several vans mounted with satellite dishes lined the drive, and a host of journalists and production assistants lugging video equipment were vying for territory.

Close-up or from a distance, Mack didn't look like someone who had made a career of the Bureau—thirty-three years, seven months, and twelve days; make no mistake, he was counting. He could just as easily have passed for a local appliance salesman or an Amway distributor. There was no uniform per se for the Bureau boys, but his plain brown suit, size forty-four regular, was close enough, even though it had turned shiny with wear and too many trips to the cut-rate cleaners. The suit really needed to be a size forty-six, but he wasn't quite ready to admit the obvious or to give in to his wife—"Go ahead, stuff yourself in there like a sausage," she'd say, "you're the one has to suffer." A new burgundy tie—new as in last Christmas—against a white button-down shirt did little to help the ensemble. Except for a downy fringe at the back of his neck and around his ears, he was gleamingly bald and had been since the September when he was twenty-nine and ate a load of bad shrimp on the Gulf of Mexico, got sick as a dog for a month and then immediately started losing his hair.

Mack pulled a pair of wraparound sunglasses from his coat pocket and slipped them on. The shades were a fluorescent yellow bleeding to purple at the bottom, something a teenager would wear. He'd found them in a phone booth in Las Vegas and, after waiting thirty seconds for someone to come back and claim them, had adopted them as his own. He liked the way the world looked through these unexpected lenses: amber, shadowy, and a bit unreal.

It wasn't the sunglasses, however, that bent the image in front of him. The hubbub over there had suddenly heated up and taken on the antics of a cartoon. Mack watched two young female roving reporters—one from Salt Lake City, the other from Las Vegas—squaring off, each with a microphone in hand, each wanting to shoot her segment from the center of the top step, the brass Sheriff's Office sign evidently making the perfect backdrop for the six o'clock news. The respective TV crews were exchanging amused and bewildered glances, while the two women pointed and shook and barked like little lapdogs. Suddenly a leggy jackrabbit who had apparently been sweating it out under a small hedge right next to one of the newswomen broke and ran, darting at top speed right in front of her. She yelped and twisted an ankle as she jumped back. It was only 10:30 a.m. Mack couldn't watch this for much longer without two aspirin and a cold diet cola.

He turned his head in the other direction and fixed his attention on a profusion of flowers in a nearby backyard. Must be irritating to live this close to the gendarmes, he thought. Must have been master planned in a more genteel time, back when residing next to the sheriff was a source of comfort. Mack himself lived just outside Las Vegas, content with his little patch of outskirts in Coral Terrace West surrounded by a six-foot fence and a view of his own making: Bermuda grass and rose bushes and his beloved white-frame pigeon loft.

He kept homers, racing pigeons, and had even used this unexpected trip to St. George early this morning as a nice little training toss. At a rest stop just outside of St. George, he had pulled over to release a basket of about thirty pigeons, blues and whites, mealys and mottles, and splashes of both. A large family of kids poured from a nearby RV, sleepy eyes and baggy shorts, already clutching video games and wearing headphones. They gathered around him and gawked at the birds, seemingly unable to comprehend anything not one-dimensional, real feathers instead of digital imagery. He set the basket on the trunk of his car and opened the canvas side-flap. As if on cue, the birds boiled out and into the faces and over the heads of the kids. The little ones covered their faces and squealed with delight, while the teens jumped back, cussing at being startled. The flock circled twice, gaining altitude and widening its reach, then suddenly veered in a beeline toward home. Mack was always amazed at how they managed to get their bearings so quickly, even on the long day-races when the birds were taken out five hundred miles and released at dawn, the good ones making it home before dark.

Today, however, it appeared he'd be the one who wouldn't make it home by dark. The call from Jack Demonovich had roused Mack out of bed at 7:21 a.m. —exactly twenty-nine minutes after the local police discovered the body of Franklin Rudd. Demonovich, the cocky young Las Vegas field manager who was probably calling from his own bed, had given Mack the assignment. More computer checks would be run, Jack said, and further info fed to him over his car fax as it became available. St. George, Utah, only 120 miles from Vegas, was part of the office's TAOR—tactical area of responsibility—which meant that all police dispatches were routinely monitored and computer backgrounds run on anything that sounded out of the ordinary. Certainly, this murder qualified. A scientist, a retired bureaucrat with a top-secret security clearance, had been killed, though Demonovich didn't view the situation as urgent enough to warm up the FBI plane.

Right, Mack thought. If they had been pulling the plane out of the hangar, one of the young hotshots would be assigned this case. Only a duffer close to retirement has to drive into the next state. But with less than five months and counting, Mack was so short he could ignore another obvious snub. Screw it. He'd just keep his focus on San Diego, the object of his affection lately, the place where he wanted to retire, though he was going head-to-head with his wife on this one. She favored Seattle for their old age, pointing out that their daughter and three grand-kids lived there. But to be honest, Mack was thinking of birds and sailing. San Diego had the flying weather and one of the best racing pigeon combines in the country. And he hadn't been around any good sailing for years now. He could easily see him-self in deck shoes and baggy Bermudas weaving up the coast-line: Coronado, La Jolla, Del Mar, San Juan Capistrano. He knew it was silly, but he loved the names as much as anything else.

Mack pulled out a handkerchief and wiped his head. It was a beautiful spring day, a great time to be out of the office and away from the paper shuffle. It had been a while since he'd done a little on-site sleuthing, so this should be fun. And as a bonus, the day was turning into pretty good entertainment. A chance to see up-and-coming TV personalities waging their little wars, giving the finger and raspberry to each other. Mack observed a familiar-looking Las Vegas reporter getting his hair combed and sprayed. Then the front door of the sheriff's office swung open.

Finally, it was his man. Tall and slender, about forty. Medium-brown hair, a little long over the collar. He was wearing loose khaki pants and brown cowboy boots—an odd combination, but it worked okay—a tan corduroy sport coat pegged over his shoulder, and an open-collared white shirt. His canvas briefcase, something from one of those trendy outback catalogues, lacked the authority of shiny brass and hard leather, but fit perfectly the image Mack had of Layne Harting. That's all Mack saw before the press crews engulfed the lawyer. Mack stood up, blew a white pigeon feather off his right sleeve, and strode toward the commotion.

"Can you tell us your client's plea?"

"What was the connection between Mr. Parker and Dr. Rudd?"

"Is it true that the murder weapon was a kitchen knife?"

"Has Dr. Rudd actually been confirmed dead?"

Dead? Mack thought. Does a pigeon shit on a statue? Of course Rudd was dead; Mack had gone down to the coolers and looked for himself. They didn't get any deader. He had snooped around the murder scene and talked to the local cops. Nothing, so far, had set off any real alarms in him, nothing that shouted national security or even interstate commerce. Of course, the local boys bragged that they already had this one tagged, bagged, and ready for court: a body, cause of death, murder weapon, motive, and prime suspect. Right, thought Mack, typical small town cops. Either they have the case solved in the first five minutes or they never solve it. He'd been to these village circuses before.

He had checked out all the players, including Layne, was aware that a Christine Parker, the suspect's niece, had been here visiting for over a month. It probably was just another garden-variety homicide, nothing the Bureau needed to bother its pretty head about. The one thing that did bug him, however, was how someone with a clean record like Dallas Parker, someone known to deal on a handshake would out of the blue commit a very violent murder and robbery. Mack was in the business of looking underneath and over the top of appearances. That's why he knew which birds to crate up for which race and why he frequently finished in the money.

Mack made his way around the edge of the crowd. Layne was trying to press forward and not having much luck. Rapid-fire questions continued and dueling microphones darted through the air. Then Mack heard the lawyer, frustrated and loud: "Will you let me pass, for hell's sake?"

"Hey, counselor, we just got that on film," said one of the reporters. "Maybe you want to slow down and help us here."

That's when Mack slipped off his sunglasses and leveled his shoulder into the crowd, waving his identification badge. "Hey, FBI, let the man through, will you?"

The crowd eased back and camera lights spun around in different directions, like giant eyes suddenly lost and confused.

Mack grinned, looked left and then right. "You boys," and he nodded at one of the female reporters who had earlier sparred with her colleague, "and girls, you seem to have left your manners at home." The reporter, as indistinctive as all the other plastic cake that presented the news, gave Mack her best piss-off-and-die-asshole look. Mack winked at her, then reached out and startled the lawyer by grabbing his arm and guiding him forward.

Harting craned his head away from Mack and stared oddly at him as they moved away from the crowd. Mack could feel the lawyer's arm stiffen as he held it.

He smiled and let go of Harting. "I guess we get used to holding people's arms in this business." He chuckled. "Don't worry, it don't mean we're engaged."

Harting laughed, seeming both surprised and pleased by a sense of humor. He took a couple of steps away from Mack and looked at him, as if to size him up. "Thanks. Being engaged is the least of my concerns right now."

"Oh, that's right," Mack said, tapping his bald head with his index finger, "a confirmed bachelor like you. Bad choice of words on my part." Mack's smile was playful, his dark eyes a little sportive, suggesting no good reason why work shouldn't also be fun.

Harting's face clouded slightly. "Do I know you? Do you know me?"

"Oh hell," Mack said, "and I'm getting on those other folks about their manners." He stuck out his hand. "Mack Sayles, FBI. Las Vegas Field Office."

Harting shook his hand and said, "Layne Harting, attorney. Saraville. Office next to a field."

Mack laughed. "That's good, that's good. I don't meet too many of you lawyers with a sense of humor."

"Well," Harting said, "you're my first FBI man. So there you go."

"Yup," Mack said, "there you do."

They were now on the border of the rolling lawn in front of the courthouse, and no one seemed inclined to bother them further. The grass was bermed here and there in a reckless, modern style of horticulture, rings of marigolds and lobelia and pansies adding splashes of color that reminded Mack of burial plots, but he liked the steep red cliffs behind the building and the gloriously clear blue sky above.

"Well, I don't mean to hold you up here," he said to Harting. "I just wanted to ask you a couple of questions. Let me walk you to your car." He took a few steps forward, his head down, then realized Harting wasn't following.

"Well, uh, look, Mr. Sa . . . Sills?" Harting said.

"Sayles. As in what my wife is always shopping for. Her hobby, you know. Save a dollar here, save a dollar there." Mack pulled a dark, tattered wallet from his back pocket. "Here, take one of my cards."

Even as Harting reached for the card, he was shaking his head. "You know I can't discuss this case with you."

"Of course you can't," Mack said. "Not the privileged communications, things you discussed with your client. I just have a couple of general questions, couple of things don't make sense here."

"Not anything," Harting said. "Nothing even remotely connected with the case."

Mack patted his arm. "Oh hell, I know all that, I know the rules. I graduated from law school myself, you know, back in 1958, little school down in the Texas Panhandle. Lot of the boys from the Bureau have law degrees," he said.

Harting turned and faced him squarely. "That's great, Mr. Sayles. You also have health insurance and a fat pension to be envied, I'm sure. But unless you inform me I'm under arrest or something like that, I'm still not going to talk to you. Period. Paragraph."

Mack watched a line of perspiration glide from Harting's hairline down his right temple. "Now, now," he laughed and waved him off, "don't get your feathers ruffled. I just don't understand why a guy like Dallas Parker, a stand-up guy from all I can see, a guy you know as a friend—am I right there?—would want to kill somebody."

Harting cast a disgusted look across the street and sighed,

then turned back to Mack. "Sir. Mr. FBI. Hello! Am I speaking a foreign language or something?"

"Okay, okay, I got you," Mack said. "How about I escort you to your car in complete silence and then ask the lovely young lady up there a couple of questions?"

It was Harting's turn to back up. "I, I, um, don't know."

"That's Dallas Parker's niece, visiting him from Phoenix. Right?"

"Look, this family is pretty upset right now. Can't it wait until tomorrow?" Layne asked. "I'll arrange it. Call me. I don't have a card handy."

Mack smiled and put up his hand. "I know where to find you. Sure, tomorrow. Tell her not to take any sudden trips back to Phoenix until we chat. Okay?"

"A team of mules couldn't drag her away from her uncle right now," Harting said. "Call me later and we'll set up a time. I'm busy tomorrow morning, but the afternoon works."

"Good enough. I'm staying right over yonder at the El Vista Motel. So you could leave a message there if it's easier."

Harting nodded. "We'll talk." Then he hustled up the hill toward his car.

Mack closed his eyes for a moment—just long enough to see the green, foam-tipped waves off San Diego—then reoriented himself, checked his watch, and put his sunglasses back on. He wondered if this town had any real pizza.

Christine wanted to know everything at once. How's Dallas? What did he say? What took you so long? What's going to happen next?

Layne seemed cool and aloof to her, more interested in getting lunch than in talking. He opened the door to Nacho Mama's for her. Christine felt like standing there, refusing to enter until she had some answers from him, but her will and resistance papery thin by now. Inside the restaurant, she felt the cool rush of an overhead fan and watched herself reach out and take hold of the cashier's counter, just like an old, unsteady woman might do.

Mama, a short Mexican grandmother, came rushing at them in a whirl of color that piqued both interest and vertigo in Christine. Mama's layered red skirt bounced as she walked and her scoop-neck blouse revealed a monster cleavage. Her brown eyes were deep set and etched with generations of a peasant mother's happiness and heartbreak.

"Layne Harting." She hugged him, her head barely reaching his chest. "Where you been? I not see you since the coon aged."

Layne smiled. "I guess it has been a while," he said. Mama continued to squeeze. "Meet Christine Parker, Mama," and Layne gestured in Christine's direction.

Christine felt her hand whisked off the counter like a foreign object and pumped vigorously in both of Mama's hands.

"Pleased to meet you," Mama said, her big, effortless smile half irritating Christine. "This is business or personal?" she asked, covering a sly grin. "I have different tables for each, you know."

"I know, Mama," Layne said. "This is business and we want that personal table in the far corner. Okay?"

Mama raised her eyebrows and the flame of irritation leapt higher in Christine. She grabbed hold of the cashier's counter again and looked away, trying to calm herself, realizing that at any other time, she would probably love this earthy woman.

Layne seemed to sense Christine's discomfort—maybe noticed her white knuckles—and quickly navigated her to the corner table. Mama followed with two menus, laid them down, and turned away quietly. Instantly, Christine wanted to say something nice or funny, wanted to put her hand out in apology, but the woman's broad hips were already gliding toward the kitchen door.

Layne smiled at Christine. "Don't worry," he said. "Mama has a heart bigger than the enchilada grande, which is huge."

He pointed at the menu, "But I recommend one of the more original dishes, handmade tamales or the light mixed grill. Mama comes from Mexico City via California. This is the only restaurant in St. George that beats out the school lunch program. Sure, you can get a baked potato and a tough steak up on the hill. But folks around here still think Al Dente installs braces. This town is so white bread it—" Layne suddenly stopped, perhaps noticing her expression. "Oooh, well. I guess you're anxious to talk."

"Yes," Christine nodded abruptly. "You go first."

"Alright, alright." Layne told her that Dallas was okay. "The jail's no Sheraton, as you can guess. But as in most of these smaller towns, it's more user-friendly, clean and well run. Your uncle is holding up well, even joking around some, as usual."

Christine heard herself say, "Dallas will be wisecracking all the way to the undertaker." The words had simply floated out, their weight and meaning hitting her seconds later. "I didn't mean," she stammered. She was determined not to fall apart again.

She felt Layne's hand touch her forearm. "I know exactly what you mean," he said. "Dallas will be popping off right to the end, but that doesn't mean the end is in sight." He removed his hand. "Not if I have anything to say about it."

"I'm okay," she said. "Thanks. Please continue."

Layne studied the menu. "What would you like to know?" he asked quietly, without looking up at her.

It was a slow and indirect approach; she couldn't quite understand his seeming reluctance to talk about the case. Was he still worried about a conflict of interest? Or maybe he felt more allegiance to Dallas than she had imagined. If he thought that Dallas was trying to take the rap for her, that might upset him. Whatever it was, Layne wasn't communicating it well to her, and he certainly fell short of her only other legal contact. She recalled the graying hair of Marsha Ebert, a gnarled, ancient divorce lawyer recommended by a friend. Marsha had stated flatly within the first two minutes of their interview, "My default fee is five hundred bucks, no harm, no foul. For five grand, I take off some skin, pain at a price, honey. If you really want the bastard's balls served up right here on the table, well, I'd need to look at your joint financial statement for that." Christine had quickly left that lawyer's office and divorced T.C. Falco herself for the price of a do-it-yourself legal kit and the fifty-dollar filing fee.

"Just tell me what they've charged him with," she said.

"Well, there's the murder, as you know."

Christine dropped her head. She had assumed that Rudd was dead, of course, but only because of Layne's statement about the murder charge against Dallas. They hadn't really discussed the details. "So he died," she said, haltingly. "I was hoping his wound wasn't that . . ." Her voice trailed off. "How long . . . when did he die?"

Layne had quit looking at the menu, his hands, and the cheap yellow candleholder in the middle of the table, and was now staring directly at her. "The time?" he said. "The time, they think, was around midnight or so. The autopsy's not in yet, but that's about the time they believe his wound would have killed him."

"Yes, of course," she said quietly. "Then there are different kinds or degrees of murder. Right? Something like that?" Maybe Dallas told the cops that he had wrestled with Rudd. That it was an accident. She'd heard about a high school security guard back in Phoenix who'd been in a terrible fight with a rough student. The kid ended up going over the balcony, hitting his head, and dying. The security guard spent one year in jail on a manslaughter charge. So there was always hope.

Layne shook his head in a gesture of resignation. Then, as if he were suddenly in the business of dashing the future, he said, "Okay. Okay. Dallas is charged with aggravated murder, aggravated robbery and burglary, kidnapping . . . who knows what more they'll come up with by the end of the day. They're throwing every book they've got at him."

"What?" she asked. "Aggravated murder? Robbery? Burglary?" She stared at Layne to see if there was a punch line or some legal mishmash that she hadn't understood.

"Dallas was found with a suitcase full of Rudd's valuables in his truck," Layne said, "things taken from Rudd's safe. And he doesn't deny any of it." Layne shook his head. "He offered me no explanation whatsoever. Just says that eventually he wants me to arrange a guilty plea."

Christine put her elbows on the table and rested her forehead in her hands. She understood exactly what was going on. Rudd had died, so Dallas had staged the burglary as a cover, to divert the attention away from her. Well, she thought, it just won't work. There was no question as to her course of action now; this business had gone far enough. She would not participate in this deception. There was no reason why the system wouldn't be fair with her. It was an accident, for God's sake.

She would calmly have some lunch—she was surprised by it, but the thick, spicy smells in the restaurant made her realize she was famished—and then, regardless of how messy or frightening, she would ask Layne Harting to drive her back to the jail and make arrangements to turn herself in. This was all one big, fat mistake, a dumb mistake, but self-defense at the very worst. True, she should not have been in Dr. Rudd's house, trespassing like that, but . . .

"And then there's more." Layne reached down to the side of his chair. "He wrote you a note." Layne pulled his briefcase onto his lap, unzipped it, and withdrew a legal pad. "Dallas made me promise to take you out to the ranch—"

"What are you talking about?" Christine interrupted. "I'm not going to the ranch. I'm going straight back over there and get this whole mess straightened out."

A young waitress, soft and rumpled and loose-boned, looking like she was made from nothing more substantial than dishrags, approached their table and set cold water down for them.

"Well, then," Layne said, "order up. Might be your last civilian meal for awhile. This is not something that's going to be easily straightened out."

She was taken aback. He had seemed almost protective a few minutes ago. Now, she couldn't determine if he was trying to be coy or just factual. Maybe he was wearing down, too.

The waitress tugged at one of her twelve earrings and clicked her pen impatiently.

"I'll have the enchilada grande. It's been highly recommended," Christine said, lifting her chin, showing more conviction than necessary. She smiled humorlessly up at the waitress, who hiked one eyebrow ever so slightly as if to say, What medications are you on, lady?

After she left, Layne opened his legal pad to the middle and rustled through the pages until he found what he was looking for. He pushed the pad toward Christine. It was Dallas's scrawled cursive, that much was sure, but she was having a hard time focusing, reading his writing, or relating to the message.

Layne lowered his voice and leaned over the table toward her. "Let me summarize. Dallas said that he has hidden something he took from Dr. Rudd's safe. He said for you to read this note, that you'd know the hiding place he's talking about. Dallas believes what he's found is important, a book or something that Rudd was writing. He, uh, talked about top-secret documents from the Nevada Test Site as being part of it."

Christine focused on the opposite wall. The cheap stained-glass windows washed the interior in flickering shades of grape and gold and tangerine. Her stomach was doing an aerial loop and she wanted to scream. She turned back to Layne. "Am I going crazy? This is all crazy!"

Layne noisily exhaled and set the briefcase back on the floor. "I thought my business was to represent people and render honest legal opinions. But if pressed to the wall, I'd have to say that everything connected with this whole case is pretty nutty—and that's beginning to include me." He leaned even closer. "Don't ask me how or why, but I promised Dallas that I'd take you out to the ranch tomorrow morning, that I'd look at a bunch of stolen government documents and . . ." He shook his head. "And I don't know what the hell comes after that."

Christine just sat there. She hadn't felt this alone since that moment in the doctor's office when they ladled the news of a tumor to her, pronounced it malignant, stage three, full-scale breast cancer with four positive lymph nodes. She had probably stared at the doctor that day in the same glazed, unbelieving way she was staring at Layne right now.

"Okay, okay. I'm sorry," Layne said, looking down, placing both hands flat on the table, fingers spread as if he were going to do some trick—suddenly pull dimes or flower petals out of his still-folded napkin. "Let's back up for a minute," he said. "Why don't you just start at the very beginning and tell me everything." He glanced up, caught her straight in the eye. "And don't leave out even the smallest detail. I mean everything."

They had been quite a pair, Christine and her uncle, walking into the bar last night. Was it just last night? Time was no steady measure of anything and it didn't seem possible that all this trouble had begun such a short while ago. Dallas had dried horseshit on his boots; she had reapplied some lipstick after dinner without benefit of a mirror, drawing outside the lines on her lower lip. Dallas laughed, told her she'd be dangerous as a blind woman, and handed her a cocktail napkin to fix herself. They were at the Ancestor Inn, a restaurant and bar embellished with old beams and new glass, worn-out saddles and rustic crockery, but whose greatest asset was the fact that it was the only actual bar in St. George serving liquor on a Sunday night. Christine and Dallas had eaten dinner downstairs, then moved up to the bar for a nightcap, which evolved into several Jack Daniels and sodas. They had been laughing, poking fun at the world, slowing things down and trying to make their moments together count.

"It's been a great month at the ranch," Christine said. She reached over and touched his hand. "Just what the doctor ordered. Even if he didn't order it," she giggled.

"Well, I sure wish you could stay longer, Chrissy," Dallas

said a little awkwardly. He brushed a cobby hand through his short salt-and-pepper hair, a nervous habit when he had his Stetson off. "I know you need to get back down to Phoenix. He thumbed his mustache, as if trying to clear the way for the words he was about to say. "Look, why don't you come on back up after your new round of tests is completed?"

"We'll see," she said. "I do have to get back to work someday. If the doctor gives me a hall pass, you know." Christine stretched and smiled. "Besides, I didn't plan to leave here until midweek, so don't be trying to get rid of your house-guest early."

"Houseguest? Hell, houseguests don't have to help with chores, cook, and shop for groceries. You've hardly been pampered, honey."

"Well, now that you mention it," she said, "I'd been wondering where the cable TV was, the Jacuzzi and the maid service." She laughed heartily. "Good lord, Uncle Dallas, if that's what I'd wanted I could have stayed right in Phoenix, got me one of those cut-rate spa weekends at a resort. I could have been waxed and rolfed. Probably even laid. Whoa, did I really say that?"

"Well, Chrissy, that laid part probably wouldn't hurt none," he said, blushing and grinning amiably. "Waxed and rolfed? I don't know exactly what that is, but it sounds ugly."

She smiled and shook her head. "You're the only one who still calls me that, you know. Chrissy. Same as when I was six years old."

"What's wrong with that?" he asked, feigning irritation. "That's your name. Not my fault you grew up and decided on something differ—" Dallas's voice trailed off. He was no longer looking directly at Christine, rather over her shoulder toward the entryway into the bar.

She was tempted to turn around, but she resisted the impulse. "Must be quite a looker," she said.

Dallas said nothing, his face becoming a mask. As Christine finally twisted in her chair to see what was so absorbing, she could hear laughter and boisterousness. A skinny old man, balding, quite short, strolled arm in arm into the bar with his companion, another older man with a heavy gut hanging out of his plaid sport coat. Obviously coming from another bar or party, they were in high spirits as they repeated in unison a joke they'd evidently just heard. "How many Mormons does it take to change a lightbulb?" And then they cracked themselves up, laughing so hard they didn't bother to finish.

Christine turned back to Dallas, who was still staring at them, his expression unchanged. They passed directly behind her, then went to the bar not ten feet away from Christine and ordered drinks from the bartender.

"Aw, Rudd, my boy," the man in plaid was saying, "it's been good to see you again."

"You too, you too," his companion replied. "Thanks for coming down from Salt Lake for the banquet. And thanks for sneaking along that flask of yours. A body can only abide so much of this teetotaling around here."

The heavyset man laughed again and clasped Rudd on the shoulder. "Well, it's a nice honor they gave you, keys to the city and all. Too bad they didn't just give you keys to the wine cellar." More guffawing.

"You sure you won't stay at the house tonight?" Rudd inquired. "A bottle of twenty-year scotch, a private guest bedroom. Don't be bashful, Glover."

"Well, I would, but my sister's only six blocks from here. Told her I'd be home with them," he paused and smiled, "just didn't tell her what time I'd be home with them." They laughed heartily.

The one named Glover dropped some bills on the bar when the bartender brought their drinks, then they wandered down to the far end in front of the television set, which was tuned to the last delirious minutes of a tied basketball game.

Christine asked, "Who are they? What's going on? You look like you've just seen—"

"Doesn't matter who," Dallas shrugged her off. "Nobody, far as I'm concerned."

"Right," she said. "Nobody always gets your jaw working like a bellows. What gives?"

Dallas relaxed his mouth, gave the muscles a quick rub with

finger and thumb. "How's that? Suit you better?"

Christine narrowed her eyes.

"Yeah, sure," he said with resignation. He took a drink and crunched on an ice cube. "Never seen the fat one. That skinny SOB is some famous scientist, I guess."

"Scientist?"

"He was a big muckety-muck out at the Nevada Test Site back in the fifties. Went off to Washington or somewhere. Then retired to St. George a few years ago."

Now it rang a bell. Christine had bought a local paper at the store while shopping earlier in the afternoon. There'd been a photo of Rudd, along with a profile piece. She had begun to read the article, then stopped as she felt her stomach muscles involuntarily spasming.

Avoidance. Distraction. Turn the page. The garden club met on Thursday, that was nice, and a man named Horace made a compelling case for why real estate agents really do earn their commissions.

Ever since her diagnosis a year ago, her mother, her father, her uncle Dallas had seemed inexorably bound through hindsight, plagued by a whispered guilt, the shared belief that they had caused, or at least could have prevented, her cancer. They all lived together on the ranch back then; Christine was conceived and born there. Her parents dumbly watched some of the test shots from the knoll behind the house and then let her play outside afterwards.

It made Christine angry that they would accept even a scintilla of blame. How were they to know about the dangers? In those days, government officials said the testing was safe; in those days, government officials never lied. For her part, Christine had tried her best to remain staunchly anti-victim. Job one, just as the doctors and support groups maintained, was for Christine to get well. Forget notions of revenge. Flush the negativity and anger. Just heal her body for now. But that advice was hard to follow when sitting near someone like this Dr. Rudd.

The bar crowd was thinning, maybe only five or six left. The bartender had a wet towel and was cleaning up in earnest. The basketball game ended in a buzzer-beater and then the high-spirited theme song for the ten o'clock news chimed in with a voice-over announcement that the lead story of the evening was centered around one of St. George's most distinguished and controversial citizens, Dr. Franklin Rudd. The barkeep hit the remote and turned up the volume.

Christine heard the man in plaid raise his voice. "That's you, Rudd. My hell, there you are, Ruddy boy, right there on the screen."

Christine couldn't believe it, felt caught in some karmic loop. A pert young blonde reporter beamed out at them from the television.

"Three people were arrested this afternoon in St. George," she said, "in this exclusive Vermillion Hills Country Club area for picketing in front of the home of Dr. Franklin Rudd, manager of the Nevada Test Site from 1952 through 1963. The protesters claimed they were on a public street and were exercising their right to free speech. However, County Attorney Jim Bidwell maintains that Vermillion Hills is a private development and that the detained individuals were asked repeatedly to leave."

The camera showed a man carrying a sign: DIS-HONOR DR. RUDD. The reporter continued, "Dr. Rudd, who retired here five years ago, was last night given the key to the city by the St. George Chamber of Commerce at their annual Lifetime Achievement banquet. As a highly respected nuclear engineer, Dr. Rudd received many awards throughout his career, including those from Dow Chemical, the Western Lands Economic Coalition, and the Free World Institute. The honoring of Rudd was not without controversy, however. Some St. George residents are class action plaintiffs in an intense trial currently underway in federal court in Las Vegas, claiming on behalf of all downwinders that they were adversely impacted by the atomic testing in Nevada beginning back in 1951. Dr.

Rudd's award has drawn fire from local downwinder organizations, coming as it does during the trial."

"Earlier, we spoke to Dr. Rudd, who had this reaction to the protesters." Rudd appeared strolling leisurely out to his mailbox, seeming to invite the attention.

The microphone was placed in front of his face and he said, pointing toward the pickets, "Welcome to America, Mr. and Mrs. Protester, welcome to America." He smiled at the camera in a twisted, spiteful way. "The reason you can protest today, the reason you still have that freedom, is because we won the Cold War." His face turned red. "But it's not a free ride. Like any war, there are casualties, sacrifices. Nothing's free, nothing comes—"

"You speak of casualties, sir." The reporter broke into his rant. "Are you admitting that fallout from these tests—"

"Idiots," Rudd hollered suddenly, "no clue, no clue. None of you has a clue." Then through clenched teeth he snarled, "Just stay tuned. That's all I've got to say." He whirled and marched sullenly back through his gate, slamming it forcefully.

Christine was stunned. She normally didn't read much from people's looks, but she had been utterly transfixed by this old man's face on the screen, the glassy hardness of his eyes. And he was sitting right over—actually, he was standing up now. She watched as he glanced around the room, his party spirit apparently sapped by the newscast. He looked weary and distrustful, but the eyes were the same as those on the TV: cold, remote.

Christine slowly turned her chair back to their table.

"Jesus," Dallas shook his head. "Where do these assholes get off? Just another son of a bitch who thinks he knows what's best for all of us." Dallas unconsciously began opening and closing his big right hand, covered with small work cuts, around a water glass. "I'd like to take every one of those bastards and stake them out in one of their own bomb craters."

Christine toyed with her napkin and grew quiet. Dallas watched her. "Oh hell, Chrissy. I'm sorry for getting carried away. But we, you especially, have every right in the world to be pissed off at guys like that. They were blasting those things off like toy firecrackers directly upwind of the ranch. And we all just sat around like dumb bastards with our heads stuck in the sand." The big muscles in his forearm stood out through his tanned skin.

It made Christine inexpressibly sad to see him bearing this old weight around, the same weight that she saw her parents struggle with, yet she simply didn't know how to release them from it.

With the expert timing of a marksman, the bartender flipped the lights on and off twice to signal closing, and Dallas was only too anxious to grab his hat and push his chair back from the table. Christine picked up her purse and put her jacket on as if the shoulders and arms belonged to someone else's body.

Casualties. That was the word Rudd had used. As Dallas settled the tab and the two of them walked outside, it chipped at her like an ice pick. *Casualties. Sacrifices.* Like in a disaster or war. And as much as she was determined not to sink into that kind of thinking, she herself was likely one of Rudd's casualties.

Dallas opened the restaurant's front door for her; the rush of night air was cool but not calming. She tried to change the mood as they approached the parking lot.

"Are you okay to drive home?" she asked, standing by Dallas's truck. He had driven himself into town after he'd finished chores.

"I sure as hell hope so, because I'm too drunk to walk," he said without smiling, taking her arm.

Christine looked at him appraisingly.

"Oh, I'm alright," he said, hoisting his dusty Stetson onto his head. "Guess I need to revise some of my old lines. That one don't fit into a politically correct category nowadays."

"You be careful," he said, opening his truck door. "I'll see you at home."

She crossed the parking lot and reached for her door handle when she heard their voices again, Rudd and his buddy, sauntering to their cars with their loud jokes and grating laughter. She just stood there watching the slovenly, grunting dance of these two old men saying good-byes. Finally, Rudd started over to his car, passing behind hers on the way, and was right behind it when he noticed her.

"Hey, sweetheart."

She frowned and gave him the evil eye.

He kept walking and his red Cadillac, it turned out, was parked right next to her. She stared directly at him across the roof of the Caddy while he fumbled for his keys.

Christine spoke loudly, "What did you mean in there by casualties?"

He froze, a short man peeking over the top of a car, as if gauging the protection it afforded.

She put a hand on his vehicle and leaned forward. "You said there were casualties! And sacrifices! Are you saying that—"

"None of your goddamn business," he cut her off. Slipping into his car, he started it and revved the engine, backing out quickly. Once out of the parking stall, the Cadillac roared forward, then screeched to a halt. She heard an electric window go down. "You people!" He seemed to spit the words at her from the cave of his running car. "You people are *sooo pathetic.*" Then he was gone.

"Bastard!" she screamed at the retreating taillights.

Christine got in her car and started it quickly. She could feel herself spinning, being sucked into a rage. That arrogant son of a bitch. She reversed out of the parking space.

What happened next was one of those rare moments, one of those inexorable "what ifs" or "but fors" that can change an entire life, can consume its options. Dallas's truck, just minutes ago, had turned right onto St. George Boulevard, proceeding west toward the ranch. Just ahead of her, Rudd's big cruiser had turned left and was now easing out into traffic, heading east. Her father was fond of quoting some baseball player as saying, When you come to a fork in the road, take it. And so she did, she turned left, acting on the barest, the rawest kind of impulse—clear, unsheathed anger.

The Cadillac was easy to follow, perhaps too easy. There was one stoplight and it was green. A couple of left turns, a couple of rights. Something was still breaking loose in her, something new and white-hot being forged. That small, hardened core of anger that she had repressed for a year or more was now cracking, taking root somewhere in her lower stomach.

Five minutes later—not enough time for calming down or second-guessing—she found herself turning between the rock pillars of Vermillion Hills Country Club Estates, following a set of red taillights well into the subdivision before stopping at fortress-like front gates hosting a large, decorative R offset in wrought iron. Mechanically, magically, the gates swung open and the Cadillac pulled into the driveway.

Christine slowed and parked across the street from the gates. She turned her engine off and sat there, a flood of ideas surging through her. If she'd had a can of black spray paint, she would have marched over to his big, clean stucco fence and added her voice to the recent protests. If she'd had a brick, it would have gone sailing toward his window.

Even at this point, with her bravado cresting on six ounces of alcohol, Christine never could have imagined what might follow. She simply wanted to pin Rudd down, make him explain himself. He had said that word—*casualties*—as if it meant no more than *flashlight* or *egg beater*. She climbed out of her car, crossed the deserted street, entered the open gates, and stood in his driveway. A huge garage door at the end of the drive was open, throwing the oddity of fluorescent light across a darkened lawn.

Rudd turned around, looking confused. He walked out to the bright threshold of the garage and peered into the dark, down the drive toward her. "Some nerve. Who the hell are you, anyway?" he demanded. "Get off my property."

Part of her was struck by the unreality of her presence here on a stranger's well-scrubbed concrete drive. The other part of her didn't care, was furious. "I asked you a question back there," she snapped. "I want to know. Why did you say casualties? And sacrifices?"

He took a nervous step back into the cover of the garage

and yelled, "You're one of them, aren't you? You bitch. Get out of here you piece-of-shit trash, before I call the cops. You're trespassing." Crouching slightly, he hit some buttons on the wall. The cavernous opening and bright light immediately began to disappear as the heavy door swept into downward motion.

"Look, I want some answers," she said futilely as the last band of light was pinched off at the bottom of the door. "You're the piece of shit," she finally shouted, standing alone in the dark. Screw it, she thought, slowly backing up. In the midst of all this lawn and concrete decadence, there was no possibility of confronting such a man, of carrying a message or making a dent.

But as she turned around to leave, the sweeping iron gates were closing as well, right before her eyes. She ran toward them, thought about trying to slip through the narrowing gap before they could shut, and wondered if they would reopen like an elevator door if she were to stick her hand or foot in at the last minute, if she were to display that kind of faith in the blind mechanical sector. The gates chunked firmly into place.

She quickly searched for another exit, trying to suppress the feeling of panic tightening in her chest, climbing into her throat. The gates featured heavy ornamental spears at the top. A few feet to the right there was a small arched walkway leading to the street, but that gate was locked as well. Moving along the stucco wall, she looked for any other opening or something that could give her a leg up. The wall was over six feet high and ran across the front of the large property, turning at the corners and continuing down the sides. At the moment, it felt more like prison than upper-middle-class suburbia, a darkened compound instead of a one-acre pedigreed lawn.

Christine grasped the top of the wall with both hands and pulled as hard as she could. The concrete stucco bit into her hands and forearms. She braced one shoe against the wall and heaved, but her foot slipped down the wall with a grinding sound and her knee slammed into the cement. Shooting pain and hot stars punctuated her frustration. Perhaps there was a time when she could have scaled this wall, but it wasn't now, it wasn't after having rounds of chemotherapy and a hefty mass of muscle and tissue removed from one half of her chest.

She turned back to the house, which was closed up tight, Rudd now evidently inside. Well, you measly little turd, she thought, and stomped around the house toward a back patio and the only light she could see. The patio door was open, with only the screen pulled shut. She yelled into the empty kitchen, "You've locked me in, mister. Come let me out."

The white Corian counters, the kitchen tile and cabinets, all white on white, looking like something out of a homeshow catalogue, gleamed at her in lavish silence. A couple of plastic grocery sacks sagged and looked out of place on the stark lines of the kitchen counter. All at once, Rudd came walking in, barefoot, tying the sash on his bathrobe.

"You've got some nerve, lady."

Christine approached the screen door. "I'm locked in," she said simply, trying to maintain a normal tone of voice. "Please open the gate so I can leave."

Rudd came part way to the door. "You got yourself in here; now you can get yourself out," he snapped. "You people are so stupid and incompetent. All you know how to do is whine and protest. Climb the damn wall. You've got about thirty seconds before I call the cops," he laughed and wheezed both at once.

Dark, icy rage filled her again and she boldly opened the unlocked screen door and walked straight into the middle of his kitchen, entirely forgetting about rules and etiquette and whatever ideas of the world she'd been taught. "What do you mean, 'you people'?" she shouted. "You don't know anything about me."

"Back off, you stupid broad!" Rudd moved to his left and, with ludicrous flair, unsheathed a medium-size knife from a black marble knife block. The flourishing blade actually prompted Christine to break out in nervous laughter, reminding her more of high school comedy than any real drama.

Rudd flushed with anger but kept some distance between them as he took a couple of practice jabs at the air. They were pathetic gestures, but then he advanced a couple of steps and the danger finally got through to Christine. This asshole was actually coming after her with that thing. She backed up slowly, keeping her eyes on him, then unexpectedly bumped into the kitchen table.

Rudd must have seen her fear, taken leave of his senses, or just been very drunk. In any event, he stood up straighter and said, "You're in my house, lady. No one would blame me for defending myself." Then he actually lunged, thrusting the knife forward.

With the table against her back, Christine grabbed his arm and twisted it away from her body. Rudd put up less resistance than she would have expected. The fact that he was frail, that he was seventy-two and small, didn't occur to her in that moment.

She felt the dull pressure of his body against her. She pushed at him with all her strength, and they both stumbled sideways over one of the kitchen chairs, tangling their feet. All Christine knew after that was that they went down hard onto the kitchen floor, that Rudd was underneath her, and that the entire force of her weight landed directly on top of him with a gushing of air. As she scrambled to her feet, she saw that Rudd didn't get up. The knife, bloody, was on the floor at his side and there was a pained look on his face.

She stood there, shocked, contemplating whether she should call an ambulance. Rudd began moving, gasping, clutching the side of his stomach. His head came up. He looked down and saw the bright streak of red against the white tile, groaned, and tried to rise up onto one elbow. "You bitch," he said. "Look what you've done. Right in my own home. You're going to pay for this."

Christine started backing up again, unable to talk, unable to conceive what to do next. How could he say such things? He'd been the one with the knife. Should she now try to help this man who had just assaulted her, maybe even tried to kill her?

"I'm sorry," she said. "But I didn't attack you. I didn't want any—"

The patch on his robe was turning darker and larger.

"You stupid bitch. Call 911. I want to see your face when they cart you off. Protesting just wasn't enough. You had to climb the wall and come after an old man right in his own home. You're going to prison for this." He was up on his elbows now, his legs flailing as he tried futilely to stand.

Christine never heard anyone else enter the room. It was as if the scene somehow skipped forward and instantly Dallas was right beside her, taking control. Rudd shouted at him to keep away, but Dallas bent and put his hand over the squawking mouth and told Rudd to shut up. The old man went limp or silent—Christine didn't know which.

Dallas took hold of her shoulders and turned her around. He moved her through the back door, over the patio, and out into the darkness of the backyard. He was talking to her in a low, assuring tone. "You need to leave here. Let me handle this. Go home and don't do or say anything until you see me. You understand? Nothing until you talk to me. Swear to it. Now!" he told her.

Christine didn't know what she had said, but she must have satisfied him because Dallas responded with, "Okay, time to get out of here. Let's go."

By then she was standing at the front wall and understood that she was going over. He boosted her up. Not just boosted, though. Dallas was strong, emphatic, and all Christine remembered was having to hang on to the top of the wall to keep from being thrown clear over.

Jillian Fetch, Chief Deputy United States Attorney for the Southern District of Nevada, walked toward the light at the end of the tunnel. She moved briskly, as if she knew exactly where she was going, her stride long and confident, her heels clicking over the concrete. As a matter of habit, she glanced at her watch, though she was sure she was on time this bright Monday afternoon. Finally, Jillian emerged from the tunnel onto the basketball court at the University of Nevada, Las Vegas, field house and stopped to look around the partially lit arena. The lights were bright directly over the court, but all seats, upper and lower, remained in darkness. Practice was closed to the press and public, although that didn't include superfan Congressman Gordon McLean or his invited guest, Jillian Fetch, whose name he had left with security at the staff entryway.

A whistle blasted shrilly from the far end of the court and immediately all bouncing balls, voices, and athletic shoes were silenced.

"On me, over on me," shouted the coach, his hand circling the air over his head. Twelve players and two assistant coaches crowded the man.

Jillian peered down past the end of the court and spotted the lone figure of Congressman McLean. He was leaning forward on the edge of a courtside seat, elbows on his knees, chin resting in his hands, totally engrossed in this scrimmage. After three decades in the U.S. Congress representing the Southern District of Nevada, he had become the number one figure in Nevada politics. And whatever his other interests, he openly and noisily proclaimed a special place in his heart for the Runnin' Rebels, the UNLV basketball team. At almost seventy years old, McLean was still relatively lanky, a tall man and only a bit stooped. Jillian vaguely recalled that he had played some small college hoops, something revealed in a sentence or two from his stock press kit bio.

She started, unhurried, down the courtside toward McLean. She appreciated the power, the money, and the determination that went with big time sports, but the games themselves didn't interest her much.

On the court, Coach Sandy Crouch, a redheaded man with a ruddy complexion, spoke in a tightly restrained voice. Everyone leaned in to hear his messianic words.

"When the ball first comes into the low post to Jamad . . .," he was saying.

Jillian tuned out the rest. She went through a kind of mental checklist, preparing herself for McLean. This was business, she was sure, though he had not been specific when he had called — when his secretary had called — with the invitation. In an almost invisible gesture, she smoothed the tight, above-the-knees skirt she wore, which was trademark Jillian, barely within bounds of acceptable dress for a U.S. district attorney.

McLean, without turning his head, without even shifting his eyes, patted the seat next to his when she drew near. He kept his full attention on Coach Crouch. All part of the pecking order, she thought, sitting down. If she had ranked a little higher, McLean would have turned to her and nodded; higher still and he would have shaken her hand and greeted her by name. Seriously high and he would have stood up, given her the two-handed shake. No matter. Just getting the invitation to this private meeting meant that she ranked high enough. At least for now, at age thirty-seven.

She crossed her legs and, in imitation, focused her own attention briefly on the coach, then shifted it to various members of the team, settling her gaze on Amon Jamad, the easily recognizable star, six foot ten inches of carved ebony, awash in today's sweat and tomorrow's dollars. The Runnin' Rebels were finally back to happy times. They were in the Final Four, starting this coming weekend. Everyone in Vegas knew that after a long absence, since former Coach Jerry Tarkanian had been forced out by the school and the NCAA, the Runnin' Rebels were finally winners in postseason action. A wave of local excitement was building, spread by radio and TV and the big electronic billboards.

The coach suddenly bounced the ball and blew his whistle, shattering his own hushed tones. Every player except Jamad sprang back from the circle, ready for action.

"Red squad at this end," he hollered. "White take the far basket. Full court scrimmage, now let's get it right this time."

McLean finally straightened up, turned, and smiled at Jillian, like some movie had just ended and the lights were back on. He was wearing a navy Brooks Brothers suit, jacket off and laid over his knees, striped tie slightly loosened at his neck.

"Counselor," he said, extending his hand. "Good of you to come."

Jillian shook his hand firmly, a no-nonsense, no dragging her fingernails across his palm, a nothing-coy-about-it greeting.

"Congressman," she nodded crisply, once.

Jillian cultivated many friendships among influential people, but to the degree that she had a patron in Nevada politics, Gordon McLean was it. He had hired her as a staff intern when she moved to Nevada right out of law school, then got her a good job as an assistant U.S. district attorney. She didn't know if McLean had put in a word or not when she'd been appointed chief deputy four years ago. Publicly, she was an active supporter of Congressman McLean, within the limitations placed upon her as a government employee. Privately, though, she made certain McLean and his staff managed to get a heads up on any important investigations or other matters that crossed her desk, including the Tarkanian gambling investigation a few years ago, for which McLean had been especially grateful, had gone out of his way to say so.

"How's my favorite prosti-cutor?" he asked cheerily.

"Just fine," she smiled. Jillian was no prude, yet he'd been calling her that for years, a prosticutor. She had always shrugged it off silently, knowing McLean as a basic cold war chauvinist. This was Las Vegas, not Oregon, and she was ambitious enough to ignore such slights.

She was unsure about the agenda for this meeting, though she had her own hopes. Her boss, Frank Neidlebaum, was retiring this December, and her best hunch said that McLean had called her here to pop the question: Was she interested in Neidlebaum's job?

Out on the court, Jamad suddenly rose like a dark hurricane and slammed the ball through the hoop.

"Yes," McLean shouted and fisted the air.

Jillian crossed her arms and leaned back in her seat. "So, how's the team look? Are they ready for the big dance?" she asked.

"Depends on how many NBA scouts show up at which

games to watch Jamad." He shook his head and narrowed his eyes as he watched the scrimmage. "Sometimes that boy can be a little hard to inspire."

Jillian watched without response. She was a first-rate lawyer, always prepared. She hated sitting here like a schoolgirl, hopeful, waiting, not in control. Come on, Jillian thought. Cut the foreplay. Yes. The answer is yes. I want Neidlebaum's job. She already did ninety percent of his work. She handled all of the case assignments, both civil and criminal, and took on the toughest ones as lead counsel for the government. Neidlebaum didn't even try cases anymore. He was a banquetgoer, a schmoozer, and Jillian was sure that she could squeeze those PR duties into her busy schedule.

"How's our favorite trial coming?" McLean asked abruptly.

Jillian was momentarily taken aback. "I . . ."

"That downwinder trial." He turned and really focused on her for the first time and Jillian could see that suddenly they had transcended chitchat. "The one in federal court that you're defending on behalf of our fair and lovely government?"

She obligingly followed along. "Fine, fine," she said. "Everything is proceeding just as I expected." The lie almost caught in her throat; she hoped he couldn't tell. The trial was in recess for a few days, set to resume this Friday. Two other attorneys and two clerks, all of whom would be back at the office right now working hard, assisted her in all phases of the case, including her pending motion to dismiss.

And until last week, everything had indeed been going just fine. The only glitch, make that a possible glitch, had come to her in the form of a rumor, nothing more. An uncorroborated rumor that a retired scientist, a Dr. Franklin Rudd, from the old Nevada Test Site days, might be writing his memoirs, might be saying some unkind things about his government and how it conducted atomic testing in the 1950s.

Since Jillian regularly utilized the in-house services of an investigator—a federal marshall by the name of R. C. Hiney—for legwork, for details, to pick up her damn laundry if she felt like it, she, of course, had instructed him to check this rumor out. Well, perhaps a bit more than just check it out. She felt comfortable telling him to discourage memoirs by such men, even to take possession of any illegal material, anything that might comprise a breach of that wonderfully broad phrase, national security. "And you take care of this personally. Right?"

R. C. was eager to please, nodding that he understood.

Now, however, here sat the congressman, all concerned. Had he caught wind of the rumor as well? The mere thought of this rumor surfacing, leading to something more substantial that could affect the trial, having McClean call her over to a private basketball practice to inquire, suddenly forced a tiny trickle of sweat to escape her right armpit and run uncomfortably down her rib cage. Deputy Hiney had not been in his office this morning, no doubt following up on her business.

McLean exhaled slowly, as if smoking a cigar. "Good," he replied, "then we're all under control?"

"That's it. Take five," Coach Crouch blew his whistle. "Jamad, over here, lemme talk to you."

"Of course, Congressman McLean," she said with more silk than she felt, her paranoia still rising, "we read the same newspapers. Why on earth would you think otherwise?"

McLean's eyes, his gray, jet-jock eyes, relaxed. "No," he said, "nothing bad in the newspapers. I just wanted to hear it from you. As you might know, I'm the new chairman of the Appropriations Committee with oversight on Labor, Health, Education, and Welfare." He said this last through his teeth without a trace of joy. Jillian knew that McClean had wanted Defense, dearly wanted Defense, but had lost an intraparty struggle. He was a conservative, but not a religious right, death-of-outrage kind of guy. Just a garden variety cold war conservative, a hawk, an ex-fighter pilot. He supported a big Pentagon and, without a hint of irony, a small government. Not to mention big business, bigger casinos. Big, big everything. But what did that have to do with the downwinders' trial?

"Anyway," McClean continued, "long story short. We have another bill coming through this summer to compensate every possible category of downwinder you ever heard of. It's a bunch of Democrats, a partisan bill good for a few sound bites. One that's easily deflected, but your case could raise holy hell in my committee if a ruling came down suggesting that my government goes around lying about this kind of stuff to the citizenry." He went on a moment longer in a rambling discourse about the problems he faced in Appropriations, how much it would cost to compensate downwinders, cans of worms and Pandora's boxes, sounding now less like the tough negotiator that he was and more like an aging man complaining about hospital food.

Jillian realized as he talked that this had absolutely nothing to do with her recent problem. She almost laughed aloud with relief, a small sound escaping her throat. "I'm sorry," she said, almost reflexively patting the back of his hand, which was flecked with age spots. "Do not worry. The plaintiffs' case is not there."

"Hey," he said, perking up, "you look nice. Good to see you smile. You always look nice, Miss Jillian."

Yeah, mister ex-fighter jock, you'll be using that line on the nurses when you're ninety. She nodded. "The downwinders are in the last rounds of their case in chief and they haven't landed one good punch yet."

"That's the spirit. So no way to lose?" He paused, "I can count on it? That's a promise?"

"I . . . well." She took a moment. What the hell was she supposed to say? *"After all, Congressman, there is a judge presiding."* Jillian was a person who rarely stammered—words-as-weapons, words-as-tools—and she hated the sound of it now. "I'm making some moves, I've got it—"

"The details are yours," he cut in, "I just like to hear a promise. A marker that I can put in the bank and move on." He smiled, "And, hey, isn't old Neidlebaum getting ready to retire, one of these years?"

Jillian would have been knocked back in surprise if she'd been standing up. The old fox never missed a trick. So she squared up her shoulders and played his game. "I promise," she said emphatically. "You damn right, I promise."

Saluting Ground Zero

August 23, 1952, 5:30 a.m.
Yucca Flat, Nevada Test Site

ALL FINAL PROCEDURES FOR SHOT HUEY WERE ON TRACK—IT was a go at H minus five seconds. The sun was due to break over the mountains at any moment. Expectation and excitement had turned into jitters and sweat.

A button was pushed, sending an electrical current from the control center to the top of a gigantic tower. A single reverberating click shattered the tense calm and then, for one microsecond, a flutter of fluorescence—the Teller Light—bathed the test area in a violet glow, immediately followed by a stark, brilliant glare, cold and gray-green, flashing across southern Nevada, so indescribably bright and powerful that it would have resembled a flashbulb popping off to someone viewing it from the moon.

In that next moment, it seemed as though the entire sky turned liquid as the raving heat of a new sun flared across the desert floor. A double mushroom cloud began to form, one billowing at ground level and the other rising off the top of a gigantic column of smoky debris. The five hundred foot detonation tower, complete with its elevator and room at the top—over three hundred tons of steel—was suddenly gone, flashburned and then vaporized, along with vehicles, dummies, animals, and all other exposed objects within a quarter mile of ground zero. Their minute particles combined with rock and sand, anything near the cloud's vortex, and were sucked upward through the stem into a molten fireball that roiled higher and higher, greedily seeking oxygen—twenty, thirty, then forty thousand feet above the southwestern United States.

Two miles away in the trench, the Marines of First Platoon, Bravo Company, tried to maintain blast position as instructed: down on one knee, head bent forward, eyes tightly closed, right arm wrapped under the helmet brim and tight across the face. They couldn't believe what they were seeing, though. Even with their eyes tightly closed, the bones in their forearms, elbows, and hands—the radiuses, ulnas, and phalanges—clear as any x-ray, glowed a bright, fluorescent green.

But the platoon sergeant, Porkchop, didn't have time to be dazzled or scared shitless by his own bones. The back of his neck was suddenly so hot that he instinctively covered it with his left arm. The first shock wave passed through the ground just after the flash of light and shook the trench with such violence that he was slammed against the narrow sides like a rag in the jaws of some monster dog. Dirt and rocks poured down, and Porkchop seriously thought they might be buried alive. An intense pressure, volumes of compacted air, pushed down on his back, shoving him even lower in the trench. Vaguely, through the dirt and powdery ruckus, Porkchop could hear his men shouting and cursing, could hear his own voice—Jesus-friggin'-Christ-what-the-hell?

The second shock wave came from behind, was a rebound of the first, bouncing off the mountains and subterranean rock formations and back toward ground zero, doubling the trench line's violent whipsawing. Porkchop tried to open his eyes, but the falling sand and debris were so thick he could barely see the Marine next to him. Even so, a light many times brighter than the sun penetrated the dust and he clamped his eyes shut again, held onto his helmet banging from wall to wall, and rode the fury out. After the longest few seconds of his life, he sensed through his gritty daze that it was letting up, that they were only buried knee deep, and that they would probably live to talk about it.

He had once been in a trench at seven miles from ground zero for a smaller shot and found it merely an exciting pyrotechnic display, but this was something else entirely. This went far beyond what he had expected or been prepared for, and he immediately wondered if there was a mistake, a miscalculation by his superiors or the scientists.

Porkchop cautiously stood up and tried to shake off the bad thoughts along with the sand and dust and debris. He heard the muddled clamor of his men as they attempted to orient themselves, calling out each others' names. "Hey, you okay?" and "Shit-a-mighty, what was that?" He waited a couple of minutes and then ordered his platoon out of the trench.

It was reassuring to be out of the ground, to see that daylight itself hadn't been blown to smithereens. The towering cloud suspended above them was an unearthly sight—dense, gray-black vapor expanding in all directions. Porkchop felt shaken and dizzy, but he had his orders: lead the platoon in a direct assault on ground zero. Purpose: gauge if troops could endure an atomic blast in the field and then pursue the enemy. He wondered now, craning his neck toward the atmosphere and back down to the base of the cloud, what enemy could possibly be holed up in the middle of that thing. But his was not to question why.

"Alright, First Platoon, listen up," he said. "Shake it out, move it. Start forming up, squads on line."

There were moans and groans and one dazed Marine, staring up at the hissing cloud, lost his balance, stumbled sideways, and went down on top of his weapon, the side of his helmet slamming into the steel barrel.

One stood with his mouth wide open. "Mother of God! Look at that."

"Son of a bitch, my balls ache," said yet another.

"Christ, my knees and hips are killing me. What is this shit?"

Porkchop's own joints were aching too, and what had started as a warm sensation in his groin had turned into prickling pain. He decided to take it slowly, give his men time to come to their senses. "Shake the dirt out of your utilities and gear," he said, stripping to the waist and brushing himself off.

Others began to follow his lead. "Walk it out. You'll be okay. We still got work to do."

Porkchop observed the confusion and decided to delay their field maneuver until they could pull themselves together. He stepped a few yards away from the platoon, taking his time to brush off his gear, bending over to reblouse his trousers, and generally trying to shape himself up. His head began to clear, the pounding in his temples eased, and the negative thoughts about what they had been through slowly subsided. Come on, he told himself. They hadn't charged a machine gun nest, just had their cages rattled. As a professional fighting man, he'd seen worse, much worse, he assured himself.

And he knew the boys in his platoon. He had trained them hard, instilled pride and discipline and molded them into a capable fighting unit. Although they were untested in battle, Porkchop had other boys in the past just like these who had followed him, hi-diddle-diddle, straight up the middle, on Guam, Okinawa, and then in Korea. And before that, he himself had been one of these boys, hitting the beaches of the South Pacific behind some hard-bit sergeant. Porkchop bled Marine green; this was his life and he knew who could take what. There were Rodriguez and Chapman, both hard chested and tight-lipped, now helping their buddies, taking the lead and encouraging the others to buck it. PFC Flood, face like a little bulldog and the confirmed screwup of the bunch, had been down on his knees puking in the sand, but even he was calming down, getting reassurances from the others. Today's exercise was just another field maneuver, the second part easier than the first. So just calm down, Porkchop thought; there'll be no Purple Hearts awarded for this business.

The sun, now up over the horizon, was blocked from their view by the towering residue of Shot Huey. Porkchop got his men loosely formed up, squads on line, three abreast in single file, and gave the hand signal to move out. Two miles to ground zero was a piece of cake. They ran three miles almost every morning before it got too hot and occasionally hiked as far as twenty miles on night maneuvers. Now, however, they started out at a walk, needing a moment to work their aching joints and regain the simplicity of movement. After a short forced march, Porkchop signaled again, raised his fist and pumped it twice, gearing the platoon up into a plodding double time.

Around them, things were beginning to clear. The prevailing winds were slowly regaining control from the force of the blast and cleansing the air, breaking up the black cloud and pushing it toward the east, into the sun and away from them. The Marines maintained their pace on a direct line toward the dissipating column of smoke. Near the edge of what had been Doomtown, they passed the waving lady, now reduced to a bent length of steel pipe, some melted plastic, and a little hanging rag of scorched fur. A twisted, pink oven door, its glass front exploded, lay at her feet. Nearby, the Darling house stood completely open, the windows and doors and parts of the walls gone, the upper half of the red brick chimney burst and scattered as if constructed from a child's blocks.

Porkchop led the platoon on a winding course through the twisted debris. All heads turned and looked, but the men passed by. The day was heating up, and rivers of sweat poured from them as they jogged over the warm sand past shards of smoking metal. Usually Porkchop or one of the squad leaders called cadence when they ran in formation, but this morning he maintained silence. It didn't matter. The Marines had run together so much that they automatically fell into perfect step, became one big machine, rifles gripped across their chests in port arms, battle ready for quick response. A mile from their objective, ash began falling, covering them like a light and dirty snow, depositing a soft gray overspread on the sand. The closer in they moved, the thicker the blanket of ash, until it became ankle deep. Each pounding step—eighty thick-soled combat boots in unison—stirred the downy layer.

In a sudden moment that none of them could have imagined, a blind and terrified pig ran straight at them, scalded bright pink and hairless, pieces of smoldering fabric seared to its skin. Blood ran from its nose, ears, and mouth, and it almost collided with squad left before sensing something, veering sharply, and squealing in agony. But not one Marine broke ranks; not one boot missed cadence. Forty rights and forty lefts rose and fell as if welded together in fear and awe.

They passed the railroad trestle, gray and skeletal, steel twisted and buckled beyond recognition, the train cars on their sides, mere matchboxes against the force of Huey. The domes of underground shelters had blown off; rebar and concrete and pipes stuck out of the ground as if in some futuristic, junkyard world. Smoky orange sunlight filtered down around the advancing platoon, casting prismatic rainbows over them and the twisted rubble. A ream of paper blew slowly, page by page, out of a demolished shelter.

Porkchop was stunned. He knew about battle stress and this qualified—a half-roasted pig in remnants, a burning no-man's-land. He fought to keep his eyes fixed on the objective. Sweat streamed down his face, into his eyes, mouth, and ears; his utility shirt was as wet as if it had been raining. Heat radiated off the sand, which had been blistered into a glassy crust, and the soles of his boots were steaming. Ash flecked his face; his mouth tasted like acetylene and his own raw nerves.

Not far off on their left, a white Atomic Energy Commission van came into view, stopped a couple of hundred yards away, and four men slowly climbed out. They were dressed in what looked like space suits—protective boots, body suits, respirators, and sealed hoods—and they carried Geiger counters, small entrenching tools, and lead-lined containers. Anywhere else, Porkchop the hardcore Marine would have snickered—those guys walking around awkwardly like overgrown boys in stifling snowsuits—but out here, the differences between "them" and "us" became dark and threatening. What was it that those men had to be protected from, while his own boys were in everyday field dress? The AEC men froze and watched them like startled deer. The Marines kept chugging noiselessly forward like some phantom locomotive, steamy ash billowing up around their flanks, their destinies joined like the long shadow they now cast over the desert floor.

Finally the platoon left behind the wreckage and entered an

area of translucent emptiness. All that lay in front of them for a quarter mile was flat, smoking ground and a dark crater; everything else was gone. Orders were to simulate a direct assault on ground zero and make it secure. Was he supposed to tactically form the squads, some positioned down for covering fire while others zigzagged in, hitting the deck, then up and charging? What? Dive into the smoldering crater? At about three hundred yards out, the heat intensified even further, and Porkchop gave the command to walk, then halt. He turned and absorbed the astonishment and fright of the young Marines in his charge—citizen-soldier-draftees standing in a silent storm of ash. If they wanted more than this from his men, well . . .

Porkchop spun around in a perfectly executed about-face and looked at the crater. He paused and then, alone, advanced twenty rigid steps. He halted, called the platoon to attention without turning, then locked his heels. He saluted smartly and held it, squarely facing ground zero. That was enough. If this damn place wasn't secure, he was one son of a buck sergeant who would never, ever see secure.

CHAPTER FOUR

THE DOOR CLOSED WITH A SIMPLE, METALLIC CLICK, BUT EVEN that was too loud for Layne, too empty and embarrassing and awkward as he stood alone out in the quiet hallway, accompanied only by foxhounds and hunters suspended in the wallpaper on the third floor of the Four Wives Bed and Breakfast in Saraville. He hadn't known what else to do or what more to say, so he'd simply backed out of the room and closed the door on Christine, leaving her sitting wearily on the edge of the bed.

Damn! He really had wanted to leave her with something kind or encouraging, but what? Try not to worry? Impossible. Everything will work out? Improbable. "Get some sleep," is what he'd grimly settled on. "I'll see you early tomorrow morning," his shoulders uncharacteristically hunched in retreat as he eased out the door.

She had simply watched him go, her eyes flat as paint, face unreadable as a Chinese newspaper. Lame was how he felt now, completely lame. He was a lawyer, a gentleman, a smart guy who could do better. Moreover, he was Dallas's friend.

He remained in the hallway, wondering now if he should go back in and try again. *"Look, don't get me wrong, I'm sorry."* But nothing meaningful came to him and he stayed fixed to his spot outside her door. Besides, he rationalized, lawyers were hired to examine hard realities and to manage bad news, not to offer feel-goods to their clients. Still, he couldn't shake the idea. Faye, his secretary, would have swarmed Christine with warm milk and tender babble. Was it just a man thing or was he "sensitivity impaired?" He felt terrible about this whole jam Dallas and Christine were in. So why couldn't he conjure up a few words to convey some sympathy?

One explanation that had haunted him since leaving Nacho Mama's and on the entire drive back to Saraville was a developing edge of guilt over not telling Christine that Rudd's throat had been cut. And any soothing words seemed rather disingenuous while he was withholding that kind of information. She needed sleep right now, though, not the next chapter in the saga. She had passed out on the drive and hadn't resisted his suggestion to stay the night here in town. "I have a friend who owns a very comfortable B & B. I took the liberty of calling him," he told her. "Dallas thought it best that you not go back out to the ranch alone tonight."

She had nodded passively.

In the hallway outside her room, Layne suddenly turned and found himself bounding down the stairs, taking them two at a time, quick as a spark, as though he were running from something. A sense of release came with his vigorous, abrupt movements. He covered two flights of the giant floral carpeted stairway, taking each landing in a single hop, banking around the smooth bends by hanging onto the venerable old cherry-wood bannister that flowed unbroken from the top floor to the bottom. It had long provided support to stair jumpers and an aesthetic core to the expansive old pioneer home.

Layne reached the main floor, slightly out of breath, and paused in the grand entryway. The house felt deserted. Trevor Mallory, proprietor of the B & B, was probably still outside working his immaculate yard that backed onto the Virgin river amidst scattered stands of century-old oak and poplar and cottonwoods. The lush two acres of lawn that seemed to run in all directions was dotted with well-mulched beds where anything that was green and had roots—the ornamental water grasses, the begonias, the ivy, the jasmine—went crazy under the shady heat and Trevor's loving care. The other guests, he expected, would be off hiking in Zion—a good little park with a bad little name, as Trevor put it—or out looking for another impossible dirt road on which to trash their rental cars.

Layne went straight to Trevor's private liquor cabinet and grabbed a bottle of Bombay gin, then walked into the spacious old country kitchen, still painted white but with yellow and plum accents now. The fridge yielded ice cubes and tonic and limes, as he knew it would, and Layne fixed himself a stiff drink. Through the kitchen window he could see Trevor kneeling at one of the flower beds. Layne was thirsty and downed the drink in a few gulps. Not smart, but he didn't care. He reloaded and then sat down at the kitchen table and waited, content to sip on this one.

He had been breathing the charged air of this case for almost eight hours now and he needed a break, needed to assess and hold the line between client and professional. The binding mummy wraps of someone else's tragedy were slowly encircling him and, as he drank his gin, he tried his best to reenter that neutral space where people feign interest in or simply ignore everyone else's problems. He was a lawyer, worthless without some trouble, but that didn't mean he should make it personal. His job was to render advice and provide steerage among the shoals, navigate the fog of code, constitution, and precedent. He was merely the lighthouse keeper, was not expected to go down with the ship. A certain detachment was required to perform this job and he would do well to remember that, to leave the cocoa and cookies and oozing sympathy to others while he focused on the case. He knew all that, but was finding it easier said.

"*I did it, I killed the old boy. Just like that,*" Dallas had said with his usual matter-of-factness, his sardonic humor, his heels planted in the ground. Just like that, Murder One, committed during the commission of a felony, a capital offense. Your choice: the lethal needle or a giddy firing squad.

"*Looks to be a book or something this guy was writing, his memories. It has copies of top secret documents attached to it,*" Dallas said.

Great. Receiving stolen property, sequestering classified documents, possession of government secrets, treason. It didn't take a genius to figure out that there were probably nine million laws here for the breaking and that Dallas was asking Layne and Christine to begin breaking them as well. But maybe this book of Rudd's was fake or declassified, maybe Dallas was getting all lathered up over nothing. That's probably why this Mack what's-his-name FBI guy was snooping around. Because it was nothing.

"She got the cancer about a year ago." Layne twirled his drink and held the glass up to the light from the window, watching little fragments of lime swirl and drift. He didn't even want to think about cancer. Wasn't this case already front-loaded enough without tossing in a curve like that?

"I just want to do what's right. I want to turn myself in. Nobody meant to hurt anyone; the authorities will sort this all out." Christine's voice reentered his head. She sounded like a broken record on this score. And as he listened to her story in Nacho Mama's, a plausible version of events had emerged. She thinks Rudd died from the accidental stab wound incurred during their struggle and doesn't know that Dallas finished the job after she left. Finished it in a final and irrevocable way that took Christine right out of the loop, so that Rudd couldn't accuse her of anything, so that she couldn't possibly plead guilty to the murder. Now it was largely irrelevant what had happened at Rudd's house before Dallas arrived. Layne was betting that the autopsy, the reconstructed facts regarding the time and cause of death, would reveal that Dallas was the killer, plain and simple. Otherwise, Rudd might even have been out of the hospital by now with just a little jab wound in his side. Or not. Who knew?

At lunch, when Layne had told Christine to go ahead and turn herself in, that it wouldn't do Dallas any good, he had mumbled something about Dallas being, at the very least, an accomplice. He knew at the time he was just copping out. What he really needed to say, but didn't have the heart, was that Dallas was cooked, well done, and that by the time the finger-print analysis came back, he'd be deep-fat-fried. "Look, lady, your uncle finished the job to save your pretty butt, slit this Rudd guy's throat and bled him, put him out of his misery like a wounded deer." Then he could have watched, really been at a loss for comforting words, as she hit critical mass right there on the spot, went facedown in her enchilada with sensory overload. But he had to tell her tomorrow morning on the drive over to Dallas's ranch. It was unavoidable; he was the chosen messenger.

"Started the party without me, huh?" It was Trevor coming through the back door. "Where's our mystery guest? Is the princess settled in the tower?"

Layne nodded, pointing to the ceiling. "Thanks for helping out, Trevor."

"And thanks for making me a drink, too." Trevor pulled a beer out of the refrigerator. "It's the first sign of alcoholism, when you start pounding them down alone."

Layne stood up slowly. "Oh, sorry man. Didn't—"

"Hey, just kidding," Trevor said, pouring a Boar's Head Red into a frozen mug. The foam swelled and crested over the top of the glass as he hurried to catch it in his mouth. "Rough day, huh? I can hardly wait to hear all about it."

Trevor Mallory, a slight man standing five and a half feet, was in his mid-fifties, but he still had the energy of three. His astute gray eyes were shot through with flecks of black. They danced with curiosity and matched the color of his long hair bundled tight at the nape and running loosely past his shoulders. In the stodgier quarters of Saraville, he was privately known as Twevy, but it was a token put-down of his sexual preferences, not really meant to be hurtful. The reality was that Trevor Mallory was a respected businessman and the volunteer head of the Saraville Planning Commission to which Layne rendered legal advice as necessary. And if an old person or couple needed a lawn mowed or the branches hauled, or if the town sponsored a highway cleanup, Trevor was always first on the job. He understood himself and the nature of these people and valued them for most, not all, of what they were.

He had been born and raised during a different era one hundred miles north of Saraville in Beaver, Utah, where even he understood himself as "that queer" in the fifties lexicon of dumb farm boys, cheerleaders, and football players. The minute he graduated from high school and patched together the bus fare, he moved to San Francisco where he stayed for thirty years, made a very good success of the antiques business, and then came back to southern Utah to open the B & B. Jokingly and in private, he occasionally referred to himself as Saraville's resident fag, but said that the threat of AIDS, which he miraculously had escaped, and age, which he hadn't, drove him to celibacy. And as far as Layne could see, Trevor's life was pretty much asexual by now. Not that it mattered. In addition to their mutual connection through the town, Layne had represented Trevor in a couple of small matters. But mostly, their friendship took place on the wide front porch of the B & B over occasional sundowners. Trevor had traveled extensively to Europe and Asia in pursuit of antiques for his business, representing some very wealthy clients who devoted themselves to either making or spending money. Trevor was smart and glib and one of the most interesting people in town.

"So, what gives? I'm dying to meet your friend," Trevor said. "Why isn't she staying over at your place? A bit of a lover's quarrel, have we?"

"No, no. Don't start that," Layne said. "Strictly business. Bad business."

"Well, a full-service firm then." Trevor wiped the foam off his upper lip. "Layne the lawyer, legal and lodging, he arranges it all."

"I'm really beat." Layne stared out the window. "Maybe I'll head on home."

"What? And leave me without a clue about my houseguest? I am the good and efficient proprietor of a reputable inn. I like to know a little something about each of my guests before they pop down for breakfast."

"Sure," Layne said. "That's only reasonable. I represent her uncle, he's been charged with a very serious crime. That's about all I can say right—"

"The cowboy killer!" Trevor exclaimed. "That's it. She's related to the guy who slit that scientist from ear to ear, bled him like a stuck—"

"Whoa, whoa," Layne said. "The cowboy killer? You've got to be kidding. Where are you getting all that?"

"The radio, TV. It's all over the place. And you're not denying it. What other serious crime is there? Oh, this is a juicy one." Trevor grabbed a butter knife covered with dried raspberry jam and inexplicably began making fencing motions around the kitchen. "The county's most brutal crime of the year is what they're saying." Parry and thrust.

Layne stepped in front of him and glanced at the swinging door leading from the kitchen. He half expected to see Christine peering through the small round window in the door, eavesdropping on the conversation. "Quiet," he whispered. "Jesus, Trevor. Stop it. She doesn't even know that bit about the throat. You can't say a word to her about this."

"Well, thank you," Trevor said. "Do I look like a putz? Hey, sissy, I hear you're related to Jack the Ripper. I look like a guy who would do that?"

"No, of course not," Layne said. "But, help me, Trevor. Help me protect . . . prevent her from talking about this until I figure out what we need to do."

Trevor raised his hand in a pledge. "Deputize me, man. Come on, you're the city attorney. Planning commission doesn't get into stuff like this."

"Trevor, be serious." Layne suddenly thought about Christine wandering down here and spilling her guts to all the dinner guests. "Don't even let her discuss the case. Call me at home if she even gets out of bed."

Trevor looked disgusted. "You're no damn fun."

"Just promise," Layne said. Then smiling, "On your mother's sacred heart."

"My mother didn't have a heart," Trevor said.

Layne stared him down.

"Oh, take it easy," Trevor said, turning away. "I promise, I promise."

In a patch of sunlight falling across the nightstand sat a vase of big white daisies, their centers so extravagantly golden that Christine felt compelled to reach out and touch them. They were warm, seemed almost like an aberration of skin, but they were not what she needed. A phone. She desperately needed a phone, as in now. She craned her head around from the four poster bed where she was sitting and scanned the room. Antiques were the theme. There was a gray velvet love seat across from her, sepia-colored photographs on the wall, and hammered tin inlays on pine furniture waxed and aged into a rich honey glow. She had been given the most expensive and popular room in The Four Wives B & B—the Sara Room, the spacious attic of the house that had been remodeled with a vaulted ceiling and angled walls and several dormer windows, creating the feel of a small, airy cathedral. But dammit, there was no phone.

She rose and walked over to the door and opened it quietly. It had been several minutes since Layne had left her, looking tired and troubled, fumbling with words when a simple good-bye would have been perfectly appropriate.

She didn't want to run into him out here, start up some uneasy dance again, but thankfully the landing was empty when she stuck her head out. Just one elegantly upholstered straight-back chair and a large asparagus fern keeping guard. She considered slipping down to the first floor, the guest phone no doubt located in some ornate drawing room, but the mere thought of tucking in her shirt and putting on shoes kept her anchored up here. There might be people down there, pleasantries she'd have to engage in. She was completely wrung out, weighted with the blitzkrieg of the last eighteen hours. Irritated, she closed the door and sat back down on her bed.

The need to hear your mother's voice—some genetically

coded impulse imbedded so deeply that there was no sorting it out or giving it a name. It wasn't as if Audrey had all the answers for the world, but Christine just wanted to talk to her, to hear the voice that, even over telephone lines, still carried comfort and a promise that everything was going to be okay.

She closed her eyes. She could imagine just how it would go. There would be the customary three rings and then her mother would be on the kitchen extension and her father on the one in the bedroom. While her father mostly listened, her mother would calmly ask the questions, then provide long, slow "uh-huhs" to let her know that she clearly, perfectly understood. In their daily lives, her parents had become shortsighted and temperamental with each other, but give them some family problem and they became a veritable domestic SWAT team, manning positions and organizing against all opposition. During Christine's cancer ordeal, for instance, they had chauffeured her endlessly and walked through every step of the treatments with her, somehow knowing the right balance between her privacy and her need for them.

For most of the day, Layne had been as reassuring about this whole mess as he could be, but he was a lawyer, it was his job to pat things into place. And at best he was only a friend of Dallas's. He couldn't possibly provide the same support as her family, which was spelled with a capital F, according to her mother. Family—as in blood and kin and all those invisible ties that irrevocably mesh lives together, good or bad, like cyclone fencing. Audrey Parker had an encyclopedic definition of family which included a host of allegiances and responsibilities, and one of the most important was never to let family members face trouble or holidays alone.

For more than three decades, her mother had insisted that Dallas spend Christmas in Phoenix, that he shake himself loose from the ranch and join the human race for yuletide. From Thanksgiving through New Year's Day, she ruled supreme, and nobody in his right mind picked a fight with her or said no, including Dallas. A few days before Christmas, he always showed up in some old truck loaded with presents and a couple of dogs, and for Christine and Robbie and Pamela, her younger brother and sister, it was as if Santa himself had arrived.

When Uncle Dallas walked through the door, the Parker household instantly changed. There was the intoxicating pall of his cigarette smoke floating through the rooms. There was loud laughter and people eating in the living room on the off-white sofa and dogs trying to howl "Jingle Bells" into the night. The dogs weren't misbehaving; they were sick, what with the Parker kids feeding them fruitcake and eggnog and cream-filled chocolates.

Her parents saw to it that there were the traditional gifts under the tree—bicycles and dolls and then radios and record players when they were older—but it was Dallas who always came through with the unexpected. One year when Robbie was eight or nine and sending them all crazy with his incessant questions and curiosity, Dallas gave him a pair of army surplus binoculars, showed him how to focus them and then sent him outside. Her father claimed they didn't see Robbie again until he was twelve years old and needed braces. Another year, Dallas gave all three of them ropes and set up a lasso post in the backyard, her mother scowling the whole time, but somehow, through the promises he extracted, they didn't hang each other.

The Parkers always stood together; it was an inviolate clan rule, so why the hell couldn't Christine do a better job now, when Dallas really needed her? Her uncle—an aging man in jail. The image brought a quick, poking sensation at the bottom of her ribs. She sat up straight and tried to slowly breathe the pain away. Dallas behind bars or Plexiglas or however jails were built—it was just too much.

For decades, he had been the same unchanging Uncle Dallas to her, but on this visit she had finally started seeing the subtleties of age: the wrinkled backs of his hands, the deepening of his eyes, a slight hollowness in his cheeks. Evenings, she noticed that he stayed seated longer in the old overstuffed rocker pushed into the living room corner. Mornings, he needed a little more wake-up time and coffee. On several occasions in the past month, she had smelled the potent herbal brew of Deep Heat or some such muscle balm smeared on him.

And if the jail image freaked her out, just think what it would do to her parents. They would ask her to repeat the details again and again. "Dallas?" her father would unbelievingly ask several times, as if his hearing had gone bad or they had the name confused. And when she brought her own name into the conversation, told of her part . . . Mom, Dad: it was an accident, I swear. How were people supposed to process that kind of information four hundred miles away? They would probably get in their car and drive here immediately, worried sick all the way and driving too fast. Did she really want to call them with this heart-battering news?

Besides, the arithmetic here was easy. If she saw Dallas getting old, the fact was that her parents were older too, not frail and ready to give up their pop-top camper and thoughts of fishing the Yellowstone, but certainly on that downward glide into old age, which they mostly laughed about. Her father was on high blood pressure medication and wore a copper bracelet, hoping it might soothe his painful arthritis. Her mother was experimenting with everything from estrogen to vitamin E for the headaches and hot flashes that had never subsided after her hysterectomy.

Did they really have to be thrown into this chaos? Couldn't she manage this on her own? It was her turn to cope and to be responsible, for God's sake. Forget the telephone. The next twenty-four hours might prove critical to clearing up these charges or at least rearranging the odds. And if nothing else, twenty-four hours would give her a chance to sleep and be able to think clearly, to be able to call her parents and smoothly take the upper hand.

She flopped back on the bed, confused and depressed. She wanted to close her eyes and go to sleep, just blank all of this out for awhile, but she felt herself pulsing and dreadfully awake in some strange electrical field.

If only she could have seen Dallas earlier, talked to him,

measured the strength and certainty in his voice herself. The man really was incredible; she had to give him that. So she and the lawyer were supposed to saddle horses tomorrow and go on some scavenger hunt at the ranch, head for hole-in-the-rock, which might as well be hole-in-the-head. She didn't know whether to laugh or cry at his tactic. Did he have to come up with something this farfetched to keep her out of the picture, away from the authorities? How the hell young did he think she was? And all this BS about Rudd writing a book—where was that coming from?

The strange thing, though, was the note he had written to her. It was brief and mostly vague, but it had definitely struck her as serious. She recalled the simple request written in all caps at the bottom: PLEASE, CHRISTINE. Not Chrissy, but Christine, a name which he had reserved for about three occasions in her life.

She had always, always trusted him. If he said it was alright to stand near the edge of a cliff, then it was. If he told her not to ride her bicycle through the irrigation ditch, then she wouldn't. When he told her that divorcing T. C. Falco wasn't as big a failure as her living a long, unhappy life with him, she knew it in her heart to be true. And now, when he wrote her a note from jail telling her to keep cool and quiet, well . . . Dallas had been steady in the water for all of her thirty-seven years. Now what?

"You know, you only have to make decisions a day at a time, here," Layne had advised her. "So you wait until tomorrow, you go out and see whatever this thing is Dallas has hidden. Then you reevaluate. Know what I mean?"

Day at a time? Another day of indecision? When fighting her cancer, she'd found indecision a real enemy. Making tough choices and going forward was what worked.

She stood, disgusted at the absurd options she'd been given in this situation, ready to forget about all of them for awhile. She unzipped her faded jeans, slipped them off, and flung them toward a nearby chair, but with her careless aim, an amber-colored Tiffany lamp on the dresser was almost knocked over. She rushed forward, appraised the undamaged lamp, shook her head. Jesus! She'd be great at a striptease. Better make sure everything in the room was cemented down.

Actually, she'd not thought about stripping or teasing in quite some time, since her illness to be exact. Cancer had made any notions of sexiness about as remote and complicated as analytic geometry. It wasn't really the loss of a breast that had stopped and dumbfounded her in the middle of her life, that had torpedoed her sexual identity—although it hadn't helped, either. It was being sick, rubbing shoulders with her own mortality that had done that. It was the recurrent nausea and terrible taste in her mouth during all those months of chemo. It was loving life too much and having that love reduced to numbers—the magic five-year survival rate. That's what she was shooting for, because after five years, chances were that she was home free, that her body was clean.

"Bullshit. Total unequivocal crap." Gwynn Rowan stood up in tie-dyed shorts and T-shirt and railed against the medical dogma. Christine had joined St. Luke's breast cancer support group shortly after her mastectomy, and Gwynn Rowan, a two-year survivor in her mid-fifties, the only woman in the group who'd flatly, of her own volition, refused implants or a prosthesis, had turned out to be the entertainment.

The women met in the hospital's basement conference room. Many of them were soft-spoken and terrified. Most of them had adopted the vocabulary of their illness and talked about themselves in medical codes. Christine identified herself to the group as a stage three with four positive nodes, though she didn't say aloud what most of them knew from this—that she had a thirty to forty-percent chance of recurrence.

Propped there among the folding chairs in her splashy outfit, Gwynn Rowan looked like a small cloudburst of color. Survival rates, percentages, statistics of any kind—throw them out the window, she urged. She called them Nazi numbers, because "if we listened to any of them, we'd probably find ourselves extinct." Everyone in the group loved Gwynn, gave her the complete right of way because she was totally fearless, joyful, and validated living. She was the antidote to those depressing little windows across the top of the room and to the "slash, poison, and burn" programs most of them were going through—surgery, chemotherapy, and radiation.

Christine had last talked to Gwynn on the telephone about three weeks ago. She had called to see how her friend had fared in a racquetball tournament, but as usual, Gwynn turned the tables and wanted to know everything about Utah and riding horses. "Is it really possible to have an orgasm on a good mount?" she wanted to know.

"Yes," Christine assured her, "but it's hard to have a meaningful conversation with Trigger afterwards."

Christine unbuttoned her wrinkled white blouse, threw it on the end of the bed, then tugged on a piece of Velcro in the left cup of her bra and extracted a dense piece of foam—the prosthesis that she was still getting used to. It was shaped like a breast, she supposed, or a mound of durable ice cream or a couple of gym socks tightly rolled up. Once, the prosthesis had even come in handy when she pulled it out in the midst of a heated conversation with her sister and threw it at her. Pamela had almost turned white, then had fallen on the floor laughing, bless her.

Christine had been given a silicone implant at the time of her mastectomy, but any hope of a curvaceous figure lasted only two days. With a fever topping out at 103, she was taken back into surgery, the implant removed because of infection, though Dr. Moritake said that later, after the infection had cleared, they could try the implant again. Six months went by and then a year and Christine just never drummed up the nerve or the fortitude to return to the operating room.

She reached back and unsnapped her bra, then slid the straps over her shoulders and off her arms. She knew women who took weeks, even months to look at their chests after surgery. She, on the other hand, had wanted to see immediately. It looked like railroad tracks, red railroad tracks, though in time the scar tissue would hopefully shrink and lighten. There were actually three scars—three incisions in almost a Z pattern:

two that were roughly horizontal at what would have been the top and bottom of her breast, and one that was diagonal between them where an ellipsis had been cut and the breast and nipple removed. The scar would always be large, sort of like a personal Gettysburg. Perhaps it was made worse by the imbalance it created: a full and shapely chest on one side and a crimped and flattened piece of real estate on the other. Gwynn had a way of evening everything out, though: "Try losing a leg or an arm," she had said.

Or being arrested for murder, Christine added now. She stared down at herself, at the body she was learning to live with. Why did it seem to take hurricanes and car wrecks and terrible events to put things into perspective? There was a man in a cooler at the morgue, her uncle was in jail for murder, and here she was in some cozy B & B. What was wrong with this picture?

She finally slung back the covers on the bed, lay down, and rolled onto her side. It was as if some blessed curtain was pulled on the whole scene. There was no tunnel, no drifting on a hypnotic sea, no groggy moment in a darkening half-world. Christine simply fell straight into the genial black arms of a dreamless sleep.

At 2:00 a.m., Uwanda Docksteader heard the front yard sprinklers come on, the pipes groaning low—an almost hurtful sound—then the sprinkler heads slowly beginning to rotate with their calming chk, chk, chk. She was in her basement, pacing, caught up in a puzzling maze of ideas and possibilities. Brainstorming. Searching. "In one of her moods"—that's how Van, her patient husband of twenty-one years, would describe it. "Whacking out" is what her son Owen would say. Shelby, Uwanda's seventeen-year-old daughter, wouldn't have any words for it, would just glare at Uwanda as if the heat from her eyes could strip her mother down to bare, powdery, loveless bones.

Van and Owen and Shelby were all asleep upstairs, well accustomed to the sound of sprinklers and the night maraudings of Uwanda. She wandered the downstairs, disconnected from any sense of time and deeply entrenched in thought, her long pale blue nightgown tenting around her ankles from the cool drafts this room was prone to. She was not exactly graceful, but at five feet, eleven inches and 173 pounds, she was firm, steady, and cut a path that would not have been questioned lightly. Her long black hair streaked with silver fell past her shoulders to the middle of her back, and sometimes, unconsciously, she brought a hand up and stroked it, as if she were gentling herself. On her feet she wore a pair of thick, purple cotton mountaineering socks.

Van—wonderful, big, bald-headed Van—had portioned off half the basement in their St. George tract home several years ago and told Uwanda she now had her own private office downstairs. He hauled in two old library tables from the city's modernization sale and had even thrown a remnant piece of olive green shag carpet over the concrete floor for her. Later, a lumpy beige sofa from Deseret Thrift was added along with two dark Lucite end tables. Not that she thought about color schemes much, but the room reminded Uwanda of camouflage, which certainly wasn't inappropriate considering the war she was waging down here.

Tattered boxes loaded with declassified government documents and others full of legal pleadings, briefs, and depositions lined the walls. For the last twelve years, she had been president of the Downwinders Coalition, a ragtag, politically charged group of angry Western residents who believed they and their families had been injured by atomic testing from the Nevada Test Site. Twelve years as president was a long time, but nobody else had the knowledge, commitment, and personality to get the Downwinders anywhere. She had never missed a meeting, court hearing, deposition or demonstration, and it was known that she had a sympathetic ear and that her home number was listed in the phone book. Even before becoming president, most of Uwanda's life had been involved with the cause. Though she could trace her ancestry to Scotland, Uwanda was born just outside of Cedar City, a small town in Southern Utah, to a third-generation family of sheep ranchers who were bankrupted, completely wiped out in the winter of 1953 by fallout from the test site. She was just a child when it killed most of their sheep. Still a child when it killed her father.

Now, finally, with herself as the primary litigant representing a large class action suit, all the facts had a chance to be proved, officially, by a preponderance of the evidence, and then recorded for history—a vindication for all to see. She hoped. God, it had been a long time, a lifetime during which they had been sustained only by anger and hope.

Uwanda knew the case was consuming too much of herself and her time, but this was their chance. At long last, they were having their day in court: *Uwanda Docksteader, et al. v. United States*. It was the biggest downwinder case in history. Filed five years ago, it finally got underway this last January at the Federal District Courthouse in Las Vegas. Uwanda had been staying in Vegas at discount motels during the week, then zooming back to St. George to reinvent her family on the week-ends.

Now, suddenly, as if some invisible explosion had taken place within her, Uwanda stopped, turned to the wall of boxes and started digging through them. To anyone else, the boxes' contents would have had no discernible filing system, but Uwanda knew exactly where to look for what she needed. For example, the Robert Mondavi boxes contained all of the coalition newsletters and correspondence going back several years. Sterling Vineyards held all of the pleadings, and the large Twirl Town Toys boxes were perfect for the bound depositions. But knowing where to look wasn't her problem tonight; it was knowing what to look for. She was simply digging, hope against hope, for something—for anything—for a miracle.

That was precisely what Joseph Attencio—lead counsel for the plaintiffs, elder statesman of environmental law and hopeless causes—had said they needed. A miracle. Normally, he was reassuring and positive, but after this latest and largest disappointment, she wasn't sure where he stood. They had been desperately counting on the testimony of an important witness last week, but the guy had fizzled on them—maybe twenty-five kiloton bombed was more like it—at the last minute. Knowing his team needed to regroup and formulate some new strategy, Joseph Attencio had asked for a weeklong recess and surprisingly got it.

Uwanda had driven back to St. George that evening, thankful for a weekend plus the extra days because she had work to do. She'd comb through every box in the basement, of course, looking for a new avenue for the case, but there was also her daughter to attend to. Van and Owen needed her attention, as well, but it was Shelby who really scared Uwanda.

Cold and impenetrable, Shelby had become unrecognizable. If Uwanda hadn't watched her own belly grow huge seventeen years ago, hadn't lain there like a mournful beached whale for twenty hours of labor with her daughter, she would never have believed that this girl-child-woman-thing had come from her own body. How could genetics have betrayed her and Van so profoundly?

Shelby wasn't like either of them, hadn't assumed Van's easygoing nature or his quiet generosity, and she certainly had been given none of her mother's individualism or her love of life and people. Shelby was intense and rigid, her view of the world so narrow that Uwanda jokingly said anyone would have to walk sideways to squeeze into Shelby's life. She was in her junior year of high school and was a straight-A student, but Uwanda would have traded any of those A's for a simple smile from her daughter, for a youthful shrug of her shoulders or a goofy knock-knock joke or a pair of faded, wrinkled jeans on her. Instead, Shelby dressed in well-pressed Oxford shirts and khakis or a pleated skirt—her "uptight, do-right" clothes, Uwanda called them.

"Better than a plumber's uniform," Shelby always replied snidely, referring to her father's gray utility workshirts with *Van* embroidered on the front pocket and *Quality Plumbing* stenciled on the back. Her embarrassment over her plumber father, however, was nothing compared to the utter humiliation she seemed to feel about Uwanda. A large, outspoken, political woman dressed in bright ethnic clothing and Birkenstocks was not the mother Shelby wanted. She was drawn to her friends' mothers—soft-spoken Mormon housewives who traded recipes and drank tall glasses of cold milk with their children and baked sheet cakes for the church's Relief Society. Uwanda had been raised in the Mormon church but had long since fallen away—a Jacqueline Mormon, she called herself—and so was all the more disgusted by her daughter's choices.

"You'd like me to be June Cleaver on a stick with a testimony," Uwanda liked to tell Shelby. She realized that most kids hate their parents at one time or another, but this wasn't just a phase for Shelby. Uwanda had recently begun to understand, in a way that made her turn cold and speechless, that there was a meanness, a vacuous stupidity in her thin, blue-eyed daughter. Shelby still lived in their house, but in every significant way she was gone. She ate her meals in her bedroom, spoke to her parents almost exclusively through yellow Post-it notes left on the refrigerator. When either she or Van tried to address Shelby directly, their daughter stared at the ceiling or glanced at them with cool obligation.

Uwanda's plan when she arrived home last Friday night had been to go straight to Shelby's bedroom, camp out on her bed, and talk late into the night with her. She'd listen to her daughter, really listen, take any attack Shelby had for her. What with the downwinders and the trial, she'd been an absent mother too long and she knew it, but love was bigger and more forgiving than that and she'd just have to prove it to Shelby.

That night, sitting cross-legged on her green comforter, Shelby had eyed her mother icily, listened to all of Uwanda's confessions, both good and bad, then asked her mother to get out. "This is my room, right?" she asked. "You always said this is my private space."

"Yes," she snarled at her daughter, "but you don't deserve it."

Why did it always seem like that—black and white, right

and left, fire and water, a huge, bottomless divide between them? She had left Shelby's room, felt sick and shaky the rest of the weekend, but couldn't prod herself into trying again. So here it was in the wee hours of Tuesday morning; she had struck out with her daughter and she was back at her usual place—down in the boxes.

"You've done all you can," Van told Uwanda repeatedly, slipping his arm around her shoulders, pulling her close. It was about the only real physical contact they had these days. During her hectic weekend visits, the strain of the trial and their children seemed to strip away much of the tenderness once between them, and the sheer mechanics of two middle-aged bodies took over. After their bedroom light was out and just before they went to sleep, Van would swing himself over to her side of the bed and she'd back into his cradled six-foot body— like parking an Olds Eighty-eight in a compact space. More and more, she was reminded of a television commercial, a Nike ad encouraging people to "Just Do It." That seemed to be the motto for their sex life now—they just did it, though less and less frequently. Afterward, she would lie there feeling as if some ocean wave had dragged over her, leaving her dizzy, disoriented, wet, and sticky behind the knees and at the back of the neck. Van would fall asleep or, even worse, sit up on one elbow, as if he was about to reveal something sweet or intimate to her, but he was only listening to one of the toilets flush or the water softener recycling, checking for the low whine and thump of a flow problem.

There was no mistaking that he wanted her home and the trial over. He did his best to take up the slack when Uwanda wasn't there, bringing home take-out food for dinner, trying to keep a pulse on Shelby's life, driving Owen and his friends to basketball and movies—all in the hours that the plumbing business didn't consume him.

She called home daily when she was in Vegas, and recently, long-distance, Van, usually not a complainer, had tiredly said, "I can't keep loving our kids for you and me both." The remark had seemed sudden and out of the blue and almost dropped

Uwanda to her knees. There was a silence that seemed to stretch longer and farther than her MCI calling card could ever handle.

Then Van's voice floated back on the line, trying to lighten things up. "Besides," he said, "you've got to rescue me. Owen has hit puberty full on. I had to have a little talk with him about showers and wearing deodorant the other day. Whew! It was getting ripe around here."

She'd had a vision of Owen's thin eighth-grade face, and the sensation was immediate and physical, a cord deep inside her that had been yanked hard. She missed him, missed them all desperately.

But how hard was it to understand that she was the lead plaintiff in this case, that she represented potentially thousands of people in this class action? People had been grievously injured, lied to by their government for over forty years. She recalled the day that Joseph Attencio had agreed to take their case; it was almost a religious experience for her. There had been a lot of work involved, but now, at least, they could point to the bottom line—win, lose or draw, this trial would be over soon. She would steamroll her way back into her family's life and nail it all back together, by God, with the same vigor that she had used to pursue the downwinders' cause, the same way she tackled everything.

Uwanda rubbed the small of her back. She walked over to the long table that she used as a desk, sat down, and placed a brand-new pad and a felt-tip pen in front of her. On the corner of the table, half of a fuzzy, green cheese sandwich sat where Uwanda had forgotten it a week ago. On the left side of the pad, she wrote the name Tesset, then drew a line through it.

Attencio had not been able to hide his dispirited attitude last Friday when he had asked Uwanda to have lunch with him. They walked and talked their way during the noon recess over to Big Ed's luncheonette, a fifty-year-old relic that was famous within a four-block radius of the Las Vegas Federal Courthouse for its smothered meat pies. That's when Attencio broke the news to her of his conversation the previous evening with Dr.

Roman Tesset, who had been scheduled to fly in the following week to testify.

Tesset's father-in-law, Colonel Lloyd Abrahms, had been one of the first Army commanders at Camp Desert Rock back in the early fifties. The reality and dangers of the whole program out there must have become apparent pretty quickly to Abrahms, who had a job to do, but who sure as hell wasn't going to allow his daughter, Tesset's wife, and grandchildren in St. George, Utah to be injured. As originally reported by Tesset, he wrote and told them in no uncertain terms to clear out of that part of the country, everything in that direction was going to be lit up by the time this testing was over.

Abrahms was now long dead, Tesset's wife had passed away, and in the political climate of the nineties, Roman Tesset had prematurely decided that it was alright to make this information public. He himself was a social psychologist at a behavioral institute back East, with three books to his credit, and the "truth" seemed a good thing to him. He'd been subpoenaed and was scheduled to fly into McCaren International in Las Vegas this coming week, but Joseph Attencio had immediately recognized trouble when Tesset called him.

The small, slack-faced man told Attencio that he would get on the stand, but that he really didn't know anything. Attencio had gone back and forth with him, taken both the soft and hard approaches, but he couldn't get Tesset to budge.

"Mr. Attencio, I'm afraid I have misled you. Col. Abrahms always made it clear that his desire for us to leave Utah back then was based solely upon his personal opinions. He was careful not to attribute his concerns to the AEC upper echelon either at the test site or in Washington." Then Tesset lowered his voice and mumbled, "And there are certain grants that I rely on at the institute, Mr. Attencio. I hope you'll understand."

Enough said. It was absolutely clear that Tesset had been tampered with, like others before him. Attencio could have forced him onto the stand, taken him as a hostile witness, but whoever had coached Tesset made sure that he repeated the magic words, over and over. Personal opinions; no actual knowledge.

Uwanda and Attencio entered Big Ed's and took a Naugahyde booth, old and high-backed, sky blue with pieces of white tape trying to restrain the cracks. "I'm sorry, Uwanda," Attencio said again. "Tesset was our best shot, however slim, of convincing this judge, of proving some kind of actual knowledge during those years—establishing any course of conduct on the part of the middle managers within the AEC." He looked directly at her. "I'm very concerned that the judge will entertain a motion from the defense for a directed verdict the moment we rest our case. I'm going to make my own motion this afternoon to recess for a week. I know the judge has other pressing matters and I think he'll grant it. But, if we don't come up with something in that time, I'm afraid . . ." He grimaced, "Sorry, Uwanda. You've poured your whole life into this thing."

Uwanda stared down at the grimy salt and pepper shakers, Attencio's deep voice lingering in her ears. She worshipped him, viewed him as a man capable of almost anything. He was an ex-congressman, a true champion of the common person. After Congress, he had served two different administrations, walked in very high places, made many friends and even more admirers. Now, at seventy-two years old, he looked like a patron saint, the one who never forgot his roots in Chimayo, New Mexico.

Joseph shook his head, his silver mane swaying like an old lion's. "It's been a long old road together, hasn't it, Uwanda? What, seven, eight years now?" At his age and at this stage of his career, it was common knowledge that, in spite of his wealth, he didn't care about material things, was obviously unimpressed by expensive haircuts or flashy suits. He wore either a durable navy or a black suit each day to trial, accompanied by his gray tie or one that had been colorfully fingerpainted by his grandson. He took this case and others like it on a pure contingency, funded much of the discovery and research on his own, and worked thousands of hours with slim chance of recovery.

"You've been wonderful," she said to him.

Attencio looked at her through large, dark eyes. She always thought those eyes had the rare ability to see beyond the present, beyond the small concerns of people, into the future and into special places that would make us all better.

"The law," he said, "normally deals only in money. It's the common language, the final result of all the deal-making and the litigation and, well, commerce. Law is basically commerce. This describes the work of a lawyer more accurately than any other word. But, once in a while, there's an opportunity to step beyond that. To actually enforce a principle, to retool an injustice, to set the record straight. I had so much hoped—"

Uwanda listened to his words trail off again as their waitress skidded to a stop and took their order, then quickly called over her shoulder, "Two pies, smothered, one brown, one bean, hold the fries." She looked back down at them, "You guys want anything to drink?"

After she left, Uwanda reached out and patted Joseph's hand, something she'd never done before. "So, it's really hopeless?" she asked. She heard her lower jaw click on the last word. It was another thing she would have to pay attention to after this whole thing was over. She had been grinding her teeth in anger so much over the last few years that she'd evidently done some damage, and now the joint sometimes sounded like a broken gate hinge.

He smiled for the first time that day. "I suppose nothing is totally hopeless. But it is pretty bleak. As you know, the judge has been hard on us. He has severely limited the scope of our discovery on the basis of national security. He has limited our own expert witnesses' testimony for any number of reasons. Our other witnesses, people like yourself who grew up with all this trouble and who saw your families destroyed, are being shut out, as always, by this sham of national security. Then there are those like Tesset, who really could help, but the pressure—" He shook his head.

Uwanda already knew the score—government galloping, plaintiffs limping—yet she'd never seen Attencio so discouraged. Maybe he'd been covering up his feelings, and she was finally catching him at a vulnerable moment.

"What can we . . ." Uwanda hesitated. She knew a lot about

the law. She had never been content to just sit on the sidelines. She had read every brief, memorandum, and relevant case and made it her business to understand them. Because Attencio and the other lawyers on her side had explained it so many times, she also knew that this type of claim was one of the hardest cases to prove. It had to be done through circumstantial evidence. In any normal tort claim, there would be witnesses, police reports, experts investigating the scene to tie it all together and crisply reconstruct it in court. Uwanda's group of plaintiffs didn't even know that they were being hurt, most until many years later. They didn't know which atomic test did damage to which plaintiff. The evidence had been lost, altered or destroyed, and whatever was left was still cloaked in all that secrecy bullshit. God bless America.

"There has to be something," she said, "some way to find a crack in the government's case and widen it. Most of those deposed government witnesses are lying through their teeth; they all know the damage this caused. They're hanging their hat on the fact that it can't be scientifically quantified. 'Definitive studies.' If I ever hear that phrase again, I think I'll—" she stopped abruptly. She wasn't really going to say "throw up" to Joseph Attencio, was she?

Now it was his turn to pat her hand. Fatherly, kindly, with great understanding. "I hate to admit it, but I had a lot of hopes pinned on Tesset," he said. "Maybe too many. Maybe it's a lesson for me."

"We're running out of time," she said. "What can we do?"

He shook his head, "Pray for a miracle, I guess."

At that moment, the waitress showed up with two steaming meat pies, one smothered in chili, the other in gravy. The thick, braised, oniony smells filled the booth as she slid both plates down simultaneously in front of them and, without missing a beat, said, "Miracle, huh? Just be careful what you guys ask for. I prayed for one once and, unfortunately, someone was listening. Look where it got me. Las Vegas." She looked sternly upward. "Thanks, Big Guy."

THE CONTROL CENTER, A WELL-FORTIFIED TWO-STORY building twelve miles southwest of ground zero, enjoyed a hotel view. Through huge, tempered windows, a dazzling 180-degrees showcased the test grounds. The building's designers had provided endless assurances about the control center's ability to withstand almost any force. Despite the fact that no prior blasts had fazed the comfort and security there, the scientists and engineers from the Green Angel team who were standing near the windows at detonation had been intimidated by the power of their own darling, Shot Huey.

After the fireball erupted, rocketing skyward, visible shock waves radiated out from ground zero as if a massive boulder had been dropped on a tranquil pond. A pelting sandstorm hit the control center's windows and instantly sandblasted the paint off the thick reinforced concrete front. The lab-coated members of the scientific team had instinctively recoiled from the windows, crouching and scrabbling backwards like so many large white crabs.

Angled for wind shear, the bulletproof glass held, but a loud crash downstairs had startled everyone. An outside solid-steel door which had not been properly secured was blown off its hinges and embedded in the back wall of the empty chamber. Meanwhile, calls were flooding in from Las Vegas, forty miles away, where thousands of windows had shattered and people awoke to watch their books drop off the shelves and their hanging lights sway. Whatever military and scientific principles Huey may have demonstrated, one thing was clear: it exceeded and defined the top limits for atmospheric testing in the continental United States.

Adam Crosswell, head meteorologist at the Nevada Test Site, had seen this show before—the earth buckling, the sky rendered, and all hell breaking loose. Weather conditions were a critical component of each shot, and he had not only witnessed but personally supervised that aspect of every detonation for the past twenty months, beginning when the test site opened for business with the Ranger series in January of 1951. With silent dismay, he watched the Green Angel team scuttle back to the windows as the wind died and the air cleared, crowding toward the glass like children. These men were hard to impress, dazzled more by theory and possibility than any simple reality. For once, however, they were speechless, not the least bit curious about the blown door downstairs, but delighted by their creation. They stared at the gigantic mushroom cloud spiraling upward and were mesmerized by the fireball, its gaseous shimmering colors. They had clearly miscalculated Huey, had not fully comprehended the exponential upsizing of those extra kilotons.

It was all becoming a nightmare as far as Crosswell was concerned. Unlike the others in the control center, he stayed at his elevated workstation toward the rear of the amphitheater-shaped main room, flanked by the two other members of his weather team, and worked to assimilate and chart the continually updated information being fed to them from the National Weather Service's strategic ground weather stations and from specially equipped military weather planes aloft. He could see enough of the blast, gauge its monumental size, from where he was. Everything indicated a good breeze running about fifteen miles per hour over the ground and just under forty miles per hour aloft, mostly heading east while bending slightly north, away from the test site. Not ideal, but well into the acceptable range.

The swaying sounds of Glenn Miller's "In the Mood" suddenly flooded the room, and Crosswell walked down the aisle and peered around the corner into a coffee lounge adjoining the main control area. Some younger members of the team were setting up a makeshift bar. An RCA sat on a coffee table and spun the record. The Green Angel team seemed to be throwing themselves a going away party. Even the word from Las Vegas about shattered windows had produced whoops and cheers—not an ounce of chagrin—from the scientists and engineers. Having a party, drinking in the control center, this was a new one for Crosswell, but it was their last shot, the end of this series. Tomorrow, a new team was due to arrive from Los Alamos and a new series was scheduled through the end of the year.

Two smiling Las Vegas bar girls clad in fishnet stockings and tight uniforms were taking drink orders. One of the team leaders licked a piece of celery served to him in a peppery Bloody Mary, then cozied up to one of the girls and slid it between her breasts. It immediately set a precedent. Others followed until a garden appeared to spring from her chest. The men began swinging the girls and each other, bourbon and hundred-proof vodka quickly torquing their excitement.

Sid Greenburg, one of the Livermore scientists on the Green Angel team, walked over to Crosswell and handed him a pack of cashews. "Enjoying yourself?" he asked. "How about a drink?"

"Hello, Sid," Crosswell answered. "No can do. Got to keep track of your baby Huey up there."

Greenburg shrugged and returned to the party. Actually, he was a decent guy most of the time, had been one of the few people around here Crosswell could have a conversation with. Most of the others were rumpled and wild-eyed, defensive, edgy enough to take your tonsils out with a ballpoint pen if you looked at them wrong. And then there was the test site manager, his boss, Dr. Franklin Rudd—Cranky Franky as Greenburg liked to call him. Surprisingly, Rudd had actually joined the celebration, was bent over, slapping his knees and hooting—Jekyll and Hyde with a Bloody Mary in hand.

Crosswell walked back up the aisle to his station and asked his two assistants for updates, trying to shut out the festivities.

The worst thing about Rudd was that you could never depend on who he was going to be—your worst enemy or a smiling, schmoozing pal. Crosswell knew better than to turn his back on him or give him more than two seconds of trust. And, as Crosswell understood only too well, Rudd was in complete charge of what information left the test site. So, when Crosswell saw that an atomic cloud was stalling out against a large weather front and then suddenly dropping, his job was to simply monitor it and see whether the fallout hit the plains of Wyoming and lit up a few ranchers and cows or congealed and dropped right on the epicenter of Denver or Chicago. "Hot spots" they were called. Similar incidents had happened before. And all he could do about it was track the cloud, submit all the updated activity reports directly to Rudd, and then be assured that absolutely nothing would happen.

So why the hell did the AEC even bother? Crosswell knew exactly why. In addition to their being information freaks, the pre-blast phase was absolutely critical. No shot was ever detonated unless the wind direction was vectored in between the east and the north. Zapping the local Mormons from St. George to Salt Lake City was one thing—it was entirely unavoidable, and Crosswell had actually heard AEC personnel joke that Mormons were so dense that a little radiation might brighten them up. But if one of these stems and clouds ever toppled over backwards and seriously contaminated L.A. or other populated areas of California, the tests would be moved back to the Pacific faster than you could say "glowing atoll."

It hadn't always been that way. In the earliest days of testing, right in the beginning, he had tracked a shot that encountered an unexpected squall and then brought a big load of fallout down on Rapid City, South Dakota. Fine radioactive debris sifted over the city, finally gathering in the lawns and gutters all over town. There had been some very discreet communications between the AEC and the town fathers, and in the end, the fire department had used their hoses to slush all the yards and streets, sending the debris down into the Cheyenne River. Not an ideal solution, but it was better than letting it lie.

On another early occasion, warnings had gone out to St. George, Utah, when a shot stalled out and dropped on that area. Radio stations were contacted and told to announce that everyone should stay indoors and that children should be kept home from school that day. However, Rudd and the other officials quickly realized that the seeds of panic were being sown by their own hand and someone quickly put a stop to it. So, for over a year now, Crosswell's tracking reports had been accepted by Rudd with a crisp thank you and no further warnings were ever issued. On the contrary, the public was told not to worry, that no harmful levels of radiation ever escaped the test site. Crosswell knew this was complete bunk, and furthermore, that the entire upper portion of the gigantic mushroom cloud called Huey, which was standing over their heads right now, had hooked into the jet stream, the "business altitude" of the cloud, and was beginning to move en masse on a course due northeast at forty thousand feet.

Even without all his data in, Crosswell could tell Huey was going to be extremely "dirty," that it was carrying a lot of vaporized metal, sand, and other debris and that the intensely radioactive fallout from this one would be monstrous. The tallest portions of the nuclear cloud would catch the jet stream and flow over Utah, Wyoming, the Dakotas, and finally light up Geiger counters well into Canada. The stem and lower part of the cloud would drag along behind and slowly settle back to earth as a strange, dry rain, putting down the hottest layer yet over the new atomic trail. And that was only if things took the most predictable path. That assumed no weather front "stopped it and dropped it" as his assistants liked to say, or that no sudden shift in the weather reversed course and took it God-only-knew-where.

Crosswell briefly glanced back toward the party room, which was noisy and standing room only. He had a short-lived inclination—deep and intense as sudden heartburn—to go in there and put his arm around Greenburg and the boys, laugh it up a little. What did it matter, since his reports would merely be filed away? But he talked himself out of it.

For the last year, this job had been creating conflict with his most basic human impulses, and a couple of months ago, he had begun waking at night with a recurring dream and a case of the sweats, thinking about a brother who lived in Salt Lake City. Crosswell would lie there in bed, desperate in the middle of the night to call him and tell him to get out, move away, leave Salt Lake, but he couldn't bring himself to do it. His job and retirement were on the line. Others, whistle-blowers who had sounded any form of alarm, had been visited by the FBI, flown to Washington, D.C., given an audience with some undersecretary of something. In a baroque, high-ceilinged office, they were sternly warned about sanctions more severe than loss of job and benefits over what were clearly categorized as treasonous acts. Just slipping away quietly into early retirement had started to sound inviting to Crosswell.

Then, yesterday, he had received word that his transfer back to the National Weather Service's Hurricane Center in Florida had been granted. He was elated. Compared to what he'd been dealing with in Nevada, hurricanes were natural and predictable and had lives—as opposed to half-lives—of only a few days or a week. His mission in Florida would be to save people and property; he wasn't sure what his mission here was any more. He called his wife in Las Vegas and told her to start packing.

He promised himself that he'd write his brother a long, friendly letter from Florida. *The ocean breezes are great. The orange juice is fine. Come visit when you can.* He swiveled his chair back toward the wall and continued to check his readings. Everything was stable. The bomb was now doing what it was supposed to—moving away from them; slowly falling out. He wouldn't be joining the party, drinking the booze or feeling up the girls. As soon as the readings outside the control center dropped back into an acceptable range, he would begin to file the required meteorological report on Huey, turn this seat over to his assistant for follow-up tracking, and then head for the gate at Camp Mercury—he hoped for the last time.

And after blue water and orange juice, he really wasn't sure what he dared to say in that letter to his brother. Their wives hadn't gotten along for years now, and in the end, he wasn't sure that he and his brother were really that close anyway.

In what seemed liked a completely different world high above the test site, information was being radioed to various military control points from an F-84 jet fighter whose mission it was not only to track the cloud, but to actually collect radiation readings and sample fallout from the cloud's interior. The pilot, Bobby Caputo, a young hotshot who had survived two hundred combat missions over Korea, flew horizontally under the base of the cloud, and at its approximate epicenter, pulled the stick, accelerated, and zipped straight up, flying blind through it. The maneuver was to be repeated until sufficient readings were gathered. In seemingly mundane lingo, the pilot radioed in the "dog" (fallout) and "rascal" (gamma radiation) indicated by his metering devices. When these readings were within the expected range, everything was "red, white, and blue."

That morning, it took three loops through the cloud for the pilot to believe what his instruments were telling him. The radiation reading was ten times what was expected. Trying not to show his alarm, he transmitted the prearranged code for a hot one. "Chili pepper! Chili pepper!" he radioed, and then flew straight back to the airstrip located only a few miles away at the Indian Springs Air Base.

The tarmac was completely deserted when he set down. No one met his plane, no enlisted man pushed the wheeled ladder out to help him down. The tower instructed him to taxi to a ramp on the far end of the strip near a seldom-used hangar, and when he finally retracted his canopy, a hollow-sounding voice over a loudspeaker ordered him to climb out of the plane and to strip right there. After some effort getting to the ground, he quickly did so, and then, buck naked, hurried across the asphalt, hopping tenderly on bare feet toward a portable shower that had been wheeled out next to the old hanger.

Normally, a decontamination crew would already have been out at the plane dousing it in Gunk—a mixture of grease solvent and water—but that far corner of the airstrip remained empty, was declared off limits. No one went near that plane for the next five weeks.

Later that morning, the cloud passed over the broad Lincoln County Range of southeastern Nevada—sheep country, where the only disjunctive sounds were bells, lots of them, clanging like a hard, stuttering music out in no-man's-land. The sky overhead turned dark, dust devils flared briefly here and there, and tumbleweeds reeled with the sudden life of artificial wind. Sheep dashed for cover, though there wasn't any, the bells on their necks clattering wildly, bringing more confusion and panic. A fine, dusty mist fell from the cloud and covered, then penetrated, the dense, layered wool of the sheep, the grass and heavy sage. The sheep veered right and left, stumbled and doubled back on themselves, bleating loudly. Finally, the wind tempered and the gentle, trailing ash became almost soothing. They lowered their heads and resumed the steady motions of grazing, oblivious to the new taste of everything around them.

Not far away in Modena, Utah, three children came out of a ramshackle trailer house and played in what they imagined to be snow, though it had never snowed in the desert in August. They spread their arms, ran in circles, and turned their faces up into the gray-white storm, sticking out their tongues, catching the ash of vaporized sand and rocks. The oldest child—the only one who could write—used her finger to trace through the dirty snow collecting on the hood of a junked car in the driveway. She licked her index finger and wrote WE. She wetted it again, not recognizing the metallic taste of armored tank, and wrote LOVE. Then—wetting three fingers—MOMMY. She stepped back, tilting her head and smiling at her message. She cartwheeled across the lawn toward the two younger ones, who were in wet drooping diapers, and then all three made themselves dizzy by spinning.

CHAPTER FIVE

MOTOQUA. LAYNE HAD ALWAYS LIKED THE NAME, THOUGHT of it as soft and pretty, just the sound, the way it rolled off the tongue in a flutter of tiny wings, like gently releasing a mouthful of butterflies. However, soft and pretty described anything but how he felt this morning. Particularly in the last hour, since he'd told Christine about Rudd's throat being cut.

He walked along the streamside trail toward the corrals, the sound of a slamming door still ringing in his ears after Christine had stomped across the porch and into Dallas's cabin. She had said something, he couldn't hear it all, about clothes. The morning sun glimmered in the ripples of the creek running shallow and wide over a fan of colored pebbles. But it was hard to appreciate small beauties through the mixture of frostbite and anger that had prevailed on the last half of the drive out to the ranch.

Rawley, a dingo-red Texas heeler, circled Layne in a frenzy, wagging his entire hindquarters in the exaggerated manner of dogs whose tails have been docked. He kept trying to talk to Layne in a series of throaty half-barks.

"Yeah, Rawley," Layne said, stooping to pet him again, "you want to know where Dallas is, don't you, pal?" Rawley looked back toward the cabin and whined. "It's okay, buddy. Come on, let's go saddle the horses."

Black Dog, an Australian shepherd and the older of Dallas's two cattle dogs, was more set in his ways. He had swarmed Christine when she got out of the car and ignored Layne completely. Now he stood guard at the cabin door, waiting for her, perhaps sensing her mood, silent and patient and faithful in ways that only dogs can be.

Bad moods and big troubles. Jesus, another morning in the saga. He hadn't exactly been in top form, after a long night of bumpy, electric sleep, when he picked her up at the B & B around 6:30 a.m. Christine, on the other hand, had seemed refreshed and settled. Her hair was still slightly damp from her shower and her skin was smooth. Layne had caught the light, brisk scent of soap as she got into the car.

"Trevor loaned me a clean denim shirt," she said. "It feels good."

"Looks good, too," he said, without thinking.

"He even offered me a pair of earrings." She smiled vaguely and fastened her seat belt.

A joke. He looked over at her: the woman actually had made a joke. She seemed more at ease, her face less full of clouds and arguments. She commented briefly on the morning, the fresh air, but mostly she just gazed out the window into the opaque light that preceded sunrise. Call him foolish, but as they drove toward St. George, Layne began to think that it was a new start, that maybe they could even be friends now. And, in contrast to his own bad night, the long sleep had done wonders for her. He glanced over occasionally, saw that she was deep in thought, but in an even, contemplative way. Her profile was strong, but feminine. Who was she, this Christine Parker, really? Score one for the fact that she was Dallas's niece, but even so, genetics was no sure bet. Just because he considered Dallas straight and honest, proverbial salt-o-the, that didn't necessarily mean anything about the woman. Okay, so score another point for the fact that she was handsome. Not necessarily pretty—she was, of course, but that's not the word he wanted—or glamorous or a babe or whatever word rang the bell. She was just downright handsome, strong features that seemed to say . . . whatever strong features seemed to say. And a great figure; he knew what that seemed to say. Cancer, huh? She looked healthy enough to him.

Knock it off, he thought, bringing himself up short. This is a client, there's a lot at stake here. Not to mention the code of professional ethics. Not to mention his New Year's resolution to keep The Bazooka out of the loop for awhile, allowing himself some time to be alone. Sex was important, very important, but it wasn't the long-distance runner. There had to be more, much more, for any staying power. Regardless, why in the hell was he having a conversation with himself about sexual ethics? Given the impending scene in St. George, his next scheduled romantic notion about this woman about ought to be off the radar.

As they exited the freeway onto St. George Boulevard, she had requested a bathroom stop and Layne asked her if she'd like another cup of coffee. "Just got a coffee shop here in The George, one that has a grinder and doesn't think the stuff grows in tin foil."

She looked over at him, "Sounds good to me."

He wheeled into the small parking lot and nosed under the brand new green and white, back lit awning with THE COFFEE GROUNDS splashed across the front and "Franchises Still Available" in small letters below. She found the bathroom while he went up to the counter. The freshest of entrepreneurs, a visibly excited young couple, fussed extravagantly over a couple of double lattes. He finally took the lattes outside where Christine was standing next to the car.

"Thank you," she said when he handed her the large, steaming Styrofoam cup.

He nodded, "Well, time to head for the ranch, as they say."

"I'm not going." She smiled at him again.

He looked up at her. She seemed to have entered some completely private space, compacted a unilateral peace agreement with herself.

"I'm not going," she repeated. She pulled back the lid of her coffee and sipped.

"Well," he stammered, "I, I can't find this manuscript without you."

"You needn't bother. I'm going directly up to the sheriff's office." She spoke softly across the warm hood of his Land

Cruiser. "I'm going to talk to them and explain the entire situation. This thing with Dallas has gone far enough." She smiled again, that dreamy, self-assured, somewhere-out-of-India smile.

"Whoa," he said, backing up. Fortunately, the parking lot was empty, the citizenry of St. George being a decade or two behind Seattle in their brewing tastes.

"No whoa," she shook her head. "I slept on it. And I woke up knowing it was the right thing—the only thing to do."

"Ohhh, shit," he said, walking around to her side of the vehicle. There were a couple of small plastic tables and some chairs off to the side, fronting the asphalt. He tried to guide her in that direction. "We need to talk."

She calmly but forcefully pulled her arm away from him. He should have remembered from yesterday that steering this woman around was less than futile.

"No. Save your breath, Mr. Harting. This is definitely my decision."

He shook his head. "This is important. Critical might be a better word. And I think you'll want to be sitting down."

"No thanks," she said. "Just spit it out if you have something to say."

In a rush of words, trying in vain to maintain an air of professionalism, he expelled the information in one long breath.

Christine simply stood there, squinting, even though she wasn't facing the sun. "What are you saying?"

"Rudd's throat was cut, that's how he died," he said, looking down at his boots. "Dallas told me he did it."

"Goddamn it," she said. "How could you keep that from me?" She turned away and then whirled back and screamed at him in the middle of the empty lot. "I don't believe it. You're lying!" She moved back a few steps like some cornered, feral cat. "You and Dallas are playing a game with me. I'm warning you—"

"Hey! Hey, wait a minute," he cut her off. "Don't you goddamn me. I didn't create this mess. I didn't go over to Rudd's house. I'm just the guy you came to for help. Maybe I'm not being very helpful, but I can tell you right now that navigating between you and Dallas under these conditions is no small job. One that I will gladly relinquish if I'm doing it badly. You just give the word. Just—"

Two heads had poked out the door of America's newest coffee franchise. Worried expressions gauged the commotion, furrowed brows asked if the police needed to be summoned. Who needs bad publicity on their sixth day in business?

Layne almost tripped over Rawley, who had been circling him all the way up to the corrals. He tried to shake off the ugly recollections of St. George. The horses were stomping around, their hot breath still opaquely visible in the morning air, impatiently waiting for someone to bunk up the feed. He dropped parcels of hay at intervals throughout the wooden troughs and watched the lead horses squabble and exercise dominance before settling in to eat. An older bay mare was clearly the boss of this outfit. Layne knew that Dallas had cut back on the stock he was keeping, was training only a couple of green horses out here right now, but Layne didn't know why and hadn't wanted to ask.

Layne looked up and down the narrow river valley that made a ranch possible. Millenniums of casual water and occasional flash flooding had patiently gouged this scarce bottomland down through the rock and sand of an otherwise inhospitable desert. Cottonwood, willow, needle, and thread grass softened the rolling bottoms even further; wildflowers added sporadic dots of color. This canyon ranch was defined on either side by hundred-foot rims of washed-out limestone. They looked like dusty cement, lacked any of the dazzling colors or staggering height embracing Saraville. No matter, this place was out in the middle of nowhere on the way to nothing. Motoqua wasn't a town; it was just the end of a gravel road, nothing but two tracks angling off from here into the vastness of the Nevada desert.

A handful of late-arriving homesteaders at the turn of the century had staked these claims along the Beaver Dam Wash because all of the good ground was already taken, and just enough water flowed through this bottom to fuel their ragtag dreams. There was no store or church or any particular attraction and never had been; it was simply a cartographer's dot on an early map that no one had bothered to erase. Layne had once asked Dallas about the name, Motoqua, and what it meant. "Damn-hard-work," came the quick reply. Then Dallas laughed and said that Layne would have to go rustle up an Indian, that he really didn't know.

Layne brought out the tack and cut out a couple of horses. He tied them outside the corral so that he wouldn't get caught in any competitive crossfires when he wasn't looking. Horses have their own agendas and he knew enough not to stand in the middle daydreaming. He had selected a pair of good, stout mountain horses that Dallas kept to work cattle. Layne had ridden one of them before, a black gelding, stable and mature. Stability was good, in horses and in people, especially today.

As he tugged a cinch into place, heard the sharp crack of leather on leather, it reminded him that he was getting real close to some sharp decision making of his own. Dallas already had his mind made up about this manuscript, while Christine was ready to gallop off in the opposite direction. Layne had somehow assumed the role of middleman, trying to balance their interests. A lawyer's unfortunate duty generally didn't involve determinations about right and wrong. That was why otherwise decent people represented child abusers and corporate predators. But even so, if you are what you do, then at some point you risk becoming your choices. And what exactly were his choices here? Was he kidding himself by confining them to something as simple as saddling a horse to ride out and "just have a look" at this manuscript?

A dozen scenarios had loomed over him like dancing ghosts late last night. Some had statutory names like aiding and abetting, failure to report a crime, accessory before and after the fact, receiving stolen property, conspiracy. God knows what else. But he didn't need God's help to take it one step further; his three a.m. imagination had been quite up to the task. If this book of Rudd's really did contain stolen documents that were highly classified—and what could be more classified than atomic bombs?—then, embellished by Rudd's remembrances, they probably had the ability to embarrass, damage, and really piss off some highly placed people. It was certainly no accident that the FBI in the form of this Sayles guy had shown up. Had this thing already leaked out? Who had Rudd confided in? Who else might feel endangered by his death, or the fact that Rudd had had a very high security clearance? And so it went, mired in half-sleep and alone with these thoughts, he had turned and tossed among the twisted sheets and tried to block all of it out, tried to forget about this whole pile of poop and what kind of flies it was bound to attract. He finally regained some sporadic slumber with a straightforward mantra: just obey the law, play exactly by the rules.

He adjusted the stirrups on a saddle and looked impatiently back down the driveway. No sign of Christine yet. Come on, if we're going to do this, let's get the show on the road. He was suddenly irritated with his own fretfulness and indecision. Stop it, he said half-aloud, reserve judgment, take it a step at a time. Certainly, as Dallas's lawyer, he had the right to at least examine this book and make a determination. That was well within the scope of his lawful duties, wasn't it? But what if this thing really was the powder keg that Dallas thought? Dallas was already charged with murder; Christine was trying to be. And Layne wasn't sure that he trusted his own rebellious nature, his propensity to not play it safe. The divorce, leaving the firm and moving to Saraville, diving headlong between the legs of a local bishop's young daughter. It was all proof enough. Why ask for trouble? Everyone who had gotten anywhere near Rudd or his book lately had been sucked into the vortex.

So what *would* he do if this book was completely legit? Would he simply report it? What if it could blow the lid off things that needed blowing? What about truth? What about his own lid? And what about that imminent sucking sound that by now even he should have heard coming from off in the distance?

Christine had a favorite cartoon. It was from Gary Larson's *The Far Side* comic strip and it pictured two adult deer casually standing on hind legs in a forest. One deer has a huge bull's-eye target imprinted on his chest and the other deer, head cocked sympathetically, says to him, "Bummer of a birthmark, Hal."

After the events of the morning, Christine felt she could not have been hit more squarely if she'd had a bull's-eye painted on her. Nor did the sight of hole-in-the-rock, as they rode up to it, do anything to comfort her. It brought back to Christine all the years and the precious history she had with Dallas, her trusted, beloved uncle who, as she was now supposed to believe, had murdered a man. Or merely a corpse—perhaps Rudd had died from the knife wound inflicted during her scuffle with him. This was all such a mess, what the hell was she supposed to believe about any of it? If only she hadn't followed Rudd that night.

Now, standing before it, hole-in-the-rock sadly reminded her of a girl as well, a girl who growing up had faithfully stored trinkets and arrowheads within; a happy, confident, smiling girl—not the woman she was now. So edgy and broken.

"Want some help?" Layne asked as she probed at the rock, working her fingers around the edges of the slab that had been shaped in place as a lid.

She shook her head quickly in response. "No, I'm fine."

They had ridden the three miles out here in virtual silence. At moments, it had felt like a punishment they were meting out to each other; at other points, the sunshine and quiet had seemed like the beginning of a small, welcome truce.

Actually, the rock lid was heavier than she remembered. She groaned when she lifted it and the raw sound embarrassed her. Layne stood nearby and let her handle it as she pleased.

She leaned over and peered into the shadowed recess, then put her hand inside, pulled something forward, and finally used both hands to remove it. The package had been wrapped several times in a big sheet of plastic, then secured with the ever-dutiful duct tape that Christine knew to be Dallas's faithful signature. She shook her head and hefted the package. "Guess he wanted to weatherproof it."

Layne was already reaching into his pocket. "He doesn't do anything half way." He extracted a small, bone-handled knife. "Here," and he took the package from her and carefully opened the wrapping.

The horses were tied nearby and Rawley and Black Dog were sleeping in the sun. She and Layne sat in the thin gray shade of a cedar tree. Rudd's book was not actually a book but more a stack of manuscript pages held within a hardbound folder. Layne opened the binding and briefly examined the first several pages. "Guess we can split this up," he said. "Let's just make a determination about this thing and get it, well, first things first. Here." He lifted the top half of the book and gave it to her. Their hands brushed in the exchange and for a moment she felt awkward. Or maybe just very aware of Layne Harting as a warm, breathing, skin-bound human being, not the enemy. She still thought that he should have supplied her with all the facts concerning Rudd's death as soon as he knew them, no matter how grizzly or depressing they were, but on the other hand, she could see the tightrope he had been walking—taking care of Dallas's legal needs as well as her own personal ones, trying to be a friend and a professional at the same time. Risking himself by sitting here in spotty shade with what looked like a bad reading assignment.

At first, Christine rifled rather nervously through her pages. What was she supposed to find and how was she supposed to concentrate? She only had about twenty things gnawing at her, but then, before she was even aware of it, she was being drawn in. She turned back and started at the beginning. It was a foreword by Rudd.

In the early morning hours of July 16, 1945, Trinity, the world's first nuclear bomb, was detonated in Los Alamos, New Mexico, and from that millisecond, this planet was forever changed. As a young man not far out of my doctoral program, I was a part of that first atomic team. In 1950, I was selected from a field of highly qualified candidates to oversee the conversion of the old Las Vegas-Tonopah Gunnery Range into the new Nevada Test Site.

A couple of years later, I became the first permanent Chief Operations Manager of the Nevada Test Site—the greatest outdoor laboratory for scientific experimentation ever known to man. During the ten-plus years I served in that position, I supervised the detonation of every atmospheric test at the site. After that, I was kicked upstairs to finished out my career in various positions with the Department of Energy. So, as you can see, my entire working life was devoted to atomic testing and later to nuclear energy. Who's Who in the World lists me as one of the ranking experts in the field of nuclear engineering. Now I am taking this opportunity to clarify history, to lay forth the real story of the testing, what we knew about fallout and when we knew it.

Don't get me wrong. I am not an apologist. I would do it all over again. Under the threat of global domination by communist powers, it was absolutely necessary. And we won. Not that there weren't casualties. Unfortunately, there were; in the struggle for freedom, there always are. But that was a long time ago, and it is time for the true facts and my own modest role in the history of this victory to come out.

What I will demonstrate in this book, in clear and convincing terms, backed by actual copies of top secret memos and documents, is that we—all of us connected with the testing—engaged in a systematic course of conduct that denied the press and the public accurate information regarding radioactive fallout generated off-site by the atomic tests in Nevada. The significance of this cannot be understated. For the first time in the entire history of the United States, a large-scale covert operation was undertaken by our government, the military and segments of the scientific community not only to deny our own people access to critical information, not only to fail to warn them, but to actually engage in a public relations campaign *assuring everyone that the tests were safe. This, when in fact, we suspected early on and knew for certain by 1954 that they were not safe. In pursuit of this goal, we had to alter or destroy data and documents that would have contradicted our story. In some instances, the only remaining copies are included in this book.*

You ask why? In short, we could not trust the citizenry or our own governmental institutions, had they been given the facts, to make the right decisions—the right sacrifices—in order to go forward, to maintain the testing.

"Shit," Layne said.

She looked up to see him intent on a page, shaking his head.

"Dallas wasn't exaggerating about this thing." Even as he spoke, he didn't lift his eyes from the page. "Unfortunately."

She noticed that the iciness invading his voice and manner since their coffeehouse argument seemed to have melted. With the weight of these pages in her lap, however, she wondered if they weren't just moving from one shit storm to the next. Last night she had imagined that this whole ride out here would be a waste of time, something done just to placate Dallas. But now she wasn't sure.

"My lord, do you think this thing is for real?" she asked. "Rudd seemed capable of about anything. And, I mean, people fabricate stories for all sorts of reasons."

Layne looked up at her and laughed strangely. "Is it real? You could ask the FBI. That's sure as hell got to be why they're here. For this little pile of paper. I don't think there's much mystery about it any more."

He picked up a page and pointed at the heavy stamp on it: Top Secret—Classified. "That's not exactly the Good Housekeeping seal," he said.

And there were plenty of other pages bearing the same stamp. From the little Christine had read, she was well aware of Rudd's voice in it, of his self-important rhetoric and his twisted quest to be joined with history, but there were also photographs, memos, correspondence, and data that originated from other sources—the military and the government—and if these documents were valid . . . My God! The allegations were gigantic and surreal. And Layne's comment about the FBI. Would it never end?

Christine flipped back and forth through the pages, just as she had with her college texts, trying to get the bigger picture. The parts she read were so goddamn detailed, so nauseatingly real—photographs of gray atomic mushroom clouds with their toylike names labeled below: Easy, Sugar, Jangle, Fox. The case could not have been more compelling, showing original fallout logs and doctored versions, side by side, and revealing official correspondence from the top levels of the Atomic Energy Commission in Washington to on-site AEC monitors: "Never again advise the public to take cover indoors after a test shot."

She flipped back to Rudd's foreward and continued reading.

We never could have continued if Congress had clearly understood all the ramifications—for example, that on the morning of April 25, 1953, when the cloud of Shot Simon, a behemoth atomic blast, was released into the atmosphere above Nevada and then traveled for two days, crossing the entire continent at 40,000 feet before encountering a high-altitude storm over Albany, New York. Concentrated radioactive debris, deadly fission by-products that are absorbed and stored in the human body, came down in that rain on upper New York State and for a short time left the streets of Troy hotter than many areas of the test site itself.

Or that Shot Harry, dubbed Dirty Harry, in that same year covered St. George, Utah, and the surrounding areas with an intense blanket of radioactive material, causing the incidence of childhood leukemia and radiogenic disease in adults to skyrocket so quickly that we knew it was an epidemic. These are just two instances. There are many, many others which I have documented as fully as possible in this book.

Some will doubt my assertions, but they won't have to take my word for it. I have incorporated original copies of highly classified documents that I personally sequestered from the test site. These trace the debate even among ourselves at the test site and within the AEC. *Handwriting analysis and other specialized corroborative techniques will easily authenticate the attached evidence.*

The fact is that science often achieves progress only because of sacrifices we make. The scientific knowledge gained through nuclear testing has been invaluable, and maintaining our position of superiority in the cold war arms race was absolutely critical. Therefore, when myself and other leading experts in the field were called upon to testify during those years in courtrooms and related hearings, our public conclusions were always the same: "There is no definitive proof that has ever been established linking cancer and other diseases to our activities at the Nevada Test Site."

I always knew that someone armed with all the facts could have challenged our position. But a large part of my job during that period was to make sure that outsiders were never permitted access to those facts. And to make sure that insiders understood in graphic detail the laws they would break and the penalties they would face should they choose to speak. We were always presented with an acute quandary: To admit the truth would have spelled disaster for our program of nuclear testing and, therefore, for this country's national security.

Regardless of what others may think, then or now, I served my country well and honorably during the cold war. Simply stated, each of us was a soldier with a different assignment. I, personally, was called upon to keep the test site operational "at all costs" in the words of Atomic Energy Commissioner Lewis Strauss.

Finally, Christine couldn't take it anymore. She stood up, dusted off her Levi's, and wordlessly walked out toward the ridgeline in the distance, leaving Layne still intent on the book. Her knees were stiff from sitting cross-legged in the dirt, so she tried to move and stretch at the same time. Rawley and Black Dog were instantly running ahead, anticipating her every move. Usually, in the mere act of walking, of steadily placing one foot in front of the other up a hill or over a distance, Christine could find a kind of quiet relief, but not today. Her body felt slow and heavy while her mind continued to race ahead in fractured segments—mushroom-shaped clouds, kids with leukemia, Dallas, prison walls, death row.

Nearing the ridgeline, she passed through a thick stand of cedars and suddenly was into a storm of tiny gnats, droves of what Dallas called no-see-'ums. She stopped, reached across her body to swat the bugs away, and as her arm pressed against the left side of her chest, was surprised for the ten-thousandth time to feel the spongy substitute for her missing breast.

God, her body. She had been conceived, carried, born, nursed, and raised for the first two years of her life on Dallas's ranch. Eaten the food, drunk the milk, and grubbed around in the dirt, right at the base of this mountain. What more did she need? A pencil and ruler to draw a straight line from the test site to Motoqua and finally to herself? In the distance, a large, dark bird floated on a thermal. She tilted her head back and looked higher. Death by wind and geography. Even by fluffy white clouds.

It was all there in Rudd's book. Not only had there been fallout, but the knowledge that people were being exposed to this fallout. Some people were injured immediately, while others became time bombs, carrying around the strange cellular and genetic damage that would erupt years and years later or maybe even in one's offspring. And if Christine could not prove one hundred percent that her cancer had been caused by that radiation, what did it matter? Rudd and his constituents understood exactly what they were doing each time they detonated a bomb; they knew that people were being injured, even killed. Whether she herself was counted among them was irrelevant to the larger picture.

The ground began to slope downward slightly as Christine reached the ridge, and for an instant, her thin-soled boots gave way, sending a small shower of scree and rubble down over the spiny crest. She gained her footing and, avoiding the extreme edge which was defined by an airy drop of several hundred feet, walked slowly along the wide rock shelf, then finally paused. An immense view flew outward from the ridge, the silhouettes of the distant mountains layered in colors beginning with light blue, then purple, then turning a deep slate gray on the most distant horizon. Suddenly she heard Black Dog growl and turned around.

"Hey." Layne stood not far from her, his hands in his pockets. "You okay?"

She had been so absorbed that she hadn't even heard him approach. She felt her lips part to speak, but nothing came out. "No," she finally said and looked back out at the vista. "But then I don't think anyone would be okay after seeing that book." She turned back to him, stared directly at him. A slight breeze crested the ridge and ruffled his hair, which was lighter in the sun, making him seem perilously younger.

"What about you?" she asked. "How are you doing?" and even at the instant she said it, she was aware that this was something new: she was inquiring after him.

He shook his head and haphazardly shrugged. "Same as you." His hands were still in his pockets; it made him look as if he were waiting for something.

She nodded out at the view. "See that? It's Nevada. We're only about five miles from the state line here."

He took a few steps forward, coming next to her, both of them gazing at this pale slice of the world. Neither spoke and it was not an uncomfortable silence, but it felt weighted and complex. The breeze picked up, prickling her skin, gently moving her collar.

"Right out there," she said, drawing an axis with her straightened arm, "middle distance, highest mountain you can see? That's Mormon Peak. And then down and to the right, farther out. That's Caliente Summit. Believe it or not, sometimes the California crud oozes this far out and you can't glimpse much of anything, but on a spring day like this one or after a rain, Dallas says you can see for more than a hundred miles from here."

She wasn't watching him, but she sensed his slow gaze south to north.

"Unbelievable," he said softly. "You get up high somewhere, get a view like this, you realize how damn nearsighted most of us are in our lives."

At that moment, as if transported in a flash from some alternate universe, an image of herself appeared. She was sitting a couple of years ago on a high rock outcrop overlooking the Grand Canyon where she had come to mourn her failed marriage. Alone on her lofty perch, with only a bottle of wine and plenty of self-pity, she had been undone by the stark, naked beauty, the immense and ancient landscape and a forceful reckoning of her own small and momentary troubles. She ended up happily drinking her wine and reveling in the greater view.

She thought for a minute of telling Layne about herself sitting on the edge of the Grand Canyon, all ready to cry, then hours later stumbling back half-drunk to her campsite, her heart as light as paper, but the revelation seemed too intimate, out of context at the moment. She sighed deeply. "Uncle Dallas has been bringing me up here, pointing out the topography, since I was a kid," she said. "Now I finally get to point it out to someone else. That's progress."

Layne laughed, then paused. "So," he began slowly, "if we're looking straight into Nevada, I suppose somewhere out there is . . . the test site."

Christine nodded. " Just about due west of here," she said, arm pointing, "a hundred miles as the wind blows."

It had been a totally unconscious choice of phrasing on her part—as the wind blows—but now, with her body standing high above the desert plateau, with this clear, indisputable view, she understood the past in a new way. The proximity, the wind, the fallout, the negligence and lies. The picture stunned her, repulsed her, but strangely, like that ethereal vista from the Grand Canyon, it also strengthened her, sorting things at long last into a clear and shining order.

"That bastard," she said, unselfconsciously. "My God."

"I know," he replied, but he didn't know, not the half of it, her breast gone, her body sick, all the bodies that had silently grown sick from this stupidity.

A flood rose and Christine couldn't stop herself from spilling forth. "Sacrifices. That's what Rudd said. Sacrifices were necessary. Guess the SOB didn't think he'd wind up being one of them." She looked out at the delicate watercolor picture that even now belied the truth. "I don't care, Layne. He deserved it. He deserved to have his lousy throat cut in his lousy kitchen. I don't want my uncle to have to pay for it, but Rudd deserved it."

"Christine—" Layne began, and though she had no idea where he was going, she stopped him, her voice down a level, more controlled now.

"Yeah, I know, this is not what an attorney wants to hear, and I'm sorry."

He looked at her, silently, his blue eyes totally unreadable. He seemed to wait, making sure that she was finished before he spoke again.

"Christine, what I started to say was that *I'm* sorry. Dallas told me about your cancer and I'm so sorry. I know that you were born out here, lived here as an infant." He paused, gazing west, seemed to seek an offering. "The truth about all of this. It must be devastating for you to read what Rudd has written. On top of everything else that's occurred. I'm sorry for all these troubles. If there's anything I can . . ."

Christine found her arms crossing her body, tightening, needing to hold herself together. Murder, arrests, her own illness: she could be stoic and angry. But someone's compassion. *Layne's* compassion. She squeezed harder.

Then he took a step toward her, time and motion skipped forward a beat, and her cheek was lightly against his shoulder as they stood there on that high place for awhile.

With his scuffed size eleven, cordovan wing tips up on the metal table, Mack Sayles leaned back in his chair and waited for Dallas Parker to arrive. He'd had a good night's sleep and been unable to resist the doughnut shop across the street from his motel earlier this morning. He'd never seen such a big maple bar before, fresh out of the deep-fat fryer and dripping a caramel-colored icing. He'd sipped a cold diet cola with it, sat by a window, and listened to some harmless chatter—guy on his right was torn between Toyota and Nissan, the young gal behind him anguished over Mormon temple marriage or a roustabout named Tom. God, it was good to be alive.

A nearby door closed with a solid echo, the sound of steel and concrete and confinement. It was a hurtful, lonely sound, but that was part of the punishment, the very reason for places like this. Mack still believed in punishment, even though it ran contrary to what he called the psychosocial-bullshit trends of the criminal justice system. He'd seen just about every kind of kink and evil and havoc humans were capable of, and it was gospel to him that all bad-asses deserved even worse than they got.

The door to the interview room swung open and Mack scrambled to his feet. Dallas Parker was ushered in.

"Thank you, gentlemen," Mack said to the guards. "I can take it from here." He pointed to an empty chair across the table.

"Sit down, have a seat, Dallas," he said, flipping the badge wallet closed and returning it to his pocket. "FBI, Las Vegas. I'm Special Agent Mack Sayles." Parker just stood there. Mack resumed his seat and leaned back again, tipping the chair up on two legs and lacing his hands together behind his head. Parker still hadn't moved, his face not quite as expressive as Mount Rushmore. Maybe he was expecting someone else, or trying to figure why the FBI was here.

"I don't know why they call us special agents," Mack said with a loopy grin. "I'm a pretty routine agent, myself. Really. If you saw some of the cases I got, you'd believe me on that one." The brown jacket that he had hung and steamed in the shower that morning now lay over one end of the table; the butt of his snub-nosed .38 was holstered on the right side of his belt.

Parker shrugged and finally sat down, slowly, the restraints confining his movements. Mack noticed that he wasn't a tall man, five seven or eight, but his shoulders were very broad and his wrists looked like tree limbs, the handcuffs just able to close around them. Late fifties, turns sixty next year, Mack recalled from the reports. But obviously strong, plenty strong enough to overpower someone and cut his throat. Not that that was any major feat.

Mack had learned long ago that motivation was the biggest single factor in any crime. Just last year, a Metro officer in Vegas, a wife and child beater, a bruiser who stood six foot five, was laid out by his two sons, ages nine and eleven. They caught the guy in the garage, stabbed him 142 times, broke three knives in the process, and finished up with the long-bladed pruners. All they could say to the arresting officers was, "He ain't coming back, is he? He ain't coming back?"

Mack stretched lazily. "So, how they treating you, Dallas?"

Parker suddenly laughed, a surprised snorting sound. "I'd be happy to trade places and let you find out firsthand," he said.

"Oh, hell. These small-town jails out here are pretty much first rate, I can guarantee you. Good food. Clean and quiet," Mack settled forward in his chair. He could see the white strip across the top of Parker's forehead where a hat had left its mark against an otherwise tanned face. Parker was a good-looking guy, rugged and all that, but Mack noticed on closer inspection that the contouring of his face was a bit sharp, the features vaguely sunken. All was not well. He must be taking this harder than he was letting on.

"Now you take the South," Mack continued. "When I was stationed down there back in the early sixties. Some of them small towns around New Orleans or up Mississippi way, why, those good old boys were using rusty boxcars side-railed off into the local swamp as holding cells. Lowered them colored boys in on a rope and just shut the lid." Mack shook his head.

"Come July, you don't think there was a little heat and humidity, a bug or two in that sucker do you?"

Parker lowered his head slightly, then looked back up. "So what does the FBI want?" he asked tersely. "I already told the local cops that I want my lawyer present for any—"

"Aw, don't worry about that," Mack cut him off with a hand gesture. "You certainly do have the right to remain silent, you have the right to blah, blah, blah." Mack examined the ceiling for a full two seconds.

"They don't need no confession here, Dallas. They could convict you twelve times with just the physical evidence alone. In fact, that's exactly what piques my curiosity." Mack had read the case notes thoroughly, gone over the crime scene, all the photos, examined the physical evidence, the written reports, and the coroner's findings. He'd even attended the autopsy yesterday afternoon, observing a couple of things that the local, part-time medical examiner had failed to note, but all of that was just the top layer.

"I'm not interested in using anything you say here against you later in court," Mack said.

"That's good, cause I hate to see you waste a trip clear up from Las Vegas, Mr. Sayles."

"Aw, you can call me Mack."

"Sure. And you can call me Mr. Parker."

"Fair enough, Mr. Parker." Mack searched his pocket, pulled out a roll of wintergreen mints. He tucked a mint against one cheek. "You're right, you don't have to talk to me. But you probably do have to listen. Us law enforcement types specialize in the captive audience. And our dearly beloved Supreme Court hasn't tossed out one *listening* case yet, not that I know of anyway." No one else was, so Mack laughed at his own joke. "I guess I can just talk to you until the cows come home."

"Oh, hell," he said, interrupting himself. "My wife says my manners are going down with my memory." He retrieved the roll of mints and offered one to Parker, who didn't move at all.

"I've been checking you out, sir," Mack continued. "I do

like to know who I'm dealing with. We don't see too many solid citizens in my line of work. Seems that folks around here hold you in fairly high regard. Old boy at the stockyard says Dallas does business on a handshake, word is his bond. Out by Motoqua, they say he works hard, helps a neighbor in need. And your record is clean, never been arrested, let alone convicted of anything, period. Certainly no crimes of 'moral turpitude,' as we in the business like to say."

Mack paused, put a hand on top of his smooth head and slowly rubbed, then examined his palm for oil. It was an old habit. "There was that little business back when, some talk about poaching deer," he laughed again and pointed at Parker. "But hell, those deer make a living off your pasture. I guess you should eat one occasionally."

"Well, pasture doesn't hardly describe what I got going on out there, Mr. Sayles," Parker finally said. "And I do believe you could talk long enough to make a fellow start confessing, just to regain a little peace and quiet." His voice had leveled off and he seemed to be understanding the game.

Mack kind of admired this Parker. He was tough on both sides of his skin, that winter bark exterior running right to the core. This guy wasn't going to give anything up easily. But everyone had his weaknesses. Everyone. Mack knew that if he had the time, if he circled long enough, he could find that one vulnerability and bring almost anybody down.

"Well, Mr. Parker, I sympathize, I truly do. It must be a real downer for a guy like you, someone who's lived out there on the desert, roaming free as a bird all his life, to suddenly find himself sitting in here, locked down and wearing that jailer's jewelry."

Mack paused for a little show of sympathy. "I'm no expert about this part of the country, that's for sure, but I had myself a little drive out there west to Motoqua, a good time abusing a government sedan on those washboard roads. The map may read Beaver Dam Wash, but it looks like quite a while since there was enough water out there to interest any beaver."

As Mack rambled on, he watched Parker closely. The man

simply sat there, offering no further insights . In fact, Parker was staring back at him, and his clear gray eyes seemed to be drilling for answers of their own. Mack was always intrigued by the reactions he got when interviewing suspects. Either they were squirming right out of their skins, unable to hold anything back, leaping forward to explain everything they'd ever done in their lives, or they were completely shut down, a deep cold well and it was Mack's job to use a flashlight and shine it down. Sometimes, as now, you couldn't even begin to see the bottom. Parker was going to be a fight.

"I took a little drive around your place, up to the corrals and all. I damn sure didn't climb out of the car," Mack said, "and make friends with those dogs of yours, especially that black rascal. And I drove over to your neighbors. Everybody is pretty shocked by your behavior, I can tell you that."

"First thing you learn training horses," Parker said, "is that things—"

"Yeah, yeah," Mack cut him off, "things are never what they appear. We've all heard that corn pone before."

Parker's jaw tightened and Mack was happy to finally elicit a reaction, knew he was pissing him off, but just as quickly, the rancher recovered and reclaimed his stony outlook.

"Problem is, I just don't take you for a petty thief," Mack said. "I could see you killing a man if you had a good enough reason, but not snitching his valuables. Nope. You can't convince me of that one."

"I ain't trying to convince you of anything, Mr. Sayles."

"Well, no, of course not," Mack said. "We're just speaking hypothetically here."

"You're speaking hypothetically here." Parker stood up and short-stepped it partway to the door, acting as if the rules of his previous life still existed, as if he was in control. "I'm not speaking anymore," he said, "and I'm not listening to another ounce of your bullshit."

"Well, I guess we got to know each other well enough for a first date," Mack said. He rose and walked over to the door leading back into the lockdown side. He opened it and peered out into the hallway. "You can never find a damn guard when you need one in these places, but I imagine he'll be along shortly."

Sayles let the door swing closed. "Maybe they're all gone to lunch. Say, speaking of lunch, I'm supposed to have a visit with your niece Christine this afternoon." It was tiny, almost not there, but Mack saw a slight grimace in Parker's face. "Can I have her bring you anything? Give her a message for you? Anything I can do, I'm happy to help out if I can."

"Yeah," Parker said sarcastically. "You can ask her to smuggle me in some Levi's, get me out of this goddamn fluorescent zoot suit."

"Well," Mack said cheerily, "it's been nice visiting with you, Mr. Parker."

The cowboy stood next to the door waiting for the guard, obviously wanting to leave the room, uncertain about how to do it without an escort. Mack leaned against the wall and watched him stand uncomfortably. He had a couple more questions for the man as long as they were cooling their heels. Not that he expected answers, but he had learned long ago that inaction was a form of action and that silence could have a telling voice.

Besides, Mack liked to snoop and provoke. After all, he was a licensed voyeur; it was one of the fringe benefits of being a cop. He had, of course, done a complete background check on Rudd yesterday and found out that the guy had developed a reputation as something of a loose cannon, an egocentric gone bitter. Rudd's early retirement had been "mutual" and his top secret clearance had been retired with him. His old department still didn't much appreciate or trust him. That alone was enough to cause Mack to dig a little deeper. In combing through the contents of Rudd's torn-up study, he found a Post-it note and a couple of other scraps containing references to a book and the word "memoir." This possibility would raise a collective eyebrow back at the agency when it involved someone who had held such a high-level clearance.

Mack didn't know why Parker had trashed Rudd's

computer—perhaps he wasn't as thrilled with the Internet as the rest of us—but it made him curious. Just to be on the safe side, he told the local authorities that he needed to take the computer back to Vegas. They showed little interest in it, waived him off and had him sign a form checking out the evidence, so now it was sitting in the trunk of his car. Mack wanted to see if one of the whiz-kids back in Glitterville could boot it up. Then he could kill a little time scrolling through more of Rudd's private life.

"Let me ask you one more thing while we're waiting here," Mack said. "Kind of a reach, a real long shot, but you wouldn't know anything about some memoir, something this Rudd fellow might be writing? Would you?"

Parker slowly shook his head. "A book? I don't know what you're . . . I wasn't exactly in the man's house trying to find something to read."

Mack pursed his lips for a moment. "Well, since you brought it up, Mr. Parker, what were you doing in Rudd's house? The interrogation reports never made that very clear."

"You're pretty good," Parker snapped. "Could I make a standing request? Talk to my lawyer."

"Oh. Right. I met him yesterday," Mack said. "Harting. Layne Harting. Seems like a nice guy. Sure has a hell of a case ahead of him."

The door swung open and a jailer looked in. Parker began to leave and then turned back. "Don't get yourself confused, Mr. Sayles. The only thing he has ahead of him is a long and happy life." He smiled at Mack for the first time. "This hell of a case is all mine."

BENDING OVER NEXT TO THE WOODEN TROUGH, DALLAS swung the big, rusted framing hammer much harder than he needed to, thoughtlessly loosing his anger and frustration, trying to put it all onto the head of a nail. The hammer glanced sideways off the long spike, then hit him squarely on the shin. A core of white pain exploded inside of his leg and he stood perfectly still, wondering if maybe it was broken.

"Uhhh," slowly released, was the only sound Dallas made, straightening up and letting the hammer fall from his hand, stoic as usual about pain. That's one reason he was always a solid attraction at the Saturday night smokers around southern Utah; he could keep a crowd on their feet, could take a punch and keep going. Until last fall, that is, when he had got too big for his twenty-four-year-old britches and tried for a headliner down in Las Vegas, had gone up against some Indian who knocked every speck of snot right out of his head. That night, Dallas had taken too many punches and stayed on his feet too long, quickly learning the difference between tough country boys and the trained circuit fighters.

"You dumb son of a bitch," he finally grimaced to himself. He could have shouted and it still would have been to himself since there was no one else within a mile. "Serves you right."

His horse had been nervously watching him and now she started backing into the trees, trailing her reins. She was a leggy young Appaloosa mare with great conformation for a mountain horse who could go for days without breaking down. Not completely broken, she probably never would be for anyone but Dallas. Her basic nature was so rangy and tough and stubborn that Dallas viewed her as proof of the old joke about why the Indians had always ridden Appaloosas into battle: so they'd be extra pissed off and ready to fight when they got there. He didn't care, didn't need a horse that just anybody could ride; the mare's stamina and willingness to work were what he admired.

"Whoa there. Don't you go spooking off on me," he said in calming, forced tones in spite of his shinbone. "Don't you be leaving me to walk home on a bum leg." The mare eyed him suspiciously. "That's right, honey. You and me, we're still okay." She must have believed him, because she quit backing away, dropped her head over a small clump of bunchgrass, and resumed browsing.

He sat down on one edge of the leaky wooden watering trough. It was fed by a length of pipe crudely plumbed into a tiny drip spring. The sturdy, rough-cut planks were deeply discolored and still slimy on the inside of the trough where he'd bailed it down less than an hour ago. It was occasionally spotted and streaked on the outside as well, showing him just where the leaks were. He was in the process of tightening and chinking it. Water was hard to come by out here and their stock, about fifty head of rangy Hereford-Durham crosses, foraged on the scarce grass and more abundant oak brush and sage as they wandered. The cattle had to work just as hard as he did to make any kind of a living out here on one homestead section and some small government grazing permits, and it showed on their bony hides.

He reached down and rubbed his leg. It was a hell of a lick—he could feel the knot beginning to swell right under his fingers—but nothing was broken. His dad also used to say that intemperance mostly damages the intemperate, but Dallas was not in the mood for wisdom or homilies this morning. This was shaping up to be a real bad month.

It had started off with Sally, Salines Goodrow, marrying a

clerk—a management trainee, as she put it—at the J. C. Penny store in St. George. The new husband also happened to be a returned Mormon missionary. Dallas had been engaged to Sally most of last year, and they had been going steady for two years before that. But her parents had always objected to him. He didn't attend church and he wasn't "career" oriented, leaving him spiritually and materially deficient. The solid fact that Dallas and Sally truly loved each other eventually came to count for nothing. Even Sally, with her mischievous smile and her good heart, was finally consumed by her family's no-nonsense attitude and married her Penney's clerk in an afternoon wedding at the St. George temple. And, like it or not, Dallas finally had to admit that Sally was right: she was a city girl, would never have been happy with the life out here at Motoqua.

Now he was wondering if it would ever suit any woman. Earlier this morning, after feeding the stock and gathering close to two dozen brown speckled eggs off their bunch of laying hens, he'd headed back to the cabin with the eggs cradled in the front of his shirt. As he stepped onto the porch he suddenly found himself frozen mid-step by angry voices.

" . . . and I'll be damned if you're going to fool around as an extra on any more of those ridiculous movie sets," he heard Audrey say. Dallas's younger brother Warren and his wife Audrey were arguing. Before he could duck away, he couldn't help overhearing them.

"Oh, hell," Warren said, "it's not full time or regular, but I gotta take work where I can find it. And the money's not bad."

"Well, it's not that good either, and it just seems to give you one more reason to stall." There was a quiet pause and then she said in softer tones, "We need to move off this place, get to a city and get you a *real* job." A pleading tone had crept into her voice, but disappeared just as quickly. "You've had your chance out here. I will not bring up our family this poor." Then Dallas heard one-year-old Christine banging on her high chair and gurgling her two cents worth in the background. He turned and could not escape fast enough to the cool, dusty refuge of their old hay barn.

Like everything else on the ranch, the water trough he was sitting on wasn't going to fix itself. Dallas allowed himself another minute to see if the pain in his shin would calm down. Sally was dead right; he needed a career, but it wasn't going to be any damn day job in town, and it sure as hell wasn't going to be fitting women into a stylish shoe. He was angry and motivated and already making his own plans, at least on paper. He was determined to make it go out here. Cattle would always be marginal, but if he could reenvision the ranch and combine it with his primary talent, breaking and training horses, maybe something could—

His thoughts were interrupted by the sound of an engine in the distance. At first, he took it for the drone of an airplane, but then he saw a dust plume rising off in the expanse. The sun was small and tight, directly above the vehicle, and he had to squint to see. He reached out and retrieved his hat from the boulder where he'd set it down while he bent over to work. By degrees, an old olive green army jeep came into view, bouncing along the rugged BLM track.

"Howdy, howdy," said one of the three men in the jeep, the one wearing green pants and a bright, plaid shirt. He jumped out of the passenger seat with greetings before the vehicle, AEC stenciled on its side, came to a complete stop. "Good morning to you, sir," he said, clutching a clipboard to his chest. Dallas stood up and accepted the man's jaunty handshake.

"Mornin'," Dallas said, blinking at the man's outfit. It was his opinion that no bad colors came with an animal, but people were a different story.

The other two men, both younger, climbed out of the jeep and retrieved state-of-the-art-looking Geiger counters, *Vic Tic* emblazoned on their sides. These boxes were by now no mystery to Dallas. The federal government strictly controlled the price of uranium and had mandated itself as the sole purchaser. The price had been set artificially high to stimulate the search for new sources, thereby creating huge fortunes for a blessed few, while hoards of luckless men from all over the country and even other parts of the world tramped back and forth through the western deserts. Devices that measured radiation were advertised to those passing through St. George, and Dallas had run into many of these modern prospectors out on the open range. One group of Australians even camped near the water a quarter mile below the cabin for a month last fall, and Warren, ever the dreamer, would visit them occasionally, bringing home stories and excitement, infecting Audrey with dreams of foreign travel and living high.

"Hey!" the older man said, grinning. "Seen any bomb clouds heading this way?"

Dallas gave him a look which the man did not seem to comprehend.

"We had a test shot this morning. Over in Nevada, that-away," the man said, pointing.

"I know where Nevada is," Dallas said.

"Oh, good," the man said, smiling. "Well, it's our job to track the clouds and take measurements. We've been running all over Uncle Sam's half-acre this morning, doing just that."

"You ain't on Uncle Sam now," Dallas replied.

"Oh. Well, gets hard to tell. Not much fencing around here," the man said. "No offense intended, though."

"None taken," Dallas said.

"Did you watch the test this morning?" His voice was nasal and sharp.

"Saw the flash," Dallas answered. "Seems you been lightin' those things off pretty regular, lately."

"That's a fact," the man said. "Gotta stay one up on the Ruskies."

Dallas nodded vaguely. What could he say to that? A lone mourning dove called out hopefully from somewhere back in the junipers and pinon.

Four years ago when the Nevada testing had first started up, an excitement permeated southern Utah, a feeling that something important was happening right in their backyard. Audrey wasn't on the ranch yet, but Dallas and Warren occasionally would climb the hill behind the cabin and watch the light show some ninety miles to the southwest. When Audrey arrived in fifty-three, she turned the preannounced shots into something festive, wearing her sunglasses, taking coffee and pastries and the two men along as if it were a picnic. As the novelty wore off, however, the morning picnics ceased and they went about their business.

Dallas alone still paid nervous attention to the blasts. He had become increasingly uneasy, if for no other reason than the tests seemed unnatural. They ran contrary to everything he saw or felt out in these windy, open spaces. When they occurred, as one had just this morning, he would turn and look up from whatever he was doing while an eerie, pale flash was superimposed over earth and sky, everything flattened into one silvery, monochromatic moment. Then, later in the morning, depending on the wind, strangely pink, roiling clouds carrying the smell of sulphur and burnt metal might pass over. Exactly as they had done earlier this morning.

No one wanted to appear unpatriotic, of course, but there were ever increasing reports circulating of stock losses and human illness. Two years ago, in the spring of 1953, up around Cedar City and other points north of his ranch at the higher elevations, some of the ranchers lost their entire herds after trailing them in off the Nevada winter ranges, the sheep and lambs wiped out by mysterious causes. The AEC claimed it was malnutrition. The ranchers finally filed a lawsuit in federal district court up in Salt Lake City during the past winter.

The brightly dressed man standing in front of Dallas continued, lulled by his own voice. The weather, the wind, the stock, what they did on a Saturday night clear out here. All the while, he scribbled notations on his clipboard. The other two men had circled away from him, occasionally calling out some numbers; then they moved back in and converged right behind Dallas, their Geiger counters clicking away like toy machine guns the entire time. They waved their wands up Dallas's back, causing him to finally turn around and see the things rudely pointed at the brim of his sweat-stained felt cowboy hat. The clicking from their counters continued and the three men were grinning at one another.

"Mister," the man with the clipboard said, "you got yourself quite a hat. A *hot* hat." All three chuckled.

Dallas didn't remove his hat, didn't reach for it, didn't even think about touching it. He could feel every bit of his pulse surging through that lump on his shinbone and it seemed to fuel a murderousness rising up in him. "Exactly what are you saying?" he asked, struggling to maintain a level voice.

"Oh, we're just kidding. Don't mean a thing, partner," the man said, patronizing now. "These readings we get out here don't mean much. Stuff is completely harmless by the time it hits the open spaces like this."

"Then why are they paying you fellas," Dallas said, his teeth on edge, "our good tax dollars to screw off and chase it around out here?"

The men glanced back and forth at each other, swiveling their heads like chickens, then the two with the Geiger counters scurried back toward the jeep. As if he hadn't heard Dallas speak at all, the one with the clipboard smiled and said, "Well, it's been good visiting with you."

And then, with the same quick drama that had marked their arrival, they were gone. The jeep roared past Dallas and continued on up the road, the three men retaining their good spirits and waving gaily at him.

Dallas's leg ached all the way home. Some part of the pain almost felt good, masked the duller ache over his loss of Sally, an ache that simply would not quit rising up in his mind with dumb regularity, when he went to sleep at night, when he woke up in the morning. It had begun to feel like systematic doses of castor oil, where knowing it's for the best doesn't make it any easier to swallow.

As he neared the ranch compound, he considered staying away and skipping lunch, not feeling very fit for human contact. Walking through the cabin door, however, and seeing little Chrissy stand up and wobble over to him, her toddler arms outstretched so he could pick her up, some hopeless, icy block melted in him. He bent down and swooped her over his head to her delighted squeals. Then, with the baby poised in the air and reaching for him, he remembered his hat. Christ, he thought as Christine kept swiping at the brim, who knew what to believe anymore? He pulled it off his head and walked back out onto the porch, leaving the hat on the back of a chair.

A little over a year ago, Dallas had been sitting next to Warren in the waiting room of the St. George hospital when Christine was born. A nervous uncle and a nervous father. She came into the world that day all bunched up and purple and squalling like a tiny storm. When the nurses waved the two men into the hallway outside the delivery room to greet the ten-minute-old infant, she landed a sucker punch on Dallas from which he had never quite recovered.

Audrey walked into the living room, wiping her hands on her apron. "Oh, you love your Uncle Dallas, don't you, sweetie?" she said, taking the baby, smiling at both of them. "Your dinner's almost on the table, Dallas, if you want to wash up."

Dallas came to the sturdy plank table and sat in his customary position at one end, opposite Warren. They may not have had the cash to buy equipment, fancy radios or new cars, but they ate as well as any family in Washington County. Audrey took great pride in her cooking, something she had learned from her mother while helping to feed four brothers. Looking around, he was reminded just how much she brought to the family, and just how much he would miss them if they pulled up and left. There were wildflowers on the table, arranged in a twenty-five-cent fishbowl Warren and Dallas had bought for her at Montgomery Ward. Gray-ball sage, deer brush, Coulter's lupine and, in the middle, a carefully placed cluster of translucent pink beavertail cactus blooms.

Today, they were eating double-bone pork chops lightly basted with maple syrup seared into a crystalline glaze, with apple-pear sauce on the side. Mashed potatoes from their root cellar and pork gravy. Snap beans canned last fall and fry bread and fresh whole milk taken from their two Jersey cows this morning. Afterwards, there would be coffee and peach cobbler.

Warren was talking about his morning and the ongoing struggle to contain their old sow and her new, energetic litter of eleven squealers. "I wish we could afford some of that iron grate they sell at Intermountain," he said, "but that stuff costs twenty cents a foot."

Dallas didn't look up from his plate. He didn't want to talk about iron grates or things they couldn't afford. He wanted to focus his energy and drive on something positive, something he could control. Last week, at the Diamond Lil's quarter horse auction in Las Vegas, several different yearlings, mostly with the new Texas Doc Bar breeding on the top, sold for about the same price as a good family car. People would pay real money to put the right training on a horse like that. Maybe someday he'd even own some decent, papered breeding stock of his own.

"I tell you," Warren continued, "if them weanlings get out at night and mama ain't around to protect them, they'll be nothing but coyote bait."

Audrey looked at Dallas, who hadn't said much since he came in. "How was your morning, Dallas?" she asked.

He reached for his glass of milk. Audrey's voice was light and calm now, not at all like when he'd eavesdropped earlier. Life out here would be stretched pretty thin and lonely if the three of them left. He took a long, cool drink. Of course he should tell them about the monitors, express his own concerns. Chrissy jabbered sweetly and played with her food.

Dallas slowly set his glass back down. "My morning? It was nothing much," he said. "Like always, more work than time. Coulda used twice the hours and another pair of hands."

CHAPTER SIX

"TELL ME YOU'RE KIDDING," SAID JILLIAN, HOLDING HER grapefruit juice and leaning slowly toward the center of the cocktail table, a movement that was both menacing and provocative. Menacing because R. C. didn't want Jillian Fetch in his face when she was angry. Provocative because the soft V-necked blouse she wore, a shade of taupe, fell slightly open, revealing a honeyed cleavage and the lacy edges of some scant underthing and reminding him of what he was missing.

"Tell me this is only some miserable joke," she continued. "Rudd is dead? As in murdered dead?" She enunciated each word so that the sentence, by the time she finished it, seemed to gather force and weigh a ton.

Less than a foot from her, Roland Clifford Hiney silently scrambled for an easy answer. Sitting slightly hunched and all balled up it was hard to tell, but R. C. at one time had cut an imposing figure with his beefy shoulders and chest tapering to a halfback's waist. That was over twenty years ago, though, before it all slid. Now it was pizza and love handles and becoming easily winded. On the table in front of him sat a cup of black coffee, as yet nervously untouched. It was just after 10:30 a.m., though deep in the bowels of the downtown Golden Nugget Casino, eternal twilight reigned, a combination of pinkish recessed lighting and murky pools of cigarette smoke. Just beyond where they sat, the craps and blackjack tables were moderately busy, but it was in the half-acre of slot machines that the action had settled.

"Don't worry, Jillian," R. C. said, "I've got this under control." But he knew, even as he was speaking, how lame it sounded, how dull and ineffectual, a blind dentist holding a drill and telling you to open wide.

"Under control, huh?" she asked, one eyebrow lifting just slightly. Jillian glared at him and leaned back into a normal position, the sexy peekaboo shot suddenly gone. "So who's this Manos guy?"

"Oh, he's just an informant I . . . we occasionally use."

"I asked you to check it out," she said sharply. "I don't recall asking you to delegate."

"Well, I couldn't exactly confront the old guy personally," he said, happy to finally have a point in his favor. "That would be a problem, lead directly back to us." He paused on the "us," but only saw her face tighten even further. He drew a breath, "Besides, when we were having this conversation, you might recall that we were a little distrac—"

"What's his rap sheet look like?" she snapped.

"Ah, the usual stuff, you know," he shrugged, palms suddenly above the table.

She spoke in short, staccato bursts. "Look. I go back to the office. In ten minutes, I have your guy's life spitting out of the printer. Start at the beginning. Leave nothing out."

Maybe it was his imagination, maybe it was the lighting, but her eyes became an eerie combination of heat and pure dry ice. And R. C. couldn't help but notice Jillian's choice of "your guy" over "our guy," even though this plan of intervention, this little scheme to snitch the book, had been hers from the start. She had sought him out, asked for his help. She told him that a witness in her downwinder case, a nuclear engineer from the old test site days who had worked with one Dr. Franklin Rudd, mentioned that this Rudd character might be trying to publish his memoirs. She had already met Rudd, personally interviewed him over a year ago, and then had stricken him from her witness list when she'd seen that the old boy was losing it, liable to take the stand and say just about anything.

"Ah, you know," R. C. felt himself hedging. "Manos is your basic—"

"I'll draw my own conclusions," she said. "Give me facts."

She continued to grill R. C. and within two minutes knew almost everything he knew about one Daniel Benito Briggs, aka Manos. He'd never been subjected to one of her cross-examinations before and now could see why she had such a reputation, why she had been appointed chief deputy. Everyone knew that Jillian was mega-ambitious, that her boss, the old political hack Neidlebaum, was retiring in December. And the hallway scuttlebutt around the Federal Building was that she had the best shot at the appointment. R. C. knew for a fact that she had a certain congressman's home telephone number listed in her address book, was regularly invited there for functions and occasionally a little tennis. Jillian was single, good-looking, spectacularly put together, and well connected. And she didn't lose. If a case was a loser, she assigned it to someone else because Jillian refused to lose. All the more reason for R. C. to be flattered and turned on last week when she had opened the steam jets on him.

"Look," she hissed, "if you've got this thing so well under control, where is this . . . guy?"

"Manos."

"Yeah, Manos." Jillian shook her head and paused. The clinking of coins hitting the return bin of a slot fueled somebody's midmorning dreams of bonanza. "Couldn't you have found someone a little more dependable? Christ, we get word that this Rudd is dead, some cowboy's been arrested, there is no sign of a manuscript, and now your guy has been strangely out of contact since when? Last Friday?"

R. C. had been dizzied by Jillian's sudden attention, so blown away when invited to explore every part of her hard, hard body that maybe he did get in a little over his head. Perhaps getting this Manos involved wasn't his brightest idea ever. He could see that now. But he had wanted to do this thing for her, do it right, hit a home run, settle her fears by finding that book or whatever it was, and incur her eternal gratitude. And if not her gratitude, then hold a little something over her.

Frankly, he didn't care. Reruns were what he wanted, a few more rides on the merry-go-round, once-a-weeks in her mirrored condo.

Last Wednesday she had invited him to her place after hours to discuss a "little problem." He had worked for her as an investigator on a few cases over the last five years and she had always ignited raging sexual fantasies in him, impossibilities, tantalizing things beyond his reach. Until she answered the door of her condo wearing a black Danskin leotard, that is, said she had just returned from an exercise class. R. C. had been totally undone watching her build two frozen Stoli martinis, every muscle and bone and fiber stretched taut beneath her black spandex, the symmetrical sweat lines still visible over the small of her back. When she finally unbuttoned his pants, she told him to go slow, that she wanted him to explore, to give her enjoyment. She smilingly said that she hoped he was the right man for the job. Eisenhower addressing the troops in the dawn of D-Day could not have been more inspirational.

Which was exactly the topic he wanted to get back to now—her, him, them—though business kept intruding, and Jillian's motto, he knew, was always business first. But the business had taken a bad turn. There was a dead body, a loose cannon out there and a possible connection back to them, all of which caused his neck and the tips of his ears to glow a bright red, his underarms to remain moist verging on tropical. Jillian, on the other hand—he had to admire her—coolly sat there, all legs and wicked intelligence, hard as new ball bearings.

"Hey, everything is cool," he assured her. "I drove to St. George myself, yesterday, as soon as I heard, to check out the scene. It's a sure bet that this cowboy killed Rudd." He leaned closer and lowered his voice. "You don't think I was worried, too? About Manos and all?" Sitting back, trying to look relaxed, "Hey, it's all there. The whole thing stacks up as a simple burglary gone bad."

Jillian looked to the right, not as if she was bringing something into her view, but as if she was shutting R. C. out.

"Nothing about this is simple," she said, "except maybe your . . ." She stopped, continued staring at the gamblers.

He knew that Jillian's downwinders trial had gone into recess beginning last Friday afternoon. It was set to reconvene in three more days, this coming Friday at nine. He phoned her early this morning with the news. He kept putting it off yesterday and last night, waiting, hoping Manos would call him, would answer his cell phone and explain everything to the last detail, put them all in the clear. It was her suggestion this morning that they walk a few blocks downtown from the Federal Building, where they both worked, over to the land of nonstop metallic whirrs and plenty of privacy. He knew she wanted to stick with the Rudd matter, but hoped that he could put her at ease and turn the conversation in another direction. He supposed he should have been more worried about the Rudd stuff right now, but the memory of Jillian last Wednesday night, her ass and the back of her thighs both muscled and smooth as she stood there in red spike heels next to that wall of mirrors, bending forward at the waist and taking everything he could give her while she taunted him for more, was simply all he had been able to think about lately. He knew that the end of a cigar, just before you burn your lips, is where the deepest flavor resides.

She finally turned away from the gamblers and back to him, cupping her chin in one long, thin hand. "So, what did we find in St. George? Anything recovered from this old cowboy?"

Tall, blonde Jillian was nothing like R. C.'s darker-versioned stubby wife, whose little bit of glamour had been forfeited to a pair of demanding infant twins and an espresso cart she operated at a local mall. "No," he said. "Checked and double-checked on that. I talked with the St. George investigators. The cowboy didn't take any files, manuscript, computer disks, no papers of any kind. Nada. Just jewelry, cash, credit cards, all the routine stuff. Old Mack Sayles from the local FBI office was up there and I ran into him. He wanted to know why the federal marshall's office was interested in Rudd's murder, but I smoothed him out, told him it was routine, we had a big down-winder trial in progress."

Jillian laughed softly, and the sound, an Arctic breeze, immediately froze R. C. "You fool," she said. "You couldn't smooth out a marble. Now we have a potential tie between the trial and this murder with the possibility of a dizzy damn memoir floating around out there someplace. And I have to just sit here and wait? Wait to see what happens? I can't believe the stupid shit that just came out of your mouth."

"Hey," he said, leaning forward and loosening his tie, his patience evaporating, "my mouth seemed to be just fine for you the other night." Behind Jillian, a big red light on top of a slot machine began flashing, signalling a lucky winner, though to R. C. the light was ominous, a silent caution.

"Look, Roger Ramjet," she snarled, "this is business and don't ever confuse the lines. I wanted to get laid the other night. You were hot for it, and none of that means squat. If I'd really wanted my brains fucked out in style, I wouldn't have turned to some nervous, married hack. Don't ever bring it up like that again."

It was enough of a hurricane that it silenced them both. There was a flurry of people toward the back of the gaming area where complimentary tokens for Caribbean stud poker were being passed out. R. C. shifted in his seat and pretended to watch the ruckus.

Jillian picked up her juice, rocked the glass, and watched the liquid swirl. Finally, she put it down. "I'm sorry," she said. "I just lost it, I guess." She reached across the table and touched his hand.

R. C. couldn't help himself. This bitch could probably make him pop a wood while working a loaded shotgun up his ass. Before last week, there had been twelve years of pleasant but uneventful marriage, late nights spent working crossword puzzles while spooning away pints of Royal Gala ice cream, Coffee Caramel and Totally Nuts being his passions. But since Thursday, he had cut out the fats, worked daily on the Nautilus machines.

R. C. smiled and accepted Jillian's apology with a shrug. "Hey, I'll stay on it. I'll find my guy and get all the answers. I can tell after looking into this yesterday, it's no problem," he said. After this display, after her little shit-slinging tantrum, it still came back to a simple fact. She needed him.

"The cowboy kills Rudd for whatever reason. He has a suitcase full of Rudd's jewels, for hell's sake. My guy gets there, sees Rudd is dead. Dead guys don't write books. The cowboy ain't got no book with the jewels. So what then? This Manos moves on to something else. He ain't exactly a day planner kinda guy. Probably stuck around to take a temple tour or something. I don't know. But nothing about this deal has our tracks on it. Okay?" He was proud of his logic, had about convinced himself, just as he'd been doing last night. "So let's relax here a little. I'll handle it."

Jillian smiled back with coppery lips and glossy teeth. "Good. Get it handled. That's all I want," she said. "I don't want to lose this trial, and I don't want to be traced back to . . . God knows what."

"Quit worrying so much. Rudd's in the freezer and this cowboy's half stiff already." R. C. wondered if she was going to mention her schedule, tell him when she'd be free. Jillian rubbed lightly at her collarbone, as if identifying it as a place to be kissed.

"Great," she said, "you stay on it. Now. I'd like you to call me tonight, say about nine o'clock, and tell me it's done. That everything is, how shall we say . . . copacetic?"

R. C. looked at her and paused. Was this an invitation, could he deliver the details in person? "You got it," he said. "Consider it done."

"In addition," she said, "get me the police report on the murder, a complete file on this cowboy . . .what's his name?"

"Parker. Dallas Parker."

"Yeah, Parker. His work, family, friends, his life. Photos. Everything."

"No problem," R. C. told her. "I already got most of it yesterday. I'll get the rest ASAP. Have it to you by five."

She tapped on the lip of her juice glass. Her fingernails were nicely rounded, medium length, painted to match her lipstick. "You realize, don't you, that if your guy is somehow implicated in this murder, he gives you . . . he gives us up in a heartbeat. We have to deal with that possibility, if you know what I mean."

R. C.'s exterior masked the turmoil he was feeling inside. He had told Jillian the basic facts about Manos—a trafficker, a hardcore get-the-job-done guy who could be charged with parole violation in a nanosecond if he decided to screw with them. What he hadn't mentioned were the more subtle details—the guy's volatility, the shrewd mind that operated in a different dimension, the addiction to other people's pain. And what worried R. C. the most was his trip yesterday, his talk with the local cops in St. George. This old cowboy up there who wasn't talking, not yet at least, just didn't fit in with the throat-cutting types. But Manos—now there was someone who could redefine the art.

"Yeah," R. C. finally said, his face clear and smooth as a boy's, "there's no part of the word *conspiracy* that I don't understand."

He wanted the moment to end with more promise—Jillian fingering her lips, slipping her shoe off under the table—but she said, "Good. Call me tonight. We'll see about . . ." Her voice trailed off into the first real smile since he'd given her the news.

And so there it was, her own little carrot and stick, a vague promise of reward. This was exactly the way he had trained his dog: obey and you might get a bone or a pat on the head or simply be ignored. And now he saw himself being just as foolish and needy, just as driven. With the dexterity of a cross-word puzzle addict, his mind realigned the moment into three perfectly interchangeable phrases. Succor. Suck her. Sucker.

Smoke from the sandstone barbecue drifted, caught a down-draft, and swirled across the patio toward Christine. The smell of charcoal and searing meat was intoxicating, as were the last few swallows of her gin and tonic. She watched the smoke as it turned on the breeze and floated aimlessly over the Four Wives' expansive lawn, toward the flower beds, through the duck wings and sunflower petals of the slowly spinning whirligigs. The sun was still ten fingers up in the sky, so she couldn't yet count the day as over, but she hoped what was left would bring no more surprises.

Dallas had killed Rudd. She was still trying to get her arms around that one, make it somehow compute, but it was going to take time and some talking to Dallas. Add the fact that, like it or not, she and Layne were now the benefactors of . . . criminy. What would you call it? An expose? Pandora's box? They'd both been pretty unhinged by the whole ordeal out at hole-in-the-rock, and when they finally arrived late afternoon at the B & B, greeted by Trevor in his barbecue apron, it seemed like a welcome break.

So here she was, sitting in a soft, floral-patterned lounge chair, boots off, feet pulled up and tucked in tightly, arms wrapped around her legs, everything hugging everything in a protective cocoon. She glanced at her empty glass, at the cubes of melting ice. Layne had assured them he was going into the house to fix three more and now she wished he would hurry. Make the most of this lull before the next shitstorm blew in.

Trevor stood with his back to her, fussing with the patties, causing the flames to momentarily leap above the grill, sizzle vigorously, and then settle back into wisps of gray.

"I call these Lamberghinis," Trevor said. "Racy burgers." He waved his stainless steel spatula in the air like a baton. Christine could see that Trevor was the perennial cruise director, the guy who always wanted to make a party, wanted to get everybody up. "I grind up some good lean leg of lamb, keeping in just a small bit of the fat for flame and flavor. Then I mix in liberal amounts of garlic and dry mustard, some finely shredded carrot, add salt and pepper, secret herbs, a touch of

Worcestershire if you like, and then form it all into patties. Cook to order just like any other burger."

There was a time, during the racking spasms of her chemotherapy, when even the thought of red meat would have sent Christine straight to the porcelain, but as she recovered she just couldn't bring herself to join the ranks of those waxen waifs who forsook all meat. She still partook, although sparingly, and was surprised now at how wonderful Trevor's lamb burgers smelled.

He arched an eyebrow. "Stole the idea from a great little place called Ruth's Diner up in Salt Lake City." He lowered his chin and his voice, "You're gonna love it, baby."

Christine laughed out loud for the first time since Sunday night, since she and Dallas had gone out for dinner at the Ancestor Inn, back in another life. This Trevor, he was trying so hard. He and Layne both were. Suddenly she felt a little pang of guilt for letting the two of them dote on her, humor her like this, like she was somehow privileged. But the guilt passed quickly. Dote away, boys.

Layne walked onto the patio, his elbows clearing a path through the screen door, his hands expertly cradling three tall drinks. "Sorry guys, the phone got me. But better late than never," he said. She watched him as he handed her a drink, walked one over to the barbecue, and then, looking over Trevor's shoulder, gamely commented upon the cooking. Christine knew that Layne, like herself, was trying to be a good guest, was trying to keep this book—the eight hundred pound gorilla—out of his mind for more than a few seconds at a time.

The manuscript had suddenly taken center stage in this fiasco. It was still foremost in Dallas's mind, according to Layne, who had stopped at the jail, as promised, on the drive back in from the ranch. Christine had taken a walk while Layne had gone inside. She wouldn't have described herself exactly as clearheaded and confident by the time Layne got back to the car, but she had surprised both of them with what happened next.

Layne had called his law office from the jail and found out

that Mack Sayles, the FBI man, wanted to meet with Christine at the public library around two o'clock, if it was convenient.

It was ten past two and Layne had begun slowly driving toward the library, a short six blocks away from the jail, when she started to panic. "What's he going to ask me? What do you think he knows? About Rudd's book?"

"Well, I don't know who else Rudd had in on this deal. We'll have to play it by ear," he said as he turned up a street. "Anyway, I'll be there with you. If he asks you any questions about the murder or the book, all you can do is take the Fifth and simply tell him to talk to me, your lawyer."

She looked at him sharply. "If I do that, doesn't it sound as if I have something to hide? Won't they suspect me of something?"

Layne drifted over to the curb a couple of houses down from the library. Christine was all too familiar with the small, single-story, red brick, generic library building out of the fifties. A town of almost forty thousand and you could fit the entire library into a basement corner of the local temple. She had visited it as a kid during summer stays at the ranch and it was okay back then, through an adolescent's eyes. Dallas had a respectable wall of books in the cabin, but she was addicted to trolling the aisles of libraries and just two weeks ago had come here to renew her card and pick out a couple of books on fine wines. She was stunned to learn that not only were there no books on wine, but that among many others *Moby Dick* had been banned because of the title and *Zorba the Greek* was tossed because he danced on Sundays.

Layne brought the Land Cruiser to a stop and turned toward her. "Just because one chooses to invoke the Fifth Amendment privilege against self-incrimination doesn't necessarily infer that—"

Before he could finish, Christine saw someone, it had to be this Mack Sayles, bustling down the sidewalk toward their car, waving and smiling like a granddad anxiously welcoming them over to Sunday dinner.

"Oh shit," Layne said. "Just let me do the talking."

"Is that him?" Christine asked.

"You got it."

Sayles walked directly to the passenger side. Christine rolled down her window.

"Oh," she said, "Mr. Sayles, I presume."

He stuck his hand in the window and Christine shook it. "Pleased to meet you, Miss Parker. Glad you could come." With his free hand, he fumbled with his dark glasses, awkwardly trying to get them off. He stuck them in the upper pocket of his jacket and patted it. "Mr. Harting, afternoon to you too, sir." He looked back at Christine. "Got a minute?"

"Actually, Mr. Sayles," Christine said, "Mr. Harting was just taking me over to the doctor's office. I told him to swing by here first, I didn't want to leave you standing around waiting. I'm sorry, but I've just felt terrible today. I haven't felt this nauseated since . . . well, I've been having some problems."

The aging FBI man leaned against the car, then seemed to realize how dusty it was and backed away, brushing his left side, hunching slightly to peer inside. "Oh, well, I'm sorry to hear that," he said. "Actually, I have to admit that I'm already aware that you've been, ah, that you've had some health problems. Routine background check, that's all. I hope you understand."

"Oh, hey, that's no problem," she smiled weakly. "I don't know how I can be of help, but I'm happy to talk to you. I just hope I feel well enough to come in tomorrow for the arraignment. Maybe I could see you then."

Christine lowered her head. "I haven't seen or talked to my uncle since . . ." She let a healthy pause take place, silently counted to four. "I'm just as dumbfounded and puzzled as anyone else about this, this . . ."

Sayles fell all over himself backing away in apology, waving, saying tomorrow would be fine. Christine wondered if the FBI trained these guys in big barns up in Minnesota, fed them nothing but corn and beets, let them listen to an occasional polka on Saturday nights, then set them loose in the world to do their work. It was her very first meaningful encounter with the law and she was obviously feeling a little smug about it.

Driving away, Layne looked over at her. "Well, that's one way of avoiding the Fifth that I hadn't thought of."

"Or even telling an outright lie," she said. "Just hope it doesn't somehow backfire on me."

Then she asked him if he could, in fact, drive by Dr. Pace's office so she could run in to pick up some medication.

Layne nodded. "Uh, sure. Are you okay?" He glanced over at her, then kept his eyes self-consciously on the road. "No problem. You'll have to remind me where he's at."

He would know about her cancer, of course. How much he knew was another matter. The grapevine that carried that kind of news was far-reaching. What struck her at the moment, though, was the difference in sexes. Women were most often open with her about it, fell all over themselves in condolences, told her hopefully about miracles and other women they'd known with breast cancer. Men, on the other hand—her dad, her uncle, male friends, and now Layne—despite their best intentions, all stiffened up, set their jaws, and stammered.

Trevor, fanning smoke away with his spatula, seemed to be addressing Layne, though he was looking directly at Christine. "Layne, the B & B has quite a little history, doesn't it?" She nodded and smiled, her eyes inviting him to tell his story, as she took a slow, refreshing swallow of the fresh G and T. Layne was already smiling, as if he knew where it was headed.

"You know how Saraville got its name?" Trevor said. "From the same Sara that lived in the room where you're staying. She was Jacob Barlow's fourth wife." Trevor was messing with the burgers way too much, turning them too often, pressing down and squeezing the juice onto the fire. God, it felt good to have a normal, silly little thought like that again.

"Old Jacob settled this entire valley back in 1877," he continued. "He already had three wives and twenty-five kids when he met Sara; he was fifty-eight at the time. They all lived right here in this big house, each of his three wives claiming a separate corner bedroom on the second floor. Sara was raised up in Cedar City. Her dad was a friend of Jacob's, had to call in a favor to get his twenty-one-year-old, old maid, mercy case daughter married off. Supposedly, she was coyote ugly and a little tempestuous, but Jacob grudgingly married her anyway. Then something happened on their wedding night. After that, Jacob got right down to business and remodeled the entire attic floor just for her, making it the best bedroom in the house, and began staying up there every night with her. Word went around that Sara might have been ugly, but she had a body and talents hidden under that bulky gingham that drove old Barlow mad. And within the year he died right up there, right on top of Sara, folks said, muzzle thrown back, trying to suppress a mad-dog howl. He was so locked up and stiff when he croaked, it took three men and a large boy sitting on his casket to get it closed." Christine was giggling and Layne grinned, shaking his head.

There hadn't been many opportunities to see Layne smile and Christine noticed that it was boyish, a little shy, charming.

Trevor walked to the edge of the patio and pointed off to the north. "See that red spire out there? Up on top of the Navajo Bench? You can't really tell from here, but that cylinder of sandstone is almost twenty feet in diameter and eighty feet high. Locals call it Barlow's Pecker; we're still trying to get that name on the topos."

Christine rolled her eyes, smiled, and hugged her legs a little tighter. Pecker. She hadn't heard that word in awhile. It was bawdy and refreshing. Having drinks, talking sex, laughing, she was almost turned on. She barely could remember—or even wanted to remember—the last time she had gotten laid. It was somewhere between postdivorce and precancer and laid was about all it amounted to. Quick and stupid with some guy she had dated three times. She quickly learned the drill, learned about the modern middle-of-the-road wing of the singles scene where the women don't do it on the first date and the guys don't do it after the fifth. As one of her single girlfriends had said, "It's a narrow window of opportunity, honey." Too narrow for her, apparently; it had been over two years since she'd done it at all.

She stood up. "And I'll bet every word of that story is true."

Trevor laughed at her. "Five minutes on the burgs," he said.

Christine nodded. "Is there a bathroom on the main floor?"

Trevor pointed and gave her directions. She walked through the kitchen and into the main foyer, found it down the side hall with a small sign on the door. Water Closet. It looked like something Trevor might have stolen in Europe.

The cool water felt good on her face and she was happy to forget for a while, to listen to some good old grab-ass and laugh at silly things. She freshened her lip gloss, then ran wet fingers through her hair, settling any flyaways and adding a little shine. She examined herself in the mirror. Everything looked pretty good, all things considered. She turned off the light, stepped out into the dim hall, and walked back to the foyer. She almost ran him down as she turned the corner. He was standing so still, watching her come, waiting so unexpectedly. It took a second for her to register that he was real.

"Oh, excuse me!" she said, stopping abruptly. "Whew, you startled me. Sorry, I'm sure I startled you as well."

"No, it's my fault. Forgive me."

She smiled. "You must be one of the other guests." She took a step backwards. "I'm just upstairs myself."

"Actually, I'm staying down the road. But I've heard such good things about this B & B that I thought I'd take a peek for myself." He had an imposing scar on his cheek, but it only seemed to add to his muscled, imperfect looks. "And I'm glad I did. It was worth the trip. But how rude of me. Trent Hanover." He put out his hand.

She took it. "Christine Parker. Pleased to meet you." His skin was unusually soft and he held her hand for a second longer than she expected.

"Likewise," he said and released it.

Christine walked across the hardwood of the main foyer to the bottom of the grand staircase into a bright well of light. "If you'd heard the story I just did. Well, it makes the house all the more interesting." She fanned a hand in front of her face.

"Ah, a story. I love a good story. I'm a writer by trade."

"Really? How interesting." He was a little shorter than Layne, certainly much taller than Trevor, and a very sharp dresser.

"I taught . . . teach English," she said. "High school. Of course, I harbor the standard fantasy about being a writer myself. We all do."

He cocked his head, clasped his hands behind his back, and nodded all at the same time. "Well, you should go for it. That's for certain. I figured it out once. Write just one page a day and in a year you have a 365-page book." He laughed gently as if he had just made a terrific inside joke.

"I'm sure that's true," she smiled. "What kind of writer? I mean, what do you write about?"

"Oh, it's pretty boring stuff, really. I'm doing a work of non-fiction right now. *Water Wars in the West* is a good enough working title. Pretty dry stuff, though." He laughed softly, another joke, and leaned toward her a little. "But I'm also working on a children's, well, crossing over into a young adult's book. That's my real passion right now. My eight-year-old daughter got me going on it. She's pretty precocious." He stepped back and sighed, "But, as a teacher, you already know about having to live in the real world, do whatever it takes to pay the old bills. And since the divorce . . ." He broke off and walked over to the banister and rubbed it with both hands. "Listen to me, will you? Don't you just hate it when strangers dump out their life story?"

"Oh, no. I didn't think—" Christine said, wanting to be congenial but also wanting to get back out to Layne and Trevor.

"Sure, you're being nice." He tilted his head way back and looked straight up through the stairwell. "I have a stairway, an old Victorian, just like this in my kids' book. In fact, this home, this Pioneer Victorian style, that's what I call it, is an exact model for the setting of my book." He released the banister and looked back down, appraising her shyly. "It's one of the reasons I stopped in."

Christine listened to him but cast a nervous glance toward the kitchen. She couldn't see out to the backyard, but she assumed that dinner was about ready. "It is beautiful," she said. "And the owner, his name is Trevor Mallory, has done a great job of restoring it."

"He certainly has."

"He's right out in the backyard. Why don't you come and meet him?"

"I'd love to. But I'm going to be late for an appointment." He lowered his voice as if he were letting her in on something. "A rather boring water interview. Member of the local conservancy district."

"Well then," she said, "it's certainly been nice meeting you. Good luck with that other book. Both books, really."

"Thanks. Nice meeting you as well." He took a couple of steps, backing toward the door.

Christine nodded and headed toward the kitchen door. "Bye."

"Wait," he said. "On second thought, could you do me a big favor?" He placed his hands together in a gesture of supplication. "It'll only take a minute."

"I, I really do have to get back out."

"One minute," he cut in, "guaranteed. I have a painting, a tentative book cover out in my car. You work with these kids all the time. You know how they think. Just take a glance and give me your spontaneous impression. It depicts the entry of a house just like this with a tall Christmas tree standing in the foyer. It's right out there. It'll just take a second."

"Well," she shrugged, and without even answering, she was following him out the front door and onto the walkway that led to the parking area, where a shiny black Jaguar was parked next to Layne's dirty Land Cruiser. Hmm, writers must be making more money these days, she thought. And it had been a long time since she'd had this much starchy male attention.

Halfway down the walk, the door opened behind them and Layne called her name. She turned to see him standing there, a strange, surprised look on his face. Of course! With all of this book business, he had warned her not to trust anyone.

Christine hurried to make the introductions and let Layne know that this was a writer—children's books, no less—seeking a bit of artistic advice. She made the offer once again to have Mr. Hanover come out and meet Trevor.

"Look, you folks are trying to eat dinner," he said, glancing at his watch and shaking his head. "And I'm late." He started down the walk again, leaving them standing there watching him. "Really. Later than I even realized." Then he opened the door to his car, stopped momentarily and called to them, "I'm going to make it back to Saraville, though." He smiled. "I'll see you again. You can bet on that."

There was a time, back in the good old days, when courtrooms reflected the solemnity of the occasion, when their Byzantine structure alone cowed most litigants into awestruck silence. They had high ceilings and elaborate lighting, real wood on the walls and intricate cove moldings, floors of marble and shining parquet. All of this had since been replaced, however, by acoustical tile and recessed fluorescents, fake paneling and industrial carpet. The judge's bench was transformed from a sweeping edifice commanding respect to little more than a raised desk.

This morning, Washington County Courtroom Number 2 suited Layne. He'd had enough drama for one week—make that a year—and downscale courtrooms felt just fine. He had appeared in this courtroom many times and even its nonde-script smells—vaguely of paper and dust and anxiety—felt oddly comforting and orderly. At least it was the devil he knew. The judge would come in with a call to order, Layne would help Dallas enter a plea of not guilty and then make his case for bail—vigorously arguing the merits, completely understanding their chances—and then listen as the judge denied his motion and that would be that. Bail in a capital case, especially down here, was almost unthinkable, so that would keep Dallas in jail, Rudd's book in hiding, and beyond that, who knew. Layne's vote was to drop the manuscript in the mail, send it to the *Washington Post* or *The Times* and just get it out of the way. Maybe he would suggest it to Dallas when they had a private moment.

Layne was thirty minutes early; the lights were all on, but the courtroom was deserted. Christine had veered off to find a bathroom. Just the thought of seeing Dallas for the first time since Sunday had begun to distract her. She was steady when Layne had first picked her up at the B & B this morning, but as they drew nearer to St. George, she began to fidget and worry again. He couldn't blame her.

A side door leading to chambers opened and Layne waved distractedly at Judge Pelton T. Andrews's clerk who walked in carrying some files, fiddled around at his desk for a moment, and then walked back out. Layne began to spread out his own case files, skimpy thus far, and two note pads on the defense table. It was the same routine he always followed. Arrive early and get set up. He liked to have at least half an hour to acclimate himself, to lay out his materials, to get himself mentally prepared for oral argument. He was fast gaining a reputation in southern Utah as one of the really good attorneys in the region and he enjoyed that. Attracting quality clients and building a reasonable practice after the first year or so had not been a problem.

The double doors behind him swung open and Don Parsons from the *St. George Spectrum*, the thin local daily, walked in. He was skinny and bustling and hunched over, with fair skin and boyish features that belied his thirty some odd years.

"Hidey ho, Brother Harting," he said.

"Hi ho, yourself, Brother Don."

"I hope you're not offended," Don said, keeping a playful distance, "but it looks as though I'm the sole remnant of that rabid press corps you had to fight your way through on Monday. They finally tagged your case as just another garden-variety murder. No O. J. here." Don was grinning from deep within his shrugged shoulders.

"Good," said Layne, and he certainly meant it. "No press,

less fuss." Every little bit helped to keep this thing calm and under wraps.

"Well, not *no* press," said Don. "I'm here."

When Layne first met Don, he thought it weird being called Brother Harting, but now it had become a standing joke between them. Don was a practicing Mormon with a rare sense of humor about it. Layne had been raised a nondenominational only child in Salt Lake City by his college professor mother and a sporadically employed "thinker," his father. They had conceived him later in their lives, finally divorced when he was in high school, and both had passed away by the time he was in his late twenties. Layne recognized early on that the non-Mormons were part of a Salt Lake City fringe counter-culture, particularly back in the fifties and sixties, before the West Coast population began toppling backwards into the Rocky Mountain states. He grew up with Mormons and counted several of them as friends, both in Salt Lake and in Saraville, but always understood that to some degree he was on the outside looking in.

Regardless, the red dirt of southern Utah was there long before the Mormons, and Layne was terminally infatuated with its landscape. He loved the mountains, the deserts, the seasons, the varied terrain, and the fact that its vast open spaces were locked away in BLM and forest lands. He had even come to appreciate the quirkiness of the Mormons because, to some extent, they kept down the flow of new, out-of-state residents. He had quit trying to rationalize or explain the ridiculous Utah liquor laws, for example, and simply shook his head in a gesture of don't-even-think-about-moving-here when queried.

Don Parsons took a seat back in the gallery and watched as Layne fidgeted through his little pretrial ritual, which was less about the bail hearing and more about the larger issues that a dead scientist and a live manuscript presented. Don covered the courthouse, the police station, the fire department, and anything else municipal. He was always lurking around the building and he loved to gossip. He was also smarter than the local cops and Layne wanted to stay cool around him.

Layne finally closed his file and stood up, stretching. "So, how's the *Rectum*, Don?"

"The *Spectrum* is fine, Layne. How's the Parker case?"

"Stay tuned, pardner."

Just then, Christine entered. She stopped in the doorway, checking to see who was there. Layne motioned her over and sat her in the front row next to the rail, directly behind where Dallas would sit next to Layne. At almost the same moment, the side door opened and Dallas was ushered in. His restraints had been removed and he was wearing his street clothes. He was clean shaven and his hair was combed. He grinned foolishly in the direction of Layne and Christine and gave them a small, waist-high wave. The deputies escorted him to his seat, then one deputy posted himself at the double doors into the courtroom while the other took up a position by the side door into chambers. Layne shook hands with Dallas, and then Dallas turned around and immediately huddled with Christine, hugging her over the rail. Upon seeing this, one of the deputies took a step toward them. Layne stopped him with a hand gesture. He could hear Christine crying softly and Dallas muttering to her. Layne stepped away, toward the front of the courtroom, to give them more privacy and to talk to the deputy. Dallas and Christine kept their heads together.

"She's not slipping him any weapons," Layne told the deputy. "I'll guarantee that."

The deputy continued to keep watch with a furrowed brow.

Layne then approached the clerk who accurately anticipated his question. "Judge Andrews has a visitor in chambers," he said. "Some FBI man. But we should get going soon. I hope."

Layne stepped back, found himself standing in the middle of the courtroom. Others were trickling in. What the hell was the FBI, probably this Sayles guy, doing with the judge? He hoped there weren't any big surprises about to walk through the door. Layne was ultra-jittery about that damn book. He had questions, uncertainties, needed to double check on attorney-client privilege. And he still hadn't been able to reach his buddy, the crack criminal lawyer in Salt Lake. He was at the Bar convention in Sun Valley, probably drinking all night, playing golf all day, and racking up Continuing Legal Education credits through osmosis.

Dallas and Christine were still huddled together at the rail. Dallas was quietly talking to her. Layne could see Dallas's lips moving a mile a minute, using this rare opportunity to get in his say, to tell her things and bolster her courage. Christine was listening intently, opening her mouth to object, being shushed by Dallas as he kept talking.

Then the elected county attorney, Jim Bidwell, came hurrying through the door in a general state of disarray, his arms loaded with law books and files. "Mr. Harting," he said congenially, "how we doing? Good, I'm not late." He noisily dropped his load on the prosecution table and stood catching his breath. He was overweight and winded.

"Morning. Need some help there, Jim?"

"Yeah, could you argue both sides of this motion? I'm up to my neck in alligators today."

"Be happy to," Layne said.

The side door into the court swung open and the bailiff said, "All rise. Fifth Judicial District Court, State of Utah, is now in session. Judge Pelton T. Andrews presiding."

Layne was back in his place at the defense table as the judge hiked up the skirt of his robe to negotiate the few steps up to the bench. Dallas had stood up but was still giving Christine a long and stern look over his shoulder. He turned and faced the bench as the bailiff said, "Be seated."

"Mr. Harting, you are here to represent the defendant. Are you ready to proceed?" Judge Andrews was almost totally bald, but his skin was smooth and he appeared in good shape for a man in his mid-fifties.

"Yes, your honor," Layne said.

"Mr. Bidwell? The prosecution?"

"State's ready, your honor."

Layne could hear the door opening behind him, more people

shuffling in. He kept his attention focused on the judge as he spoke.

"Mr. Parker, this is the time and place set to receive your plea to the various charges. I am going to ask you some questions and you may remain seated while you answer them. Are you ready to proceed?"

Dallas reflexively half-stood anyway. "Yes, your honor."

"If you have any questions, please feel free to stop me and to consult with your counsel." The judge nodded toward Dallas and gave him a tight smile.

"I understand, your honor." Dallas nodded back. Then the judge began a long recitation of his rights. Did he have counsel and was he satisfied with counsel?

Dallas nodded.

"Answer aloud for the record please, Mr. Parker," Judge Andrews instructed.

"Yes, your honor," Dallas said crisply.

And so it went: Did he understand the nature of the charges, the penalties thereon, the nature of a guilty plea, his right to take or not take the stand and testify, the inference from that, and so on and on?

Dallas answered each question without consulting Layne.

When it came time to receive the plea, Dallas and Layne stood up together. The judge read each charge—murder in the first degree, murder while in commission of a felony, burglary, unlawful entry—and asked Dallas after each one, "How do you plead?"

As he and Layne had discussed yesterday, Dallas responded in each instance, "Not guilty, your honor." When they were finished and sitting down, Layne glanced back at Christine. Her eyes were red, but her chin was up and she was watching the proceedings very carefully. She returned his gaze without visible emotion. Then something caught his eye a couple of rows behind her and he spotted the guy who was at the B & B yesterday, grinning at him like they were long-lost friends. Soon Christine followed Layne's gaze, turned around and looked at the guy. Layne shrugged it off. Mack Sayles was also in the audience across the aisle at the very back, but he had his head down reading something.

The judge continued the proceeding by asking Layne if there were any motions.

"Yes, your honor," he said. "At this time the defense would move the court to set bail."

The prosecutor was immediately on his feet. "The State would vigorously resist the setting of bail in this case, your honor. As you know, this is a capital case and—"

The judge interrupted, "Please wait your turn, Mr. Bidwell. You may go forward with your motion, Mr. Harting."

Judge Andrews peered over the top of his reading glasses. He was a tough guy. He was smart and grasped the issues quickly. He had been on the bench for a long time, didn't dance to anyone else's tune, and Layne was always happy to have a case assigned to him. The other district court judge in this county was a disaster, a younger, more recent political appointee who waffled on everything. Layne began an orderly discourse on the defendant's right to bail: the defendant's lack of prior arrests or convictions, his lifelong residency in the county, the fact that he was a ranch owner. Layne acknowledged that bail wasn't an absolute right, particularly in a case such as this, but stressed over and over that it was strictly to make sure the defendant showed up for trial, that it was purely a matter of judicial discretion, and on and on. Layne was putting up a good fight primarily for the sake of Dallas and Christine.

After he finished, the prosecutor argued as vigorously, as if he were outside making a political speech at the chili cookoff. Layne figured that they both were just going through the motions.

There was a pause and the judge asked, "Is that all, gentlemen?" He looked at Layne, "Any rebuttal?"

"We'll submit it, your honor," Layne said.

"Alright. After due deliberation, I have decided to set bail in this case." Layne wasn't sure he had heard correctly. Oh. Then he understood. Bail was going to be set at a splashy ten million or so.

"Mr. Parker, please rise." Dallas stood up next to Layne.

"What assets do you have, sir?"

"Just my ranch, your honor," said Dallas, "and a few head of stock."

"Is it free and clear?"

"Yes sir," said Dallas.

"In view of the fact that you were born on that ranch, that you have never been charged with or convicted of any crime, and your good standing in the community, coupled with the necessary presumption of your innocence until proven otherwise, I will allow you to post an unencumbered deed to your ranch property and all the stock and other assets thereon as bail in this case. Counsel may prepare the papers."

Layne couldn't believe it. What? What the hell was going on here? The county attorney was sputtering, one hand in the air toward the judge, who then dropped his gavel and left the bench. Layne spun around and happened to catch the eye of Mack Sayles in the back, grinning broadly at him. Maybe this Sayles had something to do with Dallas getting bail. What other possible explanation was there? If so, that meant the FBI might be clued in to something bigger than a simple murder, that they wanted Dallas out of jail, pointing the way.

Mack was giving Layne a little three-fingered wave. It was the Boy Scout salute, if he recalled correctly.

Big black and gold bees circled the trash can at the bottom of the courthouse steps. Christine veered away from them and Layne followed her.

She wasn't quite ready to throw a party, but things were better. With any luck, Dallas would be coming home this afternoon. Then she'd have a chance to find out what happened that night, how they had arrived at this terrible place. No matter what he told her, however, she had to accept things as they were and go on from there. He'd been adamant about that. It was all water under the bridge, he kept saying as they whispered over the courtroom railing. "We can't dwell on what's past and done. You've got to think only about the future." There he'd been with his arm around her, about to be arraigned for murder, and he was the one propping her up, giving her advice and confidence. She winced at the memory.

"I need to get right over to the title company," Layne was saying to her. "I'll have the bail documents and a trust deed drawn up and signed by Dallas as quickly as I can."

She turned toward him and glanced at his dark red knit tie set off against a crisp white shirt and blue jacket. He wore his standard-issue polished boots and pressed khaki pants, all in stark contrast to the county attorney's off-the-rack blue polyester suit. Layne's clothing was nice, classy looking, matching perfectly his own natural good looks, and she thought about complimenting him.

"I have to tell you," he shook his head and leaned a little closer, "I'm pretty dazed over this bail business. It's really, with this kind of charge, well, it's unheard of." His expression was a cross between wonder and concern, as if he was having difficulty accepting this small victory. Someone had tossed an empty soda cup into the wire trash can and more bees were homing in, climbing down into it and back up, buzzing madly, flying in small, excited circles.

Christine shrugged. "I'm just happy Dallas is getting out of jail."

"I know, I know. I am too," he hurried on, "but I'm worried about it. This FBI guy was inside talking to the judge when we arrived. Yesterday, against the regulations, Dallas was given his street clothes to wear. Today, the judge grants makeable bail in a case that oddsmakers in Vegas wouldn't give you a million to one. I don't know what's going on here, but we need to be very careful."

Christine could hear what Layne was saying, even argue with it, but she had done enough fretting for awhile and was simply taking Dallas's advice to relax a little. "Yes, we need to be careful. And grab our luck where we can get it. Right?"

Layne's jaw was tight. "Right. Luck, huh? There's no luck in that damn book. That's what . . ." His voice was low and conspiratorial and trailed off as if nothing more could be said.

Okay. He's right, she thought. But he's the lawyer and it's his job to worry. Besides, she was about worried out.

Layne breathed deeply and relaxed his neck and shoulders with a little rotating shrug. "The title company is a couple blocks down the street. Do you want to come?"

"Do you need me? Can I be of any help?" she asked, looking directly into his face.

"Not really," he said, quickly glancing away.

"If you don't need me, then maybe I'll run a couple of errands." She had in mind a few groceries to take back to the ranch, a good bottle of wine, maybe some of the little pickled sausages Dallas liked. She was going to cowboy-up now, as Dallas liked to say, get her head on straight. Dallas had pointedly asked her to be strong, had pleaded, "I need your help now, Chrissy." He had stared firmly into her eyes, not having to mention hole-in-the-rock or the rest of it.

Don Parsons, roving reporter, someone Layne had earlier pointed out and asked her to avoid, walked up behind Layne. Christine saw him coming and signaled Layne with her eyes. She was pleased and amused that they seemed to be developing these bits of spontaneous teamwork.

Layne turned around.

"Well, well," Parsons said. "That was a sweet piece of lawyering. First time, in the memory of this reporter and perhaps ever, that a capital case in southern Utah was granted bail."

"Thanks, Don," Layne said with a slight bow.

"No offense to your suave oration, counselor, but it's a little difficult to comprehend with such a brutal murder. And the amount of evidence here—"

"Still entitles the defendant to a presumption of innocence," Layne cut in. "And my client would crawl naked through a rattlesnake den to make his court appearances. He'd do anything to avoid losing his third-generation ranch."

"Can I quote you on that?"

"Yes. If you give me a ride over to Laminite Title."

Layne swung back to Christine and handed her his car keys. "I'll meet you—where? I'm not sure how long I'll be."

"Meet her over at my office." Don was crowding his way around Layne. "Hi, Don Parsons, the *St. George Spectrum*."

"Nice to meet you, Don." Christine stuck out her hand. "But I just renewed my subscription to the *Phoenix Gazette*." She faced Layne. "I'll be about an hour. Then I'll be back here."

Don asked, "Can I talk to you?"

"No, you can't," said Layne, taking hold of the reporter's arm and steering him toward the street without looking back.

She watched them go. "Thanks, Layne," Christine said quietly, speaking to his retreating figure. She looked down at his key ring in the palm of her hand. One car key, one house key, looped together on a small piece of tightly braided leather. That was it. Dallas was fond of saying—he didn't have the cracker barrel, but he certainly had the philosophy—that there was an inverse correlation between the size of your key ring and the success of your life. She tucked the keys in her pocket and looked back up at Layne and suddenly wanted to explain that she was grateful for more than just the temporary use of his car.

A woman whom Christine had seen standing outside the adjacent courtroom earlier that morning suddenly swung through the front doors of the municipal building and trounced past her down the steps. Christine had first noticed her because the woman looked so pathetic, so tired and upset and wind-blown, her long dark hair hanging in limp curls. She had been standing out in the hall next to a man in a cheap navy blue suit who seemed to be giving her instructions, probably her lawyer. Now the blue suit was following her and calling, "Gloria. Gloria." At the bottom of the steps she stopped and turned around angrily.

"Get away from me," she said. "Those are my kids, they're all I got. You can't let some judge do that."

The lawyer caught up to her at about the same time the bees did. With the trash can close by, it took only a few seconds for the insects to find the sweet-smelling, hairsprayed architecture of her hair. The bees created a soft, flying halo around the woman's head, but she barely noticed as she lowered her voice and hissed at the lawyer.

"Hi there. Remember me?" someone said quietly behind Christine, almost directly in her ear.

She twisted around and found herself face to face with the guy from yesterday—the writer she'd met at the B & B.

"Oh, you startled me. Sure, from the Four Wives yesterday," she said, backing up a step. "You following me?" she asked and smiled.

He nodded, then chuckled. "In my dreams," he said. Then he stepped back and put his hands in his pockets and stared at her. "No, no. I'm still doing the water gig. Did you know that Vegas and St. George are involved in a dispute over the Virgin River water rights? Boring stuff, but somebody's got to do it. Right?" He smiled and showed her some pearly whites—either caps or well-bleached teeth.

"Well, yeah. I suppose that's right," she said. Something about this guy was beginning to bother her, but she didn't know what. He was handsome in a rugged way, seemed pretty smart, and perhaps she should have relished the attention, the flirtation. But there was something else, some quality that set off little alarm bells. With everything going on, however, she was probably being paranoid.

"I was over here looking at records in the clerk's office when I heard about this arraignment. You know how snoopy we writers can be." He grinned again. "It's created quite a buzz in the courthouse. I guess that's a relative of yours, huh? Tough luck. Sorry."

"Oh, well," Christine said, "my uncle. Thanks for—"

"So, he has a ranch? Hell, I'll bet water is always a problem for ranchers in these parts. In better times, I'd like to meet him and talk some water, under different circumstances, of course."

"Um, I'm sorry," Christine said. "I seem to have forgotten your name."

"Oh, Trent Hanover. Almost like hangover, but not quite," he laughed.

Christine laughed softly. "So how's the work coming?"

"Oh, you know. Water. What can you say about water?"

"Well," she pondered, "I guess there's a lot to say if you don't have enough."

"Hey," he smiled, "I'd like to quote you on that."

"Be my guest." Christine sighed. "Well, I'd better get going."

"Sure," he said, "can I drop you anyplace?"

"Oh, no. That's fine. Just have a couple of errands to run."

"Well, how about that opinion you promised me on my book cover?" He had a hopeful, almost boyish expression now. "My car's right there at the curb and you did kind of promise."

Christine shrugged. "Well, I'm no authority," she said. He kept pressing, so she started toward the sidewalk, to get rid of him if nothing else. He was right beside her. "But remember," she said, "advice is cheap and you get what you pay for."

He laughed heartily. "Okay. Fair enough."

She felt a sudden, slight weight in the small of her back. His hand was there, guiding her, escorting her—touching her. She stopped midstride. He quickly removed his hand.

"Miss Parker, Miss Parker." She turned back toward the courthouse. Several people were walking down the steps and she could hear Mack Sayles before she could see him. He emerged from the crowd, huffing and waving, his jacket draped over one shoulder. He hobbled down the stairs and she greeted him.

"Good morning, Mr. Sayles."

"Hey, you folks got yourselves a bit of good luck in there." He was doing everything but twanging like Festus. "Bail, that's dang good luck."

"Well, uh, thanks Mr. Sayles."

"Mack, please. Call me Mack."

"Alright." She suddenly remembered Trent Hanover. "Have you met Mister . . ." But Hanover was walking away, waving at her.

"You're busy," he shouted, half-turning and backing up, "catch you later."

"Hanover," she finished.

"Friend of yours?" Mack asked.

"No, no. Just met him." She waved back. "Last night, in Saraville actually."

"Just keeps popping up, huh? Kinda like me." Mack Sayles was watching Hanover when she turned around. "That his car?" he asked.

Christine shrugged. "I suppose. It was parked at the B & B last night." Hanover seemed to be having a little trouble with his key in the lock. "Why?"

"Oh, I just appreciate exotic machinery, I suppose. So, anyway, how you feeling today, Miss Parker? Any better?"

Christine struggled, going momentarily blank, and then recovered. "Oh, a little better, thanks. Frankly, I'm just dying to get home, get Dallas out of here and back to the ranch. This has been a trying couple of days."

"I'll bet it has," he said sympathetically, "I'll bet it has." He jangled coins or something in his pocket and rocked back on his feet. "Just a few quick questions, before you run off, though?" he asked.

Christine did her best to look calm. "Shoot," she said, wishing that she'd gone with Layne, not in the least wanting to be here alone with the FBI.

"You were with your uncle on Sunday night. Correct?"

"That's right," she nodded. "We had dinner here in town."

"Then you went home, back to the ranch, I mean. That correct?"

"Uh, yes. We each had our own car. Well, Dallas had his truck."

"What time did your uncle get home?"

Christine paused. She had rehearsed this part many times in her mind. "He didn't . . . I didn't see him. I waited, but he didn't come home. So I went back, afraid there'd been an accident. Trying to find him."

"Did you?"

"No. I didn't see him again until today."

Mack appeared to let that sink in for a minute. "Now, let me see if I have this straight," he said, shifting gears. "You'd met this Dr. Rudd before, is that right?"

"No, no. I saw him on TV, that's all." Christine froze up inside, waiting for what might be coming next. "No," she heard herself say again.

"Oh, well," Mack Sayles scratched behind his ear as he watched the black Jag pull away from the curb. "Guess I must have been mistaken."

Home on The Range
Spring, 1953
Newcastle, Utah

OVER IN THE CORNER IT LAY, FLESHY AND DARK, LIMP AS A
bloody glove, humpbacked, no wool and where the two front
legs should have been—nothing. There was a head of sorts, if
you wanted to call it that: a knotted bundle of skin with two
large eyes, the milky, almost transparent lids still closed.

Nate Docksteader, wearing the same dark green shirt as he
had for the past two days, stood in the dusty slants of sunlight
streaming through the cracks in one of their low ceilinged
lambing sheds, pointing down at the contorted form lying in
the blood-soaked straw. "You tell me just what kind a ungodli-
ness that is," he said, shaking his head disgustedly.

Back in the shadows by a doorway into the feed room,
eleven-year-old Uwanda Docksteader peered between two
shaggy cedar rails in the wall. She willed herself to move away,
but couldn't. She didn't want to hear her father's voice when it
was like that—angry, helpless, full of nails and tacks. And she
didn't want to watch old Dr. Threadgill over there, bending
down, poking around, rolling it over, examining, then straightening back up, patting her father on the shoulder, and trying to
calm him with soothing words. But even to the inexperienced
ears of an eleven-year-old, Dr. Threadgill sounded completely
hopeless.

"I just don't want to hear any more of that bunk," her
father stammered, "the County Ag boys comin' around talkin'
about poor range feed. It was a mild winter and the damn feed

was all close enough to normal." The veins were standing out in her father's neck as he spoke; it didn't happen often, but when it did Uwanda knew it to be a bad sign.

"Keel," her father said, "how many years we been winterin' in the Timpiute? And up in the Pancake? You see any difference in the feed?" Her Uncle Keel stood in the circle with them, but he was silent, his arms folded across his chest, his face turned away from her so that she could only guess what kind of storm cloud he was wearing.

Uwanda leaned her forehead against a post and breathed in the deep, sweet headiness of fresh straw bedding and feed grains. She was exhausted. Up until nine days ago, almost everything in the world had been perfect. She had raised her math grade up to a B-plus, had earned nearly six dollars from babysitting, and was looking forward to an overnight trip to see the Salt Lake Mormon Tabernacle and the Temple grounds with her Beehive girls' group in April. Her mom had even said maybe when Uwanda had asked if she could paint her bedroom lavender.

Then, last week, her father and Uncle Keel had come home. It had always been wonderful before, the big herd trailing back in after wintering on the public grasses in Nevada, a real time of togetherness and celebration, all confirmed by the fact that Uwanda, a late baby and only child of a couple who had almost given up on having children, was born in November. For more than twenty-five years, these two third-generation Iron County sheep ranchers had pushed their herd of pregnant ewes west out onto Nevada's open range, then slowly trailed them back home in the early spring, in time for the lambing. Tending sheep was a rough way to make a living. Nate complained about Keel's cooking. Keel complained that with the amount of dust they ate each day, neither of them should be hungry. It was a lonely way of life, but something they wouldn't have traded.

This spring, however, they might have reconsidered. What had straggled in from the winter range was frightening, almost unrecognizable. The herd of two thousand rambouillets, a tough and mangy breed particularly suited to range conditions, had taken sick, many of the pregnant ewes aborting out on the trail over the past few weeks. Normally a ewe would hang around a premature fetus, try to coax it back to life, but these ewes were half-dead themselves and simply walked away from the twisted, bloody, stumplike creatures they dropped. By the time the men and sheep arrived home at Newcastle, it was more than just winter that had leaned on them.

"As I've said, I haven't ever seen anything like it." Dr. Threadgill walked slowly with Nate and Keel down the length of the open shed. Uwanda's grandfather, who worked this same ranch and western range like his father before, always said that Doc Threadgill, the only vet in Cedar City, about thirty miles east of the ranch, had bought his degree through a magazine. But if there had been any speculation about the man's credentials, there was certainly none about his empathy and loyalty to the Docksteaders and other ranchers. Dropping whatever business he had and hurrying as much as his heavy frame would permit, Dr. Threadgill had made it out to the Docksteader ranch almost every day.

Even on these house calls, he always wore his white lab jacket. Uwanda had seen him in Cedar City wearing it at the gas station and dime store, too. She wondered if he wore it to bed. Most of all, she wished that he could fix the sheep, give them some kind of medicine to end all of this craziness. Her grandfather claimed almost every other day that Bromoseltzer saved his life; she wondered if there was something like that for sheep.

"Well, I'll tell you one big difference in the range out there." Nate stopped, his face bright red. Uwanda worried because her mom said that he was going to blow a gasket if he didn't calm down. Uwanda didn't know what a gasket was, but she sensed that blowing one would bring even more trouble.

"Twice in early January, in the same week, heading down the Railroad Valley," her dad continued, "we got completely covered by burnt ashes from two of them atomic blasts. The whole damn place tasted like a welding rod. For a full week, until it finally rained."

"Now, now," Dr. Threadgill rose slightly up on his toes, "I wouldn't go jumping to conclusions. The AEC sent people around. They've assured us that there is no—"

Keel uncharacteristically butted in, "Ain't no other conclusion. Something poisoned these sheep, plain and simple. And it sure as hell wasn't the bunchgrass or the sage."

"What about the water?" Dr. Threadgill asked. "Any chance of bad water?"

Both men went silent for a moment and looked at each other. Keel Docksteader had always been the quiet younger brother, but even that was changing since they had returned. Now he walked to the feed crib at the rear of the shed, told Doc Threadgill to come have a look. Head down between the stanchions and into the hay, a ewe had died standing upright. She was still balanced against the rail, on her feet, stiffening fast. Keel gave the ewe a shove with his foot and it fell noiselessly. He reached down and tugged at the wool around the throat. A large clump easily came away in his hand.

"You shave these ewes down," he was saying, "they have sores all over their throats and backs, inside their mouths, like somebody went along and burned them with a hot poker."

"Yeah, I know," sighed Dr. Threadgill, "I've seen it on your other ewes."

Keel was down on one knee, pointing. "So, you think maybe bad water causes these burns and sores?" He threw the handful of loose wool to the side in disgust. "Besides, we drank almost all the same water the sheep did. Ain't no damn bad water."

Dr. Threadgill hesitated. "I admit, it's got me stumped. All I can do is pass along the recommendations from the County Bulletin and tell you boys to beef up the protein. Feed the best diet you can afford to build them back up."

Nate's face hadn't even begun to return to a normal color. "We just got back from the bank," he said, "borrowed for more specialty feeds. If we make the feed any damn hotter, they'll accuse us of burning their throats." Nate laughed, like something out of a can.

Uwanda stepped back and ran out of the rear door of the

feed shed. She stood in the breezy arms of a late Tuesday afternoon. She knew she shouldn't have been there listening. But why did her father have to talk like that, make it sound so . . .

Sarcastic. That was the word her mom had used a few days ago in the kitchen. She had turned to Uwanda's father and told him not to be so sarcastic. They had been talking about the only subject that seemed allowed within the walls of their house for the last nine days—sheep—and her mother, frying eggs at the stove, had said that maybe the worst was over.

"Sure," her father had replied, holding his cup of Postum at the table, "maybe we ought to buy a gallon of ice cream and celebrate."

In the midst of all this black talk, Uwanda had wanted to scream at everybody, "I'm eleven, not twenty." She wanted to remind them that she was just a girl who wished to paint her bedroom lavender because lavender stood for a long, happy life full of travel. It was supposed to be Chinese or something. Jeannette Knutsen, her best girlfriend, had read that to her straight out of a borrowed magazine. Jeannette herself had chosen yellow which meant the opposite sex would find you very attractive. Uwanda had slugged Jeannette in the arm and told her to think again.

Uwanda climbed on top of an unused oil drum at the end of the shed and folded her legs Indian style. The spring day was bright and the steep afternoon sun warmed her against the wall. She watched the three men walk into the sunlight.

Dr. Threadgill waved. "How you doin', Uwanda?"

She heard a strong, well-composed voice—her own—answer, "Fine."

Nearby, the men stopped and stood in a half circle, their arms folded, each looking off in a different direction.

"I know it's no consolation, but there are other sheep men just off the range with the same problems," Doctor Threadgill said. "Old Harold Perkins over in Veyo has lost almost two-thirds of his herd and is about to go crazy."

Nate nodded and scraped his boot through the hardened, hoof-packed dirt. "I know all about that. We're having a meeting in Cedar City at the stockyard tonight." He looked up at Doc Threadgill. "So that's the whole score with those boys from the Atomic Energy Commission? You talked to them again and they said the atomic tests are safe? There's no compensation for this? Nothing they're willing to do about it?"

Uwanda could see that it was the same each time Dr. Threadgill came to look at the sheep. Surprise, amazement, confusion. Doc Threadgill would shake his head and wander, stupefied and aimless, around the sheds. He'd listen to Uwanda's father rant for an hour or more, until he'd talked himself out for the time being. And before he left, the doctor would always go to the house to give Uwanda's mother his regards, sympathize, eat a piece of her pie.

Uwanda glanced over her right shoulder toward the house, which had turned dark and dreamless, an unfamiliar place where some new and different family slept these past nights. Not the Docksteaders. Not the people Uwanda knew. On the clothesline off to the side of the house, laundry tossed in the wind, white and angry.

Uwanda pulled her knees up to her chest, encircled her legs with her arms and squeezed herself tight, balancing on the top of the drum. More than the bloody lambs, more than all the tense discussion between her parents, what she remembered most was part of a conversation her dad and Uncle Keel had been having earlier that morning when she came up behind them.

"At this rate," Keel was saying, "won't be much left. To take to market or to summer range."

"At this rate," Nate replied, "there won't be anything left. If we lose the herd, we lose the ground, we lose the whole place. We're gone, period."

Uwanda didn't understand what that meant. We're gone. Period. Where would they go? What about school and her trip with the Beehive girls? And what about her bedroom? Would it ever be lavender?

CHAPTER SEVEN

THE ATHLETIC YOUNG QUARTER HORSE WAS EXECUTING A tight spin to the right, the soft dirt billowing up and obscuring the precise movement of its hooves. Christine set two glasses of lemonade on top of a broad fencepost and stood with her forearms on the top rail of the corral, her chin resting on her hands. The sweating horse suddenly braked to a halt, stood momentarily, backed up five steps, then walked forward. Dallas sat erect on the horse, the reins in his left hand poised directly over the saddle horn. Then, without any overt signal from Dallas, the horse began an equally agile and impressive spin around the near side.

Christine brought her hands together a few times, clapping softly, trying to be a good sport, trying to accommodate Dallas. Rawley and Black Dog, sitting at her feet, simultaneously looked up at her. "Pretty good, huh boys? What do you think?"

During this past month at Motoqua—back in another time zone it seemed—she had enjoyed watching Dallas work his promising young prospect, this black filly registered under the name of Motoqua Pride's Daughter. Christine was amazed again at how the horse responded instantly to such subtle moves from the rider. She knew that the filly was obeying Dallas's leg pressure and weight shifting, trained almost to the point where the reins were extraneous. She fully appreciated what she was seeing and couldn't help speculating as to how much longer it would last. Dallas was out on bail for the time being, but the legal problems would come knocking again soon, and then all of this—horses, dogs, land, a lifestyle, his life— were certainly in jeopardy. And it was all because of her. That was the most painful part. The way that she had stupidly, self- ishly, set this whole mud slide into action.

Dallas stopped the spin and let the horse stand. The filly was alert and straining, her muscles bunched as she awaited more direction. Then, slowly, she visibly relaxed as Dallas relaxed, reading his body language correctly. Smoothly, he swung off in a dismount, dropped the reins, and stroked the side of the filly's neck and crest, speaking softly at the side of her cheek. She lowered her head slightly and her eyes drooped, and finally, her entire body seemed to slacken under Dallas's cooing praise.

He left the horse standing and walked over to Christine. "Hey, girl. Thanks," he said, reaching for the lemonade, then raising his glass, "here's looking at you." He took a long, greedy drink, emptying the tall glass. He smacked his lips as if he were determined to enjoy every moment of his new freedom. Black Dog came over to Dallas's feet and whined softly until Dallas bent down and rubbed the dog's neck and shoulders with both hands. He put his face inches from Black Dog's nose and a pink tongue caught him on the chin. Dallas laughed, "Everything's going to be okay, old fella. You missed me, didn't you?" He moved his gnarled fingers over the dog's ears, putting it in a trance. "You and me, Black, we're alike. Just a couple of old work plugs, happiest in the traces. We'll go shoo us up some cows tomorrow morning."

Christine smiled. This man and dog might well have been attached, Siamese twins of a different sort. Whereas Dallas trained the horses to his subtle moves, the dog seemed to read Dallas's mind.

"That filly still looks great," Christine said. "Hasn't missed a beat."

Dallas leaned against the fence and looked back at the horse. "Sometimes a short break, a few days off, is right," he said. "She's really alert, anxious to get to work today."

Christine studied her uncle in profile as he watched the filly, the brim of his Stetson pulled down low, hindering a good look at his eyes. This was his "inaccessible" pose, where he peered out at the world and didn't allow the world much of a look back in. When Dallas wanted to open that door, the hat was raised by degrees, until it finally sat on the back of his head, sort of hanging out the welcome sign. It had always seemed to her that this was merely an extension of the artful body language he used training horses. And today Christine had no doubt that she was being manipulated as well, with the same forceful subtlety as this young filly.

"Dallas," she said.

"Yeah?" He reached up and pulled the hat down even tighter, his eyes on the horse.

"Dallas, can you talk to me?"

"Sure can," he said. "That Layne Harting must be some kind a lawyer, gettin' a fella *and* his truck out of jail like that."

Christine saw a slight grin spreading. "Yes," she said, "he seems very nice." And competent, she thought. He had Dallas out of jail and sent them on their way pretty quickly. She had told Layne about Mack's questions, told him that she had lied to the FBI.

He didn't seem alarmed. Said they had bigger problems. "If Mack or the cops approach you again," he told her, "tell them you want me present."

She had readily agreed. It was time to start agreeing on some things. And that's all she wanted from Dallas as well—some agreement on things.

"That Harting's smart, too," Dallas went on. "And available." He swiveled and looked at her. "Not too hard on the eyes, either. For the gals, I mean."

"Oh, Dallas," she said. "Not now. Not at a time like this. Please."

"Suit yourself," he said.

A minute later, Christine tried again. "You know what I mean. I want to talk about Sunday." She paused. "At Rudd's house—"

"That reminds me," he butted in, "I have to get a plan

together here. For that book." He looked at her, fully serious this time. "I mentioned it to Layne. Told him I'd take care of it now I'm out."

"We'll see," she said, "but that's tomorrow's news. Right now I'd like to talk about some yesterdays."

"Done's done, Chrissy," he said, almost sharply.

"Dallas! It's not that easy." Her exasperation mounted. "I got this ball rolling and it's also my problem—"

He stopped her with a look. "You didn't get a damn thing rolling, Christine. That Rudd was a big boy, fully responsible for his own actions. Same goes double for this old boy."

"But if I hadn't—"

"Hadn't scha-madn't. If none of us had been born, nothing ever would happen. You didn't do a damn thing." He stopped speaking, his features quickly softening under his hat brim. "Aw, hellfire, Chrissy, this buck just got out of a jail cell. It ain't how he wants to spend his first moments of freedom."

Christine nodded. The thought of Dallas in prison was more than she could handle. And she didn't want to be pushy; after all, Dallas was right, he had just been released and needed some—deserved—some time. She tried to keep that in mind, and yet she still had the need—more like a pressing compulsion—to talk to him, to make some sense out of that night.

"I'm sorry," she said, "I don't want to be difficult."

"You're anything but that," he said quietly, "and I do understand."

In the silence that ensued, she contemplated when would be a good time to talk.

As if sensing her thoughts, Dallas ambled back toward the horse. "Don't want her to cool down too much," he said over his shoulder, "she's still got some work to do." He swung himself up, standing in the stirrup, and she thought she noticed him wince a little as he settled onto the saddle, but he quickly began working the mare again, warming her back up and then putting her through some lead changes, stopping, starting, moving her through quarter pivots and rollbacks.

Christine watched how happy Dallas was in the saddle,

living perfectly in the moment. He would stop and correct the filly when she missed something by talking to her, reassuring her, then doing it over again. Here was a man just out of jail on a murder charge and he was acting as if this were just another day. Perhaps it was therapy for him, she thought, or perhaps he was just that rare individual who, if informed that he only had a month, would do the exact same thing tomorrow that he had done yesterday.

For the last ten years, Christine's own life had felt bogged down in a lot of second guessing, a long series of woulda's, coulda's and shoulda's. And that Greek chorus, those faceless voices whispering from the dark recesses of her mind, had been driving her crazy since yesterday when Layne told her about the cut throat. Damn it! That stark and singular image was haunting in a way that she couldn't escape. And it was fed by a vivid memory from years ago, an all-too-real apparition almost forgotten that welled up and kept replaying back to her.

She was about nine years old and spending part of her summer vacation with her family at Motoqua. One morning, while escaping her younger siblings by playing up in the loft of Dallas's hay barn, she heard her uncle and father talking outside in the back. She crept up and over the tight bales of hay, playing Indian scout, until she reached the rear of the barn. From there, almost twenty feet up, she had a clear view out through the hay door of the loft. She kept her head low as she spied on them.

Dallas and her father had a rope tied around the horns of a steer. The animal was snubbed tight against one of the support posts of the loading chute and couldn't move. Christine was lying down, right at eye level with the second story block and tackle fastened to the center beam of the barn's roof. She had seen them use it to hoist hay bales up into this loft. Dallas got some slipknots around the hind legs of the steer while her dad removed the slack and fastened the other end of the pulley system's rope to the rear bumper hitch of Dallas's truck.

She watched, unable to look away, as Dallas picked up a large knife and, without any formality, stuck it squarely into the side of the steer's neck, rotating the handle of the knife downward, leaning his full weight through the cut. The animal struggled briefly, gave one short bellow before the knife sliced through its wind, then dropped to its knees, and before Christine could even think of moving, even comprehend what was happening, her dad was driving the truck slowly forward. Dallas slipped the rope off the horns and the truck hauled the hind quarters and then the entire thousand pounds of beef into the air, head down, blood gushing onto the ground directly below her, creating a bright red river of nightmares.

She jerked herself back from the edge of the hay door and hid in the dark corner of the loft while they gutted and dressed out the animal. Sitting tight between two big bales, she shook and brooded. Before the steer, the sum of her exposure to death had been a couple of backyard ceremonies for deceased goldfish. There in the loft, she felt that maybe it had been wrong to spy on them, wondered if that had anything to do with the death of the animal.

The image of Dallas cutting the throat on that steer so quickly and efficiently kept recurring to her last night as she tossed and turned. She had tried to push it down, but it persisted and today had begun popping up at unexpected times: watching Dallas in court during the arraignment, on the drive back out to Motoqua, and finally, right here in plain view of that same hayloft .

She turned away from Dallas and his work with the horse, leaned against the fence, and stared directly at the barn. Now the old images of the steer were overlaid onto quirky new images of Rudd and his bloody throat. She could envision Dallas cutting the old man exactly the same way, through the side of his scrawny neck in one clean swipe, much easier than that steer. She even flashed on an image of Dallas putting a rope around Rudd's ankles and stringing him . . . She tried to stop herself. She looked at Dallas again, then down at the dogs, then up at the limestone rims, but she knew that it would be an ongoing struggle to stop this absurd theater running in her head.

Why had Dallas killed Rudd? Was it Rudd's rambling, hysterical threats that had pushed him? "You'll pay for this. You're going to prison for this." She should have stayed there, handled the situation with Dallas and not left him alone. But given the fact that she had been boosted over the fence and willingly fled the scene, what did she expect of her uncle? Rudd probably had continued with the threats, even pointed them toward Dallas. It wasn't that her uncle had a quick temper. He had enormous patience, at least with horses, but when he made a decision, he always seemed to quietly carry it out. And, as far as the logic behind cutting someone's throat, what the hell else did she think Dallas was going to do? Club the guy to death with some blunt object? Flail away with the knife, stabbing and mincing Rudd up like some hysterical woman or weak man might do? No! It all made sense, given who Dallas was. After he'd considered his options and his decision was firm, he would have handled it in one clean motion, simply put the old bastard out of his misery.

The filly was blowing hard now, but Christine continued to stare up at the crisp line described by the chalky white rims above them and at the enormous blue-bird sky. They were so different, earth and sky—the colors, the texture, the knowable and the unknowable—and yet they fit together so well. Christine desperately wanted to know how everything she was dealing with fit together. Guilt, for instance, a silly, stupid guilt that Dallas had evidently been carrying around for awhile, especially after he learned of Christine's cancer. Her mother as much as told her that Dallas blamed himself for not sending them away from Motoqua earlier, back in the fifties. He had confessed just how badly he had wanted the family to stay together, admitted that he had serious reservations about the atomic testing and its safety, but chose to remain quiet. She knew that hindsight made a pretty effective weapon for people to batter themselves with.

Her uncle was right. What was done was done and certainly unimportant in the scheme of things now. So why did she have such an overwhelming compulsion to ask this man who was loping a pretty horse around the arena to recount the gory details? She watched a powdery cloud of dust move back and forth across the corral.

Then, bright and out of nowhere, a moment of clarity surrounded her. What she really wanted was to be exonerated, to hear that it wasn't her fault, wanted to hear it again and again until she could believe it. That was it, wasn't it? That was at the bottom of all of this. She wanted to be absolved, to have Dallas bear the cross for both of them, and the very thought was so mean and bitter when it came to her that—

Her thoughts were interrupted as Dallas suddenly rode over to the gate and opened it without getting down from the horse. "Hey, girl, I'll take my next lemonade without lemons," he said as he went past her, the young filly lathered now. "Make mine Jack over ice. Back in twenty minutes." Then he reined the horse up the river bottom, just as he always did after a good training session, gave it a chance to stretch out, to run and do a little sightseeing—a reward for paying attention and working hard. Dallas's broad shoulders and back seemed to barely move as the filly broke into a swaying canter and loped up the gently winding trail.

Layne opened a Boar's Head Red and sunk into his desk chair. In the three days he'd been away from his office, the sludge had accumulated—a growing pile of mail, a new stack of case files set out each morning by Faye, requiring his attention. There were interrogatories to send and others to answer, two motions to compel, a complaint to file, et cetera, et cetera. A heap of pink message slips had been carefully arranged front and center, topped by a note from Faye in her loopy, schoolgirl handwriting: *Hey, big guy. If you call some of these people back, they just might quit calling me.* There was no signature, as usual, just a smiley face.

Layne cracked a humorless grin back at her note. Thanks, Mom. I thought I'd left home about twenty years ago. She had a point, of course. He had neglected returning calls since Monday morning when all this Parker business had hit the proverbial. He knew, however, the demands and expectations of clients. When people said "my lawyer," they meant it, literally.

He removed Faye's note and examined the first message. Anything to get his mind off the Parkers. Oh, hell. Cassandra Noakes. He wondered again if that was her real name. Too bad lawyers couldn't dispense prescription drugs as part of their profession, because people like Cassandra needed that screwy, magnetized edge taken off before their legal problems could even begin to be rationally addressed. There were six messages from her, all of them frantic. She'd been a very attractive lady in times gone by, before the sun and age and endless anxiety had leathered her face. A childless woman of four divorces and countless live-ins, she had set up her modest-but-mod desert home as a crystal palace. She made a portion of her living there by reading cards, tea leaves and palms, tinkling bells over clients' heads, and brewing who-knows-what potions for them to drink. Recently, a wealthy woman from L. A. had sought Cassandra out, become a "patient," and flown in regularly to be under the magic pink cliffs of Saraville and to have Cassandra chant and wave sagebrush over her prone body. After about a year, and with a fair amount of money exchanged, the client had become disenchanted with the future according to Cassandra and was suing her for malpractice. The woman's L. A. lawyer alleged, in rather hurtful language, that Cassandra wasn't really in touch with the future, the past or much of anything at all. Poor Cassandra. Now she was being held hostage to judicial blackmail and vengence, being threatened with a mountain of legal fees.

He mustered his energy and dialed the number. A voice as thin and wispy as high drifting clouds answered and told him that Cassandra had gone to Sedona for a few days of renewal.

"Be sure to tell her that I returned her call—her calls—if you would," he told the friend, the housesitter, the whatever she was, trying to make everything as brief and uncomplicated as possible, then hung up, feeling that he'd gotten a reprieve on that one.

He thumbed through the other messages and checked his watch. If he couldn't reach the other callers, then he could at least leave responses on answering machines and voice mail, explaining. Let people know that an emergency had come up, that he hadn't suddenly become neglectful or uncaring toward their respective dilemmas. He massaged the back of his neck and rotated his head, hearing little seltzer-like popping noises bubble up from his middle-aging vertebrae.

It had gone pretty smoothly getting the title work done, the documents drawn, the deed to Dallas's ranch escrowed into the court. Throughout, Layne had not been able to stop second-guessing Judge Andrews. The decision to grant Dallas bail had come from so far out in left field as to not even be in the same ballpark. Layne had compulsed about bail and the manuscript, how they might be related, until finally, when Dallas was out of jail, he had a chance to talk to him about it. They had a private conference standing at the tailgate of Dallas's truck. Christine was sitting in the passengers seat, waiting.

"I know," Dallas said. "Not to worry."

"What do you mean, you know?" Layne asked, his face full of bewilderment.

"That Sayles guy, he came to the jail yesterday, not long after you left." Dallas paused, "He's a cagey one, have to be careful around him."

"He knows about Rudd's book?" Layne said, alarm continuing to rise in his voice.

"Well, I didn't say that," Dallas said, seeing Christine watching them through the rear window of the truck. "One minute, we're on our way, Chrissy," he waved. Then quietly back to Layne, "Sayles asked a question, that's all. Asked if I knew anything about a book Rudd might be writing."

"Great," Layne exhaled. "That's just—"

"Hey, counselor, like I said. Not to worry. You did a great job springing me outa there." Dallas grinned broad and sincere.

"I wasn't really expecting to be back out when I asked for your help on this. But here I am. So I can take it from here. You and Chrissy both, wipe it out of your minds, forget you ever laid eyes—"

"No disrespect, Dallas," Layne said more sharply than intended, "but the only reason you're standing out here right now is because the FBI wants you standing out here. Bail had nothing to do with me. It's plain. You're their intended tour guide to something. And I think we both know what it is."

"I can do some guiding if they want," Dallas shrugged. "I got some routes they won't believe."

Arguing the point any further was futile. The old cowboy was incorrigible, upbeat, just happy as hell to be going home. There was no denying that he looked slightly gray and festering around the edges, but he was heading back to the ranch, back where he belonged, with Christine in tow to supply the chicken broth and tender mercies. Layne was sure that the open space and fresh air of Motoqua would provide, at least temporarily, whatever else Dallas needed.

Tempted to take Dallas at his word, Layne had come to a different decision on his drive back to Saraville. He would stay involved—Dallas wasn't calling all the shots—if for no other reason than to protect Dallas, who was acting far too fatalistic, from himself. And to make sure Christine was okay. He knew that the best way to uncomplicate this case was to immediately get rid of that damn manuscript. He was making that a top priority. Get it to the downwinders—that was Dallas's big brainstorm. Do it anonymously, under some form of privilege or confidential-source protection, in a dark parking lot. Whatever it takes, but he was giving Dallas this evening to relax, and then tomorrow that manuscript was job one. Slip it under someone's door and mail copies to the press. Once it was in the public domain, Layne, Christine, Dallas, they weren't important anymore. Once the press published it, everyone in America had a copy.

Layne leaned back in his comfortable leather chair, propped his boots up on the desk, and took another slug off his beer. He picked another message slip from the pile and grabbed his portable phone from its cradle. Any small act of settling back into his office and its knowable routines was balm to his troubled mind. He looked around his living-room-cum-office. Layne felt a wave of gratitude and beer pass through him and he appreciated anew this little world of his own making. There was nothing like someone else's troubles to make you relish your own.

His eyes halted on the blanket covering the back of his couch; it was backward, facing inside out. Faye must have been messing with it, but it wasn't like her to leave it that way. His eyes wandered upward. A couple of pictures were drooping slightly to one side. He put his feet back on the floor and set down the phone. It was strange—more a feeling than a visual observation, at first, but things were different. He turned toward his credenza and studied the bookshelf for a moment. The binders were canted and out of place, as if they had been examined and carelessly restocked. Faye wasn't one to leave anything sloppy. She was a master organizer, in fact, said you had to be if you had six kids and a lobotomized husband. He returned to his desk and opened the drawers. Same thing. He couldn't be positive, but was almost sure someone had been in there. He walked back to the bedroom. It was subtle, nothing tossed and strewn, but it was definite now. A feeling—cold, gray, and slimy, like the first time he ate raw oysters—overtook him. Then he was pissed off. What the hell was going on? And then apprehensive. Maybe someone was still here. He quickly covered every inch of the house and had found that he was alone by the time he opened the bedroom closet, which had definitely been gone through. Whoever had been here had finally lost patience, begun throwing things aside and onto the floor. A jacket, shoes. By now his breath was coming in short, choppy bursts.

He scanned the yard from the back window, then walked through the house to the front porch. The road was empty except for his Land Cruiser and Christine's car, which had been sitting right there since Monday morning. The sun was beginning to drop, angling through the big cottonwoods and their millions of shivery leaves. Suddenly, everything took on a surreal quality. He had viewed this same street thousands of times, standing on this very spot, but now it seemed vaguely threatening. Just outside the fence, a cat meowed and Layne felt himself jump.

He hurried down the front steps, his senses heightened. Christine's little Honda was smothered in dried dirt from all the trips to Motoqua and now the sharp, reflective sunlight made it doubly hard to see in through the windows. He noticed that the trunk was ajar, however, and opened easily with a lift from his finger. He spotted the marks where it had been popped, then rushed around to the driver's door, found it unlocked, and swung it open. Slowly, he bent and peered in. The seats had been slashed, one long gash in each, the white stuffing protruding.

He whistled under his breath. "Jesus." He slammed the car door and stood there in the road, turning and gazing in all directions, not sure what he was looking for or even confident that he would recognize it. He didn't have Christine's keys, couldn't easily move the car to a more discreet spot back by the barn. Across the street, a screen door slammed and he damn near jumped out of his skin. He was suddenly sweating, little rivulets running cold down his ribs. He tried to breathe deeply and slow the pace of his heart. Nothing threatening or unusual came into view.

He rummaged in the back of his own vehicle and pulled out a lug wrench. Acting confident and casual, he strolled around the side of the house and stopped in the backyard. Kids, letting out occasional squeals of terror and delight, jumped on the trampoline over in Faye's backyard. He gave them a quick wave. The neighbor next to Faye had three sheep and a fat steer, all heads down, contentedly grazing their way toward the freezer. His own mare and gelding raised their heads from the pasture grass in unison and began to amble toward the barn. That seemed like a good place to be right now and he moved through his back gate and out to the feed shed, peering in cautiously, tire iron still in hand. He bucketed some grain for the horses and scattered a little on the ground for the mad goose, who was at least smart enough not to harass him when he was passing out the goodies.

He hoisted himself up and sat on the sturdy top rail of the corral, giving himself a little better view. Everything quiet and normal as cherry pie.

Shit! They were way past dealing with Rudd's death now. That manuscript was evidently the object of someone's affection and was the only thing keeping this case alive beyond the local precinct. He couldn't imagine that the local cops had anything to do with this. They didn't rifle a lawyer's office around here. He was positive of that. His instincts, his fears of a much wider circle, were validated now. Somebody was hot on the trail of Rudd's book. Somebody besides Mack Sayles. That guy might get into a snoopy little illegal search, but a seat slasher? Layne couldn't imagine it. That was done to send a message, to let them know that people were getting impatient, that it was time to quit screwing around. But who? The CIA? The ATF? The Military Intelligence Whatever? These were all just movie names and acronyms to him, but he began imagining vans with listening devices in the headlights and mini-satellite dishes disguised as sideview mirrors. The possibilities started jumping toward him exponentially.

Then he stumbled on another reality. If they'd come to his house, done this to the measly lawyer, what might Dallas and Christine be in store for? He bounded back toward the schoolhouse, then slowed and cautiously entered the back room and looked under the bed and into every corner once again before sitting down at his desk. He dreaded the possibility that the phone at the ranch might go unanswered, all the conjuring he would get into on the long drive over.

"Christine?" he said with great relief. "Everything okay?"

"Yes." She paused. "Layne, is that you?"

"Yeah, sorry. I, um . . . is Dallas there?"

"No, you just missed him," she said. "He's out tending stock and irrigating."

He tried to settle on the best way to proceed. He didn't want to frighten her unnecessarily. "I need to talk to you two right away. But not on the phone. I'm going to drive out."

"What's wrong?" she said, her voice rising in alarm.

"Not on the phone," he said. "In fact, don't use the phone if you can help it. Especially not for anything, and I mean *anything*, related to this case. Okay?"

"Uh, sure," she said. "Are you alright?"

"I'm fine. Sit tight, it'll take me about an hour and a half."

Christine's "okay" was followed by a click, then dead air. So he was going to rush out to Motoqua and warn them to be careful. Then what? Then a firm direction, a plan. If the book was going to the Downwinders Coalition, then fine, it was going there carefully and quickly.

Layne gathered up a small suitcase full of clothes, locked his door, as if that really mattered anymore, and finally caught up with Faye over at Winnie the Shampoo.

Winnie Engle had run her beauty shop out of the split-level half-basement of her and Fred's brick rambler for several years now. The city council agreed that as long as applicants stayed within strict limits on the traffic created in residential areas, such cottage industries were a desirable tradition. He spotted Faye's car and parked right behind it, apologizing silently to Winnie for the unwanted congestion.

It was a small shop. Winnie was the only beautician. Faye's hair was in perm curlers and she was gabbing away with Suzie Lambert, the part-time manicurist, over some newly installed false fingernails. Winnie appeared a little panic stricken when Layne burst through the door like it was a raid, like she knew having an employee, even part-time, was pushing the rules. Suzie looked up from the last spot of red paint she was applying to ten long fingernails that dramatically lengthened Faye's pudgy hands.

"Sorry, Winnie," Layne said as the tinkle bell over the door bounced around on a loose spring and would not quit chiming. "I'm just chasing down Tonto here. Never can find my faithful companion when I really need her." He was doing his level best to contain his breathing—he should have walked from his car instead of jogging across the lawn—and not spread panic or beer fumes among these secular sisters bonded by funky religious underwear. Winnie nodded his way, her mouth full of bobby pins, and kept working on another customer.

"Hey, everybody, it's Layne Harting," Faye said cheerfully. "That missing person's report I filed this morning must have done some good."

The last thing he needed to worry about was the smell of beer. The room reeked of ammonia, hair spray, and peroxide. His eyes began to water.

"Howdy, Faye," he said, squinting. "You guys all come down here to get your sinuses cleared?" He sat on a small, backless stool with casters and glided in one move across the linoleum toward Faye and Suzie.

"Nope," Faye said. "We come here to talk about guys and get beautiful." She raised a hand and waggled five flashy red nails at him. "And you should hear the stuff I say about you. Whoa! We don't even need perm solution, curls the hair just thinking about your escapades."

"Be careful," he said, "I got a couple of things on you, too, lady."

"Pabulum by comparison," she said, admiring her nails. "Advise me, counselor." She draped a hand in his face, her nails just inches away. "The nail accents. On the index or pinky? Whada ya think? A star? Moon? Gold or silver?"

"What's the big occasion?" he asked, suddenly comforted that someone he knew right now was untroubled and normal. "What are you getting all duded up for?"

"Oh, big doin's," she said. "My high school reunion up in Cedar City. The big Twenty Year. We all get together to count kids and wrinkles."

"Wow, that is big," he widened his eyes. "Plenty of lime jello, I'll bet."

"Absolutely! You should come along as my guest. I hear you share a keen interest in those good old high school days." She gave him a wicked wink.

Layne admitted defeat. "Are you about finished here? I need two minutes."

"Hey, don't get sore and run off," Faye laughed. "Suzie, you warm up the sparkles and the glue, dear. I'll be right back."

Out on the front lawn, leaning against the etched wooden sign for Winnie the Shampoo, Layne tried to act casual when he asked Faye about two things.

"No, no," she said. "I didn't see anybody come or go from your office."

"Well, I was up and out early, didn't really have a chance to look around this morning," he said. "How about last night?"

"Nope," she said. "You got home, your lights went on at about ten. I'd say roughly 10:22."

"Roughly?" he said.

"You ain't got nothing, honey, if you ain't got snoopy neighbors. Remember the little blon—"

"I already got that one. Thanks."

"Want me to call the neighbors, then?"

"No," he said, "but let me know if you hear anything."

"Hmm, sounds serious. Something wrong?"

"No, no. It's probably just early Alzheimer's," he said, hoping that no one would notice Christine's slashed seats. Then he asked her about the Downwinders Coalition. Who headed it up? Who was the leading activist? Did she know any of the plaintiffs representing the class action he read so much about, that trial currently under way in Las Vegas?

"Yes, yes, and yes," she said, "one answer to all questions. Uwanda Docksteader. She's a lifer in the cause. Lives over in St. George. You can find her in the phone book because she's the only married woman in The George that ever kept her maiden name." Faye held up both hands in the early evening air, swishing her nails dry. "Only name you'll need. Second cousin of mine, I went to high school with her. Tell her to quit being such a dang stick-in-the-mud and come to our reunion this year."

"Yeah, sure, I'll try to get the message to her," Layne said. "If I don't make it back tonight, feed Limbo for me, will you?"

"Are you kiddin'? That dog's always begging at my back door. Why do you think he's so fat?"

"We should all die fat and happy," he said.

"So, why do you suddenly need a downwinder?" she asked.

Layne thought about the answer. "Oh, some other time."

Then she held both hands up, admiring the shiny new nails, and wiggled them in front of him. "So, tell me seriously, counselor, whadayathink? The stars or the moon?"

Ten cents. A dime. Just one little shiny coin that stood between pain and relief for Uwanda Docksteader's aching bladder. And she didn't have it. She had hunted through her wallet, found a few quarters, lots of pennies, and a couple of small safety pins that she used in emergencies when some weak seam in her clothes wouldn't hold or when one of her fatigued bra straps broke, but she couldn't locate a dime. She opened up her bulky leather purse, a slouchy shoulder bag with two inches of refuse collected at the bottom, and began to sort through it. Ballpoint pens, keys to she couldn't guess what, bronzing gel for her cheeks, more pennies, wispy tatters of Kleenex and long-forgotten notes to herself. But no dimes. She tossed her wallet back in and looked around for help, but there wasn't any.

The women's restroom at the Clark County Law Library in Las Vegas was deserted. It was almost 5:30 p.m., dinnertime for normal people, whoever they were. Now she wondered what her chances of finding a custodian were, someone with keys who could let her into one of these high-security lockup stalls. Criminy! She tried to always remember to carry some dimes for the stalls. Why was there a charge for using a toilet, anyway? It was pathetic, and Uwanda gave herself a pinch on the wrist as a reminder to write a letter to the County Commission and post it with Ms. O'Dell at the front circulation desk, but right now her bladder was talking straight at her in some kind of code that was pulsing right down through her tapping feet. Maybe she could go borrow a dime, but there really wasn't time for that. Childbirth and middle age had left her relatively whole but not unscathed, her plumbing now permanently torqued.

She bent down, checking out the condition of the floor, actually considered trying to slip her bulk under the door of the stall, when she heard the tinkle-jingle of her earrings. She straightened back up, went over to the mirror, and watched herself reach up and grasp one—costume jewelry, a showy affair that dangled almost down to her shoulder. Mock-Chinese coins strung on a tongue of low-carat silver. Uwanda plucked one of the coins, walked back to the nearest stall, placed the coin in the turn slot, and bingo, she pushed the door open and whirled around. The gleaming seat was cool. The air conditioning was marginal in the rest of the library, but for some reason it was on overdrive in here. The clean stall suddenly felt like a refuge.

It had not been a good day. Or a good week, or a good year for that matter. Lately she had been wondering if it was even a good life. Her family was awash in trouble and her downwinders, her beloved downwinders were on the verge of losing it all in their class-action suit. She knew it; everyone knew it. With less than high hopes, she had returned to Las Vegas this morning for another round of legal meetings .

Uwanda sat there longer than she had intended or needed to, getting her coin's worth. She sighed and gazed casually upward at the ceiling, the only real view corridor in a restroom stall, she supposed. Suddenly, and in spite of her troubles, she blurted out laughter.

Last fall, not long after Bridger Junior High had started, Uwanda was called into the office of one of the counselors, a Mr. Pierson, to discuss her son Owen's proclivities as a troublemaker. It seemed that he had demonstrated some brand-new prank entirely of his own devising—at least, in the memory and experience of Mr. Pierson—for a select group of boys from his fourth-period gym class. His fellow eighth graders had watched him drop his gym shorts, then climb onto the top of one of the bathroom stalls. With the showmanship that seemed to come naturally to Owen, he straddled the sides of the stall, bottom down, suspending himself directly over the middle, his hands and legs planted on either side. Spread-eagled, he took aim over the toilet, his buddies hooting and applauding as he yelled, "Geronimo," and demonstrated what would become forever known at Bridger Junior High as "the long drop."

Of course, Mr. Pierson, hidden behind a bushy graying mustache, didn't use that term. Rather, he mumbled something, which Uwanda, still with a blank look on her face, asked him to repeat.

"Defecated!" he said too loudly, looking and sounding completely exasperated.

Honestly, Uwanda didn't know what made her explode at that moment with a braying laugh—embarrassment, shock, Mr. Pierson's own humiliated countenance. And she couldn't seem to smother it, in spite of Mr. Pierson's smoldering glare.

"I'm sorry," she said, choking in earnest, "I'm really sorry, Mr. Pierson," then made the same dutiful apologies and promises regarding her son that this counselor must have heard from a thousand parents.

She had marched home and confronted Owen, having by then worked up just the right amount of parental indignation. At first he denied it, finally confessed, and then actually seemed proud that he had squarely hit his target. He was a headache and a handful, but even so, she loved that kid, loved his spirit of adventure and constant grin and generous heart.

The long drop. Jesus! Not only was it an all-too-vivid memory as she sat there on the toilet, but it suddenly loomed above her as a quirky metaphor for what the government was doing to them in this case. Stalling, using "Top Secret" as a means to sequester the damning documents that the plaintiffs really needed, lying and covering up under oath—taking a big, fat dump, again, right on downwinders' heads.

Uwanda got up and left the stall. She freshened herself at the sink and exited back out to the library. As she passed the front circulation desk, Ms. O'Dell stopped her.

"Uwanda, dear," she said. "I've located the catalogue numbers of the microfiche files for those newspaper articles you requested from 1963. The files are over at the main library, though."

"Oh, thanks so much," Uwanda said. "I didn't mean for you to go out of your way."

"Oh, my, it's no trouble. No trouble at all." She smiled and waved Uwanda off. "Our database is tied in to the central system and it's not exactly rush hour in here."

The entire law library was empty except for the two of them. Actually, Mr. Wolfkien was there as well, so that made three, but then Mr. Wolfkien was always there, almost part of the furniture. He was stationed at his same long table, his back against the far wall. As always, he was hunched over his big piles of books and articles and note pads and colored pens and markers, all carefully spread out, giving him the appearance of a tired, overage law student.

Uwanda was thankful he was located on the far side of the room since he usually smelled of body odor and herring. With his bald head and bushy eyebrows protruding over the tops of his black horn-rimmed glasses, he looked up now and nodded, tersely acknowledging their voices, more precisely the interruption they were creating.

Ms. O'Dell padded over to her desk and picked up an index card with the pertinent catalogue numbers written on it. A month and a half after having her bunions operated on, she was still wearing the blue, soft surgi-shoes prescribed for her. They were so comfortable, she had told Uwanda, that regular shoes were going to be hard to go back to. "How's the family, dear?"

"Fine, just fine," Uwanda lied. "And yours?"

"Fine, just fine as well."

She and Ms. O'Dell always inquired about family, always said "fine," and then often, toward closing time at ten o'clock, as if the hour loosened something pent up in each of them, they ended up confiding a bit. Ms. O'Dell lived with her mother but had wispy, nostalgic hopes of something different, had found her podiatrist quite gentle and charming. Uwanda, for her part, poured her heart out about her daughter, that female child she perhaps loved the most. Beautiful, dark-haired Shelby, a total mystery to her.

Uwanda took the index card and wandered back to her study carrel, not a full-size table like Mr. Wolfkien hogged, but enough. It was her own space where she could keep the books and periodicals that she needed. All of the librarians knew her and never hassled her, or Mr. Wolfkien for that matter, about keeping things in circulation.

She plopped down on her sturdy wooden chair. If the damn air conditioning was at its best in the bathroom, it was at its worst right here, on her side, the west part of the building. The sun was low and blasting against the windows right next to her, in spite of the closed blinds. She slipped off her cotton African wrap, the type of garment she frequently wore to break up the expanse of her wide shoulders and arms, and hung it on the back of the chair. Half-moons of sweat soaked under the arms of her aqua-colored dress. She picked up her notebook and fanned herself, but that seemed to produce only more waves of heat.

Maybe she should go back over and chat with Ms. O'Dell. Or return to the cool restroom. She knew she was in a funk, which only worsened the heat, but she couldn't help it.

Earlier this afternoon, there had been a meeting of the downwinders' ragtag legal team. Four of them sat around a table talking doom and gloom. There was Attencio, of course, and Ben Harper, a young lawyer who practiced in Las Vegas and acted as local counsel for their case. He had just opened his private office last year, after a two-year stint prosecuting drunks and barking dogs for the city attorney, but still had enough time on his hands to go along for the experience, for the privilege of learning from Attencio. His legal mind, in Uwanda's view, didn't add that much, but he allowed the team to operate out of his less-than-uptown law office in the Via Linda strip mall over on Carson Boulevard.

The tail end of the legal team had always been composed of various law students serving brief internships. The current intern, Carla Littlefeather, had come up from New Mexico last month and was scheduled to be with them for three more weeks, though Uwanda had no confidence in Carla's abilities.

As they sat there, Attencio, in his deep baritone, disclosed that the judge had convened a meeting in chambers with counsel early that morning. He had asked Attencio what remained of plaintiffs' case in chief. After some discussion, the government's lawyer—Uwanda's favored candidate for vampire of the year—indicated that she would move for a directed verdict and would like to begin briefing the issue. The judge agreed and indicated to Attencio that if the plaintiffs couldn't come up with stronger evidence on the key issue of intent, he would consider granting the government's motion.

"I'm sorry, folks," Attencio had said. They were spread forlornly around Ben Harper's secondhand conference table, their coffee cold, some uneaten Danishes drying out. "Even with Roman Tesset's testimony, I doubt that we would have enough going to surmount this particular judge's views on the 'hoary verities of sovereign immunity,' to quote a dear old associate of mine. And we must decide whether or not to vacate the subpoena for Roman Tesset. We can still call him as a hostile witness. At best, however, his testimony is circumstantial and thin."

Attencio was slouched in his chair with his head drooping and seemed to be studying the length of his long and slender frame. At such moments, he reminded Uwanda of a clean-shaven, almost swami-like version of Abraham Lincoln.

"It's a shame," he continued, "because we have proven all the other elements of our case to my relative satisfaction now. What we need, however, is one really strong piece of evidence on this key issue of intent."

He paused and looked over at Uwanda. She had gotten to know him well, had always been so impressed by the astounding energy of this man in his seventies, but today he appeared worn and disconsolate.

Attencio said, "Of course, we have proved that government officials failed to inform the public. That they put forth all kinds of statements, various forms of propaganda, for general consumption, all aimed at convincing citizens that the tests were completely safe. And, as you know, therein lies the problem. We have not been able to satisfy this judge that the people making those statements actually knew they were incorrect, that the statements were intentionally misleading at the time they made them. He is going to require proof rising to a level that clearly demonstrates bad faith. Suspicions, disagreements among the ranks, compunctions on the part of certain staffers, as we have shown, simply will not be enough. We must convince the judge, just as we are convinced, that the test site managers knew to some degree of scientific certainty they were injuring, possibly killing, segments of the population. And that they made a conscious decision, for whatever reason, to proceed with the tests."

He stretched and pulled himself upright in the chair. "Then, we might have a shot. And all of this is coming to a head when we rest our case, perhaps as early as next week."

Uwanda already knew everything that Joseph had said, but hearing it again, enumerated in such bare, rocky terms, sent her panic level soaring. It was one of those days when her whole life, everything that she'd ever worked for or done or identified with, seemed to be hanging in the balance.

"What about all the new documents," Uwanda said, "the ones they finally produced? How's the search going, Carla? Are you finding anything that might open up a new avenue for us?" Uwanda realized that her voice was tight, sounded shrill and uncontained. Carla was young, slight, soft-spoken. And completely terrified of Uwanda.

There was a pause. A ruffling of paper. An unattended telephone rang in the lobby.

"Carla?" Uwanda repeated. "How's it going?"

"Okay, I guess," came the weak reply.

"How about those newspaper articles from the sixties, Uwanda?" Ben Harper interjected, defending cute little Carla by deflection. Uwanda wished that he and Carla had just screwed, gotten it over with, and booted that strange, sexual tension out of this conference room once and for all. Carla made a big deal of being engaged, though, off-limits, which caused Ben Harper to sniff around her all the more.

Besides, this trial had been going on since January, and Ben was ready to have his office, his small practice, and his life back. Uwanda had read the signs for some time now: his abruptness, his lack of enthusiasm, his well-placed barbs. If it weren't for Attencio, Ben would have kicked them out long ago.

"I'll have the articles by morning," Uwanda said. "Then I'll come over and help Carla plow through the rest of the new documents."

"I have a deposition tomorrow," Ben said, "here in this conference room."

"Well, where do you suggest we go then?" she said, too sharply.

"Hey, that's not my problem, big U." He had called her that once before when he was really angry. "And you don't see my meter running on this case."

That little interchange had ended the meeting and sent Uwanda straight back to the law library. She couldn't bear to just go and sit in her cheap motel room with its cheesy floral bedspread and smelly carpet—the kind of place where a single deadbolt didn't feel right so she had taken to pushing the noisy mini-refrigerator in front of the door each night as well.

Now, planted here at her carrel where she had logged so many hours since this trial started, she began to wonder. Maybe she should have just gone back to the motel after all for that nap she craved. She took a Kleenex from her purse and blotted her damp forehead and behind her neck.

She glanced sideways, noticed that the top of Mr. Wolfkien's head was gleaming with sweat, too. His face was fervently buried in an open book. He was retired and spent every day here, at least since Uwanda had begun camping out here the same way. It was as if breaking the backs of enough law books, keeping them permanently open and spread before him, could somehow magically solve his problem.

Mr. Wolfkien's current problem—there was always some cause or problem in need of his attention—was with the State Department of Transportation and the proposed new beltway route. Uwanda personally thought Mr. Wolfkien was a little nuts, in a sympathetic sort of way, and she could barely understand him when he launched into one of his rants, forgetting his English and mixing in his native Hungarian. She definitely felt sorry for the little guy, felt sorry for all the little guys, but he had to quit torturing himself.

Then she recalled her own feelings about being the little guy and silently chastised herself. Legislation had been passed through the Congress a few years ago to "compensate" the downwinders without admitting responsibility. In Uwanda's opinion, it was a pure, unmitigated joke. The compensation amounts were insulting and the tests for who might qualify were more difficult than Olympic trials. Moreover, the fund was administered by some of the same agencies that had originally caused the damage. She considered it just another photo opportunity for Senator Hatch and other politicians.

A small family picture was taped to the side of her carrel, taken a few years ago when Shelby would still sit next to Uwanda for a picture. A few years ago. Why did they have to grow up? Why did they have to become something else? Something besides her children. Even in the midst of the law library, they were here with her, at her carrel among the long, shadowy row of books. They never asked anymore when she was coming home, when the trial would be over. Van asked, although not for himself. He was an adult, he said, and had his plumbing business and loved her and knew that what she was doing was important, but he wanted to know for them.

Faithful Van, never-wanting-to-cause-any-alarm Van. On her nightly calls home, he always tried to buffer the truth as best he could, but he was tired and stressed.

Well, yes, it was true. Owen had pierced his navel. No, it didn't look infected.

Yes, Shelby still preferred to communicate with him mostly by notes.

Actually, Uwanda had talked to Van this afternoon, after leaving the lawyers. Shelby had just arrived home from school, he said. She'd had a fight with Marsha, thought she'd be staying home tonight. In fact, he was going to buy pizza for the three of them, him and Owen and Shelby. It'd be nice to have them all together for dinner.

Then tentatively, like he was walking on ice cubes, "They miss you, honey. Me, too. When do you think this'll be over and you'll be home?"

Uwanda knew with hundred percent certainty that guilt was not just an emotion. It was a real, undeniable object that lodged at the bottom of her throat like a stuck chicken bone or sometimes rested sharp as a stiletto between her shoulder blades.

There in the library she picked up her notebook and fanned harder. The titles on the law books turned a little fuzzy. She laid her head down just for a moment, and as she did she saw the little snapshot of her family again.

She closed her eyes, drifted, and out of some deep, inky pool of memory, a different image of her children came to Uwanda. It was summer, years ago, before Van had even started his own business, before her children had taken their grow-up pills and started distancing themselves. Shelby and Owen were eight and five or thereabouts, and for all of June and July that year, Uwanda watched them in the backyard playing on their Slip 'N Slide, a long banana-colored piece of heavy vinyl that attached to the garden hose and became a wet, slippery playground. The kids would back up clear to the fence, get a long running start, and then hit the vinyl at full speed. Out of control, they'd surf or slide or tumble or cartwheel for twenty feet, their little hands waving riotously. Of course it ended, even before Labor Day, with Owen breaking his arm, not a horrible fracture, but an itchy cast for eight weeks, nonetheless.

Suddenly, she jerked her head up off the desk, bumped one of the oversized law volumes and sent it thudding to the floor. Her children, sliding uncontrollably, struggling to keep on their feet. Even now—especially now—that's what they were doing. And if Uwanda didn't get to them, wasn't there to help and guide and oversee and love and kiss and make it better, there would be worse casualties than that long-ago broken arm.

She stood up noisily, grabbed her purse, and draped her wrap over her arm. She was up and moving now, firmly on the go. She thought about asking Ms. O'Dell to use her phone, but the lobby pay phone offered more privacy. She was going to call Van and the kids, reassure them that Mom would be home in a couple of days and they were going to get everything back together again.

As she approached the heavy glass doors next to the circulation desk, she caught sight of Mr. Wolfkien again. He happened to look up at her simultaneously. She paused briefly and held his gaze and that was the moment when she knew that she was really bailing out of here. They could clear her carrel, put all her books back in the stacks where they belonged.

She strode into the lobby, picked up the receiver, and authoritatively punched in her credit card number.

"Hell-o." Van always said the word as if it had two distinct parts.

"Hi, honey. It's me," Uwanda said. "How are you?"

She thought Van said something, but couldn't grasp what it was because of some kind of static or thumping on the line in the background.

"Honey?" she said, slightly louder. "I guess we have a bad connection."

Van raised his voice, too. "No," he said. "It's okay. Go on."

"Honey, I'm coming home Saturday morning. This trial's about over, but even if it weren't, well, I've decided. I'll finish up this week at the trial and then it can go on without me." She paused, a little surprised that Van had no reaction. "I've left you and the kids too long. I know that. I'll make it up, though."

There was a short silence. For some reason, Uwanda sensed that Van had his mouthpiece covered momentarily.

"Great, sweetheart. That's really great." He sounded as if he was reading script cards. And that banging was back.

"Honey, what's going on?" she asked. The banging was louder. Uwanda was sure she heard Owen call, "Dad."

"Just a sec honey," Van said. "I'll be right with you."

Uwanda heard rattling and turbulence, like someone had turned on the garbage disposal.

When Van came back to the phone, he seemed slightly out of breath. "So, you're coming home?" he said.

"Yes. As soon as I can. Home to stay." The banging had not subsided. It was rhythmic, like a hammer, she decided. "Van, what's wrong?" she asked in a tone that was flat and serious.

Van let a couple of seconds go by. Then, in a weary flood that even the microfine wires of the telephone couldn't disguise, he said, "Shelby. She's in her room, nailing the door shut. She says she hates pizza and wants to die."

Minute by minute, he was getting more pissed off. Nonetheless, Manos kept moving, bruising his feet and a new pair of three hundred dollar snakeskin boots, over hump and gully, through the deepest part of night, around some desolate cactus junkyard called Motoqua. He'd parked almost a mile away from the Parker homestead and started out cross-country. Shortly, he had come to the back side of the rims and found the steeper ground hard to gain. Trudging up the hill, losing the light of the moon in shadow, he planted his boot heels sideways to gain purchase, but kept sliding back in the sand and slippery talus. He wasn't particularly winded—vanity, not health, kept him in shape—but his feet were killing him, all hot spots and blisters, and he was beginning to sweat through his shirt. He stopped, removed his sport jacket, tied it around his waist, and out of habit reached back to make sure the cool, arched handle of his snub nosed .38 was free.

Earlier, when he'd pulled on the snug cowboy boots and selected a loose-fitting sport coat to wear—his mistake, he was tracking a cowboy—he hadn't figured on a workout. If he'd wanted a damn sweat, he'd have gone to the gym. He'd have snapped on some tight spandex, a muscle shirt, and gone to pump iron and watch the showgirls whose jobs demanded that they look lean and sassy, with high, tight asses and long, flawless legs. Their names were all short and singsongy, chosen for some dreamed-up star quality: Chloe, Kip, Jenna, Stace. Manos caught them on either side of prime—new in town, dead broke, and struggling to break in, or getting a little older and fading out of the limelight. Either way, he specialized in girls who needed help and he traded that help for what they had to offer. Not that they were his only line of business. Manos was vertically integrated—drugs, burglary, sex, anything with low overhead and high profits—and he was always scouting for his next good deal. And from the desperate messages that Mr. Deputy Marshall R. C. Hiney was leaving on his mobile phone, Manos was getting the impression that this old dead guy's book might just be that next good deal. Regardless, he intended to follow its trail until he found out.

Manos finally struggled up the last of the talus slope and crested a small bluff where he hoped to gain a vantage point. He wasn't disappointed. There, under a bright three-quarter moon, was the Parker place—cabin, barn, corrals, the whole sorrowful thing dribbled across a rocky creek bottom. The cowboy's truck was parked out front and the lawyer's Land Cruiser stood in the towering cottonwood shadows. Manos sat down and took off his boots and socks. He was in no hurry. He wiggled his toes and aired his fiery feet.

Scanning up and down the narrow valley, he tried to hone in on anything unusual. Had they circled the wagons yet, posted a lookout? Probably not. They were just a bunch of hicks who had no clue about the kind of trouble ready to descend. Even if they were alert, they weren't equipped. Like most people, they didn't know how to deal with fear. Or pain. They turned inside out, became easy prey when that first bone-crunching bolt busted their nose. That was always Manos's edge, the ability to deal in pain. It was part of his currency, to be able to give it and take it, to use it, get pumped on it—unless, of course, it involved something like blisters or a hard day's work.

He sat, slowly rubbing his bare feet. The cabin below was

completely dark. Why in the hell would anyone live like that down there? He had no understanding, no theories about these people. Such a boring, low-octane life. Jesus! Watching the sun creep from east to west, watching the trees grow. He heard a horse stomp and blow down in the corral and minutes later some coyotes yipped off in the distance. What he was looking for, listening for, was a dog. All these hillbillies had dogs, right?

The acoustics off the cliffs lining the sides of the valley were so good that he thought he could hear someone snoring. Maybe not. An owl hooted gravely through the treetops. Manos waited and listened. Finally, he jerked his boots on and selected a loose chunk of sandstone about the size of a baseball. He wound up and lobbed it as hard as he could, wincing at the instant pain in his shoulder, thinking that perhaps he should have warmed up with a few tosses down the back side of the slope. The rock carried well, though, and kept dropping and dropping, cleared the creek bed and finally bounced in the dirt. Instantly, two dogs rushed forward off the porch and barked furiously near the area where the rock landed. He sat back down and rubbed his shoulder as urgent voices erupted from the cabin and then the shirtless old cowboy Parker stepped out into the moonlight with a rifle in hand. He looked to be barefoot from the mincing way he walked.

Lawyer boy Harting straggled out next. "What is it? Can you see anything?" he asked.

"Nothing yet," said Parker. Manos could hear them so clearly he might well have been sitting in a tree right above the house.

Finally babycakes, Parker's tasty little niece, stepped off the porch, pulling a robe closed around her. "What's wrong?"

Manos grinned. Kind of a jumpy bunch down there. Makes a guy wonder what they have to be afraid of, what they're hiding. He watched to see if anyone else came out of the house, but knew they wouldn't. He could hear the cowboy speaking, telling the dogs to settle down, telling the others that it was just the coyotes making the dogs jumpy, that everything was okay.

The old boy sent the other two back inside as he stepped

into his irrigating boots standing on the porch. He stayed outside with the dogs, doing a little tracking under the moon, trying to pick something out. He circled the entire cabin twice, looking at the ground. Manos had learned as a kid growing up in L.A. that people always looked straight ahead or down, but they rarely looked up, seldom checked out the tops of buildings. Just in case, Manos remained seated and still behind the rock ledge, careful not to silhouette his figure against the silvery night sky.

Parker came around the house again, apparently satisfied that something harmless had roused the dogs. He reassured them and went back inside. Everything was working perfectly. Manos would let them get back to sleep and then toss another rock. He'd let the dogs cry wolf one more time before the real wolf made his debut. He quietly passed the time with speculation about how much this dead scientist's book might be worth.

After he winged another rock less strenuously over the edge, the dogs rushed off the porch signaling a second false alarm. Manos took his time getting back down to his car. He wished he'd thought a little more about shoes and a little less about guns in preparing for tonight. His blisters were growing to the size of quarters.

He opened the trunk of the Jag and placed his small, holstered .38 back in a metal suitcase, then extracted a Heckler and Koch P7 in an oversized shoulder holster with two extra clips, just in case. He pulled out a new silencer from a small pocket on the holster and checked it. A meaningless precaution clear out here, perhaps, but sound carried. Maybe there were neighbors somewhere or campers nearby. Whatever. He wanted to take his time once he got into the cabin; didn't want any interruptions. His plan was to put down both dogs as he encountered them on the way in, then circle behind the cabin. Parker and his people would be slower in coming out the front, less cautious after hearing the barking for a third time. He'd get the drop on the cowboy and his old lever action rifle. He'd shout, FBI or police as he jumped them, giving them some hesitation about shooting back. And then it would all be over.

They'd be tied up in the cabin and he'd be having a good talk with them about this book. The local cops didn't know anything about it, he was convinced of that, but some well-placed people in Las Vegas did, and they were very, well, concerned. Deputy R. C. Hiney, in fact, was shitting all over himself. So, this book was in demand. By morning, he intended to find out just how much.

He selected a straight razor from another suitcase in the trunk, thumbed the catch and flipped it open. It flashed silver and emphatic in the moonlight. He snapped the razor shut and put it in his pocket. Manos himself wasn't all that fascinated by straight razors—he thought they were rather cliched, his exact word—but it was an effective tool; it got people's attention. He figured the old boy would crow like a rooster when he saw all that wickedness against his niece's throat. Or edging between her legs. Then Manos would pop the menfolk off and spend the rest of the night getting to know the lady. He had actually liked talking to her over at that B & B and again this morning in front of the courthouse. She was so straightforward and naive. He got a little stiff just thinking about it. He liked women who weren't afraid to show their fear, who begged like little girls not to be hurt. He'd find out everything there was to know about this book deal and have a little fun in the process. Besides, somebody had to pay for these damn blisters.

Manos closed the car trunk and headed off through the sagebrush toward the creek bed where the cottonwoods would shield the moonlight and the tall willows would serve as cover. He wanted to get close in and then use another rock to bring the dogs into view and within easy range. He moved carefully, a hundred feet at a time, and then stopped, straining for any sound or movement. He peered ahead, unable to see the cabin yet, but feeling sure of his position. He'd had a good overview from above and was able to recognize the terrain. He wasn't formally trained in stalking, had never been in the military or gone hunting as a kid, but anything predatory seemed to come naturally. He scanned the shadows, then closed in on the perimeter of the cabin, using static movements, concentrating his weight on one foot at a time. He stopped again and listened and waited to pick his spot. Once he found it, once he drew the dogs in, he would have to move fast.

Suddenly and without warning, he heard something in the brush directly ahead of him. He froze and pointed the gun toward the sound, but he didn't see the movement from his left side until it was too late. The dog sprung at him and he barely got his free arm up as it bit down solidly on his wrist, puncturing the skin and clamping hard against bone. Manos whirled, and yet the dog held on, fifty pounds of seething anger tearing away at him. He reflexively strained against the animal's weight, shoved the gun hard into its ribs, and pulled the trigger. There was a muffled pop, the dog exhaled a soft yelp and then went limp, releasing its grip and sliding to the ground. Almost within the same instant, Manos heard a low whistle. Spinning around, he saw the vague form of another dog retreating from its position in front of him.

That whistle had been extremely close by. Before Manos could analyze further, a blinding muzzle flash and a booming retort went off in front of him, and a bullet tore by his head, ripping noisily into the bark of a cottonwood tree.

"The next shot takes your goddamn head off," said a quietly angry voice in the close darkness. "Drop it. Who are you?"

Manos didn't believe in discussions in someone else's conference room. He dove sideways into the brush, scrambled to his feet, and took off running, cutting back and forth down the wash through the heavy brush, expecting the other dog to immediately be on him. He halted behind a cottonwood to protect his back and looked around. He strained for any sound that would give him a direction to shoot. Nothing. He began running again, quickly made it to the road and back to his car.

His wrist ached and blood soaked his sleeve where the dog had taken hold. His silk shirt was ruined and he needed stitches, probably even shots for all those shitty dog diseases. So it was going to be like this—more complicated, more interesting. That old man must have lain in wait, held the dogs back until Manos was close, put them on him, and then taken a shot at his head.

Mistake one: he had underestimated an adversary; but there would be no second mistake. That book must really be something. And now it all felt, well, it felt really fucking personal.

CHAPTER EIGHT

"I'M GOING TO RIDE OUT TO HOLE-IN-THE-ROCK," DALLAS said forcefully, standing in the living room of his cabin. "I'm going to get that book, take it to Vegas, and find that Docksteader woman. I want you two to head back over to Saraville and find a safe—"

"Oooh, no you don't!" It was Christine. She was on her feet and suddenly face to face with Dallas. "Not on your life, Dallas. No way. This is my problem too, and I'm in it all the way."

Layne listened and stayed out of it for the moment.

They had quietly buried Black Dog, Dallas's constant companion of ten years, out in the predawn at Motoqua. After the dog was killed, Dallas had tracked the assailant all the way out to the county gravel road, found where the car had been parked, seen where it had turned around and headed back east. He returned to the house and wordlessly began digging a grave. The moon dropped behind the horizon, but all three of them continued to work—Christine insisting on helping—spurning lanterns or flashlights, each taking a turn shoveling while the other two stood off, straining their ears in the darkness.

Rawley lay down next to Black Dog, his muzzle across the dead animal's back, and refused to move. After they buried the dog deep enough and put some rocks over the grave to keep the coyotes from digging into it, they returned to the cabin. Layne's nerves were frayed. It could have been him or one of them or all of them lying in a grave. Whoever was after this thing—the government or whatever they were—had some pretty strange methods, which he had no way of contextualizing.

"Chrissy, damn it," Dallas said. "Don't fight me on this—"

"I'll do more than fight—"

"Wait a minute, hold on there," Layne finally interrupted both of them. Then, with a labored sigh, he said, "Forget it, Dallas. You're never going to shake your niece off of this. Or me, for that matter." Layne tried to manage a look of conviction. "To do what you want, Dallas, we have to find this Uwanda Docksteader. To protect ourselves, we have to find one of the lawyers involved in the trial. We have to get them to accept the book under some kind of attorney-client privilege." They were both staring at him. "Besides, there's safety in numbers. And the judge agreed to include Las Vegas in your permitted travel area, due to your horse business. So as long as we don't go any farther, you won't be jumping bail."

Truthfully, Layne felt as if he had a half-dozen agendas pressing on him and all of them were important: friendship, professionalism, the sickening truths that the book could expose. And most importantly, keeping the three of them out of harm's way. The safest way to do that was to make the postal service their ally, to make copies and mail them all over the place. But Dallas was adamant. It was his book now and he wanted to be a part of this, wanted to put it directly into the hands of the people it would help the most. Given the complexities of dealing with the press and the pressures of time, Layne had quietly given in. Maybe it would be okay. They might be able to find Uwanda Docksteader this morning. Then get the thing into the hands of her lawyers and the court and the press too. They might be able to dump the damn thing by lunch. Then the dog-killing, seat-slashing sons-a-bitches could take it up with the federal judiciary.

Dallas saddled his best mountain horse. The corral was still dark, but black had turned to smoke in the east, signaling the impending dawn. He rode off alone toward hole-in-the-rock, saying that he could travel a lot faster that way, would be back in under an hour. He asked them to stay in the hayloft of the barn and keep the Winchester with them, and ordered Rawley to stay behind to stand guard. They did exactly that, each pretending to catch a little sleep after the hoofbeats faded up the trail.

Dallas returned quickly, surprisingly so, and they quietly packed and left for Las Vegas. It was still early, the sun not up. For all the calm and beauty surrounding the new morning desert, the mood in Layne's Land Cruiser was tense. Layne felt himself lapse into an austere, skeptical silence, broken only by fiddling with the heat vents and asking if everyone was warm enough. Christine tilted herself in the backseat so she could nervously watch for cars from behind. Dallas rode shotgun, literally, up front in the passenger seat, chin up and posture stiff, a holstered .22 pistol at his feet, the Winchester 30.06 loaded and upright between his knees.

They headed south, quietly rumbling over the dirt and gravel. Finally they hit the blacktop and coasted through a deserted edge of the Shivwits Indian Reservation. Crumbling adobe houses, overgrown grassy pastures, the dull light among the dead branches of old, splayed apple and peach trees: it all seemed more haunting than Layne had ever noticed before. When they finally picked up Interstate 15 with its steady stream of traffic, he immediately pinned it at seventy-five, the speed limit, and kept it there. He didn't really believe that anyone was following them at the moment, but he knew people would be looking for them. The book was in a battered leather briefcase stuffed behind the spare tire, where it rode like a hump on his back, a tangible weight that he was aware of each moment.

By half past eight, the shabby, misguided outskirts of Las Vegas began to appear. The first thing Layne realized was how thirsty the somber and dry mood on the drive had made him, and how much he craved a cup of coffee and, since he had completely forgotten about dinner last night, something to eat. He pulled off at the first freeway interchange and into a McDonald's. Egg McMuffin and watery piss-coffee and reconstituted orange juice never tasted so good. Dallas had never eaten an Egg McMuffin in his life. He turned it over and over in his big, gnarled hands and then inhaled it in two bites. Layne took his steaming refill of coffee and a load of quarters outside to the pay phone. Through the window, he could see Dallas, who had ordered two more McMuffins and was eating them more slowly now, sitting across the small table from Christine, the two huddled into themselves like refugees.

Someone had dropped a giant brown soft drink in the parking lot right next to the phone. The sun was well up and doing its Las Vegas thing, heating the brown fluid mixed with oil stains and grime and dirt into a congealing, gooey mass. Layne stood to the side of the phone, checked out the receiver for gunk, wiped the receiver on his shirt sleeve. He leaned around to dial, avoiding the goopy coating on the ground. In this fashion, and with the aid of information operators, he called Uwanda's motel again—"Hey, man, I already tol' you once, we ain't got phones in the rooms and we ain't no damn messenger service," click; the Federal Courthouse—"I'm sorry, sir, that trial does not resume session until nine a.m. tomorrow"; and Uwanda's husband, Van, whom he tracked down on a cell phone.

"Mr. Docksteader? Layne Harting. I talked to you yesterday afternoon? Looking for your wife?"

"Vulkenburg," Van said, breaking up in some static.

"Excuse me?" Layne said. "What, what was that?"

"She's Docksteader, I'm Vulkenburg. She keeps her maiden—"

"Oh, I'm sorry," Layne rushed to apologize. Then, trying not to be specific, Layne said how urgently he needed to find Uwanda. "Would you know any other numbers where I might reach her?" he finally asked.

"Talked to her last night, right after you called," Van said. "Told her you were looking for her."

"Oh, great," Layne said. "What did she say?"

"Well, she called again this morning. Said you could try her at the library. Or Ben Harper's office," Van said, the line crackling again.

"The library? Ben?" Layne tried to suppress his panic. It felt like he was getting somewhere, but might lose the connection, wouldn't get it back. "What library? Ben who?"

"Harper. Ben Harper, lawyer down there in Vegas," Van said, and then, "the library," as though it didn't occur to him that there might be more than one. "Sorry I don't have the numbers with me, I'm on a job. Can I leave her your number?"

Layne explained that he was just getting to Vegas, didn't have a phone number yet, would try these other places, might need to get back to him. "I really appreciate your time, Mr. Vulker . . . thanks a million."

He could see now that he had some serious phone time ahead of him, so the next order of business would be to round up the Parkers and get checked into a hotel where he'd have the comfortable use of a private telephone. They settled on the Oasis, a forty-year-old hotel sporting a recent and less-than-successful facelift in the cut-rate Middle Eastern motif. Four blocks off the Strip in a seedy industrial area that was a little less noisy and a lot less expensive, it was six stories high with a ground-floor bar and a restaurant featuring ZaZa the belly dancer undulating between dishes of lamb curry every Friday and Saturday night.

Layne signed them in under false names, surprised at how quick he was: Doewina Rollhauf, Buck Montana, and Harold Rivers. A combination of things—former clients, familiar places, and animal genders. He bought three rooms, paid in cash, then, as casually as possible, handed the brown briefcase containing the book over to the desk clerk, who promptly issued a receipt and deposited it in the hotel's old walk-in safe.

Safe—it was a word Layne had never considered much, but now, it was everything. There was no telling who they could trust, who was after this thing and them. He had to go forward carefully. He had to find this Docksteader woman or someone like her. To that end, he went up to his room and began making calls, flattening one ear then changing to the other, sitting on the edge of the bed and working the phone like a tumbled politician.

The human body was not made to dangle from a piece of rope, to spin and flip in a breathless pocket of air seven stories above the ground while a heartless crowd below vaguely oohed and aahed. At least that's what Layne thought, but then he wasn't in the most appreciative of moods, wasn't part of the vacation-minded ant farm that was milling excitedly through the main lobby and along the various balconies opening out onto the gigantic atrium of the famous La Carnival Hotel and Casino, one of the brand-new billion-dollar jobs pushing the Las Vegas Strip ever closer to Barstow. He was cranky and tired, and definitely not into trapeze artists. Nevertheless, he craned his head back and watched two glitter-laden men, billed as the Amazing Amario Brothers, prepare for their airborne finale. A drumroll resounded through the place and spotlights swirled high in the air. An invisible ringmaster wished them Godspeed in hushed tones over a gigantic sound system. Suddenly, the brothers swung toward each other, curling and crossing, twisting and somersaulting through space, then barely snagging hold of each other's trapeze bar just in time to avoid plummeting to a large safety net. The applause was scattered, muted by the clanging of slots, bodies shuffling about, and lush carpeting.

It was lunchtime on the mezzanine level here at La Carnival, where the show—the Amazing Amarios being just one of four daring noontime acts—almost never stopped. A loss-leading $4.95—preteens half price, preschoolers free—bought multiple trips through the All-U-Can-Eat Buffet along with a balcony view of the aerial show. Cheap meals brought in the families, then Mom and Dad parked the kids in the video arcade while they spun their dreams on the wheels of fortune. Judging from the spare-no-expense opulence of this place, the model seemed to be working.

Layne sat at a table next to the atrium railing along with Christine and Dallas. They had an unobstructed view of the whole scene. The family sitting next to them—four kids, all ages—seemed to be absorbing the food and the frantic energy of the place with vigor. By comparison, Layne thought, he and Christine and Dallas were virtual zombies.

"Well, that was special," Christine said as the Amarios took their bows.

Dallas looked up from his food dully, nodded concurrence while gazing out over the vast atrium. "Well, speaking of special," he said with the first spark of humor since last night, "nice scarf, lady."

Christine came to life. "Well, that hat," she proclaimed, "certainly has 'Dallas' written all over it." And it did. DALLAS COWBOYS. A brand-new blue and white baseball cap with a dead-level brim. "But you better work on the bill, shape it or something. My high school kids would laugh you right out of the place."

Dallas took the hat off, checked it, shrugged, and plopped it back on his head. Then all three of them looked at each other and smiled in spite of it all.

The new hats, scarf, and glasses had been Layne's idea, just to take down the edges, make somebody have to look twice to identify them. He said that Dallas in particular was too distinctive in his Stetson. That had drawn a grumbling objection, but Layne stopped anyway at the first big gift shop he saw as they were driving along the Strip toward lunch at La Carnival, chosen for its crowds and hoped-for anonymity. Layne had pulled into the parking lot and more or less pushed them into it. And he had been right: Dallas appeared clunky and different in the baseball hat, just another old geezer here in La La Land.

"A disguise?" Christine had said dazedly, standing in front of a small mirror, but she quickly got into it and spent the most time modeling hats and glasses. She finally selected a scarf of brightly colored polyester with pictures of the Eiffel Tower and Casino de Paris printed on it. She tied it snugly under her chin, then draped the two corners behind her neck. With her cheap new cat-eyed sunglasses, she looked like some wannabe forties starlet.

Layne halfheartedly tried on one of those gag headsets with an arrow going through his head. Examining himself in the mirror, he was startled by the crude metaphor: *What* was he doing? What kind of foreign object had pierced his brain, had put him out on the lam here in the dreaded time warp of Las Vegas, in possession of stolen documents and dodging who knows what kind of trouble? He finally settled on a pair of very dark, bug-eyed, wraparound sunglasses. He wasn't sure if they made him look different or simply like the fool he might actually be.

There was another drumroll from the hidden speakers at La Carnival and the jocular moment over their disguises passed, each of them lapsing back into silence. Initially, the buffet had smelled appetizing, but now a wave of lethargy overtook Layne. The knife and fork felt clumsy in his hands; his chicken and roast beef and potatoes and four kinds of salad might just as well have been crepe paper. Dallas and Christine didn't appear to be doing much better.

"Maybe you should try Uwanda Docksteader again," Christine finally offered. "Maybe she's gone back to her room for lunch." She had cut a slice of cantaloupe into several small pieces, then put her fork down without eating more than two bites. The next aerial act had just been introduced—a man, a woman, and four chimpanzees.

Layne checked his watch. "Let's give it another ten or fifteen minutes," he said. "Our last try was less than twenty minutes ago."

"Yeah, you're right," she said. "Besides, I wouldn't want you to miss this. Monkeys on wheels." One at a time, the costumed chimps jumped atop unicycles, chrome gleaming in the spotlights, and pedaled across a tightrope from one platform to another. With each successful run, a man and woman on opposing platforms raised their arms along with the chimps and garnered applause from the crowd below. A loud medley of Monkees songs played in the background.

"Doesn't do much for my appetite," Dallas said, head down, sawing through the gristle in a slice of undercooked pot roast.

Layne knew, they all knew, what was wrong with their appetites, and it had nothing to do with monkeys acting like people or people acting like monkeys.

The chimps finished their high-wire show and received hearty applause. "Okay. Guess I'll try phoning again," Layne told Dallas and Christine. They nodded; Christine wished him luck. It wasn't a receptionist's voice that greeted him this time at Harper's law office, but an irritable lawyer answering his own phone during the lunch hour.

"Ben Harper," he said.

"Mr. Harper. I'm from Utah, looking for Uwanda—"

"Wait," the voice cut him off. He could hear some mumbling in the background and then, "Please, you take this."

Layne's breath caught as he prepared to finally talk to Uwanda Docksteader. He had to handle this right, not scare her off, bring her into the circle, see if she could be trusted, and make her feel safe as well. Not all over the phone, of course not, but set up a meeting, quickly, close by.

But another male voice came on the line. "How may I help you?" it said.

Layne felt instantly deflated. "I was hoping to speak to Uwanda Docksteader," he said, the disappointment clinging to his voice.

"She's not here today, and she's not expected." The voice was low, magisterial, and now vaguely familiar. "She will be in federal court tomorrow morning, however. I can take a message. Or you could try her motel later."

"Sir," Layne began without understanding why he was being so deferential, "it is of the utmost importance that I speak to her." Layne found himself falling into the other man's rhythm and formal style, hoping to be taken seriously.

"As I said, she is not here today." There was no irritation or impatience creeping into his voice. "My name is Joseph Attencio. Perhaps I could be of some assistance?"

Layne immediately recognized the name and now the voice. He knew from the news accounts that Attencio represented the downwinders in this trial. Clear back when Layne was in law school, he had been aware of Attencio, who had been heavily involved in Washington politics but even then took on his share of hopeless cases. As time went on, Attencio became a singularly disenchanted voice that seemed to hover above, then disengage from, the clanging noise of Washington. Over the last fifteen years, what few glimpses Layne had caught of him in the media projected a deepening image of despair, a Quixote-like figure, lean and bony but still tireless, aged and ageless in his tilting.

"I'm pleased to meet you, or speak with you, Mr. Attencio. My name is La . . . well, Buck . . ."

"Excuse me," Attencio said, "Lowell Buck? I didn't quite—"

"Mr. Attencio," Layne rushed to save himself. "I'm an attorney myself. I know you by reputation and have a high regard for your work." Christ, what should he do now? Blurt it out? *Help me, help us.* We have this hot goddamn thing on our hands that you can use. It will blow those slimy suckers right out of court, *pow*, right to the moon.

But what if Attencio blew the whistle? He was an officer of the court, after all. An ex-congressman. He might patronize them, only to decide that the CIA need be summoned. And there was no doubt that he and his friends and relatives were all deeply imbedded, at least on some level, in the system. It was safer to deal with the plaintiffs first. Layne could feel the moment stretching thin.

"I, I must speak with Uwanda Docksteader."

"Well, as I said," the sonorous voice patiently restated, "she's not expected here today." There was a pause in which Layne recognized he was being extended the opportunity to leave his number or message or state his case. It passed. "And as I said, you will surely be able to speak with her at the Federal Courthouse when our trial reconvenes tomorrow morning."

Thick, spicy steam rose from the stainless steel pan and billowed around Mack Sayles's head, slightly burning the tender edges of his ears and causing him to momentarily lose his focus as he stood in the buffet line at La Carnival. He backed up a step, trying to avoid the heat off the fresh pan of chicken enchiladas. He wasn't really hungry, but he could always eat. Right now, in fact, it might be considered part of his job. He scooped a small mountain of enchilada casserole, smothered in a rubbery melted cheese, onto his plate, then absently spooned up sides of verde and rojo sauces as he craned his neck and gazed over the glass-topped buffet.

They made a sad, scattershot threesome this noon—Parker and his niece sitting over there on one side of a table, while across from them, their ever-vigilant lawyer seemed unable to get his coffee right, adding one packet of sugar, then a second, then more creamer and stirring discontentedly. The niece finally had removed her silly-looking sunglasses halfway through lunch, then reversed herself and put them back on. Parker's plate was full, though he seemed to be only dabbling with his fork. Mack shook his head. Whoa! That ball cap Parker was wearing and the gal's get up? One thing was certain. If their intent was to be incognito, well, it was more like incompetent.

Mack picked up a serving spoon and briefly examined the remains of a large pan of scalloped potatoes, dry and curled at the edges, strangely reminiscent of his wife's cooking during the first years of their marriage. He put the empty spoon back down and decided, instead, on the rice pilaf. If Parker and company were merely seeking a respite from their troubles, a break from the mean and unreliable world, he could have told them that the La Carnival noon buffet could not be counted on. Raucous laughter, children on the loose, people and animals risking it overhead. In fact, the place wasn't sitting at all well with him either. He had other places he'd rather be. Home, for instance, at his backyard pigeon loft, waiting for his race team to make it in from their final training toss. Today was Thursday and he was giving them one last tune-up before the big race.

Mack reluctantly passed up the spareribs—just too messy—

and settled on the ham. Saturday was it. The much anticipated Las Vegas Racing Pigeon Combine's annual five hundred mile race, the biggest of the year, winner take all. The entries were now closed and the prize money stood at $18,500. Not bad work for a bunch of pigeons. The birds, over five hundred top entries, would be driven all night up I-15 in the combine's specially outfitted truck and trailer, clear up past the Idaho border and then simultaneously released. They'd fly nonstop in a beeline right back to their home lofts, all the best ones making it by dusk, doing it in a day. Counting a couple of side bets, Mack stood to make almost twenty grand if one of his birds came in first, though he knew there was only one real contender from his loft: a yearling blue-check hen, band number 4260, who had won three low-stakes races last year as a young bird and now carried all of his hopes.

But the Parkers and their lawyer, by so unexpectedly driving down here to Vegas this morning, had disrupted his plans. He had known since yesterday that it was a possibility, their trip to Vegas. Why else would the lawyer, Harting, have included travel to this area in the judge's bail order? But Mack had no reason to believe they would come here this morning. In fact, he had intended to head for St. George bright and early this a.m., check on them at their rural outpost and see if his little helping hand in arranging bail, his little game of trolling the suspects, was producing any results. One of his motives for going, however, was so that he could stop on the freeway at the fifty-mile mark and drop his race team off. It was the perfect prerace training toss, but then, before he could even get the car loaded, he had discovered, through the wonders of modern technology, that Harting's vehicle was headed his way.

TL 14's. More commonly known as tadpoles. High-frequency homing devices with the round, fat, dark appearance of small amphibians. They were good for about a hundred and fifty mile radius. A couple of days ago, Mack had checked out a monitor and a couple of tadpoles from the equipment office, and though they were dinosaurs—Radio Shack-simple compared to the current technology—they were easy to use and often came in handy. He had attached one to the underside of the Harting vehicle during yesterday's arraignment, then gone over to the county impound yard and put one on Parker's truck, too.

After the judge had announced Parker's bail, Mack had hustled back to Vegas, to the downtown FBI office where he dropped off the hard drive from Rudd's computer, left it with Gordo, a techno-geek with slicked-back hair. "I know we're all up to our butts in work," Mack had said, "but see if you can't boot her up and get into the directory for me. I'll check back, see how it's going tomorrow." It was a long shot, a hunch based on one little Post-it note, but maybe there was something there. And if not, Mack wanted to know that, too. Call it intuition or indigestion or just having lots of experience with troubled people, but nothing still added up to nothing in this whole Parker drama.

Then he'd stopped by Ellen Grayfield's desk, given her the license-plate number from that black Jag he'd seen sporting around St. George, and asked her to run a check. "I owe you one," he told her.

"Yeah, you already owed me one and this makes two," and she promptly suckered him for two Junior League lottery tickets before he could get away. Twenty dollars for a chance at what? A weekend at Spa Dante. Jeez! How come he could never say no to Ellen's big, soft, schoolgirl face?

The buffet balcony was filling up faster now. Frantic fun hogs, boisterously attired, were arriving in droves, seeking cheap fuel and lots of it. A tiny woman with hunched shoulders and white hair so thinned that he could see down to her pink scalp began tailgating him in the buffet line. Mack helped himself to a sturdy, decent-looking cinnamon roll and snagged two pats of butter. Grandma inched closer, seemed to be breathing into the small of his back. Mack turned around and gave her a quick, false smile. Her plate was close to heaping. She slipped a strawberry off it and began nibbling.

He stepped aside and bowed slightly over his plate, gesturing in a sweeping motion with his free hand. "Miss," he said, because it usually flattered the old ones, "please. Be my guest."

She looked up at him through thick plastic lenses, her head bobbing on the front of her deformed little back, and peered like a small animal stranded on the bottom of its cage. Her black-and-gold name tag read: Wild West Tours. Ida Burns. New Jersey.

"Well," she said, some fruit stuck between her teeth, "only *two* hours to eat and gamble. Then it's back on that damn bus." She shuffled past him, immediately reencased in the ever-shrinking bubble of her own world, and began fishing with a ladle in a bright bowl of pickled herring. "And a *damn* long time since this one's been a Miss," she said to the dead fish.

Suddenly the whole busload seemed to be backed up right behind Mack, and after glancing down at the absurd amount of food already on his plate, he veered out of the line. Without getting too close to his threesome, he angled his way toward the balcony, looking for an open table. He couldn't see one any-where and suddenly had a contrary impulse, an urge to walk right over and join them. Just sit down and begin eating, then flat-out ask them what the hell was going on.

Give it up, he'd say, tell me exactly why you're down here. If he got any kind of a straight answer, anything that made sense, he'd go right to the office, fill out a report concluding "local jurisdiction only," case closed for the Feds, and file it. He had not come up with one thing to corroborate a vague rumor and equally vague sticky note, nothing firm about an illegal book. Hell, the guy could have been writing his genealogy, and crazy murders happen every day; that ain't a federal case.

By now, his racing team, if all was going well, should be . . . he glanced at his watch. It was almost 12:30. Mack had ended up having to impose on a friend and fellow fancier, Irv Henderson, to get his birds up the freeway, and release them exactly at noon. They should be roughly halfway home by now, which is where he should be too, awaiting their arrival, watching the sky for that first dark little spot to see exactly which one made it home first. Then it was extremely important to observe their condition. After all, the birds couldn't tell him how the flight had gone or how they felt. They had to depend completely on his powers of observation. And if he wasn't a professional observer, then what was he?

Surveillance. It was his area of expertise. He'd even bragged a couple of times to his wife, touting his "sixth sense," until she started calling him Old Eagle Eye and shut him up. Unlike the new agents in the bureau, Mack had honed his skills back in the J. Edgar days, back when they appreciated good gumshoe. Just watching people, interpreting their nuances, their movements, the way they used their hands or read a newspaper.

"Ladies," Mack said and nodded, standing next to the only empty chair from which he could still observe his trio. Two small tables had been pushed together, one of them empty and the other occupied by a couple of teenage girls. They wore cutoff Levi's and boobless halter tops that exposed pale, emaciated waists. Their hair was shiny and long except where it had been buzzed on top. They immediately began giggling. "I was wondering if you might share your table with me?"

There was a high, squeaky "Okay" from one of them and then more leaning into each other and giggling. Mack hoped it wouldn't last throughout the meal. He sat down, nodded at them again, and put a napkin in his lap. Just then, across the balcony, the lawyer Harting rose and, looking vaguely disturbed, wandered off like he was going to the bathroom. The other two, Parker and his niece, continued to sit there in the same opaque and deflated attitude.

Suddenly, both girls turned to him, were facing him with painfully rebellious complexions and exaggerated eyes. "Is it?" the girl on the other side of the table asked him.

Mack shook his head. "Sorry, sorry," he said. "I didn't get your question. Guess I'm daydreaming over here."

There was a slight tittering, like a sprinkling of salt, Mack thought.

"The sundae bar over there," the girl gestured with her head. "Is it free or do you have to pay extra?"

He glanced toward the area in question—two soft serve

machines lit by a revolving neon ice cream cone on top. "Oh. It's included, I suspect. Being that it's dessert, you'd think I'd know." He laughed and patted his stomach, but the girls had already turned their attention away, were quietly plotting which of them would stand up first, which of them would lead the way.

"You are so uncool," one said to the other.

"Try looking in a mirror."

"You're too fat for ice cream anyway."

Oh my God, Mack thought, the sheer gravity, the sheer torture of being trapped in a teenage body.

The girls excused themselves. Would he save their place? Of course he would. He picked up his fork in unison with a loud drumroll from the ceiling and began eating, trying to ignore the antics overhead for as long as he could, then finally looked up. Four damn monkeys were zipping through the air. If he was going to sit around and watch anything fly, he knew what it would be.

That little blue-check hen. She was in the air, should be home—he looked at his watch again—in fifteen minutes?

Mack shoved his plate aside. It was empty and he was not at all tempted to go back for more. Nothing happening over yonder. The lawyer hadn't come back yet and the other two were beginning to get antsy. At first, he thought they might be meeting someone else here, but he could tell by now that they were just hunkered down, having lunch, not looking out for him or anyone else. Unless the lawyer was off doing something by himself. Where the crap was he, anyway? Ah, give 'em enough rope . . .

"Oh, hello girls," he said. He'd totally forgotten about them. Now they were back, holding two of the biggest banana-nut sundaes he had ever seen.

They shrugged in unison. "The line was long," one said.

"My God, you'll each need hollow legs to—" Suddenly, Mack saw a looming figure standing right behind the girls, dwarfing them.

"Gooood afternooooon, little ladies," the person said in an unforgettable drawl. He was six-feet-six of slender cowboy wearing black smudged makeup to create just the shadow of a beard and thickened brows. His chaps were so new that Mack could smell the swarthy leather.

The two girls turned around, startled at first, protecting their ice cream, and then began laughing. "Oh, dude."

"No, Duke," Mack said.

"That's right," the cowboy nodded. "John Wayne, at your service."

"Gawd," the girls said in unison.

"Just wanted to invite you all downstairs. There's a great show in the main ballroom. World's biggest collection of John Wayne memorabilia. Got some discount coupons for you here." The cowboy dealt them three coupons, then tipped his ponderous hat. "See you later."

"Jesus," Mack muttered. And people thought pigeon fanciers were strange.

He casually glanced over in the direction of the three musketeers, but they were gone. Mack jumped up and moved quickly to where they had been seated, scanning the crowd, stopping the busser who was beginning to clear the table. A new group of gamers, loaded buffet trays in hand, stood nearby, looking like they were ready to fight him for the table. He hurriedly checked out the top. Nothing. An empty glass, a wadded napkin, a couple of gravylike spills.

Mack searched the crowd, walking toward the exits. Shit! He hustled downstairs, excusing himself, wending his way through the amoebic traffic, until he was standing in the vast parking lot. Nothing. Now he'd have to find them again, reel them back in through the trusty tadpole. He hoped that they'd soon make a move. The time spent following them this morning had certainly produced less than sparkling results. He liked giving his subjects plenty of rope. He didn't always like waiting for them to hit the end of it.

At the same moment that she opened her eyes, Christine heard a low-pitched, massive boom, a sound so deep and tangible that it seemed to pass through her body in a discernible wave. She lifted herself up onto one elbow in the heavy silence that followed and tried to make sense of the world, tried to put the sound into some rational context, but she'd been asleep, napping after that ridiculous lunch at La Carnival.

Slowly, she rolled off her elbow and dropped back on the bed, closed her eyes again, and let comfort and drowsiness and warmth ripple around her. This time the noise was shorter, less bass and rumble, with more of a vicious cracking at the end. She bolted upright. Jesus, what's going on? She threw the bedspread off and stood up, dizzy from the sudden movement. Were Dallas and Layne okay? A flash of blue light illuminated the room as she walked unsteadily to the window and peered out her sixth-story room at the Oasis Hotel. Outside, the deep gray of clouds and weather churned. She glanced at her watch. God, she'd been out for almost four hours. Wind lashed at the oleanders and bottlebrush trees and the tops of palms below her. Litter danced down the street and wicks of dust swirled up from the curbs and off a vacant lot next door. Another cluster of lightning shredded the middle distance of the horizon with thin, medieval fingers.

She pulled the curtains together, went to the bathroom and flipped on the light, yawning at herself in the mirror. Adjusting the knobs on the shower, she stepped into a wall of thick steam and soaked under the hard jets of water until her shoulders began to tingle from the needling spray and the grogginess fell away in layers. She threw on a clean pair of khaki hiking shorts and a T-shirt, combed her damp hair, then gave herself a little color with lipstick and blush. And, as she always did these days before finally walking away from any mirror, she cupped her hands beneath her bust and lightly shifted her bra into alignment.

Now that she was completely awake, that earlier edginess began creeping back. She opened the door and looked both ways down the hall. It was completely empty. She grabbed her sandals and closed the door behind her, moving hastily, then knocking quietly at room 632, Dallas's door.

"Yeah?"

"It's me, Uncle Dallas," she said.

The door opened and she was instantly assaulted by the smell of onions and garlic. "What?" she asked, sniffing. "You started the party without me?"

"Sorry, darlin', but I just couldn't wait," he said. "After that sorry attempt at lunch, I was feelin' a touch light." Christine noticed a film of perspiration on his forehead. "Room service chili, Middle Eastern style," he said, wiping his brow. "You know me, why just eat when you can set yourself on fire."

Christine smiled at his resilience. That was a lot of what made Dallas who he was. Take notes, she thought. There was plenty she could learn from him.

Even after the long nap, after being hunkered down here in the safety of these anonymous corridors, she still felt trapped in the same runaway dream, constantly on the verge of a panic attack. She leaned her back flat against the wall and breathed deeply from the abdomen, just the way she had been taught in the yoga/meditation classes she had taken to battle the mental and physical aspects of her cancer.

"You okay, girl?" Dallas said, peering over at her with fatherly concern. "Let me call down and order you a bowl. This stuff will take your mind off anything."

"No, no," she pushed away from the wall and straightened up, continuing the breathing exercise which seemed to be helping, "what I really need is a bottle of Xanax and several stiff drinks." She quickly smiled, giving him her brightest *I'm kidding* look. "Don't fret about me. I'm okay," she said.

Dallas pointed at the television set, its picture on but the volume low. "Got us a fight comin' on. Pedro Mendarez and somebody called Wailin' Tyrell Hawks. Mean looking middleweights, both of them." He looked down and must have seen that she was barefoot. "Headin' for a walk on the beach?" he asked.

She swung the sandals in her hand and shrugged. "Don't I wish. How about the next flight to Madagascar?"

"Not a bad idea," he said. "How's Layne? You talked with him?"

Christine shook her head. "I've been asleep all afternoon."

On television, the fighters were in their corners, awaiting the bell. They were frenzied, fisting their chests, hopping around, and acting like they were ready to kill each other. Dallas picked up the phone. "I'm going to give Layne a call, see what's going on."

In a few minutes, Layne arrived in Dallas's room. "How's everyone doing?" he asked. Naps, it seemed, had been the order of the day.

Layne filled them in on his latest round of phone calls. "Anyway, it looks like federal court tomorrow morning is our best bet," he said. "I think that's where we stand."

Dallas nodded slowly. Layne looked over at Christine, presumably for her acquiescence as well. Christine nodded. She certainly didn't have any better ideas. Sensing herself staring at him, she turned away, feeling embarrassed, though she didn't know exactly why. She gazed at the floor, at her own bare feet which suddenly seemed inexplicably unattractive to her. There was a time when she could have wiggled her toes and gone to the ball barefoot, but the mastectomy had removed more than her breast. It had excised some part of her physical confidence, something that she had yet to recover. She sat on the end of the bed and wordlessly put her sandals on. The leather straps only covered small portions of her feet, but she felt dressed.

"I was thinking about dropping down to the bar for a drink," Layne said. "Anybody want to ride shotgun?"

Dallas gestured to an empty beer bottle on the table. A second bottle, unopened and sweating, stood by. "I'm set. You guys go ahead. But be careful. Wear your sunglasses," he said without smiling.

Christine found herself weirdly on autopilot walking with Layne, down the long hall toward the elevators in awkward silence. It felt like a thousand empty steps between here and there. Maybe room service would have been a better idea, she thought.

They finally arrived at the elevators and Layne pressed the down button. A handwritten "Out of Service" sign had been posted on one of the doors. The corridors were airless and deserted, the vague scent of industrial-strength cleaner drifting from the carpet. Avoiding Layne's eyes, she riveted her own above the elevator door, watching the little lights that marked its China-boat progress downward. She glanced over and saw that he was gazing directly at her, his face mildly questioning, earnest and disarming. It struck her in that single moment just how much they had been through together and, more importantly, how much she trusted this man. Perhaps the stakes weren't the same for each of them when they had begun this journey on Monday, but now, four days into it, things had changed. They were joined in this now. She recalled those news reports of disaster victims, strangers hugging each other, and understood the quick bonds that trauma creates.

"How are you doing, anyway?" Layne finally said.

"I . . . ah . . . I . . . don't have a *damn* clue," she said.

Layne's hand came up and touched her shoulder. She reached out toward him and without warning he was standing closer, patting the back of her shoulder, the way one might comfort an old person or a baby. She allowed herself to lean into him slightly and realized how good it felt.

There was no warning, no ding, no whistle or bell. The elevator doors simply sprang open. Christine jumped in surprise. Inside, at the back of the elevator, stood a lone man in black warm-ups and black athletic shoes, his hands folded over his chest. His dark hair was short and he wore tinted aviator glasses that obscured his eyes.

The man stepped out of the elevator and said in a gush of words, "Oh, heavens, sorry, sorry. Didn't mean to startle you. These elevators are kinda dark." The man backed down the hallway a few steps, his hands still in front of him, still apologizing.

"Hey, not your fault," Layne said, smiling. "We're just tense tonight, going to the tables to make up our losses."

He guided Christine into the elevator and kept his eyes forward as he said, "Sounded more like a CPA than a CIA to me."

Christine snorted out a bolt of surprised laughter. Embarrassed, she giggled even harder. "Oh God, I'm sorry," she rushed to explain. "I've been so jumpy, so frazzled with . . ." Quickly, as if words had become insufficient, she grabbed hold of his arm, tugging downward on it and leaning into him, laughing, mocking herself, wide-eyed and horrified.

"I think I'm losing my damn mind," she said.

Layne laughed along with her all the way down to the lobby and when the door opened they were still laughing. A tired-looking bellhop, an older man with gray hair and a tattered uniform complete with shrunken pants that showed all of his white socks, stood in front of their elevator holding onto his cart loaded with suitcases. He gave them a glare of quiet disgust, as if he'd seen enough goofy vacationers for more than one lifetime.

Christine couldn't have cared less. She kept shaking her head and chuckling as they crossed the lobby to the bar. "Boy, *now* I think a drink is really in order."

"No argument from me," Layne said.

Ali's Den was a funky little bar with dim lights, oversize palms, maroon carpeting, and so many people packed in for a late happy hour that the interior seemed almost liquid.

A sign on an easel at the door said: WELCOME OKLA-HOMA STATE CORVETTE CLUB.

"Wow. I don't know," Christine said, peering in through a row of bushy palm fronds.

"Let's go down the street," Layne suggested. "Find a quiet corner in the Monkey Bar, it's only a couple of blocks."

Christine welcomed the idea. Just walk over to a bar, act normal, have a drink with this tall, handsome guy.

"Let's go," she said, leading the way out the front doors and into the turbulent air of the impending storm.

The hostess at the Monkey Bar had to be over six feet tall

with reddish-purple hair framing a long, horsey face rendered exotic by Maybeline. "Bronze Bomb Arrow," she said, seating them at a window table and sliding two menus onto it.

Christine looked up at her. "Excuse me?"

"That's who's playing later tonight, over in the other part of the bar," the hostess answered, motioning thataway with her head. "I'm supposed to tell you." She smiled, revealing a wealth of blocky white teeth. "It's called suggestive selling."

Suggestive selling. Christine liked the idea, the implied manipulation.

They each ordered a double margarita, rocks, no salt. As the server turned to leave, Christine said, "In fact, bring me two, first one's purely medicinal."

"Suits me," Layne nodded to the waitress. He glanced away, out the window at the traffic. The silvery-white beams of car headlights swept over the glass and lit his face in soft relief. He was angular and cool, a thin but sturdy nose, distinct cheek lines, a square chin made more sincere by a small cleft. His eyes were pale, washed out in this light, but the lashes, appearing long and almost feathery, made him seem boyish and vulnerable. Christine eventually turned and looked out the window, pretending to watch the cars as well.

Since the elevator ride a few minutes ago, she could feel her tension beginning to ease, to release its vicelike grip and dissipate through laughter and swearing and acting a little silly. And she could feel something different, something promised. Everything between them since they had met on Monday morning in his office had been riddled, utterly dripping with self-consciousness. And she was thoroughly bored with it. She was dying for a normal, friendly chat. A harmless flirtation. Whatever. Anything but all that other stuff.

The server brought their drinks and Christine finished her first margarita more quickly than she should have, but she was thirsty for the greenish liquid courage, cold and sweetly sour, the perfect remedy for strange twilight and nerves. She pushed her empty glass toward the center of the table and leaned back. "That's better," she said.

It was strange. She really felt that she knew who this guy

was at his core, but almost everything else about him—his daily life, his family, his habits—was a complete blank. She'd learned that he was divorced and building a different version of his life in southern Utah, but those things just barely skimmed the surface. On the other hand, he probably knew even less about her.

"I'd like to apologize," she said. "I've been a real pain in the posterior much of the time since we met."

"Understandable, with all you've been going through."

"Tell me something about yourself," she said firmly, as if giving an assignment in class. "Something that has nothing to do with murder or atomic bombs.

"Humm," he thought for a moment. "How about turning forty, no kids, one ex-wife, the Turk, a lawyer up in Salt Lake."

"The Turk?"

"Just a little term of, oh, I don't mean to be snitty." He sipped on his second drink. "Just another young lawyer. Still has the energy to take herself way too seriously."

"She sounds pretty aggressive," Christine said, immediately regretting it as presuming too much intimacy. And regretting anything cast her straight back, against her will, to recent regrets, such as someone prowling in the dark at the ranch last night. Mack Sayles came to mind and she dismissed it quickly. He didn't strike her as a prowler. Or a dog killer.

"Earth to Christine." It was Layne who no doubt had noticed the sea change in her face. "I thought we were taking a time out from all that," he said, giving her that little half-smile again, revealing a row of white, but not perfectly straight, teeth.

"Right," she said, drumming up a smile in return, "unless somebody comes through that door over there waving an Uzi, it's time out on trouble."

"Here, here," he said, raising his wading-pool-size margarita glass. "Tell me something about yourself. Time to turn the tables."

Christine clinked glasses with him and took a healthy swig of margarita number two. She thought about it only briefly, breathed deeply, and told him her story in just two long breaths.

"I married my boyfriend, a rock star, the day I turned eighteen. I was pregnant by the time I was nineteen and then, tragically, eight years and four kids later, he was killed in a small plane crash while rushing home in a blinding snowstorm to be at the birth of Jovi, our fourth child."

Christine lifted her glass and finished the drink.

Layne chuckled softly. "That's some story."

Christine could feel the booze punching through her veins and pointed at their empty glasses when the server appeared. "Sprinkle the infield, girlfriend." She looked at Layne and lowered her voice in mock villainy, "I'm just as capable of interesting fictions as the next guy. After all, I do teach Shakespeare."

"I'll not doubt you again, fair lady," he said, lifting his eyebrows and grinning. "That was good."

She could tell that he was happy to sit and shoot the breeze about nothing, if only for awhile. And that smile! It was getting to her. She had noticed it a couple of nights ago at the B & B, and now she had to admit it could easily lead to a lady's undoing. Then some part of her stepped back for a moment. Jesus! Keep your damn head on straight, Christine!

"I'll bet you're a hit with your students."

"Sure. Until grades come out. Some of my story was true," she said, waving a hand through the air as though she were pushing the falsehoods to the side. "My ex, T. C., was a musician alright, a broken-down sax player. We met after college, forgot to have kids, and he forgot to die in a plane—" She stopped and shook her head.

"Hey," he cut in, "I think we can stipulate that neither of us wishes our ex-spouse would go down in a plane." Then hesitating, "However, a little nonfatal fire? Something merely disfiguring?" he said, eyes narrowing, twirling a mock mustache.

She laughed.

Then he took her completely by surprise. "What since then? You seeing anyone now?" he asked, seeming awkward, glancing away.

The server dropped two more drinks off at the table. "Don't forget," she said, turning to leave.

They stared at her and said, almost in unison, "Forget what?"

"Bronze Bomb Arrow."

"Oh, right," Christine said. "More suggestive selling."

"Uh huh. You already heard. Cool," and then the server was gone.

The first raindrop, a big fat one, hit the window next to her, followed by another and another. She exchanged glances with Layne.

"Want to try to beat it?" he asked.

Hell no, she thought. I want to answer your question. Ask it again: Am I seeing anyone?

Christine reached for the drink, then pushed it aside. Slow down, she told herself.

"This sucker is about to hit, real good," said Layne.

And then she knew that the moment had passed.

"Come on. Let's go," she said. "You don't know who you're looking at. Girls' track team, Arcadia High School, 1970, '71. The hundred yard dash, the 220, the girls relay. That was me."

"Well, alright. If you say so." He signaled the server for the bill, and by the time they reached the front door, the storm had arrived in earnest.

Rain can be to the desert what a newborn albino alligator is to the zoo—a total, unexpected mystery; something that people can't help pressing their noses against the glass to ooh and ah at. Las Vegas is dry, alkaline dry, but every once in a while it snags a real thunder-boomer. The clouds burst and rain fills the dry, reptilian city, flooding the streets and bringing traffic to a crawl.

Layne and Christine stood at the glass-fronted entrance to the Monkey Bar and gazed out at the free-for-all. Water monsooned downward and was quickly a foot deep in the gutters and almost half that right over the streets. Heavy spray fanned off the wheels of cars. Those pedestrians with umbrellas tried to navigate against the wind, while most held newspapers and plastic shopping bags over their heads for protection. At the hotel across the street, a crew of valets and bellhops, suited up like maroon-and-black drum majors, scurried under the covered entryway, trying to attend to the sudden onslaught of customers. A line of taxis jockeyed for position along the hotel's circular front drive, honking their horns and flashing their lights to let everyone know they were available.

"Maybe it's not such a good idea," Layne said, perching on his toes to watch the action over the top of the crowd gathered at the doors.

Christine was feeling her liquor, but there was something else at play. Her welcome mat was out for a small, manageable challenge, something to feel good about alongside all the rest. "No problem," she said. "Dallas may think I'm sugar, but I don't melt." She grinned at Layne. "Try to keep up."

Then they were outside, running as the water hit them. By now, most pedestrians had the sense to find shelter, so Layne and Christine had the sidewalk to themselves. They splashed their way down to the corner, dodging a trash can tipped and rolling in the wind, ducking an awning that was seriously bowed and ready to break. Layne had offered his hand when they started out and she still had a firm grip on it, matching him stride for stride. Finally, they turned off the main drag and headed down the side street toward their hotel.

They were completely soaked, but perhaps because of the running, Christine wasn't cold. In fact, she felt exhilarated, glowing somewhere inside. After resisting the initial blasts of water, she had straightened her shoulders, raised her head, and felt the strong, rhythmic movement, splashing water with every step. The running, the rain, it all felt like release.

They finally ducked into the lobby of the Oasis. Much of the Corvette Club had left the bar to watch the storm and now greeted them with drunken cheers and hoots. Christine squeegeed the water out of her hair and then quickly crossed her arms to make sure that their wet sprint hadn't unsettled her bra. This was just the kind of crowd that would get a kick out of Tits Akimbo. Not to worry. Her fifty-dollar brassiere had done its job and everything was in line.

Layne followed her onto the waiting elevator and up to the

sixth floor. Without much thought and even less memory, with some internal guidance system handling the course, Christine wordlessly opened the door to her room. Both of them entered and then the door swung closed. She didn't bother to go for the towels. She simply turned around and there he was.

They came together easily and predictably, one move leading to the next, their bodies touching, arms entwining, face to face and then kissing. Deep kissing. She didn't know how it happened, nor did she care. It was like the only car accident she'd ever been in. She was seventeen, driving her father's green Caprice, and the next thing she knew the front of the car accordioned toward her and the shattered glass of the windshield, some of it as fine as sugar, sprinkled her lap, her hair, filling the cuffs of her jeans.

Christine was breathing heavily and she could feel water dripping off their bodies, soaking the carpet; thought that steam was beginning to rise off their heads and shoulders here in the dark. She moaned, a soft, odd sound that seemed to start around her knees and work its way up. Christ, it had been *so* long.

Now she felt her need and more, her pent-up attraction to Layne. It was instantaneous and growing, as if for a moment her world had been released from gravity, from cause and effect and logic. Layne was making small noises and breathing against her open mouth. They toppled sideways onto her bed and he pressed his body against hers, his leg, his thigh coming up between her own. The fulcrum, the point of no return, was approaching fast, and she had not one corpuscle of toughness organized around this exact situation yet. How was it supposed to play out? Didn't she need to talk about this? Prepare him for what lay beneath her wet shirt and expensive bra? Or maybe it was she who needed more preparation, more time to think. Other than the doctors in the hospital, no male had seen her this way—that scarred declivity alongside her normal right breast—and whatever else happened, she simply could not bare to face her own chest here in the dark with this man tonight. She dreaded it beyond words. What if he registered surprise or hesitation or, worse, if he was repulsed . . . if his body language gave even the slightest hint?

His hands were at her waist, inside her shirt, had found bare skin and crept to the bottom of her ribs. His warm, wonderful hands.

"Please, no. I'm, I'm sorry." Christine pulled away and sat up, swinging her feet off the bed. It took a monumental effort. "This is just too fast for me," she said softly. "I'm sorry."

He dragged himself up slowly and sat beside her, their breaths slowing and softening now, his arm lightly around her shoulder, his lips on her cheek and her ear, whispering to her, "It's alright. Don't worry. There's plenty of time."

Mack Sayles didn't often think about windows. Tonight, however, sitting in the glassed-in cubicle that he called his "orifice," watching water pattern down the thick, tinted glass, he wished he could throw the windows open, lean back, and smell the elegance of desert rain, let his lungs feast on nitrogen-enriched air while this cloudburst spilled its guts over Las Vegas. Most people-files housing office workers didn't afford such human luxuries, and this faceless, nameless office building occupied by the local branch of the FBI was no exception.

He glanced at his watch, 8:45, and closed the manila folder lying on his desk. A neatly typed blue tab on the file read "Daniel Benito Briggs, aka Manos." Maybe he should stroll down and check one more time to see if Gordo, the sleek geek of Brooklyn, was any closer to copying the data off Dr. Franklin T. Rudd's banged-up hard drive. Mack felt tired and a little depressed, but hauled himself up anyway. The other offices were dark as he walked slowly down the broad corridor toward Gordo's office and what passed for their local crime lab.

The real lab was in Washington, D. C., of course, but he couldn't really justify sending the hard drive there. D. C. was

backlogged into next year and they now required lengthy prioritization forms from the local supervisors to jump the line on
anything. What could he possibly say? He'd found a suspicious
Post-it note? He wasn't sure yet what the computer might show,
but the file on this Manos guy had certainly set off his alarms.
Nothing he could prove, but scum like that didn't hang around
St. George or keep seeking out Christine Parker without a
damn good reason. Unfortunately, the prioritization forms
didn't have a box to mark for gut feeling or gumshoe intuition.

Mack poked his head into the lab. It was open and well lit.
Gordo was perched on a stool at an island workstation, head
down, staring into Rudd's computer drive through specialized
heavy black-framed magnifying lenses fixed to his head like a
welder's hood. The lenses were illuminated around the edges.
He was surrounded by computers, wires, tools, meters, spare
parts, and a splayed pizza box containing several pieces of dis-
carded crust and one uneaten triangle. The room smelled of
anchovies. Now Mack really wished there was a window he
could open; he hated anchovies. He and his wife, when they
were young, had visited Virginia Beach for a long weekend,
awakened late on a Sunday morning famished with only half a
tank of gas left to get home and two dollars in change between
them. They had just enough money for a pizza and ordered the
Beach Supreme Combo down on the boardwalk. Two western
kids in the fifties who had never even heard of anchovies, who
couldn't gag that pizza down even *after* picking off the slimy
little bastards. Mack had ended up tossing the whole thing to a
rough-looking bunch of seagulls.

"Hi, Mr. Mack," Gordo said, looking up at him through the
big back-lit magnifiers. He wore them when examining little
things like carpet fibers from a rapist's knees, bloodstains or the
circuit boards from a dead man's computer.

"Hey, Gordo," Mack waved. "How's it going down there in
digit-land? Any progress?"

Gordo rolled his eyes, knowing full well the effect. Each eye
appeared three inches in diameter, moist and diaphanous
globes, exotic twin aquarium dwellers sporting hot, red veins.

"You know what they say about a watched pot, Mack."

"Not true, Gordo." Mack pulled up a stool across the work-bench from the technician, parked a cheek on it, and concentrated on anything but anchovies. "I've tried it and it boils every damn time. Just takes patience."

Gordo shook his head and looked back down at his work. "Oh yeah, forgot who I was talking to."

"Well, the hell," Mack mumbled. "Don't take my word on it. You're the scientist." Mack realized he wasn't making any sense and straightened up on the stool. He toyed with a cold Bunsen burner on his side of the workbench. It was the first time he had played with a Bunsen burner since eleventh grade, back in his one mandatory chemistry class when he, along with ninety-five percent of the students, had decided that atoms and molecules and saturated solutions were well beyond his ken. He watched Gordo work, probing at this circuit and that, glancing at a gauge each time to see if the needle jumped. That was Mack's trouble tonight; something about this case was beginning to make his needle jump.

This Manos character was just the latest example of things that didn't feel right, were in the wrong place at the wrong time. Ellen Grayfield had left a message for him late this afternoon saying she had the rundown on the owner of the black Jaguar. It was quite a rap sheet, the message said; she'd leave the file on his desk. He'd had to go to his Thursday evening racing pigeon combine's meeting at six, register his birds, and pick up the special time clock settings that would stamp the exact time each bird arrived home on race day. All the combine members were buzzing around the little meeting hall, pumped up for this weekend, the biggest race of the year. Twenty grand had everyone's attention, and Mack knew he definitely had a good shot, better than most, at winning it. He was already halfway to spending the money, torn between a used sailboat or a new racing loft when they got down to San Diego. So the absolute last thing he wanted right now was to be distracted by any new developments in this case. What he really wanted to do was close the file on Dr. Rudd, tell his boss that it was just another homicide, that the local authorities had their man and were headed to trial.

But his conscience and curiosity had gotten the better of him, and he had swung by the office on his way home from the combine meeting. On its face, nothing about this Manos character tied into the Parkers or Franklin Rudd. With a rap sheet this long, the only surprise was that the guy had only one alias. So why would a sleaze like that be cruising the streets of St. George? Why had he sought out Parker's niece, not once, but on two separate occasions in two completely different locations? What was the tie-in—why was he circling around her? Mack had run a check on Christine Parker two days ago; she'd never had so much as a bad report card. And, perhaps most importantly from where he was sitting, why should the Feds give a shit about any of it?

Gordo stopped and scribbled numbers on a pad, then began probing again. "Gettin' there," he said, without looking up.

Was it really possible that the answer to all these questions lay hidden in this partially fried and battered maze of circuitry? Probably not. And if this dead-ended, if nothing new cropped up by tomorrow afternoon, Mack resolved even more firmly to close the case. Hell with it, then he'd be free to kick back on Saturday and wait for his birds to come home.

"Go home, Mack," Gordo said. "I'll buzz you if . . . when I get a readable copy off this thing. It's just a matter of time. It got fried in a few spots when your boy popped the tube and winged it onto the floor. Actually, I could've had it by now, but I was busy all day with that little counterfeit matter."

"You go home, too, Gordo," Mack sighed, feeling a little guilty. "I'm just casting the net here; this isn't a top priority."

"I'm just fine, Mack." Gordo kept his head down. "I can work on this. Or I can go home and keep trying to break into the Federal Reserve. At least this keeps me out of trouble." Gordo squinted and worked a probe in deeper. "What you hope to find here, anyway?"

"Wish I knew. Probably nothing on there but some genealogy charts and the guy's Will Maker. Probably sat around and updated his will every day, depending on which relative called or visited. Background check shows that under the glossy surface, our man Rudd was something of a weirdo." Mack stretched and craned his neck to see what Gordo found so intriguing. "But this is probably my last gig before retirement," he continued. "Guess I should be thorough. Wouldn't want to screw up on my last case, now, would I?"

"That's some kinda heavy shit, man," Gordo muttered.

Mack knew his shit wasn't really that heavy these days. Quite the contrary. But, what there was of it, he liked in tidy piles, neatly organized with no loose ends.

"Well, I'll get it," Gordo said. "No original science here, just trial and error." Gordo glanced up from behind the magnifiers, widened his eyes and then crossed them directly at Mack. "*Go home!* You're making me nervous."

Mack wandered back down to his office, feeling out of sorts. He scribbled a note to Ellen Grayfield, paper clipped it to the Manos file, and dropped it on her desk on the way out.

Ellen, I'm going to visit this guy's probation officer first thing in the morning. Have one of the runners figure out where this character lives, works, plays, etc. Credit cards or cash. Who fixes his car. The girls (or boys) he dates, complete copies of all his phone records, who he talks to and why—the works. Thanks a million, Mack.

Then he rode the elevator down to his car, pulled out of the underground parking, and drove the short distance home. As he swung into his driveway, only vaguely warmed by the porch light, he pushed the automatic garage-door opener, but stopped short of pulling in. He reached into the back seat and brought forth a small aluminum case. He set it on the passenger seat, opened it, plugged it into the cigarette lighter, and flipped some switches. The green lights of the monitor board for the TL 14's came on slowly, began the work of tracking the radio signals from the tadpole homing devices that he'd put on Parker and Harting's vehicles. Before calling it a day, he wanted to make sure his Utah folks had run safely to ground for the night.

A radio signal off one of the tadpoles came in and gave him

a reading. It was almost out of range, up north in Utah. He checked the number. It was Parker's truck, parked right where it was this morning. He switched frequencies, searching for the other tadpole, but got nothing, unable to locate even a faint signal from Harting's vehicle. He ran through different sequences and finally reverted to a basic test series. A message came up slowly, glowing green: "Signal unreadable, battery function low."

"Goddamn," Mack slapped the steering wheel. "Damn it all to hell." Now he'd have to hit the streets tomorrow, possibly blow off the whole day just to find these guys lounging by some pool drinking Mai Tais and grooving on the hula.

Son of a bitch, he should have done it. His wife wanted him to do it. Why hadn't he? Because he was a mule, that's why. They had offered him early retirement two years ago for a slight discount in his pension, not that much, really. But he'd held out, feeling that faceless bureaucrats had nicked him one too many times. They'd done everything in his career but assign him to Saudi Arabia.

He snapped the case shut and entered the garage. Turning the ignition key off, he reached for the door handle, but paused and waited, not completely understanding why he was feeling this way, why he was receiving these signals that his own battery functions were low, so very, very low.

The Atomic Whores

September 1960
Round Up Ranch, Indian Springs, Nevada

"HEY, COWBOY, IT'S BEEN AWHILE." IT WAS THE ONE WHO
called herself Fortunata, the one with very large breasts hoisted
up in a black camisole and settled there, under her small chin,
like fleshy ponds with freckles floating on the surface. She was
standing in the doorway and directing her comments toward
Dallas as he walked up the front steps and then under the small
red-and-green neon sign—Round Up Ranch—blinking feebly in
the colorless glare of the afternoon sun.

"So, Dallas," she asked playfully, swinging aside to let him
pass, "when you gonna give a girl a chance at some of that
money you been takin' off of Bea?"

Dallas smiled and touched the brim of his hat, removing it
with two fingers and sidling past her into the darkened bar. He
wore Levi's, a white Western-cut shirt with a large silver belt
buckle at his middle. She let the door swing closed behind him
and he had to stop, stand there momentarily, blinking and
trying to let his eyes adjust from bleached white to deep twilight. As usual, the place smelled of perfume and scented pow-
ders, whiskey and money.

"Your Cheatin' Heart" was playing on the jukebox in the
corner. Dallas became uncomfortably aware of eyes on him
and, as the room slowly materialized, he could make out the
shapes of a few men and several women folded into the semi-
privacy of high-backed velveteen booths. There was never much
business here at 3:30 in the afternoon: a couple of servicemen, a

salesman or two. But later, around midnight, after plenty of booze and rationalizations or after the swing shift got off at the Nevada Test Site just fifteen miles to the northwest, then the men would come in droves.

Right now, the women in the booths were mostly chatting and playing cards. They shared certain attributes—young, pretty, shapely—except for Fat Betty, who must have appealed to a very select clientele and who could be recognized from afar or even in the dark by her shrieking giggle, something she now let loose upon spotting Dallas.

"Yeah, yeah! Come on Dallas," she squealed. "Give a fat girl a chance, too."

Everyone in the room laughed, and Dallas felt himself blushing, thankful for the covering shadows and dim light. He had matured into a darkly handsome man and females generally noticed. His face held the traces of constant wind and sun, but that only seemed to enhance his well-cut features and strong jaw. His gray eyes—deep-set, reflecting a light of their own—sometimes seemed to betray everything about him, sometimes nothing. He wasn't a tall man, but he walked comfortably in the broad shouldered, powerful body that he'd inherited.

"Sorry, girls," Dallas mumbled, "just gotta talk to Bea, that's all." He hurried to the back of the room and a small bar with six empty stools, set his hat on the first stool, and leaned his tired butt on the next. Fran, the longtime bookkeeper and bartender for Bea—she not only chilled beer and mixed the drinks, but made sure that the tax returns and the operating statements matched—was at work over the double sink, soapsuds foaming at her elbows, sloshing bar glasses and mugs onto the upright brushes. She nodded to Dallas. Middle-aged and no longer marketable, she had apparently done some retraining to stay here at the Round Up with Bea.

Dallas didn't like coming into this establishment, but occasionally he had no choice. He did independent contract work for the madam, Bea Murdock. He trained some of her best horses, helped her out with her twelve-year-old stallion who had been standing stud now for several years, but whose confirmation was quickly being outdated by the Texas breeders whose new Doc Bar blood line had boosted the standard and raised the bar for all the competition. Which was what brought Dallas here today. He had gone all the way to Austin in Bea's new truck and two-horse trailer to pick up a horse and bring it back here to the Round Up, discreetly sited down a long lane well off the highway. Bea had just bought herself a stallion, paid more money for it than the average tract house. She was now the owner of Doc's Dandy Man, the best quarter horse, at least on paper, in all of southern Nevada. Though she employed two full-time stable hands and a handler, she insisted that Dallas, who was gaining a genuine trainer's reputation, work with any important or promising horse.

Bea owned five thousand acres: two miles of highway frontage on either side of the Round Up, some of the dead flattest, chalk-dustiest do-nothing ground Dallas had ever seen. But it was all hers, twelve bucks an acre, cash on the barrelhead. Her whorehouse must have made her rich, especially since the test site had been installed in 1950, because another half-mile down this private lane, in the middle of her property, she had built a house and guest house, barns and stables, training arenas and facilities for one of the best quarter horse operations in the state. She planted five hundred trees along the lane and around the buildings, put in acres of lawn, created an oasis in the middle of desolation, and then invited every politician, business leader, and bureaucrat that dared show up. And Bea knew how to throw a barbecue—whole roasted pigs, linen napkins, a band of serenading troubadours moving over the lush green grass.

"Boss lady around?" Dallas asked Fran, whom he knew only through brief but important conversations. This was where he presented his bills for services rendered and this was where he got paid, in cash.

"Yeah, she's here somewhere," Fran said. "Take a load off, she'll be back up soon. Get you anything?"

"Oh, no, well, a tall glass of water, if you don't mind." Dallas had never bought a drink in here before, never patronized the establishment. He was fidgety, not only about the environment—he didn't quite understand the sex-for-hire attraction—but about that expensive stallion parked out there in the shade. He'd left Austin early last evening so that the animal would have the benefit of the cool air, have an easier time with the drive. Moving a horse always put some stress on it, and how it got moved could put even more. Now he wanted to tell Bea he was back and get the stallion unloaded.

Just then, a heavy swinging door leading into the back hallway—where the real business was located—slammed into the wall with a loud bang. Bea Murdock came around the corner like a linebacker, red faced and cursing. "Goddamn. Christ-on-a-crutch!" In her right hand she held a plunger, the angry look on her face suggesting she might be ready to use it on someone out here in the bar. All heads spun around to watch her.

Bea was near fifty, but she was nobody's grandma. She had the energy, mannerisms, and bottled red hair of a much younger woman. Make no mistake—the road miles were there in her face when you got up close, but from a distance, and holding some weapon such as a plunger, she was an intimidating figure. Mother to her girls, but also the boss. She strode toward the bar, the large yellow flowers in the print of her dress swaying like moving targets.

"Told those girls a hundred times not to flush those things down the toilet." She shook her head and then her face changed. "Hey there," she said, "when'd you get in?"

"Just did," Dallas said.

"You wouldn't know the name of a good plumber, would you?" She stood at Dallas's elbow but didn't take a seat. "Here, Fran, got a present for you," she said, extending the plunger's handle over the bar, then turned back to Dallas. "So, how's that horse of ours?"

"Yours," Dallas said and pushed his empty water glass to the back edge of the bar. "He's probably better than I am," he grinned. "Don't teach him to drink coffee and drive all night. Did you decide where you want to put him up yet?"

"Larry took out two walls in the south stable," she replied. "He'll have his own triple stall."

"Good enough," Dallas said. "I'll take him around and introduce him to his new surroundings, try to give him a little exercise. What do you think, keep it to the indoor arena for now? Until he adjusts to the place a little?"

"Well, you decide, you're the expert here."

"Oh, no!" Dallas said, half chuckling, half serious. "Not on a horse that's worth more'n my ranch."

The main door suddenly swung open wide; a square of sunlight obscured the man walking in. "Hey there," he said. He hadn't peeked in first or tentatively pushed the door open like most. He was wearing dark glasses and took them off with his free hand, the one not carrying a briefcase. His eyes must have adjusted quickly, because he began acknowledging some of the girls by name as he saw them. "Hi, Pattie, Fortunata, Rose," he nodded and smiled and kept naming the ones he knew. "Hey, Betty, been getting any lately?" he snickered.

"If you wasn't so dang cheap, I might, Tom," she said in her loud, pitched voice.

He walked to the bar, at once nodding toward and ignoring Dallas.

"Hi, Bea," he said.

"Hi, Tom-mie," she said, feigning no affection.

He didn't blink an eye. "Hey, Fran. How about a beer?"

Fran set a long-neck bottle on the bar. "Two bits," she said.

He gave her a look, then dug a quarter out of his pocket and slapped it down. He set his briefcase on a stool and took out some materials. The first was a pile of brochures that he placed on the counter right in front of Dallas. "Okay to put these out for the customers, Bea?" he asked.

"This look like the library to you, Tom?" she said. "You already got my girls wearing those rad badges. Ain't that enough?"

"Civic duty, Bea," he said, reaching into his briefcase, pulling out a carton of new film badges, called rad badges because the encased filmstrip was said to record the exact amount of radiation it was exposed to. "We're all enlisted in the cold war," he said.

Dallas glanced down at the pamphlets sitting on the bar. The cover was a rendering of a cowboy tranquilly riding his horse over a desert landscape with a big mushroom cloud behind him—certainly a new kind of sunset to ride off into. The byline proclaimed: Fallout Does Not Constitute a Serious Hazard to Any Living Thing Outside the Test Site. Dallas didn't bother to pick it up and open it. He'd seen flyers and pamphlets similar to this before, generally distributed off the counters of businesses, churches, and civic buildings around southern Utah. They were always couched in simplistic terms, written in fourth-grade English, the AEC boys talking down to the local yokels.

Newspapers, radio, lectures—there was no end to the AEC's "there is no danger" chant. If it was really all that safe, Dallas wondered, why the hell did they have to keep saying it, beating on it so hard? And why should anybody need to wear a little badge?

"Okay, girls," Tom said, "everybody turn in your rad badges. Time for a new one."

Renee and Desiree, dark-eyed, exotic identical twins who could fool any customer, drifted toward the bar. They wore matching outfits: knee-length red silk kimonos, black nylons, low-cut bodices, and high-heel bedroom slippers with fluffy fringe on the toes. "Guess where my rad badge is today, Tom," one of the twins cooed. "Same place mine is," the other followed up. "Two for the price of one, if you guess right," they said almost in unison.

Fat Betty came bustling over. "Tom, Tom, did you see that article on us yet? There was a reporter in here last week, from California. Said he was doing a story on us, heard about us in Vegas, called us the atomic whores," she squealed. "He must have been on an expense account, because he did plenty of research." They all laughed with Betty.

"So that makes us the atomic twins," Desiree said.

"Yeah," Fortunata chimed in, "I told that reporter that I could make at least part of him glow in the dark." She batted her long false eyelashes. "And I think I made him a believer."

"How do you read these rad badges anyway?" one of the girls asked. "Do they tell you if you're really hot?"

It was getting way too thick for Dallas and now he wondered why he had stood here this long. Driving twenty hours, no sleep, gallons of coffee—that might immobilize a fellow. Suddenly he was heading for the door. He turned and waved to Bea. "Indoor arena, okay?"

She nodded and waved back. "I'll be down in a few minutes."

Dallas pulled the trailer down the lane to the Round Up's real ranch and unloaded the stallion, who was more than ready to get out. It was dim and cool in the building, just enough sunlight filtering through the open door and a couple of skylights. He didn't bother to turn on the overhead lights, didn't need any extra excitement for the pent-up stud. The horse took off around the large indoor arena, kicking up the soft dirt under his hooves, checking out every foot of the steel enclosure. They were alone, the horse and Dallas, and he sat down on a bleacher seat and watched the powerful animal. It broke into a wild gallop across the arena, skidded to an abrupt halt, whirled about, and jogged back toward him, tail high, neck arched, in a sweeping gait so smooth that the stud appeared to be floating, its feet barely touching the ground. Its grace and power amazed Dallas; that's what made the horse worth so much money.

As Dallas watched the horse begin to wind down a little, the vague scent of perfume lingered, mostly in his head. Dallas enjoyed the company of women, there was no doubt about that. From time to time he had himself a girlfriend, usually down in Vegas, someone who enjoyed a Friday night here and there, who didn't have a lot of expectations. Dallas's ranch was still the same jealous mistress.

He stood up and sauntered down the aisle of the bleachers. He wasn't the spectator type, usually didn't find himself sitting in these places, but he remembered that only about a month ago, he had sat in the bleachers at Dixie High to attend a meeting of the Washington County Cattleman's Association.

Like any other stockman, Dallas was nervous about the safety of his horses and cattle and had specifically come to this meeting to hear the AEC representatives address local grazing concerns. There had been those devastating losses incurred by the local sheep ranchers, with a consequent lawsuit filed, but the AEC was trouncing the sheepmen soundly in the courts.

The government's star witness and head honcho at events like this cattleman's meeting was a Dr. Franklin Rudd, manager of the Nevada Test Site since its inception in 1950. He was a small man, short and very slender, with a pencil-thin mustache and wire-rimmed glasses. He looked almost frail, but when he spoke, his voice was full of tension and he conveyed a curious kind of energy and vigor. Behind him on the stage was a panel of five men seated in a row. A gigantic American flag, by far the largest Dallas had ever seen, hung from the ceiling and pro-vided a dramatic backdrop. Rudd introduced one and then another speaker. A big-name veterinarian talked for a crisp ten minutes about radiation and animal science, another scientist about the effects of radiation contained in sunshine and the similarities it shared with the radiation in the bombs. The pre-sentation was friendly, but well orchestrated.

One of the scientists talked about the rad badges, explaining the disarming simplicity of them. Dr. Rudd did a summation and used one of the film badges as his visual aid.

"If you are concerned," he said in a clipped voice, "and I assure you that there is no reason to be, then sign up on this sheet after the presentation," he rapped his knuckles on a clip-board on the table, "and you will be issued a rad badge by our monitors. It will be collected monthly and a new one issued. Where you go, it goes. What could possibly be simpler?" He paused and grinned very slightly for the first and only time, "And if you want to fasten one to a cow, be my guest."

Then a fifteen-minute film was shown. It opened with march music turned up high and swelling to the rafters, as a picture of an atom bomb flashed and then towered dramatically. There followed a series of old news clips from the forties—World War II footage of fighting men hitting the beach, the bombs going off in Hiroshima and Nagasaki—dramatic pictures with a newscaster's voice-over talking about how many American lives were saved by dropping these two big bombs. Then it switched to scenes of Joe Stalin, Mother Russia and dreary music.

Abruptly, they were watching a sunny spring day in Nevada. The tone of the film changed, went from dark and shadowy to light and airy, the music becoming something off a Bendix commercial. The subject was now the future, everything from atomic-powered ovens to automobiles. Power too cheap to meter. At the center of all these glowing future promises was the Nevada Test Site. With every shot, every test that went off, the scientists were that much closer to realizing their dreams. Our dreams. The end.

The lights came up. Dr. Rudd walked to the middle of the stage, stood erect with his feet apart, and asked for questions. He slowly looked around the room, stopping to lock eyes with any man who dared hold his gaze. Dallas was in the back row, up top, and watched this Dr. Rudd, this skinny little man, bully a bunch of tough cowboys and ranchers. Not one unpatriotic hand went up; not one Russia-loving question was asked.

The stallion, Doc's Dandy Man, finally stopped near the center of the arena, went down on its front knees, and prepared to roll over in the dirt. "It's about time," Dallas said absently, leaning on the fence. This was what he had been waiting for from the stallion, knew that it would help calm the horse, rub some of that long ride off. And he sure as hell didn't want it to try rolling around in its stall.

"So I pay that much for a dusty horse that likes to roll in the dirt?" It was Bea, finally coming down to see her new stud.

"I'm about ready to join him," Dallas said.

"Tired?" she said.

"Yeah, but I'm alright."

"You're young," she said wistfully.

Dallas saw that Bea had one of the rad badges pinned to her dress now. "That guy even got you wearing one of those things, huh?"

"Got to humor the test site, whatever it takes," she said.

Then, lowering her voice conspiratorially, "You have any idea of the money I've—" She caught herself, though, before she said too much, even by her standards.

"You really think," said Dallas, "that those badges mean anything, that they work?"

She broke up laughing. "Are you shittin' me? This is . . . what do you call it . . . a placebo?" she said, fingering the badge. "Look it here. Does it change colors? Or give off a little whistle if it gets too many rads, too much radiation—whatever the hell that is, odorless, colorless, flavorless? They come around and collect them every month, but they don't mail you a report or anything like that. I've never heard of them contacting anyone and saying, 'Whoa, get in here, your rad count's up!' They're the only ones who even have a clue about how to read them. Do I think they mean anything? They mean whatever the hell those boys over there want them to mean."

"Well, if they don't analyze them or," Dallas's vision seemed to blur a bit as his weariness suddenly deepened, "what do they do with them?"

"Let me give you a clue," she said. "Charlie, my day janitor over at the bar, was picking up papers and beer bottles outside, policing the grounds awhile back. He found a pile of these badges dumped in the ditch out yonder. Brought them inside, gave them to me in a sack. I saved them for souvenirs."

"Maybe they were new ones, defective or something, maybe somebody tossed them." He had driven through the night, fought oncoming headlights and a strong need to sleep. Did he have to have this conversation now?

"Oh, you are young, you man-child you," she said, rolling her eyes. "I don't know the truth about radiation doses around here, maybe nobody does. But I do know that these morons are just jerking us all off with these badge things. And if they did show something, we'd sure as hell be the last to know."

Dallas was used to Bea's rough talk, but he was also used to her intelligence and solid reasoning. He'd never known her to be flaky about anything. "How do you know all that for sure?" he asked.

"Dallas," she said, "we got customers, people like you wouldn't believe. Monitors, scientists, lab technicians, laborers, you name it. And they all blab endlessly to their favorite girls."

"I thought all that stuff was supposed to be classified, so hush-hush. Top secret." He looked at her cynically.

"Don't kid yourself, honey," she laughed. There was a sudden coolness in her voice and a blue, almost dreamy distance. "It's like our kind don't really exist or something. You'd be simply *amazed* at what a man will tell a whore."

CHAPTER NINE

LAYNE SHIFTED UNEASILY ON THE HARD OAK BENCH, CONSCIOUS of the space between himself and Christine. Even though they hadn't gone much beyond kissing last night, he had wanted to badly, would have if she hadn't stopped. Now he did his best to ignore this bit of morning-after awkwardness and tried to focus on the proceedings.

A slender, well-groomed woman in extremely high heels was giving the downwinders' team of lawyers a strenuous tongue-lashing. "This whole motion is a charade," she said, pointing to the plaintiffs' counsel table where Uwanda Docksteader and her lawyers were sitting. Layne didn't know Ms. Docksteader by sight, but he assumed it was she up there, the hefty, long-haired woman who had been greeted by a dozen or more spectators when she entered the courtroom.

The defense's tirade continued. "They claim to need more time in order to review documents received a month ago, but this is, in reality, just another of their delaying tactics. They are seeking *another* continuance, having already been granted two such motions. The truth is that they are running out of time."

There had been a scattering of other spectators when Layne, Christine, and Dallas arrived in Courtroom D-2, Federal District Court for the Southern District of Nevada, Judge Thomas Sanders presiding. As if through some shared intuition, they furtively sought out the very last, back-to-the-wall row and slid in, blending in as best they could. This was probably one of the safest places they could be if someone were trying to kill them. Or not. Who knew about the faceless, nameless ones who were after the book? Almost immediately the courtroom began to fill to capacity, though, with a variety of people—downwinder friends and supporters who waved at Uwanda, gave her the thumbs-up; old-timers and a few kids; professionally dressed people and some who looked like casual, tropical tourists. Layne thought that the three of them needn't have worried so much about fitting in with the crowd.

He felt someone's eyes on him and reflexively glanced sideways. Christine tilted her chin up and studied the proceedings. It was a very nice chin, indeed. He knew they were both sharing the same jittery compunctions, had sensed it earlier this morning when the three of them met for breakfast back at the hotel. Christine had greeted him but kept her eyes mostly focused on her coffee, the dry toast she ordered, and the swirling patterns in the carpet.

Layne wasn't sure what to say or do, whether to reach out and touch her or maintain a modest distance. He could sympathize, having awakened in the early hours with a serious case of the yips himself, all sorts of sleepy scenarios rattling around in his head. After all, he was her attorney; she was a client. This was the way professionals got themselves into trouble, which is just what he needed right now—more trouble. Then there was the issue of her cancer, which they had never so much as whispered about. Other than that, she was terrific, really great.

Not that he had much room to talk as he waded deeper and deeper into the swamp of felony aiding and abetting himself. Good-bye bar license and cute little schoolhouse down by the river. Hello federal prison. This was one merry chase that could have some real consequences. Not to mention the fact that the CIA, the KGB, the mafia—somebody who took this seriously was on their trail. Somebody who was unpredictable, disdainful of the normal procedures in pursuit of Rudd's book. He could only hope they'd given their pursuer the slip and bought enough time.

Christine shifted positions, crossed her right leg over her left.

She was wearing a brown skirt this morning which crept up over her knee now, causing him to glance quickly at the ceiling. The room was extremely high and magisterial with an abundance of ornate, turn-of-the-century fluted moldings, oak and marble craftsmanship. The judge sat high up on the stately throne of his bench at the far end of the room.

The government's counsel, the stiff lady in heels, suddenly increased the decibels. "They have *failed* to produce any evidence to overcome the strong presumption of governmental immunity in cases of this nature," she said, smoothing the light gray fabric of her expensive suit and straightening her back, lifting the full bustline of her sleek double-breasted jacket. "Your honor, the government at this time would like to present its own motion to the court for a directed verdict. The plaintiffs clearly have not met the required burden of proving actual knowledge or intentional acts leading to the damages alleged." She stood there defiantly, arms now crossed, as if she expected the judge to rule immediately in her favor. Her hair was full and shiny, her lips bright red and in a pout. She reminded Layne of the Turk, of all the things he didn't like about what ultimately became her barracuda style. When he'd first met his ex-wife she was capable of charm and fun, though by the end, a "nobody fucks with this gal" mentality extended from the law practice into every area of her life. The more he resisted the notion of life as one big assault, the more she expanded it, as if he were creating a vacuum which she had a duty to fill.

The judge spoke softly, as if to offset some of the lawyer's scabrousness. Layne leaned forward, placing his forearms on his knees, and focused his attention toward the bench. "Do I understand plaintiffs' position correctly?" Judge Sanders asked. "You are requesting additional time to examine the government's latest production of documents?"

A tall and distinguished-looking gentleman, a man in his seventies whom Layne had no trouble recognizing as Joseph Attencio, rose slowly, and in a deep, rumbling voice that would have done well on stage or screen, answered for the plaintiffs.

"You understand our position correctly, your honor."

Attencio's Mount Rushmore profile looked just as it did on the TV news reports that occasionally followed the ex-congressman's twenty years of public battles.

"When, sir, did you receive your copies of the documents that you requested?" the judge asked, respectfully.

"Just three weeks ago, your honor." Attencio extended a palm toward the government's side of the aisle and continued. "But if I may, your honor. These documents were covered in any number of plaintiffs' motions for production going back at least five years. If they were, in fact, classified on the date of the initial and ongoing requests, as claimed by counsel for the defendant, and I have no reason to doubt that they were, then, since they were clearly covered in the plaintiffs' request and the defendant's denial based upon the blanket grounds of national security, I would propose that it is clear that the government had a continuing duty to plaintiffs and to this court to make them available immediately upon declassification.

"According to the government's own statements, these memos and exhibits were declassified about four months ago. About the time this trial began. Therefore, I find it ironic that defense counsel would resist our request for more time to examine rather voluminous and complicated documents after the government sat on them for several months beyond the date of their declassification."

Attencio paused and clasped his hands behind his back. "And, your honor, with all due respect and as a loyal citizen of the same government we are now suing, I can't shake the feeling that has been germinating inside of me for the last thirty years. I harbor the strongest conviction that the key to all of the plaintiffs' claims lies squarely within the remaining classified documents housed under the jurisdiction of the Department of Energy. Our problem has always been how to get at them."

Attencio turned slightly to include the gallery and spoke with his chin tilted upward, as if he now conversed only with a higher power. His booming voice echoed down the length of the room. "And I am equally convinced that the government's position denying access to most of the documents we have requested solely on the grounds of national security is but a convenient means by which the government can deny its own citizens access to the truth. What began as a shield against out-ward foreign aggression clearly has been turned inward against ourselves."

Layne was mesmerized and excited. This was it, a perfect fit. Rudd's book addressed the precise issues that Attencio was raising here in court. Attencio was right: the government had no legitimate national security interest left regarding the era of atomic testing. The technology was passé—any hack scientist from any hack country could build a bomb if he had the mate-rials. And the Cold War was over; old enemies were now allies.

This was exactly where the book had to land; they had to get it to Joseph Attencio and convince him to use it. Here was a man who understood the entire governmental apparatus, its public as well as its secret workings. Attencio would have the best chance of shepherding Rudd's allegations toward some fair conclusion, would know how to bring them to light within the context of these proceedings and in the press. Layne suddenly found himself waxing patriotic and wanted to rally for the cause, to feel less threatened or more heroic.

It was a quick bubble of euphoria that felt quite good just before it burst. If life were only that simple. This must be how criminals feel just before they forge a check or go in the bed-room window. Later, they have plenty of time in a small cell to wonder if bungee jumping would have served their purposes just as well.

No, Layne had to remain calm and rational. He still had a duty to protect himself and the others—and that, frankly, included Attencio and his associates. Someone with a violent nature was almost surely still after this thing. If Attencio decided to accept the package, it had to be with full knowledge of the facts—Rudd's murder, the theft, the shadow dangers. All cards had to be on the table. And for their part, his and Christine's and Dallas's, Layne must obtain the cooperation of and some assurances from Joseph Attencio personally. They might even engage him as their own attorney in the matter of the manuscript and thereby invoke client privilege. In any event, Layne had to use all legal means to allow them to remain anonymous.

Realistically, just getting an audience with Attencio would be difficult. Layne couldn't stop him in the hallway and breathlessly tell him a tale of intrigue any more than he could over the phone yesterday. They'd all be dismissed as nutcases or possibly criminals. So they were right back to Uwanda Docksteader; they needed to start with that woman sitting up there. She was the main cross-bearer in this cause. She would be far more accessible than Attencio. Probably she could give them the lowdown, advise them whether Attencio would be open to receiving such materials. Then she could set up a meeting with him, hopefully this afternoon, and they could go from there. If Attencio turned them down, Layne reasoned, they could still mail it to someone in the press.

The judge called a thirty-minute recess to consider the motions of both counsel. He requested that lead counsel approach the bench for a quick conference. The rear doors swung open and the courtroom began emptying noisily. Uwanda Docksteader finished talking to a couple at the rail and then walked out of the courtroom. Still seated, Layne looked over at Dallas and Christine, then motioned his head toward the hallway. They followed Uwanda down the hall to an alcove housing some vending machines.

"Ms. Docksteader," Layne said tentatively. "Uwanda Docksteader? My name is Layne Harting. I spoke to your husband yesterday. Can I speak to you for a minute?"

She was studying the beverage selections and had one hand blindly rooting through her purse for coins. A large, imposing figure with flowing material draped across her beefy torso, she straightened up and gave him the same scrutiny she had been applying to the machine. "Another reporter?" she snarled. "Asking if we're ready to throw in the towel?"

"Um, no," Layne said, backing up a step. "I'm not with the media. I'm a lawyer."

"Oh great. Swing a dead cat these days and you'll hit a

lawyer," she said. "I've got all the lawyers I need right now." She went back to digging for change in her purse.

Layne stepped forward. "Please, allow me," he said, producing some of the quarters he'd secured for the pay phone yesterday. "What would you like?"

Uwanda sighed. "Diet Coke," she said, displaying little gratitude.

He punched the button. There was a high-pitched whirling noise and the machine disgorged a can. Then another. And another. They kept coming, spilling down the chute, piling up, then hitting the floor and rolling in every direction. Finally, the machine issued one last metallic belch and quit. Layne and Uwanda Docksteader just stood there with Coke cans rolling around their ankles and looked at each other.

"I'm also a lucky lawyer," he said. "And I think I have something that can help your case."

She stooped and began picking up cans. Layne bent down to help her and they stacked them on top of the vending machine. "Well, you're not *that* lucky," she said. "After all, it's just Coca Cola."

Layne laughed at her joke and heard Dallas and Christine chuckling behind him. He glanced at them and saw Christine smiling. The ice cap that had begun to form might be melting away. He genuinely hoped so. Being with her last night had been—

"So how can you help us?" Uwanda asked.

"We, um, have something that we feel could . . ." Layne pointed to Dallas and Christine to include them. "This something could greatly help your cause."

"Super," she said with mock enthusiasm. "What is it? I've looked under every rock and in every box of documents between here and Washington, D.C., for the last fifteen years trying to come up with some piece of thunder to help our cause. If you've got something, let's have it."

"Well," Layne said, "it's not quite that simple."

"Right," she said, "it never is. Money? Is that the angle here? Well, let me tell you—"

"No, no. Nothing to do with money," Layne hastened. "It has more to do with . . . well," he glanced around. They were alone in the alcove. "It has more to do with confidentiality."

"Well, there's just us four chickens here," she said, craning her neck, seeming to mimic his caution. "So, no problem. Shoot. What you got, Mr. Harting?"

Layne was developing a rapid and intense dislike for this woman. Couldn't she even respond with minimal politeness? "I can't possibly explain it all to you standing right here," he said, reverting to a more formal manner to match her rudeness. "If you care to meet us for lunch, we'll be happy to explain the situation."

"Well, I can't possibly make it for lunch. I'm tied up tighter than Houdini all afternoon." Then she patted one ample hip and softened her tone a notch. "God knows, it's not something I like to miss."

Layne sighed, "You call it. When and where can we meet you today?"

"For starters, why don't you introduce the rest of the *we*?" she said.

Layne stepped back, checked the hallway to make sure that they weren't being overheard, then lowered his voice. "This is Dallas Parker. His niece, Christine Parker."

Uwanda's eyes quickly passed over Christine and fixed on Dallas. "Wait a minute! I *thought* there was something familiar about you . . . Rudd." She aimed one large, rude finger at Dallas. "Aren't you—"

"You've got it," Layne intervened.

"And . . . Harting!" she exclaimed. "You're his lawyer."

Layne nodded. "Your cousin Faye is my secretary. So how about dinner?"

A rhythmic tap-tap-tap of high heels approached and all of them looked toward the hallway to see the blonde lead attorney from the trial. Her hydraulic stride slowed as she saw them. She was all eyes, gazing first at Dallas, then Christine and Layne, then cementing her stare back on Dallas. Layne understood the practice of a lawyer checking out the opponents, but there was definitely some kind of rub here. The woman appeared visibly startled or upset, her perfectly composed face slipping, for a few seconds, into a slack, open-mouthed exclamation. She recouped quickly, however, regained her stride, and passed by.

Uwanda watched the woman's retreating figure. "Oh, so you've met the government's lead bitch, Chief Deputy Jillian Retch—I mean Fetch?"

"No, no," Layne said. "I've never met her, but it appears that she knows who we are." His mouth went a bit dry at the fleeting thought that she might know more than just their identities, might know about certain unauthorized possessions in their tow. "Anyway, I think that's our cue. So how about dinner?"

Uwanda stared at Dallas, apparently speechless for the first time in quite awhile. "Okay, okay, wait a minute here." She shook her head and shoulders.

"Then you'll meet us?" Layne asked.

"I . . . Jesus!" she said, pausing, as if she needed a moment. "Well, if you're buying. "

Then she straightened up to her full height and stepped crisply toward Dallas, extended a surprisingly dainty hand and said, "I'd be *honored* to have dinner with the man who, who nailed that Dr. Franklin Son of a Bitch Rudd."

Illicit sex was pathetically overrated, R. C. Hiney thought as he unzipped his pants. Fuckin' fantasyland stuff, always gets you moving in the wrong direction. He stood over the urinal in the old, marbled men's room on the fourth floor of the Federal Building and tried to calm himself, but the words "incompetent little prick" kept circling back at him. Why did she, the esteemed U. S. Attorney, Ms. Jillian, seem to think that she could do that every time she saw him lately—mix body parts and insults. True, she could be considered one of his supervisors.

He had been assigned to investigate specific matters for her on a case-by-case basis, but that gave her no such rights. She could just tell him that she was concerned, needed more help, and leave it at that.

He nervously stretched the limp bat, changing the trajectory of his steady stream. Mr. Batman here had flown into the wrong cave for sure this time, had gotten him into enough trouble to last a year. No, make that a lifetime. If he came through this deal with Jillian unscathed, he was going to say a thousand Hail Marys and cut the nocturnal forays, retire and stay home with mama where he belonged. He knew it was trite as hell to blame his dick for doing his thinking, but he also knew that if he didn't have one, he wouldn't be in this jam. There was an old Irish tradition of repenting and making promises right at cliff's edge, but, by God, this time he meant every word of it.

He took a deep breath, still pissing hard—Jesus, ought to cut back on the coffee too. So he'd had a hard-on for the broad, lusted after her as she strutted around the Federal Building, sticking those tits out like some kind of Proud Mary. Yeah, sure, there had been that one night last week, one time at her condo—the king-size bed, the mirrors, the booze, the music and lights. Godzilla visits the Holy Land. But, Christ, he had to pay every day of his life now?

Truth was, R. C. had been avoiding Jillian for the last couple of days, sidestepping those moments when he had to shrug and admit to her that he had not seen or talked with his "guy." But he'd also told her, a million times by now, that they had some old cowboy in custody up there, that Rudd's murder was open and shut. He'd been up to St. George himself twice now and everything was cool. No sign of Manos, but then, like he kept telling her, the guy wasn't exactly known for his dependability. He could be off anywhere, doing something else by now.

Just moments ago, Jillian had caught up with R. C. out in the hallway, not far from his office. He knew she was back in that trial, downstairs on the second floor, so he had thought he might get a reprieve today. Fat chance. Court was in morning recess and she had tracked him down.

"Where the hell have you been?" she hissed quietly. "I've been looking for you."

"I was across the street, having coffee at—"

"You incompetent little prick." She leaned up and damn near whispered it in his ear. Her face was smooth, airbrushed, glazed with perfect makeup. She'd had her teeth done, he guessed. Capped. Polished. Then she tilted her head slightly to the left and moved even closer to him. "Do *you* realize . . ." Her voice wound tighter.

He had just about let go of his Irish temper right there. Not just prick, but little prick. Instead, he had taken a step back, could still smell mint on her breath, then turned and walked away, strode down the hall and into the men's restroom.

Now he wasn't quite finished peeing when suddenly the men's-room door flew open and Jillian stormed in. R. C. struggled to look back over his shoulder and still keep from pissing on the wall. "Jesus!" he said.

She locked the door, then her heels clicked over the white tiles as she moved to the only stall and pushed it open to make sure they were alone. The door swung wide, banging hard against the inside of the stall, the sound echoing off the high ceiling. She turned to him.

He quickly finished and zipped.

"I don't know if you're deaf or just stupid," she said. "I suspect the latter, so I'll put it bluntly, asshole. They've made your guy."

R. C. walked to the sink and put his hands under the faucet, making a show of hygiene and normalcy. Lukewarm water hit the back of his hands. He felt dizzy as he reached for the paper towels. "Manos? Who made him? For what? What the hell you talkin' about?"

Jillian sighed heavily, as if this conversation was proving too long and circuitous. "Local FBI," she said.

"Look, Manos has been made more times than a ten dollar

whore." R. C. shrugged, but he was already trying to turn down his panic response. "Where'd you get this from, anyway?"

Jillian crossed her arms and leaned against an edge of the marble stall. "What the hell's the difference? I make it my business to know things."

"Well, what is it you know, then?" he asked.

"I know that he's been seen up there in Bumfuck, Utah. I know that they've got his mobile phone records and that your number has shown up, home and office. And I know that the FBI is checking into your phone records. As we speak." She almost seemed to smile, but it quickly veered off into a sneer. "I also know that your man Manos made calls on said mobile phone as recently as yesterday, late yesterday. From Utah. From St. George, Utah." Her words were clipped, as if she were shooting them at him. "The above finally putting to rest your bullshit theory about him being gone, dusted or otherwise out of the picture."

R. C. fumbled with the paper towel and leaned against the counter. His lung capacity suddenly seemed cut in half. When he was just fifteen, he had watched his father have a heart attack on Thanksgiving day during a heated argument with his oldest sister, right at the dinner table. Watched the old man go down, clutching at the linen cloth, pulling the whole shittery right off the table and down on top of himself: turkey, gravy, cranberry sauce, everything.

"Not only that," she said, "Dallas Parker, your so-called dumb cowboy, is downstairs right now with his niece and, I presume, their lawyer Harting." She paused for dramatic effect. "Talking to, imagine this, that Uwanda-lead-nutcase-plaintiff-Docksteader." She fairly spat the last parts at him, then breathed deeply, "Jee whiz, I wonder what they could be discussing."

R. C.'s head began going light. He hung on to the sink for balance as spots floated before his eyes. He tried to speak, but a heavy, clogging weight had parked in his chest. Maybe he was going down, right here on the tile, just like his father. He forced himself to take a long, slow inhalation and then another, as he fought to regain his composure. No way. He wasn't dyin' here, givin' this chick an easy out. Worse comes to worst, he'd take her with him, they'd go down together. Period.

"Okay," he said, rubbing his temples. "Let me check it out." He walked past her over to the frosted window. He stood there with his back to her, gazing as if he were enjoying some kind of view, until he felt his lungs open up and return to normal. Think, he urged himself, think, breathe, think.

"You never know how these things come down," he said. "Worst thing can happen is to panic." He pivoted around. "We don't know why Parker's here. Just got out of jail, could be looking for a vaca—"

"Don't be an idiot," she cut in. "I didn't get this far with such shit-for-brains logic."

"Well, whatever, we still need to stay cool. See how it plays. Worst thing is when people freak out, start talking to other people. Happens all the time, they step in their own shit when it ain't necessary. Let's just find out where all this is comin' from."

He went to the mirror, feeling slightly better, the shock receding. He was straightening his tie when he saw the damn stuff—an orangy glob right on the lapel of his suit coat. Shit! Not only was he caught flat-footed by new information that he should have known, but here this broad stood, immaculate, her gray suit tailored and merciless, while he sported Sears and a boutonniere of Gerber strained peaches from his twins' early-morning feeding.

Jillian pushed away from the edge of the stall, her posture demanding that he face her. She shook her head, as if commenting on something pathetic. "You think I'm looking to you for advice? That what you think?"

R.C. raised his hands, palms out. "Hey, we're on the same team."

"Cut the crap. This isn't baseball."

Jillian's eyes, filled with utter contempt, started at R. C.'s stained lapel and traveled down his length to his shoes. He didn't look down, just hoped to God he didn't have strained peaches on them, too.

There was a brief silence, but it was in no way calming. An automatic deodorizer spit for a couple of seconds, venting an invisible cloud that smelled exactly like bubble gum.

"Look," Jillian said, "this whole game is about over. Maybe I'll visit you in Lompoc sometime."

R. C.'s eyes squinted slightly, searching for meaning. "Lompoc? What the hell you talkin' about, lady?"

"Here's how it plays, stud," she said. Jillian flicked at a nail with her thumb as if her manicure took precedence at the moment. "You come to my condo. Last week. It's after dark. I let you in, of course. As a U.S. marshall assigned to render periodic assistance in my cases, we have ongoing business to discuss. You, however, can't keep your mind on that business. You make a pass at me. I try to settle you down. You've been drinking. You tear my blouse, get a little rough. I finally get you out, but not before you leave a deep bruise on me."

Jillian reached up, unbuttoned her suit coat, then undid the buttons on her blouse. Yanking down the edge of her satin bra, she revealed her right breast. A purple bruise spilled across her pectoral muscle. She left her blouse open, her breast exposed, sticking out there longer than it needed to.

There was a small space marked "Donor" on R. C.'s driver's license, and a Y printed below it for Yes. But they were supposed to wait until you were dead. He got the feeling that she was about to remove one of his vitals while he was still kicking, right here, right now.

"Anyway, you keep calling me at home," she said, cupping her breast back into her bra but leaving her blouse completely unbuttoned, the seductive undergarment exposed. "Finally, on Tuesday, I meet you at the Nugget for coffee, try to talk some sense into you, try to save your career. If not for your sake," she paused, "then for your wife and children's." She was completely in control, speaking softly, using her practiced voice of small, sharp arrows. "Unfortunately, you are beyond reason. And you've been stalking me at odd hours. That's why I have to file a formal complaint of sexual harassment."

R. C. blurted out a laugh, high strung, full of disbelief.

"What? You actually filed a written complaint?"

Jillian nodded. "Just listen. You'll catch on soon enough." She made a show of checking her watch. "I do remember, of course, mentioning to you, in your role as an investigator, a rumor that I'd heard about some retired administrator from the Nevada Test Site, a Dr. Franklin Rudd, about some exposé he might be writing. Apparently, you took my remarks way out of context, took the situation into your own hands—perhaps to impress me or to make up for assaulting me. Or maybe just to get in my pants. It's hard to know. Bottom line is I've never met this Manos, never heard of him in my entire life, my number's not in his cell phone records. Never met Parker either, never called or, God forbid, set foot in St. George, Utah." She stepped forward. "You're all on your own now, idiot child—"

"You call me one more fuckin' name—" he cut her off, his temper finally over the top. They could both go down right now, right here in this bathroom. "I've about had it with you, bitch. I'd like to change the shape of your face."

She took a step closer. "You don't have the guts."

R. C. started toward her and then abruptly stopped. Come on, man, come on! He wasn't born yesterday. She wanted him to hit her, to validate her claim. She'd laid it out for him, but everything she said could be a lie. Why would she file a harassment complaint at this point? It made no sense. But if he nailed her, right here in the Federal Building, she could file any damn claim she wanted. And she'd win it. More importantly, his credibility, his word against hers, would be shot to hell.

Seamlessly, without a sound, she reached up and slapped him. Hard, a single shot echoing off the tile walls.

His fist came up instinctively, a big Irish ham that could have sent her through the wall. It would have been interesting to see how many pieces he could break her perfectly straight nose into, but he checked himself. Instead, in a single moment of clarity that had been missing ever since he saw this broad, he veered past her over to the restroom door, snapped the lock, and opened it. Then he stepped into the hall, searching both ways. He motioned to a secretary who just happened to be passing by, explained that he needed her help. "Please," he said, "this woman . . ." He opened the door wide and pointed to Jillian. "She's my supervisor, followed me into the men's restroom and has been harassing me, making threats. She even bared her breasts."

The secretary stood there motionless, staring wide eyed at Jillian. There was an awkward, frozen moment, and then Jillian's hands, as if wounded, fluttered back down to her sides as she quit futilely trying to button up her blouse.

"I need you to witness what's going on in here," he said. "Please." R. C. turned his back to the secretary and smiled for the first time in days at his favorite U.S. attorney. He couldn't help it. From the very first, he had told Jillian that he liked being on top.

The evening air felt cool and friendly, a surprise to Dallas, who had just stepped out the double doors of the Oasis Hotel. The street was mostly deserted. Sidewalks and gutters had been scrubbed by last night's storm and a slight, revitalizing breeze flowed in from the desert south. Daytime's glare had been replaced by a deepening blue, but he could see that twilight here would have no chance, was already being overtaken by all the lights from the nearby Strip.

Boredom and restlessness, a combination he hadn't experienced much in his life, had taken over, pushed him up and out of room 632. He began walking down this side street parallel to the Strip. He wore well-broken-in dress boots, a tan Western-cut sport coat, and his weathered Stetson, but it was the walking, the sheer mechanics of movement, that gave him comfort. A block behind the Oasis, the street became deserted. It was after hours, and this area was exclusively light industrial— linen supply, heating and refrigeration, a House of Hose. It didn't matter; he was making little attempt to hide, duck his head or wear silly hats. If someone wanted a piece of him, bring it on.

Christine and Layne had gone off to meet Uwanda Docksteader for dinner. Standing dressed and ready in his room, they had initially insisted he go with them.

"That's your bailiwick, counselor," Dallas said. "Work it out so you're comfortable with it all." Layne had been discussing strategy and guarantees of confidentiality from Attencio. "If it was up to me," Dallas continued, "I'd take it to her and just hand it over. Right after I made a copy to mail to the newspaper."

"Well, maybe that's what we should do then," Layne said, exasperation creeping into his voice.

"Oh, don't listen to me. What have I got to lose—"

"Dallas!" Christine cut him off. "What kind of talk is that?"

"Shit, Chrissy, I'm sorry." He knew exactly what Layne was doing—protecting Christine, protecting his own lawyerly behind, and Dallas wouldn't have it any other way.

"Ah, hell. Truth be told," he said, "I don't *want* to have dinner with the Docksteader woman. She'll be all over me with questions, wantin' to know about that night. And . . ." His voice trailed off. The three of them stood there for another moment, but little more than awkward good-byes were exchanged.

He continued to stroll along the sidewalk. The scenery wasn't much to speak of—gravel and weeds in the parking strips, storefronts separated by occasional vacant lots. This desolate little business artery probably bustled with service vehicles during the day, but it was past dead now. Scraggly Chinese elms struggled here and there to survive where the cracked curb occasionally trapped water. He moved aimlessly, stopping to peer into the dirty bay window of Calico Brothers Plumbing, Home of the Royal Flush. He shook his head. Son-of-a-bitchin' omens were everywhere.

A skinny dog crossed the sidewalk up ahead and then crept

into the street, keeping a wary eye turned back on Dallas. Abruptly, a shadow from the alleyway moved and then a shabby homeless man stepped in front of Dallas.

"Hey, man, spare a buck for a cheap bottle of wine?" He stood there with his matted hair, wearing a ragged thermal jacket, peering out through yellowed eyes.

Dallas was caught off guard. He didn't see panhandlers much, and this one's candor surprised him. He reached for his billfold, saw that the smallest he had was a twenty. Half-embarrassed, he tossed the bill toward the man. The money fluttered to the ground between them, and Dallas immediately regretted having thrown it.

"Sorry, pardna," Dallas said, bending and picking it up, "didn't mean to toss it at you."

"You can toss all those you want, mister," the man said, taking the bill from Dallas. "Thanks. Thanks a lot."

Dallas nodded and moved on with no idea where he was going. A siren started up in the distance, followed by another. He considered wandering back toward the Strip to play a little twenty-one or poker, but only if he could find a smoke-filled room full of grumpy men bent over green who felt similarly disenchanted with this new Vegas as Disneyland. On second thought, gambling seemed like a pretty pointless recreation at the moment; he'd been gambling enough lately, waging stakes that were higher than he could really afford. Maybe he'd find a newspaper, see if there was a horse show or rodeo in town.

The mechanical wailing drew closer and then a squad car zipped past Dallas and down the street, sending a pink playbill fluttering in its wake. It was soon followed by another, then by a fire truck and a couple more emergency vehicles, their red lights dicing the night. They all turned right at the block ahead and drove toward the rear of one of the big hotels.

When Dallas arrived at the next intersection, he could see down the block and all the commotion, cops and cars and people, more emergency vehicles pulling up. He stopped on the corner, not particularly wanting to get mixed up with that scene, but his street dead-ended in the next block. He thought for a minute, then walked toward the lights and sirens, staying on the opposite side of the street, trying to keep clear of the hotel and the police lines being strung to manage a scattered but noisy crowd.

A cop car whisked to the curb just in front of Dallas, and then, as brakes rumbled, a large truck with a spotlight mounted on its flatbed pulled up and parked. An officer hurried out of the black and white and began stringing more police tape, blocking the entire street. Dallas slowed, then stopped beside the truck.

A fat man leaned out the passenger side of the spotlight truck, craning his neck and squinting toward the top of the hotel. He was wearing a tie and a sausage-tight sport coat. He opened the door, stepped out onto the high running board of the truck, and raised a walkie-talkie to his mouth with the same hand that held a stubby cigar clamped between two fingers.

"Yeah, yeah, that's right," he said into the mouthpiece, "tell him we got a flier on the roof." The man was sweating profusely despite the pleasant evening temperature.

"I don't *know* how the fuck he got out on the roof. I'll ream the building engineer tomorrow, okay? But tonight I got Streisand, in about an hour. She's a flippy broad, wigs over any kinda shit.

"Well, we got to get him off. What? Yeah, that's right." The fat man leaned back toward the driver inside the truck. "Aim at the roof, light that bastard up.

"Damn," he said back into the walkie-talkie, "hired a giant spotlight for Streisand and now we gotta use it on this dumb cocksucker. What? I don't give a shit. Just tell that fruitcake to get off our roof. One way or another."

Suddenly a noisy generator fired up and the big revolving spot on the back of the truck clicked on. It was pointed straight in the air, the needle beam instantly stabbing toward infinity. Dallas moved away several paces. The operator rotated the mirrored canister until he found the top of the hotel, quickly fixing the beam on a lone man balancing on the roof ledge. The man raised one hand, as if he were going to wave to the crowd, but shielded his eyes from the intense light.

Dallas backed up again, trying to escape the generator's noise. He bumped into a woman standing behind him, stepping on her toe with his boot heel. "Oh, sorry, ma'am," he said.

"Don't worry, I walk on 'em, too," she replied.

Dallas nodded apologetically.

"It's okay," she laughed. "These dealer's shoes are made to take a beating."

"Well, I'm sorry," he said again.

"Hey, that poor sucker's the one who's sorry." She pointed up to the man on the ledge. "But I almost can't blame him. What a jam."

Dallas was confused and she must have seen it on his face.

"House security, they were sayin' that the guy . . . I just finished my shift in there at the hotel. The guy up on that ledge gambled away his family's life savings. They sold the house back East and he was supposed to meet the wife and kids and buy a new one out West. Tried to double the down payment, I guess."

"Jesus," said Dallas, "ain't no amount of money worth dying for."

"I don't know," she said, shaking her head, "he may as well jump. If I was married to the dumb bastard, he wouldn't have much to live for after a stunt like—"

A sudden noise, an unmistakable collective gasp, escaped the crowd. Dallas and the woman watched as the man on the ledge, illuminated like a rock star, casually stepped forward into thin air. He disappeared from the spotlight, but Dallas could still see him outlined against the building, his arms and legs rotating in frantic swimming motions as he trailed downward through all the other emergency lights. Dallas looked away just before the man hit.

"Holy shit," the woman said. "I didn't mean to . . ." Her voice tapered off.

The fat man jogged past them on the sidewalk. "Talk to

me," he said into the walkie-talkie, oblivious to anyone around him. "They get that airbag infla. . . . No? Not quite, huh? Christ." He shook his head. "Soon as they stow the body in the bag, get the cleanup started. We still have a show to do." The fat man glanced toward them, caught Dallas's eye, then shrugged and walked away.

Quietly, the dealer woman turned, slump shouldered now, and walked toward the rear of the large parking lot without saying another word. Dallas began retracing his own steps, sorry he'd ever wandered down here. There was a whole big city to walk in, and damn if he didn't make his way straight to this poor guy to watch the last few minutes of *his* bad luck.

He turned left at the intersection and reentered the industrial neighborhood he'd come through earlier. He moved slowly, feeling the drag of a tide that had been pulling at him for days, a devastating sadness that he'd refused to acknowledge since, well, since Sunday night, since Rudd. He'd been fighting that reality, of course, struggling for a hold on all of this, but there wasn't one, just like there wasn't anything left for that guy out on the ledge. In a stark, split-second image, he saw the flier again, churning through the air, leaving it all behind.

Dallas walked faster. And it wasn't just the Rudd ordeal, though that in itself was enough. Something was going on inside him, something he hadn't told another soul about. A doctor had confirmed it a couple of weeks ago. Some blood test or other was flipping off the charts, substantiated by the doctor's own finger-of-fire rectal exam and a needle biopsy. But Dallas didn't really need a doctor or lab tests to tell him that his body was letting him down, that his prostate was burning, swollen, and terribly wrong.

So what was the point now? Was he going to sit in a cell with cancer? Turn into some emaciated old man waiting to die in prison? If it was fair to contemplate your life, it was certainly fair to contemplate your death. He, of all people, having lived hard and remote and mostly off the land, understood that as a natural part of the cycle.

Within sight of the Oasis, he spotted a weather-beaten bus

bench and took a seat. Gradually, the noise of traffic dulled as did the rumble in his head. Dallas looked up, but any chance of seeing the stars was obliterated by the city light. He slumped in the seat and pulled his hat down tighter on his forehead, then folded his arms across his chest. He wondered if it was balls or the lack of balls that would finally make a man take that jump.

CHAPTER TEN

SWANK. THAT'S THE WORD CHRISTINE THOUGHT OF WHEN SHE and Layne entered the Saltwater Grillade. Its interior was all deep red leather and mahogany wood, and it was beautiful in its bygone way, one of the only authentic old-time supper clubs still existing among the flotsam of fast food and Roman-casino chic on the Las Vegas Strip. The Grillade's specialty was lobster, Maine lobster flown in fresh, huge blue and gray and yellow shelled creatures moving sluggishly in bubbling tanks behind a wall at the rear of the restaurant. Layne had picked the place, saying privately that drawn butter and violin music might help soften this warrior named Uwanda. Christine glanced around nervously—they were almost fifteen minutes late because of road construction and bumper-to-bumper traffic—but she couldn't spot Uwanda Docksteader. She realized her palms were sweating and discreetly dried them on the sides of her linen pants.

The tuxedoed maitre d' bowed slightly and addressed them in thick broken English. "Bonjour, mademoiselle. Monsieur. How may I be of service?"

"Layne. Party of—" he paused. "Actually, we'll be three, tonight."

A small dark cloud crossed the maître d's face. "Yes, of course. Your *party* is already seated." He spun on his heel and beckoned them to follow. They were escorted to a large, horse-shoe-shaped booth, high-backed and private. The table was draped in crisp linen and a single candle burned inside a thick crystal goblet, refracting glittery light over the tablecloth. In contrast, a toe-tapping Uwanda Docksteader, dressed like a gypsy, was hunched over a glass of white wine and several Xeroxed copies of Las Vegas newspaper articles whose tabloid headlines were clearly readable the moment they rounded the corner: "Cowboy Killer Slices and Dices Mister Bomb"; "Kitchen Knife Nukes Atomic Scientist."

Christine felt her stomach tighten.

Uwanda continued to stare at one of the articles for an additional rude second. The maître d' departed wordlessly without waiting for them to be seated or performing the obligatory unfurling of napkins across their laps.

Uwanda eventually looked up at them, scowling. "Where's Mr. Parker?" she asked.

Layne took a step backward. Christine quickly slid into the booth next to Uwanda, who moved over just a little. Christine had dealt with her share of unruly students, haughty principals, and cranky fellow teachers. Don't buy this woman's act, she told herself. We need her, need to figure out where her soft spot is. Layne sat down next to Uwanda and opposite Christine.

"I'm so sorry we're late," Christine said. "Everyone in town must have decided to drive all at the same time."

"And Uncle Dallas? Is he coming?" Uwanda leaned back, placed a beefy arm on the top of her seat, and tapped her fingers against the rich leather. "I hope you guys aren't putting me on here."

"No, no," Christine reassured her. "My uncle isn't . . . believe me, we're not putting you on. He's just not feeling well." As the thought formed and then the words spilled out, she was reminded that her statement was deeper and more personal than just a convenient excuse for Dallas's nonappearance.

The waiter appeared and a silent truce was declared while they ordered drinks.

"So I get the supporting cast," Uwanda half-growled as he left. "If Rudd made some deathbed confession—and I've racked

my brains all afternoon over what else it could possibly be—
we're going to need your uncle. I'm not taking anything to
Joseph Attencio that I don't one hundred percent believe, that I
don't hear directly from Mr. Parker." She seemed to pause for
effect. "Unless one of you wants to tell me you were his accomplice that night."

Layne jumped in without warning, and now Christine was
happy for the help. "Ms. Docksteader. We sat in on your case
this morning. I listened to counsels' arguments. I listened to
both motions, including the basis for the government's motion
for a directed verdict. It appears to me that—"

"Mr. Harting. Excuse me! I've been working on this case for
over ten years. No, I've been working on this case *all my life*!
You don't have to tell me what happened this morning."
Uwanda glared at him. Below the scarf wrapped and tied into
her hair, a slight sheen had begun to form on her broad forehead, in spite of the perfectly conditioned air.

"No offense to your lawyerly perceptions," she continued,
"but my teenagers could have told you that those were not
exactly Kodak moments for our side today. If Judge Sanders
gets a wild hair up his rumpola and grants the defendant's
motion for a directed verdict, it's pretty obvious that it's all
over. Not just this trial, but years and years of work, by Joseph
Attencio and myself, and a whole lot of other people." She
brought the glass of wine to her lips and sipped almost daintily,
leaving a petal of bright orange lipstick on the rim. Her hand
was shaking slightly. "But it's not really the work that's important," she said, her jaw set and jutting forcefully. "It's real
people who have suffered true injury and death. Families torn
apart. Hardworking rural families who don't have the desire or
the sophistication to march on Washington. They are not accustomed to being lied to by their own government. They are not
cynical. I cannot begin to describe to you the entire scope, all
the damage that goddamn test site has done to people like —"
Abruptly, she stopped and looked down into her lap.

Christine watched this large and combative woman begin to

dissolve, watched as her lips bunched together with the effort of fighting back her emotions. She instinctively reached out and put a hand on the woman's shoulder.

There was no denying that next to Uwanda, Christine felt wimpy and self-centered, a cop-out. She recalled being up on that ridge above Motoqua a couple of days ago, reading Rudd's manuscript, looking out toward the Nevada test site. She didn't really know Uwanda Docksteader's story, but having had a few moments of single-minded clarity up on that breezy lookout, she thought perhaps she could make an educated guess. And now she was ashamed of herself for falling back so quickly into fear and immobility, once again surrendering and deferring to the menfolk because someone killed a dog.

She heard Layne mumble an excuse about needing to go to the bathroom. She removed her hand from Uwanda's shoulder, while shooting him a hopeful look. He nodded in silent encouragement as he stood, giving her one of those little half-smiles that seemed to say *keep the faith, we don't discourage that easily*. She looked back at Uwanda, who was now tracing an enlarged circle over the linen tablecloth with the bottom of her wineglass.

Uwanda finally said with her now customary bluntness, "So what's your involvement here? Do you have a vested interest in some part of this? Or are you just a supportive relative?"

Christine didn't reply. She simply looked directly at Uwanda, at her dark eyes and the dark circles under them. For a moment, it appeared that the stare might become competitive, but Uwanda broke off with a sigh.

"Oh, don't mind me. I'm just . . ." Uwanda turned her head without finishing, appeared to examine some abstract and unknowable painting on the opposite wall.

"Do you happen to know where Motoqua is?" Christine said. She had known other women like this, women whose scorched and tattered exteriors belied the truth of what was inside.

Uwanda shook her head. "Never even heard of it. Until today, that is. It was mentioned in one of these articles. Out near the reservation." Uwanda waved her hand over the papers in front of her. "Even mentions you in passing, says you're visiting your uncle, up here from Phoenix."

Christine nodded. "Could you please put those clippings away?" She said this evenly, without rancor. "Please?"

Uwanda looked at her, then, almost shyly, gathered up the papers, placed them in files, and inserted them back into a large, overflowing briefcase. "I'm sorry. I can get pretty wrapped up in my own little world at times." She slipped the briefcase off the seat, placing it at her feet.

"Do you know where Gunlock is?" Christine asked.

Uwanda nodded. "A quiet little place. Nothing much there."

"Well, Motoqua is west of that," Christine said, "ten miles from the Nevada border, pretty much out in the middle of nowhere."

"I think I know the general area. The Beaver Dam Wash, Bull Mountain, Gunlock, Veyo. It's all just southwest of where I grew up in Newcastle." Uwanda shrugged, but had begun to eye Christine suspiciously. "That whole area down there, that whole corridor really got plastered by fallout back in the fifties. Even so, we have a hard time making the connection in court. The government still holds all the cards. It did all the monitoring, has all the data. We should have been more self-protective, but we just didn't know enough."

"No, we didn't," Christine said quietly, "at least my parents didn't. Uncle Dallas didn't. If they had, I'm sure they—" Christine stopped herself, a sudden swelling lodging in her throat.

Uwanda reached over now and touched Christine on the arm. "Go on. I guess I know where you're going with this now. I'm a lifer, Christine Parker, like my mother before me. I've heard—and seen—it all. Please go on."

Christine took a sip of her martini rocks, thankful for the smooth but potent vodka clearing her throat. "I was born on Dallas's ranch. My father was raised there, met my mother. I'm the oldest. They tried to make a go of it, but . . ." Christine shrugged, "but couldn't. We moved to Phoenix when I was two. Not because of the testing—no one really knew enough. Because of the money. Not enough of it coming in." She dug one small, stubborn olive out of the bottom of her glass and ate it. "I guess we never gave it much thought after that. Even though we heard things. You know, about problems. But we were far away by then and nothing ever . . ." Christine paused again and tried to clear her throat, "Excuse me, I'm kind of new at this. Until, until about a year ago. That's when my life turned . . . upside down."

She was looking into her lap. She felt Uwanda watching her, felt tears finally escaping her eyes, splashing down on her hands. Uwanda let out a great, unsmothered sigh, slid over next to Christine, and hugged her, enveloping her into practiced arms. She had the grip of a mother bear, and it was not unpleasant. The fleeting scent of Chantilly or some old-fashioned fragrance lingered on Uwanda's neck, and Christine felt herself squeezing back, genuinely liking this woman, this strange, wonderful amalgam of bluster and beauty, who now seemed to be officially welcoming her into that club of hers called Downwinders.

Christine became aware of another presence at the table. She drew away and looked up to see Layne standing there. Awkward, eyes questioning, vaguely shaking his head in total wonderment. She burst out laughing, a sudden and unexpected release with a blubbery bubble at the end. Uwanda stared at her as it popped out of her mouth, and then completely lost it, hee-hawing so loud that diners at all the adjoining tables turned to stare.

"Guess I won't go to the bathroom again," he said, sitting down, "miss all the fun."

"Aw, we were just telling dirty jokes," Uwanda said.

"Gotcha," he said, "Us guys, we always hug on our best jokes, too."

Men are so linear, Christine laughed silently, they just don't get it. Her friend Gwynn called it *women in a heap*—one small confidence leads to a meaningful secret, leads to pledges of unending support until it all crescendos, until they were all spent and exhausted—more or less in a heap.

The server arrived just in time. Recommendations were made, orders were taken. Bottles of wine were presented, sampled and approved. All during which, there was a bit of chitchat, some coded statements from Uwanda to Christine, and an informal welcoming of Layne into the club.

"Okay, so tell me, guys," Uwanda finally said, "you got to know, I'm just dying, dying of curiosity. Whada ya got?"

Christine and Layne exchanged glances. He spoke first, "A couple of things. We need a promise, a serious commitment from you."

Uwanda dropped back for a moment into her suspicious, guarded self. "You want me to promise without—"

"Just a simple promise, that regardless of where we go from here, you didn't hear any of this from us."

Uwanda's face brightened. "Confidential sources, of course." She huffed a little, "I've got finks, excuse me, I mean *sources* in several government jobs. It's just that they don't know enough. But I've never ratted off a source. You can set your clock by Big U, tell time by that one," she said a bit smugly.

"Number two," Layne said without hesitation, "this thing is dangerous. We don't even know how dangerous. Or which direction it's coming from. But you have to know that getting involved with this is risky as hell."

"Risky, schmisky," she said. "If you have something good, I'll do the low crawl to get at it. Let's get on with it."

Layne shook his head. "Okay," he smiled, then paused, looking at Christine. "Go on. It's your show."

Christine said, "Well, you are not going to believe this. Rudd was about to publish his memoirs. He wrote a four-hundred page book. He goes through a complete history—"

"His memoirs?" Uwanda butted in, impatient, speaking fast. "We could care less if he ever wet the bed or hated his dad. Does he rat 'em off? Say yes, please say yes. Does he nail the test site?"

"Hold your water, lady," Christine said calmly. For the first time since Sunday night, she felt herself filling a natural role;

she felt like a player. "Memoir or whatever you want to call it. It's all about the test site. Rudd cites chapter and verse, documents, dozens and dozens of instances where the managers covered things up. How they shredded documents and replaced them with—"

Uwanda suddenly looked stricken. "What's wrong?" Christine asked.

"Shredded. That's what's wrong," Uwanda said. "I've had this conversation with Joseph many times. Even if we can get someone to tell us what happened—before they all die off—including Rudd, even in writing, the court will be skeptical of anything but actual documents and—"

"How about copies?" Layne broke in.

Uwanda looked over at him. "Sure, copies, copies are . . . what the hell are you saying to me?"

"Just that Rudd was handy with a little spy camera or something." Layne was still smiling. "His book includes over a hundred exhibits, somehow smuggled off the test site, every last mother one stamped classified, top secret, the works."

Christine watched Uwanda fall into a kind of slack-faced trance. Her eyes were almost blank, her jaw hanging. "It's true, Uwanda," she said, "not only are the documents there but Rudd tells a completely believable insider's story explaining them. Many of them are, according to Rudd, the only copies in existence. Most of the originals were destroyed. They wouldn't exist today if he hadn't copied and smuggled them out."

"My God almighty," Uwanda said, "tell me that you're not kidding. Where is this thing?"

"You'll find that out when we deliver it to Attencio and the press," Layne said. "Until then, for your own good, you don't know jack. Or his cousin shit."

Uwanda said, "So you'll be delivering it?"

"You just clear a path," Christine said, pleased with a new bit of authority in her voice. "But you better have another drink, dear," Christine continued, "there's more."

"More? More than this? That's not possible," Uwanda said. She lifted her wine glass and drained half of it.

Christine wasn't smiling now. She looked at Layne. They'd had their little occasion to revel in Uwanda's reaction, enjoyed this moment in the sun in an otherwise very cloudy week. Now they had to tell her about the rest. Layne came in right on cue.

"The news isn't all good," he began. "As you might imagine, something like this is bound to attract other interested parties."

Uwanda had recovered. "Sure, sure. Go on. I hear you." She leaned in conspiratorially, gearing into serious mode right along with them. "Need someone to rumble?" she said, massive forearm planted on the table. "Big U's your gal."

"This is way beyond rumble," Layne said. "Rudd's dead, and if Dallas hadn't—" he stopped. "Let me rephrase that. The FBI has caught wind of this thing. I'm convinced of that. An agent named Mack Sayles has been asking questions. They just don't know exactly what we've got or where we've got it. If they did, we'd be in jail. Or worse." Layne paused, seemed to want his words to sink in. "And I think that there are others. Last night, someone tried to get to us at Dallas's ranch. Dallas took a shot at them. Whoever it was killed Dallas's dog when it attacked. In addition, my office and home were searched, illegally. Christine's car was searched and vandalized." Layne leaned back and took a drink. "Someone is trying to get us alone or scare us. They haven't succeeded on the former, but the latter they've got well covered."

Christine had listened carefully. It suddenly felt very serious again. Back to reality. She marveled at how one minute they could be laughing and talking about Rudd's book in such glowing, save-the-day terms, and the next minute be sitting around waiting for the hammer to drop.

"This is dangerous, Uwanda," she warned, "you've got to believe that, you've got to be careful. It was our only compunction in telling you."

For the first time, Uwanda nodded without any wisecracks. She kept her face stern, but finally couldn't hold it. "They're not going to gun us down in here, are they?"

Layne looked puzzled. "I . . . er, certainly don't think so."

"Well, then, Lord sakes," Uwanda grinned, "let's celebrate."

Her timing was perfect. From there, the courses began hitting the cloth with orchestral precision. By the time dinner was finished and the heated Grand Marnier served, their group had become chummy beyond all reckoning, chummy and modestly profane. Rudd, that mother-fuzzer, and his manuscript had been hashed and rehashed and its future course charted. Uwanda would call Attencio tonight; they would meet first thing in the morning. Layne stressed and restressed the need for caution to Uwanda, who brushed it all aside, saying that her whole life had been lived for this moment and she sure as heck wasn't going to sit around clucking like a chicken now. Everyone's problems were solved. Except Rudd's, but at least the old dick's life hadn't been a complete waste after all. By tomorrow morning, the manuscript would be enshrined in a proper home—the consciousness of the American people, as Uwanda put it. Christine hoped so. God, did she ever hope so.

Uwanda was giggling at Layne and being a little flirtatious as she sipped on her after-dinner drink. "I can hardly wait to call Joseph. He'll drop his teeth on this one." They all hooted laughter, were all getting tipsy. "Oh, and, by the way, regarding that crack I made during dinner about my cousin Faye. I hope you don't mish . . . understand." She giggled again. "It's just that I have a running war with the Mormon Church, and if you live in southwest Utah, that's sort of like belonging to a small, starving band of Apaches trying to avoid the U.S. Cavalry."

"Tell me about it." Layne raised his glass. "Here's to heresy, here's to anarchy, here's to—" he paused, "living in the only place on earth where a Jew is called a gentile."

Uwanda tossed her head back and hooted again. "And," she leaned forward, whispering, raising her glass conspiratorially, "to the manuscript."

Christine raised her glass, too, her sides sore from laughing. God, it felt good to enjoy the moment, relish some small victory in their saga.

"It's a perfect fit," Layne was saying to Uwanda, "there's no better home for that book. And," he smiled, "you ain't half as mean as you walk around pretending to be. In fact, here's to you and here's to your cause." He raised his glass and they all toasted again. "You're a real sweetheart, baby," Layne drawled in a bad New York accent.

Uwanda rolled her eyes at Christine, pursed her lips in mock embarrassment. "Lord," she said, "you better calm your man down. I don't think I've made a guy this happy since—the drive-in movie when I was nineteen."

Friday night, and this particular segment of the human race was eating itself to death, ordering expensive four-course crab and lobster meals, plowing every mouthful through warm butter, washing it all down with expensive French wines—at least that's how it looked to Manos sitting in the bar of the Saltwater Grillade. He had avoided the busy maitre d' in the lobby and floated up a few steps to the split-level bar that overlooked the starched elegance of the dining room—perpetual twilight, servers moving about like marionettes, airy violin music floating above it all. Manos knew all about the fancy Grillade. Occasionally, when he met a new girl—he might even think of her as a "Saltwater" girl: young and impressionable and fresh off the bus—he would represent himself as an "investor" and bring her here and insist that she try the hundred-dollar live lobster feast. Then buzz her up with moneyed talk of real estate deals and mergers while speculating silently about the muscle tone between her legs. This was a long way from Topeka or the hills of Chattanooga and it worked every time.

Tonight he was sitting alone, however, impatient and pissed off after two and a half hours of hiding behind the smoky glassed-in architecture of the bar, sipping on his shot of Porfidio, raking the crowd with his eyes—more bored than predatory by now—and watching Lawyer Harting finally, finally request the bill. Observing the three of them in their plump, high-backed leather booth ordering more wine, yukking it up, huddling over the table and whispering, eyes wide with excitement, the hippo broad noisily cruising through a lobster the size of a violin: all of it had taxed the last ounce of his patience and fueled his fantasies of payback—the Parker girl for instance, still a part of this unfinished business.

He lifted his glass of tequila—clear, sun-blazed, sharp—and drank. His wrist was wrapped in white gauze, still looked like hamburger, but it was nothing really, just a little pain, an unexpected souvenir, a motivator from two nights ago. Things hadn't gone exactly according to plan, but no matter. He was here to pick up the pieces. He shifted on his stool, popped the knuckles of his left hand, and listened absently to the couple, tanned and middle aged, sitting at the bar next to him.

"Now?"

"No. Tomorrow."

"How come?"

"Just forget it."

"No way."

"Whatever."

A woozy young counselor finishing an internship by visiting inmates once told Manos that the only thing harder than living with someone else was living alone. Jesus Christ. He looked up at a row of slow-moving fans high overhead, feeling choked up about his loss, about missing all those cozy little cycles of bickering and irritation.

He glanced back down at the Three Musketeers. Pay the bill, people, let's get out of here. The lawyer finally signed the receipt, tore off his copy as they gathered themselves then started toward the lobby. Manos dropped a couple of bills on the gleaming surface of the granite bar and followed. Out in the parking lot, the two women hugged each other and laughed and hugged again. The lawyer leaned against the back of a blue Ford station wagon, grinning, seeming unable to contain his own joy. The hippo broad thrust her arms outward and upward, operatically, the giant florals of her loose sarong hanging like curtains, then whirled on the lawyer and gave him a big, fat kiss on the lips.

Manos observed this heartwarming display as he skirted the edge of the parking lot, moving slowly toward his own car. So long as there was progress, it was okay, their joy was his joy. They could be ringing their little bells gladly about only one thing—the book—and he was getting closer, he could feel it.

He'd lost their trail yesterday but picked it up again at the Federal Courthouse this morning. The lawyer's secretary had initially been very close-lipped. Manos finally got a female "associate" to pose as Judge Pelton T. Andrews's clerk, saying that the judge was going to revoke Mr. Parker's bail within the hour if his whereabouts were not immediately made known to the court. Manos, listening on an extension line, could hear a pause on the other end.

"And what did you say your name was?" Harting's secretary asked.

"Haberman. Nancy Haberman," the name spilling out as smooth as oil from a young woman who hadn't uttered a word of truth in over ten years. "I'm Judge Andrews's clerk."

On the Utah end of the line, a baby cried in the background. "Yeah, okay. Federal Courthouse in Las Vegas," the secretary said over more squawking. "Lisa, quit torturing your sister. Heavens. Just tell the judge it's official business. They're meeting with witnesses in the Parker case."

"Who are they meeting? The judge will want to know."

There was another pause, shattered by a child's broken-hearted shriek. "Levi! Stop. Give that back to her. Sorry. It's Docksteader, they're meeting a Uwanda Docksteader."

Manos had been able to spot all of them at the trial this morning without being seen himself. From there the pieces lined up like refrigerator magnets: Federal Courthouse, big lawsuit over atomic bombs, old geezer scientist murdered, tell-all book about atomic bombs, Deputy Dog Hiney's office in said courthouse, he does legwork for the government on this downwind case, and so on. It didn't take a genius. A few phone calls, a little research and deductive reasoning, and the value of such a book to the downwinders was obvious. Which made it even more valuable to certain persons or agencies, the ones who cherished secrecy, the ones that abhorred arriving at their unnumbered offices and finding themselves confronted by a reporter's surprise questions that could only be no-commented upon. And if the spooks' embarrassment factor didn't translate into sufficient funds, then Manos was certain that he could wiggle through the channels of a foreign drug lord or a Middle Eastern arms dealer, someone who could easily spring for mid-six figures, pocket change, just to have a little anti-U.S. government bombshell in their portfolio.

Manos knew, however, that he was running out of time. It was becoming obvious now where this manuscript was headed; he had to get his hands on it before they turned it over to the court. Once it went public, all his leverage evaporated.

As he reached the black Jaguar, the immediate question became who to follow. This afternoon he had tailed the Land Cruiser back to the Oasis Hotel, was able to bribe a clerk out of three phony names and room numbers. He could keep following them now, probably back to the Oasis, but there was a new player, a new option to pursue. And Manos's world ultimately came down to the risks versus the rewards—go in after the jewelry, pull a gun in a drug deal or have beans for lunch. It was a continuous and prickly assessment. He didn't love the odds at the Oasis: the old cowboy's guns, three people to control, other guests getting in the way, the possibility of getting trapped on the sixth floor.

His determining factor, however, finally turned on the obvious. When he had followed the Land Cruiser from the Oasis, he was taking all precautions. They knew his black Jag; they might know by now that he wasn't a guy named Hanover. At any rate, spotting the car, spotting him, might send them running again; no point in pressing his luck. When they reached the Grillade, Manos had again kept his distance as the lawyer pulled into valet parking behind a screen of those damn oleanders. The Docksteader woman was already inside, so who came with what was uncertain, but one thing was for sure: Docksteader had padded out to the parking lot after dinner with an overstuffed briefcase in hand, the contents of which presented his best option.

The woman's blue Ford station wagon pulled out and he went with her, keeping a few lengths behind. She didn't know him or his car so he could stay a little closer. At a red light on the Strip, he could see her tilted back comfortably in her seat, staring straight ahead, paying little attention to anything around her. They headed north. The going was slow and noisy down the crowded street. It took time to reach the downtown area and then longer to get through it. Dazed gamblers wandered through the streets, a trillion blinking and humming lights in the background. Manos stayed close behind her. It was like driving through a herd of sheep.

Eventually they emerged on the north side and everything changed within a few blocks. North Las Vegas was an abandoned and abysmal island of poverty and crime. To Manos's grinning wonder, the Ford continued on in that direction, finally picking up Paraldo Run—The Runs, as the cops called it—a six lane main street that bisected this blighted area.

The traffic thinned out and he dropped a short way behind her, watching the stoplights ahead and gauging them to keep up. The overhead glitter of downtown and the Strip was now replaced by a more earthbound sparkle—a thousand points of light off broken glass littering the curbside and barren parking strips under each streetlamp. Unlicensed sidewalk entrepreneurs sprang up on every corner, vending goods and services from their pockets and bodily orifices. Manos knew all about business in The Runs—he was uptown now, but this is where he'd had to start when he first got out of the joint.

The blue Ford wagon stopped at a light and Manos braked, easing up slowly from the rear, not getting too close. His shiny Jaguar with its chrome wire wheels stood out like a drug dealer's cell phone down here. Two young hookers, one black and one white, about fifteen or sixteen he guessed, were standing on the near corner under a streetlight. The black one—wearing spike heels, pink tights, and a yellow halter—was doing the vertical splits, one long pink leg running straight up the lamppost. She hugged the pillar, smiling innocently and provocatively toward Manos's car.

The Docksteader woman glanced over at the hookers. A white Ford Escort—had to be a rental car—pulled around him and eased over to the curb to open discussions with the ladies. Manos knew that the cops rarely hassled these girls or set up decoys to snag the patrons. Live and let live was the motto in Vegas, so long as the streetwalkers stayed over here and out of the way, didn't push their luck.

The blue wagon pulled away when the light turned green. They passed a storefront bar with loud music and patrons spilling out onto the sidewalk, glasses of beer and whiskey in their hands. A pawn shop and a run-down motel on the other side of the street. Mama Eddie's Ribs was lit up farther down the block and doing a good business. Manos continued to be amazed that this big, conspicuous, middle-aged, middle-class white woman was driving deeper and deeper into The Runs. First she has dinner at one of the swankiest places in town, then comes down here. Was she a nut or a thrill seeker? Perhaps she had business down here—that was an intriguing possibility. On the other hand, he just hoped that she wasn't lost and trying to find her way onto the northbound freeway, that some bout of homesickness wasn't driving her all the way back to St. George for a quickie tonight. That would bum him out; he'd seen enough of that hick town.

Then, a few blocks farther on, the station wagon abruptly signaled left and swung across traffic into the Starlite Motel, a dilapidated two-story, brick complex of rooms. Manos killed his lights and waited across the street. The Docksteader woman parked her car, got out with her briefcase, walked to one of the lower units, fished a key from her purse, then let herself in. He'd be damned. That was the last thing he expected. She was actually staying down here, in one of the cheapest places in town. Rented by the hour, day, week or month. He shook his head. A seedy desk clerk was sitting in a well-lit, thick-glass booth that had been tacked onto the front of the building like a gun turret. The clerk barely glanced up from his magazine as the blue Ford pulled in.

Manos drove farther down the block, then parked the Jag in the shadows. He preferred to be directly under a streetlight, deter the punks from messing with it, but he also wanted to be less visible if things went wrong, if he needed to scoot out of here quickly. He reached into the backseat and grabbed a UNLV baseball cap and a lightweight black jacket. He slid out the passenger side and onto the street. Pulling the hat brim low, he locked his car and headed back toward the Starlite. Now he could smell what part of town he was in: heavy car exhaust, uncultivated dirt, overripe garbage cans and dumpsters. The side door of a tiny cafe oozed a gray haze of smoky oil and fried fish. Manos crossed the street and was approaching the parking lot when the Docksteader woman came out of her room, locked her door, and rumbled toward the front of the motel and a pay phone mounted there, next to and in plain view of the desk clerk.

Manos kept walking, then circled through the far side of the parking lot where the lights were burned out or broken. He stopped on the other side of her station wagon, comfortable with the darkness, and watched. If she was going off somewhere, this is where he'd intercept her, this is where they'd talk. The woman was on the phone, talking a mile a minute, waving her arms, very excited. The desk clerk began giving her malevolent looks. She noticed and simply turned her broad back, hunkering into the phone. Manos pulled a plastic toothpick from his pocket and idly pried between his white teeth.

She must have been on the phone fifteen minutes before she hung up and dug for more quarters. She made another short call. Finally, looking around more carefully now as if she felt him staring, she returned to her room while he held perfectly still in the shadows on the far side of her car. He waited a few minutes longer. It appeared that she was in for the night.

He worked his way toward the edge of the parking lot, ground glass and gravel crunching under his shoes. Headlights suddenly swung into the lot and Manos stopped next to a tree, turned to it and acted like he was taking a pee. A Latino prostitute and her client pulled in, paid at the booth, and went into a room at the very front of the Starlite. He waited for them to get settled and then continued in leisurely fashion toward the Docksteader room.

Finally, he stood directly in front of her door, leaning into it so that no one could see his face. The outside light was conveniently broken off at the fixture and it was dark. He knocked gently. He heard the bedsprings squeak as she must have stood up. The footsteps were tentative in their approach and her voice broke slightly in an attempt to sound in control and commanding. "Who is it?" she said.

"Ma'am, don't mean to disturb you, ma'am," Manos said in a southern nasal tone, something he'd perfected in prison to mock some hapless con. "The desk man ast me come down here and fetch you, ma'am. Said you had a phone call."

"A phone call?" There was a pause. "From whom? Did they give a name?"

"Don't know, ma'am. I'm new here. Desk just say come tell you." Manos paused and shuffled his feet noisily on the concrete. "I tell 'em call back tomorrow. That you sleepin' now, ma'am."

"No, wait." Another pause. "Look, you go tell them to hang on, stay on the line. Tell them don't hang up. Okay?"

"Yes, ma'am. I tell 'em." Manos took a couple of loud, scratching steps away from the door and heard her add in grunting tones to no one in particular, "Yeah. Tell them to hang on the line, because now I have to wrestle . . . this heavy damn refrigerator away from the door again."

Seldom were waking dreams so connected for Layne. Deep and hazy, but at the same time, stunningly clear. Christine was sitting on top of him, naked, her legs wide apart, eyes closed and head back, taking all of him, every last possibility deep inside. The radio was playing, neither loud nor quiet, and mixing in odd dissonance with the random sounds of traffic, an occasional horn far below. There were no lights on in the room, but lights from outside shone through the window onto the ceiling, a glancing rainbow of muted, flickering colors. Christine was moaning softly, a breathy sound that wove among the other noises and made him wonder abstractly if he was hurting her, if he was too deep, but at the same time, Layne understood completely as her hips undulated, her hands braced against his chest, that any hurt came from somewhere much deeper inside. The small alarm radio on the bedside table read three-something-a.m., but time held no meaning for him right now. They had been doing this, and variations of this, then resting quietly and resuming, over and over for the past three hours. Christine hadn't uttered a comprehensible word and neither had he since they'd first begun making love. Layne was by now afraid of words, afraid of breaking this fragile spell, and was resigned to the vocabulary of their bodies, moaning shudders and short breaths and blunt, salacious sounds to say it all.

They had returned to the hotel after leaving Uwanda Docksteader in the restaurant parking lot. By then, they were completely intoxicated on red wine, each other, and their unbelievable good fortune in accessing Attencio. All the draining stress and fatigue of this past week, all the restrained feelings and attraction and their individual loneliness had collided wildly the second they stepped over the threshold into Layne's hotel room and began tearing at clothes. They kissed hard, pressing into each other, sidestepping toward the bed and stumbling, garments fluttering like leaves. Layne pushed Christine back onto the edge of the bed and fell between her bare legs onto her stomach, his hands and face and tongue roaming over her chest. He heard her begin crying, softly, but he didn't stop. He wasn't sure what he had finally said or done in those first moments, in his awkward attempts at reassurance, but one thing he knew and knew with bone-drilling certainty: It didn't matter. Not one bit; not for one instant. She had one beautiful breast and one beautiful scar. It still added up to a beautiful woman. Those were his exact thoughts as he slid his body up further between her legs and entered her in slow and even motions. Her crying turned to gasping and he resolved that she would never, ever again have cause to mourn a missing breast.

And now, after hours of lovemaking, of falling deeper and deeper through indescribable layers of feelings he barely knew he had, her missing breast was just too far down the list of things that mattered. Layne elevated his hips and slid a pillow under them, settling even deeper inside her. Christine straightened up fully in response. He raised his knees behind her and she reached back and gripped his thighs, arched her back, dug her fingers into his legs, and tried to connect them there, too. Their hair was damp, their faces glistened, their stomachs—neither had a dry spot anywhere.

Christine spread her legs wider, moving and rotating over that exact spot, as if she wanted to engulf every part of him. Swallow him up inside of her, he thought, put him in that safe place and carry him, protect him. A new song came on the radio, something with a swaying steady beat and a woman's breathy voice that occasionally rose and lilted over the top of chanting monks. The mood of the song settled over the room, penetrated and fit with their own. Layne had been through athletic, endurance sex before; been humped over the top and fucked flat by women who gave as good as they got. He'd enjoyed most but not all of it. Never, however, had it even approached this. The magnetism of new and unexplored flesh combined with the repressed fact that he had been falling in love with her all week; and now the tenderness, the protectiveness that he felt toward Christine, merged on that blazing red scar zigzagging over her chest. The scar was, in some obtuse way that he had yet to understand, becoming a symbol in his mind, a welcome rebellion against the cultural norms of perpetual youth and beauty.

He moved his hands to her chest. Her right breast was full and voluptuous, the nipple hard and erect, the aureole pretty. On her left side was a long ragged scar in the shape of a Z, extending from under her arm almost to the middle of her chest and then back to the side of her rib cage. It was still red, hadn't settled to a flesh color.

Layne touched it, ran his fingers along the rough furrows in her otherwise smooth and even flesh. Watching her, touching her, he suddenly felt himself stirring toward another climax. He'd already come twice, the first had been fairly quick, the second following an hour or so later. As his excitement increased, it struck him that the last time he had made love—had sex—was in Las Vegas, and it had no relationship to what was happening tonight. Tonight, he was actually making love, flat out, and he was falling in love with a softness that he had never before felt toward a woman. The possibility of pregnancy—they had discussed nothing—crossed his mind just for a second, but he couldn't stop himself. Maybe a boy or a girl or twins.

And he became aware that her big, angry chest scar, her once fabulous and now missing breast, in some unfathomable way made it all the more intense and delicious to him. Layne lifted his hips, heard her moan in response. Bringing some sense into it, he realized, didn't matter so long as he could keep feeling this way.

The Conquerer

WARREN PARKER HAD NEVER NOTICED BEFORE HOW SAD THE sound of a hammer was. Metal against metal, it echoed with loss and emptiness. His wife, Audrey, barefoot and wearing a blue chenille robe, had stepped out of the house and into the garage to see what all the racket was.

"Lord God, Warren. What are you taking apart now?" she asked.

That woman, though he loved her to pieces, had a way of phrasing things. He looked down at her through the upper part of his glasses. Short silvery hair. A small, slightly rounded body. A face that still said pretty to him.

"Honey, I'm just trying to fix that little run-in you had with the garage door," he said, bringing the hammer down again.

At close range, Audrey must have heard it too—the pain and heartbreak—because she took two steps back and swung her hand up through the air. "I just wish . . . whatever," she said, then turned and walked slowly back into the house, the blue hem of her robe swaying right and left.

Warren tried to refocus on his task. Usually he would tackle a job like this—repairs, tinkering—with gusto, savoring the refuge of his garage with its smell of sawdust and motor oil, its orderly matrix of worn and useful tools.

Why, why, why? The word repeated like his relentless hammer. Why did it have to be his Christine who was sick? Or diseased. Or whatever the hell was the right word for it. Warren thought for a minute and decided that there was no right word. Your child facing this kind of trauma at age thirty-seven—there was no vocabulary for that. Or fairness. She was just getting back on her feet, getting over her divorce from that rat's-ass husband, Falco, then yesterday they had received the verdict after a biopsy: cancer.

Christine's doctor was a woman. Tiny, Asian, and young. Dr. Moritake was her name, but standing in the recovery room, she had told them to call her Sue. Still in green scrubs, she sat on the side of Christine's bed, placed her hand on top of Christine's as she explained everything.

"The results are just preliminary, but it looks like a middle stage malignancy," she said. "We would have liked to have caught it earlier. On the other hand, it's not terribly advanced."

The three Parkers nodded in unison, riveted on her every word.

"We'll get it," she said flatly. "With measured, aggressive treatments, your chances are very good." She squeezed Christine's shoulder. "I'll be back in shortly and we'll talk everything over and make some plans to get started."

Warren swung the hammer around hard, slamming it into the garage door. Gray paint flakes flew. A round ding appeared in the metal. Oh great, make it even worse. Of all the emotions in a father's repertoire, what he kept feeling this morning was outrage. Goddammit, why? A large part of him knew it was a useless, imponderable question, but in a strange way, he'd been asking it for years.

It all began almost forty years ago, during his "Hollywood days," as he called them, back in the early fifties when he'd been hired as an extra in a few movies shot in southern Utah. Most of them were no big deal—he was indistinguishable in a cavalry charge or a horde of space aliens—but in one, the biggest and best known, he rode a horse right alongside John Wayne who was starring as Genghis Khan. The movie was *The Conqueror*, a gigantic epic of its day produced personally by Howard Hughes, costarring Susan Hayward, and directed by Dick Powell.

Warren never considered himself particularly sentimental, but he bought a spiral notebook at about this time and began collecting autographs in it, local news articles, souvenirs, paycheck stubs, photographs—anything having to do with *The Conqueror*. The scrapbook even included Warren's own handwritten narrations. Back then, he could not have imagined a better time than those thirteen well-paid weeks of filming in the summer of 1954. He was twenty-two years old, living at Motoqua with Audrey and Dallas. The world seemed suddenly new, full of hope and possibilities and fine people. Like Christine, his one-month-old daughter. And John Wayne, that bulky six-foot-four figure standing at the edge of the set in the early morning, black coffee in hand, sizing up the day's scene. In his slow, gravelly voice, he wanted to know how the cameras would be set, which direction the horses would run.

Warren, who was being paid both as a Mongolian extra and as a wrangler to help with the feeding and care of the horses, found himself being buddied up to by Wayne. While most of the other starring cast stayed in their trailers until their scenes were ready to be shot, Wayne roamed, sweet-talked another small slice of pie from the deluxe chuck wagon, and then grumbled to Warren over at the corrals that the studio had him on a diet—cottage cheese, hard-boiled eggs, salad—but worst of all, he claimed with bullied good humor, they were making him go thirsty. His usual bourbon and brandy were totally off limits. Warren even observed Wayne working out with a fencing coach, smoothing his moves for the movie's required swordplay. It was impossible for him not to add a cowboy's touch to his swashbuckling, but that was alright since even the director had described this movie as an Oriental western: "Some good guys, some bad guys. Some fighting, some loving."

Susan Hayward stepped in for the "some loving" part. When she arrived on location, Warren was surprised at how quiet she was, reserved and almost shy. With her gorgeous red hair and hazel eyes, she walked demurely around the set, seeming more a southern belle than a Tartar princess, despite all the sun and sand and wind.

Filming started in May, and as June proceeded, temperatures climbed toward 110 degrees. In the glaring sun and blistering heat, it was easy to see southern Utah as a desolate chunk at the end of the earth. For Warren, however, it was heaven. He'd been born out in this country, and a little sand and heat was nothing compared to all the excitement.

Snow Canyon, the movie's location just twelve miles west of St. George, was already a desert, but for the purposes of the big screen, it had to be transformed from tourists and Mormons to warriors and nomads. It had to become the Gobi Desert, complete with howling wind and ravaging sandstorms. To that end, industrial-size fans were brought on site to stir up a gritty brew; then the extras, dressed in blousy pants and furry snow boots, many of them shirtless, mounted their horses and rode through it, first one way and then the other, playing both sides of warring Mongol tribes. Warren, who rode his own skittish Appaloosa bareback during those scenes, felt sand in every pore of his body, had to scrub himself raw to get the yellow makeup caked with sand and dust off his arms and face and torso. It felt as if they all had permanent grit between their teeth. Even without the giant fans blowing, two hundred cast and crew members made their own cloud of fine powdery dust by merely walking around the set. The camera and support crew, who took to tying bandanas around their lower faces, looked like a mass of stagecoach robbers. And then, to stir things up even more, a half-dozen big dump trucks arrived on the scene in the last few weeks of shooting and began loading sixty tons of sand for transport back to Hollywood, where RKO would use it to recreate an indoor desert set for retakes and close-ups.

"To Warren, my favorite cowboy and Mongol. Thanks a bunch, pardner!" Signed John Wayne. It was written on a plain white napkin and given to Warren just hours before a silver limo arrived to take the departing Wayne to the airport and back to California. The napkin, of course, went immediately into Warren's *Conqueror* scrapbook, which for several years thereafter mostly sat in a drawer, coming out on a special occasion or a nostalgic Sunday afternoon. Then, in 1958, after

Warren had relocated his life and family in Phoenix, he noticed in a copy of *Movie* magazine that a *Conqueror* costar, Pedro Armendariz, had been diagnosed with kidney cancer. Warren cut out the article and tucked it away in the scrapbook, never imagining that a few years later, in 1963, another news article would be paired with it: Armendariz, at age fifty-one, had killed himself soon after being diagnosed with lymphatic cancer as well.

It seemed like only a strange fluke when *Conqueror* director Dick Powell succumbed to lung cancer later that same year. Warren added Powell's obituary to his scrapbook, remembering how he had genuinely liked this man, had felt sorry for him and the rest of the cast when *The Conqueror* was practically laughed out of theaters on its 1956 release.

By 1974, another costar was dying, this time of uterine cancer. Agnes Moorehead had played Ghengis Khan's mother and was quoted as saying to her dear friend, Jeanne Gerson, that "Everybody in that picture has gotten cancer and died." This news was not well received by Gerson, who had also played a role in *The Conqueror*. She later developed breast cancer.

The next death came in 1975—Susan Hayward, who had secretly been battling skin, breast, and uterine cancer for almost a decade. Warren felt queasy at the macabre turn his scrapbook had taken, but he continued his chronicle nonetheless. It was the year 1979 when Warren added the most pages to his scrapbook, however, the year John Wayne's fight with lung, throat, and stomach cancer finally came to an end.

Not only had a Western icon been lost by the American public, but the deaths of so many closely connected movie stars stirred up a controversy around atomic testing and related illness, with one Hollywood cancer specialist calling *The Conqueror* "less a movie than an epidemic." Warren didn't have to dig for the information. Articles appeared frequently in national magazines and newspapers, adding new words to his vocabulary: *iodine 131, plutonium 283, radioactive cesium 137, strontium 90*; deadly fission byproducts that, along with many others, had been found in recent Utah soil tests along the Colorado Plateau, in the Salt Lake Valley to the north, and at the site of *The Conqueror* filming—Snow Canyon, its towering sidewall landscape acting as a funneling device, a virtual reservoir where radioactive fallout had gathered from Shot Simon, Dirty Harry, and other 1953 tests in the Upshot-Knothole series. One of the articles that Warren saved in his scrapbook even quoted, anonymously of course, an official from the old Atomic Energy Commission—which had been disbanded by the time of the Duke's death and rolled quietly into the Department of Energy—in a banner headline, "Oh My God. I Hope We Didn't Kill John Wayne."

Warren was no scientist, but it wasn't especially difficult to understand the deadly details being batted about in the media. During atomic explosions, vast amounts of sand were scooped up and vaporized, often carrying new elements, some of which were radioactive. The time it took for this radioactivity to dissipate from an element was known as its half-life. Rubidium 90, for instance, had a half-life of only 4.28 minutes—the time it took for the beta radiation to decrease by half. Strontium 90, on the other hand, had a half-life of 28.9 years, and the real problem was, as Warren found out, that this element resembled calcium and was absorbed by the human body, finding its way into the bones and emitting radiation there throughout its half-life. Cesium 137, with a half-life of thirty years, also targeted the bones, Iodine 131 ended up in the thyroid, uranium often went to the kidneys, and zinc to the prostate. And it was hard for him to even comprehend plutonium, with a half-life of over one hundred thousand years.

Shaken by Wayne's death and the host of disturbing facts appearing in the media, Warren sat down one afternoon and drew vertical lines with an old wooden ruler to make a ledger in his scrapbook. Then, with a complete list of cast and crew provided by the California Historical Filmmaking Institute, he entered all 220 names from *The Conqueror*—including his own.

Looking over his shoulder, Audrey had shaken her head.

"It's morbid, Warren. Kooky and morbid," she told him.

"The scrapbook's just a hobby," he told her.

"What?" she said. "Are you waiting to check off your own name?"

"These are some people I knew and cared about. Part of a fateful, endangered group," he explained.

"Aren't we all?" she answered.

By then, Warren realized that his scrapbook was serving a different purpose than the one he'd intended, but it wasn't his to determine fate, merely to record it. And so he began keeping track—counting coup. Of the cast and crew who worked on the film, an astonishing ninety-one had contracted cancer, and of those, at least half had died.

Warren had moved over to his workbench now and was fixing a section of the chain that raised and lowered the garage door, replacing some links that had been twisted and tweaked. Working in the quiet of his garage, he wondered half-aloud if he had created a jinx. Never for a moment did he imagine that the deadly legacy he had been chronicling would fall to his daughter Christine.

"Dammit," Warren said as the needle-nose pliers slipped off again. Normally, he was the epitome of patience in handling such a task, but not today. Despite some encouraging statistics bandied around yesterday by Dr. Sue, Warren knew the score, had been collecting and studying it for about thirty years in that damn scrapbook.

His glasses slipped down the bridge of his nose and he pushed them up with the back of his hand, knocking sweat down off his forehead, the salt stinging his eyes. Suddenly, with the concentrated effort of a lightning bolt, he threw down his tools, turned away from his workbench, and marched into the house.

The scrapbook was in a spare bedroom that Audrey liked to call the study. Warren picked it up out of the bottom dresser drawer, dirty hands and all, and started back toward the kitchen. He didn't know exactly what he was doing—just that one step was leading to the next—as he pushed the sliding door to the patio open with his elbow and went outside.

Audrey watched him from the kitchen sink and followed him to the door. "What?" she asked him. "What is it?"

Without answering, he approached the barbecue and opened the lid, grabbed a wooden match and turned the gas on high.

"Honey," she said, "don't you want to talk."

He removed the grate and tossed the bulky scrapbook directly onto the flames. He already knew the headlines— "Golden Girl Gives In." "The Duke Goes Down." "Officials Deny Link." The cover didn't burn, but melted and shriveled like some slinky thing from the deep. Warren didn't feel a thing until the pages began to burn, curling one at a time, closing slowly like black flowers. Wordlessly, he watched pieces of ash rise, less the weight of smoke, then drift on a slight breeze over the patio and into the sunshine covering the emerald lawn.

CHAPTER ELEVEN

THE RED DIGITAL NUMBERS OF THE CLOCK ON THE BEDSIDE table showed 6:10, too early for Christine to be pulled from sleep, too soon for her to become restless with Layne's sweet warmth stretched there at her side. They had slept this way, cradled and facing each other, their feet touching, their hands nested, their faces so close that they had breathed each other all night long, but she was awake now, fully and inexplicably awake after only three hours of sleep. And she was silently talking to herself, a conversation, as if there were two of her: a rational, cool, smart Christine with a case of the jitters, and an impetuous goof, ready to toss it all to the wind.

She rolled onto her back. One week, she told herself. You've known this guy less than one week. It was a reasonable admonishment, but as she glanced over at the dark, blanketed form that was Layne, her argument immediately softened. He had felt so good—all of it had been so good! Of course she was sex starved, but last night had been . . . about something so much more. Oh shit, she thought, trying to apply the brakes. This is crazy!

She closed her eyes and took a long, slow breath. Sex had a smell, a definite smell, and this hotel room was full of it. Ripe cantaloupe or ocean water—musky, thick.

Christine jumped slightly at the phone's first ring and, before a second rude, cold noise could fill the room, picked up the receiver on the nightstand next to her. "Hello," she heard herself say, her voice still rough with sleep.

"Layne Harting, please." It was a full, smooth, vaguely familiar voice.

Christine felt Layne lazily roll over, spoon his back to her, and pull the covers over his head. She lifted herself onto one elbow and tried to quietly clear her throat.

"He isn't . . . um . . ." She quickly sorted through her vocabulary as if it was a half-missing deck of cards. ". . . isn't available right now."

There was a pause on the other end, a silence in which Christine felt something more than just dense air and circuitry. Maybe it was her experience with cancer and all this trouble with Rudd, but she seemed to be more acutely aware of such pauses these days, and of the unexpected and random course life often took afterwards. She sat up. It was light outside and the first thing she saw in the disheveled room was her underwear and other clothing, crumpled out there in the middle of the floor, floating like tender debris from some wreck. She swallowed. "This is Christine Parker," she offered. "Could I help you?"

Until that moment, she hadn't actually thought about this situation—this little slumber party—and the need for discretion, but she'd answered the phone and identified herself now. She hoped it wasn't going to cause any problems.

"Oh. Ms. Parker." The man on the other end said her name as if it made sense to him. "This is Joseph Attencio. Uwanda Docksteader mentioned your, told me about you."

There was another pause, shorter this time.

"I'm sorry to be calling so early," he said, then tumbled forward. "It's about Uwanda."

Finally Christine heard something she could lock onto. "Oh, Uwanda," she said cordially. "Yes. We spoke with her at length last night and—"

Attencio broke in. "Ms. Parker, I don't mean to be abrupt. Truly I don't. I know about your meeting with Uwanda last night." His voice trailed off. "I'm sorry to have to tell you," he continued, "but Uwanda, she was, she was murdered last night."

The wallpaper below the wainscot was something Middle Eastern, mosque shapes that swam together as Christine gazed at them and tried to comprehend Attencio's words.

"What?"

"I know," he said. "It's . . . unbelievable." His voice kept breaking.

Somehow, Christine could feel the ragged control that Joseph Attencio kept summoning to continue this conversation. She squeezed the receiver tighter.

"It happened in her hotel room, probably sometime around midnight. The room had been ransacked. I don't know many more details. The police are investigating."

"My God," she said. A string of vivid images from last night ran through her mind: Uwanda sitting in the restaurant with them, so funny and alive and capable. They had only known her less than twenty-four hours, but Christine couldn't help thinking about the connection she had felt.

"I know. I'm sick, absolutely crushed," Attencio said. "I don't know quite what to do right now." He paused as if she might have a suggestion. "But there's unfinished business that was of great concern to Uwanda. And to all of us. She called me last night. About eleven. She explained your situation, about you and your uncle. All of it to me. I thought that perhaps I should come . . . that we should talk."

Christine pinched the bridge of her nose and closed her eyes. The book, that goddamn book. Somebody thought—a wave of nausea overtook her—that Uwanda, that they had given her the book. "Hold on," she managed to tell Attencio. She lowered the receiver and covered the mouthpiece. "Layne," she said. "Please," shaking his shoulder, "you need to take this call." She stared straight ahead, but felt Layne rustling next to her. "It's about Uwanda Docksteader. She's been murdered."

Christine knew it was a terrible way to wake him, but it was all her repertoire held at the moment. He sat up immediately, the sheet dropping to his waist. He peered at her, confused and groggy, waiting for some explanation, but Christine simply handed him the phone. "It's Joseph Attencio," she said, and with no thought to her normal self-consciousness, slid bare from under the covers and walked to the bathroom.

She didn't bother to turn on the light, just stood there naked and dazed, her palms flat on the countertop where she tried to absorb the distant coolness of the tile. Feeling lightheaded, she slowly backed over to the toilet, closed the lid, and sat down. She cradled her head in her hands and vaguely heard the rise and fall of Layne's voice. She pushed the door closed and retreated to silence.

God almighty, Uwanda was dead. Not just dead. Murdered.

Christine raised her knees, set her feet on the toilet, and wrapped her arms around her legs. Cancer: it carried pain, real and identifiable, right there or right there, but this pain was worse. Unexpected. Uncontrolled. Exploding as you inhaled or burrowing into some region you couldn't even point to. And, was this . . . all her fault? Beginning last Sunday night? All her fault?

Layne knocked on the bathroom door. "Christine?"

"I'm alright," she called weakly from the darkness. "I'll be out in a minute."

Shortly, she stood and turned on the light, and through sheer mechanics, washed her face, borrowed some toothpaste, swished it through her mouth, then fixed her hair with Layne's comb, which lay by the sink. Under normal circumstances, using Layne's personal items would have brought a small, secret pleasure to Christine, but now all postcoital fuzziness had dissipated. She wrapped a large white towel around her, opened the door, and began to round up her clothes: panties here, blouse on the other side of the room. It felt like an awkward scavenger hunt with Layne standing there already dressed, but he turned his back and made a show of studying something he'd written on a pad of hotel stationery.

"You okay?" he asked.

She dropped the towel and began slipping into her clothes,

though they felt strange, like a skin she had shed in some other lifetime. "Yeah," she said. "I guess so. I mean . . ."

She had just put her arms through her sleeves when Layne turned around and came to her, hugged her tight, her blouse still open. "God, I know. I just can't believe it," he said softly.

It was amazing, truly amazing, but even in the midst of this, Christine felt a warmth run through her as he breathed into her hair.

"Do you think it had to do with . . .," she began tentatively, and then stopped herself, already knowing the answer. "It's Rudd's book, isn't it? Everything it touches is a disaster."

She felt, more than heard, his sigh. "We should have been more careful, it's my fault. I never should have . . ." His voice seemed to fail.

"It's not your fault," she said in a rush, "it's my fault. And it's that damn book."

He put his finger to her lips, held her a moment longer, then backed away a foot or so and looked into her face. He appeared older this morning, the tiny lines around his eyes and mouth testifying to the velocity of time, to the endless wear and tear of life. His face truly touched her, but it was what he did next that crushed her.

With the naturalness and ease of someone who had known her forever, he reached out and began buttoning her blouse from top to bottom. It was a simple act of caregiving so full of love that Christine thought her knees might buckle. Instead, she dropped her eyes, watched his hands at each of those six tiny closures.

"I've already called Dallas and told him," he said. "He'll be over here shortly. He was going to call your room, wake you, but I, uh, told him you were here, that you already knew."

Christine nodded her head, then began looking for her shoes.

If Dallas noticed the earthy after-smell of sex or found the two of them strangely rumpled this morning, he didn't let on. Nevertheless, all the clues were there. The only thing lacking was a big neon arrow pointing at the bed, the fact that all of it had been slept in.

Dallas nodded a good morning to them. "Whada ya think?" he asked Layne, wanting to get right to business. He stayed near the door, his arms folded over his chest, his Stetson slightly askew this morning.

Layne leaned against the edge of the desk. "The Docksteader woman—" he said, shaking his head. He looked at Christine. "We need to get the hell out of here. We've got to unload that book now. Somebody killed her thinking she had it. They may have even seen us together last night."

Christine sat at the end of the bed. Part of her listened while the other part kept returning to Uwanda. She remembered their good-bye, their hug out in the parking lot last night, and the strange way their two lives had intersected for just one evening with that delirious Vegas skyline as the backdrop.

Layne held up the pad of hotel stationery, as if it were some kind of legal evidence, and said that he'd worked it out with Attencio on the phone, taken down his address, agreed to get Rudd's book over to him. "There's a copy machine at the law office and Attencio has agreed to bring some security. Dallas, you've got your gun. I'm not suggesting that you'll need it, but you and Christine stay together in your room until I get back."

"Bullshit," Christine said. No way she was going to be separated from either one of these two men now. They'd come this far together. "Bullshit," she repeated, adding an edge to the word's cadence.

Layne and Dallas looked at each other.

"Three of us are safer than one or two," she said. Christine stared at her uncle.

Dallas sighed in resignation. "The woman seems to know her arithmetic."

Even at 6:30 on a Saturday morning, Paraldo Run appeared to be the city's de facto landfill for human debris. Cruising down the broad street in his brown sedan, Mack Sayles noted that the hookers and dealers had all closed up shop, but the drunks and druggies were still here, some in varying degrees of stagger while others lay curled around a fire hydrant or in such a misshapen sprawl that they seemed to have been dropped from the sky.

In Mack's business, a lot could happen in twenty-four hours. And it had; the whole shitery had blown its top yesterday. Now the Vegas FBI office was on red alert; district and regional supervisors and even Washington had been notified. Mack had been rousted early, for the second morning in a row, this time to check out the death of one Uwanda Docksteader, to see if there was any evidence of a possible connection to the death of Dr. Franklin Rudd, if it was suddenly fatal to have a little historical interest in the Nevada Test Site.

First had been the 7:20 a.m. call yesterday from Gordo. Mack was in his pigeon loft feeding the birds, getting ready to fill the water containers with a special prerace mixture of vitamins, garlic and Gatorade. He was always nervous about these last-minute preparations, not wanting to forget anything or screw up, because by noon it would all be out of his hands. That's when he had to drop the birds off at race headquarters for their long trip north to Idaho.

His wife had opened the back door and yoo-hooed him to say that his office was on the line. Early yoo-hoos could only be bad yoo-hoos. Whatever else he thought about the FBI, they were still career civil servants right down to their wing tips and easy-stride pumps.

"Tell them I retired yesterday," he hollered way too loudly, echoing through the wooden loft and startling the birds. A flurry of wings rose from the floor where they were eating breakfast, a sudden blizzard of soft colors and lustrous highlights that spun up around him in 360 degrees of feathered confusion. Outside the loft, Floppsy, their old cocker spaniel asleep on the lawn, jumped up too quickly for her arthritic pangs and started barking, then howling in pain.

"It's okay, Floppsy, calm down," he said in soothing tones.

It was over as quickly as it had begun and Mack cussed himself silently. His racing team was well settled and performing beautifully; he didn't want to spook them or change a thing. He spoke to his birds in reassuring tones, "You boys and girls just eat up there, this is your last meal before the race."

As soon as he picked up the phone, he could tell that Gordo was tired and irritable.

"You live out in that pigeon coop or what?"

"I . . .," Mack paused, "good hell, are you still there?"

"Aw, old Rudd had a couple of tricks up his hard drive. Even without the damage, he intended it to be difficult to break into," Gordo said wearily.

"Well, I sure as hell didn't mean for you to stay up."

"Challenge of the nerds," Gordo answered dismissively, "don't sweat it. Look, Mack, after I got a clean copy, I couldn't resist a quick peek. You better get down here and look at this thing. This guy has scanned what appears to be dozens of classified documents into his computer. Maybe they're declassified by now. I can't tell. But one thing's for sure. They're part of a four-hundred-page rant intended to put a giant hex on the old test site. And on all the related agencies."

Now, twenty-two hours later, Mack found himself pulling into the unkempt parking lot of the Starlite Motel for the sole purpose of probing a possible connection to the Docksteader woman's murder. The sedan slid to a stop over pocked asphalt, gravel, and broken glass. Discovering Rudd's book had been just the beginning of things. This Manos guy's cell phone records led to a Deputy Marshall R. C. Hiney, who overflowed like a clogged toilet and led to one Assistant U. S. Attorney Jillian Fetch, who led to the downwinders trial in federal court, who might now lead toward the murder of the primary plaintiff, Uwanda Docksteader. Mack personally doubted that the Docksteader woman's death would be a pure coincidence, just a bad choice of venue, but he'd be able to tell soon enough.

He approached the uniformed officer stationed outside room number 18, apparently to keep the curious at bay, though Mack doubted there'd be even one curious person here so long as the *poe-lease* were around. He flashed his badge. "Morning, officer."

"Sir," the young cop nodded to him. The motel had been

here for a long time, randomly overgrown with tall cotton-woods and box elders, built in a different era when this part of town was new and respectable.

Mack walked into the seedy room and saw that the place had been completely wrecked, ransacked from floor to ceiling, as if a pit bull had rocketed into an insane rage. The mattress and an overstuffed chair had been shredded, patchworking the room in heavy gray clumps that reminded him of New York slush. Adding to the blizzard were sheets of white paper scattered everywhere. Manila files were dumped from their boxes. The floor was ankle deep in legal documents, briefs and other typed materials. Perhaps, thought Mack, the killer has a special hard-on for jurisprudence.

"Well," a voice said from the dim-bulb interior, "if it ain't the FBI. What are you doing on this side of town, Mack?"

"I'll be darned," Mack said, turning, "Lieutenant Franks."

"Long time no sleaze," said Franks.

The two men shook hands. They had worked together before, most recently on a double homicide involving interstate commerce; i.e., two very young and very dead white women from the Tennessee hill country transported across state lines, presumably while still alive, for immoral purposes.

"What's happening, Mack?" said Franks. "How can we help you? Or maybe it's you helps us?"

Generally, Mack's experience with local law enforcement agencies had been good. There was seldom any rivalry between the Feds and the Vegas cops. In the trenches, any assistance in solving crime was just ducky as far as Mack knew, since there was so much of it to go around.

"What do we have here?" Mack asked.

"Somebody pops her. One bullet, small caliber, point-blank, base of the skull. But only after beating her to a stump. The body left about fifteen minutes ago, headed for the medical examiner's office. Don't know if she died from the beating or the bullet. You'll have to talk to the hacksaws about that one."

"Yeah, I'll swing by later. Thanks," Mack said. "So what's with the shit storm that hit this place?"

Lieutenant Franks shrugged. "Hard to say. Hell of a struggle though. Our gal's got beaucoup blood and skin under her fingernails."

"What about the neighbors?" Mack asked. "What did they see or hear?"

"Neighbors?" Franks laughed.

"You telling me somebody comes in here, breaks all the furniture, pushes over the fridge and nobody hears anything?"

"You kiddin'?" Franks said. "As this here *lo-commotion* gathered steam, the other guests, the entire populice—all registered under names like Smith, Jones, and Doe—deserted like rats in a barn fire. We checked every other room; place's a ghost town. Body's already four hours into stiff when we get called. The desk clerk was too far down the row to hear anything, holed up in a cubicle with his TV blaring."

Franks kicked a little wadded stuffing to the side and quickly looked at Mack. "Sorry, don't mean to mess with the crime scene. Down here, you get used to assuming it's some zinged-out crackhead. But I guess that wouldn't explain your presence."

"Right," said Mack. "A druggie who beats her for . . . whatever, then finishes her like a pro, then figures she stashes her money and credit cards in the mattress every night." Mack knelt down and brushed some papers aside, examining a large blood-stain on the worn-out carpet. Motive was not a big mystery here.

Mack had been informed yesterday that Rudd's classified documents were not only still classified, they were possibly the only copies still in existence, having somehow avoided the shredder. The Feds didn't want that manuscript hitting the street. The word came with emphasis straight from Washington. Possible suspects in possession of Rudd's manuscript included this Manos and, as far as the bureau was concerned, too many others to count. That also included the Parkers, Mack figured, but for entirely different reasons. They were a completely different kind of float in this crazy parade.

Lieutenant Franks walked over to the kitchen counter and

pointed to a big, floppy woven bag collapsed on the broken formica. "Her purse. Two credit cards, twenty-one dollars and change, still here," he said, hoisting the heavy bag for effect.

Mack opened the Docksteader woman's bag. The first thing he saw inside was a fistful of rolled-up newspaper. He unfolded it and immediately recognized a copy of the *Las Vegas Review Journal* from earlier in the week: "Retired Test Site Chief Murdered, Utah Man in Custody".

"Mr. Sayles?" It was the young cop standing in the doorway. "Dispatch just put out the word. You're to call your office, they said it was urgent."

"Okay, thanks." Mack started out of the room toward the mobile phone in his car. He turned back to Lieutenant Franks. "If you don't mind, have your lab guys be careful, treat this as a priority. Our own techies will be here soon to help out. I'll call you and explain what I can later."

Mack made his call, then started the car and squealed through a hard right turn out of the motel parking lot. Even a gutless government-issue sedan can spin its tires on pea-size fragments of broken glass. Mack could hardly wait to talk to the Parkers and their trusty lawyer. He hadn't been able to find them yesterday; they had somehow managed to evade him and the local police, by design or accident, by not using any credit cards, cell phones or Christian names. But the lawyer Harting had just called his secretary a half hour ago from room 616 in an off-Strip hotel called the Oasis.

Mack disliked the theatrics, but nonetheless reached down and fumbled for the red light sitting on the floor. He plopped the magnetized device onto the roof and plugged the small cord into the cigarette lighter. He felt a sense of panic. What if he was too late? What if the killer or killers were there now, doing the same number on the Parkers and the lawyer? Maybe he had been taking his retirement a little too early, or his pigeon race a little too seriously. He wondered if a bit more investigation and homework on his part could have prevented Docksteader's death, but then he stopped himself. Those kinds of feelings could become a real occupational hazard. He'd learned years ago that you could see the mountains on Jupiter with enough hindsight and one naked eye.

Mack abruptly hit the brakes and found himself sliding through an intersection, laying on the horn, and heading toward a truck. The truck spotted him, braked and turned away, narrowly avoiding a collision. Mack straightened the sedan out and kept going, slowing down a bit and paying more attention. He skirted downtown and the Strip by using the arterial routes. Finally, coming to a stop in front of the deserted entrance to the Oasis Hotel, he jumped out of the car and ran inside.

The young clerk, who hastened to explain that he just got to work two minutes ago, didn't hesitate when Mack flashed his badge. The clerk grabbed a passkey and they rode the elevator to the sixth floor. Mack motioned to the clerk and told him to wait a minute. He preferred having a witness as he took a quick look through each room. All three were empty and none had been ransacked, although one was questionable. He didn't see any files or a manuscript box, nothing but clothing and personals. They apparently had left in a hurry. Mack just hoped it was voluntary, that they weren't headed toward the desert with a gun at their heads.

He went back down to the lobby and was met by the night manager, an erect fellow with a thin white mustache. "I understand you are looking for three of our guests," he said.

"Yes, that's correct," said Mack.

"They just left," the manager said, "you just missed them. While you were upstairs, they were in the back office, retrieving a package from the hotel safe. I assisted them in that, and then they departed toward the parking lot." The manager, clearly troubled, pointed to the rear exit. "They did seem a bit hurried and nervous," he said. "I do hope there won't be any trouble for us."

"What kind of package?" Mack asked.

"A standard brown briefcase," he said, holding his hands apart to indicate size.

"Thanks," Mack said, heading down the hall, following the

exit sign toward the rear door. Maybe he could catch them, head them off, or get a glimpse of where they were going. He was going to haul them into custody, mostly for their own good.

As he came through the back door, Harding's gray Land Cruiser pulled out of an old parking structure directly in front him. Mack could see them clearly; old man Parker was driving the lawyer's vehicle.

Mack stepped off the curb, waving his arms for them to stop. All three of them stared at him through the windshield, the two men in front, the niece in back, and then the Land Cruiser swerved sharply, finished the turn and sped up, zooming down the hotel driveway toward the street.

Christ, the idiots. They were in much deeper shit than they could possibly know. Mack stood there for a long second shaking his head and catching his breath. If he were in a tenth the shape of one of his pigeons, maybe he could sprint back up that long hall, through the lobby to his car and catch them. Then, from the corner of his eye, he saw the sleek black Jaguar move slowly off a side street, staying back, but following them.

Dallas sped over the winding curves in the gravel road, jerking the steering wheel of the old Land Cruiser back and forth, throwing the vehicle into a curve and then quickly correcting back in the direction of the skid. With both hands on the wheel, his elbows and arms worked high and quick, almost as if he were boxing again, throwing punches and counterpunches. Overcorrecting, he began another drift in the opposite direction, finding it hard at this speed to get good purchase in the dirt. He quickly spun the wheel again, this time letting off the brake and stomping down hard on the throttle. No stranger to driving fast on the back roads, Dallas tried to accelerate his way out of the slide and into the next turn, all four wheels churning a thick, dusty cloud in their wake.

"Hang on back there," he shouted as he missed the bend in the road, bumped off the low shoulder and onto the flat desert terrain, violently whip-tossing the rear end of the Land Cruiser in the process. Everything in the back, including Layne and Christine, went up in the air and settled down with a thump. "Try not to bust your heads on the roof," he said above the strained roar of the engine.

They careened over the tops of sagebrush and small cactus; a rock clanged hard against the front skid plate directly under Dallas's feet. He kept the throttle down, spinning the wheels over the sand and back onto the dirt road. He knew he was lucky that he hadn't gone off the other side and into the crumbling arroyo, into the early grave they were trying to avoid. It wouldn't advance the cause here, wouldn't help them get away if he punched a hole in the oil pan on a rock, or let that crazy bastard in the black Jaguar catch them turned over and bleeding in a deep wash. Slowing down a little, he settled on a more sensible speed, knowing that he shouldn't get too excited and make some stupid move. He believed that he had already neutralized the Jag's speed advantage by taking to the unpaved back roads. That was his rational side. The rest of him wanted to stop right here and now, turn around, and go head-on at that son of a bitch. Have it out face to face. If he'd been alone, swear to God, he would have done exactly that. A joust, a game of chicken—car to car, gun to gun, man to man—winner take all, screw the odds.

The gravel portion of the road soon gave out and then turned to plain dirt leading farther and farther north into the vast alkaline desert. Overhead, the sky was unfolding in a flat, transparent morning blue. Knowing exactly what he was doing, exactly where he was going, Dallas kept moving away from Vegas into the barren wasteland, understanding that for desert rats like him, this environment could be a great equalizer.

As the road bed became increasingly crude and unattended, granular dust billowed up behind them more and more vigorously. Some of it was sucked into the Land Cruiser on the backdraft and poured in through the shattered rear window, blanketing them, the entire interior, with a fine white grit. Each bump dislodged more pieces of broken glass from the gaping hole in the rear. Christine coughed and put her sleeve over her mouth. Dallas opened the driver's side window and yelled back, "Layne, could you roll down that front window over there? Maybe it'll help keep some of that dust pushed out the back."

Layne reached over the seat and rolled down the passenger window. Earlier, when they'd left the Oasis Hotel, he had been in front holding the briefcase containing the manuscript while Dallas did the driving. Between the two of them, it was Dallas who really knew the town of Las Vegas, who could probably get them over to Attencio's office most quickly. But they had not even made it half a mile from the hotel before Christine spotted the black Jaguar right on their tail. "It's the guy from the bed-and-breakfast, the one who showed up in court, who kept trying to get me to . . ." She was thrown sideways midsentence as Dallas took a sharp left turn, accelerated down a broad avenue, then drove straight under the freeway, toward the thinly populated west side of town. No way did he want to deal with this guy in traffic and amidst stop signs. The Jag stayed with them effortlessly, dropping back, then closing the gap, as if toying with its prey. The Jag became tired of the game once they reached the outskirts of town, though, and pulled abreast, then swerved toward them, as if considering a muscle move. Dallas swerved right back and tried to hit the Jag, tried to spin it or run it off the opposite side of the road, but the car was too quick, darting away and backing off. Then, getting into position directly behind the Land Cruiser, the driver of the Jag put his left hand out the window and fired two running shots at them, one of which hit their back window and put a hole in the metal roof. Christine let out a high-pitched scream from the backseat while being showered with small particles of shattered glass. Layne quickly pitched himself over the seat.

"You two okay?" Dallas yelled back at them.

Layne pushed Christine toward the floor. "Yeah. I guess. Considering somebody's shooting at us," he answered.

That's when Dallas abandoned the pavement and headed off cross-country through a giant new subdivision under construction on the edge of the desert. Just in the process of being graded for utilities, it was nothing but trenches and roughed-in dirt tracks. Dallas was able to put enough distance between them and the Jag to stop momentarily and get into four-wheel drive. Then he kept going, crossing to the other side of the subdivision and finally encountering the gravel road they took north. Five minutes, ten minutes, Las Vegas blurred and was finally consumed in the graying background and, at least for the time being, the Jag along with it.

Dallas monitored the condition of the road, moving at a steady pace as the terrain gradually changed from mostly flat to rolling hills. There hadn't been time to get scared, to fixate on danger when all that fast driving and shooting had been going on; now, however, his breathing was noticeably shallow, his hands a bit jittery.

The road swung wide and then switchbacked up onto a low bench. Up ahead, in a blessed veil of familiarity, Dallas spotted Sheep Peak. He stopped the car and got out. The rolling dust overtook him, smothering him in a thin white coat and making him cough. He ducked under the brim of his hat and moved away, over to the edge of a small cliff. Back in the distance where they had just traveled, there was only one other vehicle in sight, four or five miles off, easy to spot by its dust-up. Dallas squinted and watched it for a moment, then glanced up. Thin skeins of waterfowl resembled tiny gnats against the sky, heading north, taking high passage over the parched desert.

He had to assume that the other vehicle contained their guy, their pursuer. It was too far back to see the car clearly, but it had to be him. It would have been easy enough for the man who shot at them to have found his way around that subdivision and then follow their dust trail north.

"You better not let me get my hands on you, mister," he muttered. "There won't be enough left to haul." For a moment, the image of Black Dog, a steady hand with the cattle and ten years of good company, floated through his mind. He really didn't know the Docksteader woman, but that was certainly unfortunate as well. Christ! What had he gotten them into here? Dallas took his hat off wearily and rubbed his head for a moment, as if sore thoughts could be excised that way, then replaced the Stetson. Layne stood a few yards away, watching the oncoming vehicle.

Dallas turned around and surveyed their potential routes north. At the base of Sheep Peak, about ten miles away, there was another dirt road that he knew quite well. He wasn't particularly familiar with the one they were on now, but there were hundreds of roads just like this one that intertwined like spiderwebs crisscrossing the entire Colorado River Basin—heyday remnants from the uranium miners, timber companies and ranchers, back when they were more or less free to treat federal lands as their own.

He and Layne returned to the Land Cruiser and they started off again.

"Still back there?" Christine asked. Her voice sounded cramped and small.

"Yeah, but he's a ways," Dallas said, shifting down a gear, climbing. "We need to lose this guy and then wait him out until dark. He won't be able to see us or our dust cloud if we're driving at night. We can't go back to the ranch, too easy to find us there, but I know a remote spot, a slot canyon with plenty of water. Right at the base of Sheep Peak, not too far from here. It should be a safe place where we can wait him out. After dark, we slip out. The old highway's only twenty miles east of there. Find a phone, maybe make a try for Vegas again."

"Jesus," Layne said, "I wonder what Attencio thinks. First Uwanda. Now we turn up missing."

"Where's your car phone? We could find out," Dallas said.

"My mistake," Layne said. "But I mostly try to avoid phones."

"I thought all you lawyers had one of those things."

"You must be thinking of dentists and real estate agents," Layne said.

"Oh, yeah," Dallas said, "I forgot. Lawyers don't use the phone without a billing sheet handy."

Christine laughed, short and abrupt, a little too shrill, then fell quiet again.

"So, you guys okay with the plan?" Dallas could see them in the rearview mirror, looking at each other, unconsciously consulting the other about the future, already seeking a consensus. He didn't know all the details, but you don't have to see the flash to know where lightning has struck.

It was Christine who finally spoke. "What choice do we have?"

"We're gaining ground on that guy," Layne said. "Maybe we should go ahead and circle back toward the freeway and Vegas."

Dallas paused for a moment. "I . . . that makes me nervous. We don't know how many buddies he's got. We don't know who all might be after this thing. Who might know this gray truck of yours." He didn't want to say it outright, but who were they supposed to trust? How did this maniac find them? How many others knew where they were this morning besides the Jag man and the FBI guy? "To tell the truth," said Dallas, "I'd like to slip back into town in the dark, find an out-of-the-way copy shop, and get a duplicate off in the mail to some reliable press outfit, even before we contact that lawyer again."

"Let's ditch this guy first," Layne said with an air of resignation. "Then we can talk through everything, come to some mutual decision."

The place Dallas had in mind was only another few miles north. It had been completely overlooked by hikers because it wasn't part of a bigger canyon system and was located out in the middle of nowhere. A few ranchers knew about it, but the word hadn't circulated among the nut-and-berry set or been put into a guidebook yet. It was a deep slot canyon off the Beaver Dam Wash with only one way in or out, and it had several vantage points that would make it easy to defend, at least in the daylight.

"How you doing, Chrissy?" he asked.

"I'm doing," she said.

He tried to give her a little grin in the rearview mirror, but his face felt slack and nonresponsive. He'd taken charge here and he hoped to hell he knew what he was doing. Used to be that he never questioned himself; always had full faith in his logic and choices. Now uncertainty was creeping in like some pitiful fog, and Dallas hated it.

They were still slowly climbing and with this new altitude, the vegetation had changed—bunchgrass, wildflowers, pinion, and juniper dotted the hills around them. On the roadside, felled for no apparent reason, lay a pinion, its needles still green and intact, some bozo from the suburbs probably out walking his chainsaw. Dallas abruptly braked the Land Cruiser and got out.

"You got any rope?" he said to Layne.

"Some nylon webbing," Layne replied, following him out of the Cruiser. "You going to clothesline the guy?"

"Naw, just a little trick of Roy Rogers's and Gene Autry's."

Dallas found the one-inch tubular nylon and dragged the bushy eight-foot tree over to the car. Layne stood by with his head cocked and watched. Dallas threw a couple of hitches around the tree trunk, looped it behind a stout lower branch so it wouldn't slip off and then, playing out about ten feet of slack, snubbed the nylon strap to the ball hitch below Layne's bumper and tossed the extra cord into the back of the Land Cruiser through its broken rear window. Dallas turned to appraise his work.

By now Christine had gotten out of the car and was watching him as well. "What are you doing?" she asked.

Dallas smiled at her. The world would never be set right by just one trick, but it was a start. "I hope to confuse the situation."

Christine looked at the tree and the red nylon cord tying it to the Land Cruiser. "Good so far," she said. "I'm certainly confused."

CHAPTER TWELVE

FEAR HAD A TASTE, A DISTINCT TASTE, TO CHRISTINE. THE metallic edge of old mayonnaise. The bitter white pith of grapefruit. Dallas was asking them to climb into a dead-end crack in the earth while some bloodless psychopath hunted them down. Her lips were bruised from last night, dried and cracking from today. She was covered with a gritty white alkaline soot dusting her hair to a paltry gray. Still feeling the effects of too much wine and too little sleep, she couldn't shake the invasive fear that lay curled in her chest, making each breath quicker, shallower than it should have been. She longed for a cool drink of water.

The three of them tottered at the brink of the deep, narrow canyon which ran like a hidden vein through the desert and gave little evidence of itself until they were close. Standing back a couple of hundred yards, it was nearly impossible to detect and Dallas seemed to be counting on that. He had worked the Land Cruiser as best he could into a sparse stand of junipers. He and Layne had hiked back to the dirt road, smoothing out any part of a tire track that might give them away. Hopeful, they rejoined Christine at this sudden crease in the desert floor.

"You have to squint to see it," Dallas said, pointing out the beginning of a steep and indistinct game trail. "No other way down. Everything else is dead vertical. Been years since I tried it, but the deer and other critters around make it down to water. I suppose we can too."

Christine wearily nodded her assent. Time and events had started tumbling forward uncontrollably the second she'd answered that ominous dawn phone call in Layne's room, and here she was, dressed for anything *but* an outback frolic, having quickly thrown on the linen pants and shirt she'd worn to dinner last night. Instead of a fast crosstown drive to meet Joseph Attencio, they'd been chased and shot at, hunted by who knew what. She looked down at her feet, at the Sierra Clubber's nightmare, the one shoe splurge she'd allowed herself all last year: Italian brown leather slip-ons, comfortable and gorgeous as cream on her feet, but with soles like parchment. She might as well tackle this precipitous, rocky trail in ballet slippers.

Layne went back to the Land Cruiser and quickly stuffed a few items—sweatshirts, the bound length of tubular nylon, an empty water bottle, a large flashlight—into a tattered green day pack. When he returned, her feelings must have been plastered all over her face, because he stopped suddenly, reached out, and took her arm, giving her a faint smile of encouragement and then a tender kiss on the forehead.

"How you doing?" he asked, making no attempt to hide his new affection or his heightened protectiveness.

Christine was happy about that much, at least, and a few daring images from last night flashed through her mind, but given this morning's outrages, there was no context, no comfortable way of allowing herself to dwell on what had happened. "Oh, I'm hanging in there," she said, reaching up and squeezing his hand lightly.

Dallas had already started carefully picking his way down the radical slope, scanning the terrain with a route finder's practiced eye. He halted and extended a helping hand to Christine at the first crux point. Layne brought up the rear as they traversed their way into the earth like ants descending from view.

"Careful about dislodging rocks, rolling them down on the person below," Dallas said, turning back toward her and Layne. "If you do, holler out a warning." He moved slowly, negotiating around some small, broken limestone cliffs. Just when it appeared that they were rimmed out, Dallas would find a way to skirt the obstacle. He carried the .30-06 rifle and the brown briefcase in the same hand, switching, always keeping his free hand toward the hill. Layne was wearing the day pack along with Dallas's holstered Colt .44 casually slung over his head and shoulder, the ammo belt draped across the front of his knit shirt like some golfer in a spaghetti western.

Christine supposed she should take comfort in their display of firepower, but she was not in the mood for more gunplay and, book or no book, would have welcomed the entire cavalry about now. Let the cops have the damn thing, let officialdom take over, and let the law run its course. Anything to put an end to this crazy chase. No one else needed to get killed. Certainly not Dallas or Layne. She wasn't quite sure when enough was simply enough, but knew that she was within one fried nerve ending of being there. Initially happy to be out of the Land Cruiser, out of that tight, jarring box, she now felt way too exposed out here on this slope as they continued their slow descent. Into what? Some special hell that she'd begun fashioning six days ago? If the killer—whoever this guy was, whoever he worked for—caught them here, if this place was destined to be their grave, it could be years before anyone found them.

Small showers of scree were occasionally and unavoidably dislodged by one or the other of them on the slipperiest parts of the trail, echoes rising up at them from the bottom of the canyon. Now and then, she passed a stubborn desert plant clinging to the slope or to a crack in the rimrocks, blooming prickly pear and hedgehog cactus, yucca with its white pods funicular and straining. She felt just coherent enough to be impressed by the plants' tenacity, clinging to anything they could for survival, and hoped that her own instincts were that intact. The slope they were descending faced due south and the sun beat mercilessly down on them. A heavy sweat broke through the dull layer of dust clinging to her face and arms. Any chance of a breeze, any hope that the air would stir, had been left up on top. When rocks weren't crashing over the next ledge, any other sound, however slight, seemed to ripple with alarming resonance as they cautiously moved deeper and deeper.

About halfway down, her feet suddenly slipped out from under her, and she caught herself hard against the rocks, felt a sharp pain in her hand. Scrambling, she righted herself quickly, sending even more gravel and debris down. The others stopped and watched, worried.

"You okay, Chrissy?" Dallas asked, craning his neck back up the slope at her.

Regaining her balance, she nodded, trying to catch her breath. "Forgot my hiking boots," she said, without really looking at either man. She stood erect and still for a moment and examined her left palm as a thin trickle of blood emerged from the soft skin and traced a bright line down her wrist. The surge of red conjured an image of Uwanda Docksteader. Had her blood trickled slowly like this? Or did it gush forth, Christine wondered, letting Uwanda's life out because she'd gone to dinner with the wrong people, made some new friends who couldn't wait to unload Rudd's book onto . . . goddamn everything anyway. Almost everything she had touched since last Sunday night had completely turned to crap. Where was her intelligence, her normal smarts that should have made her leery of the creep in the Jag? Even so, it was useless. What would she have done, report him? Christine smeared her hand over her thigh, onto her fancy dress pants, bloodying an angry smudge on the fine linen.

But this was no time to indulge her remorse; she was going to fall off the trail and kill herself if she didn't pay attention. She stepped carefully along their tenuous route, focusing directly on her feet, which were hot and blistering. The adrenaline flowed harder because of her fall and her breathing came even faster. Fear and panic fluttered around inside her chest, banging against her rib cage like trapped and frantic birds. If it was this hot at the bottom, how would they ever survive? She hoped once again that Dallas knew where he was going and what the hell he was doing.

They finally came to the shadow line running horizontally across the slope and moved into the blessed relief of shade. She was still dry, dirty and fearful, but getting out of the sun eased her crushing downward spiral. When she paused, she realized that she was dizzy, was literally going a bit out of her head.

Closer to the bottom now, the trail became easier and Dallas moved a little more quickly. She could feel cooler air welling up as she walked and it reminded her of standing at the entrance to a deep cave, the kind where someone charges admission. She wondered about the price of this one.

Finally, they all stood on the sandy canyon bottom, a narrow slot less than twenty feet wide. It was cast in perpetual dusk, the sun quite apparently having been absent since the beginning of rock time. A tiny stream cut its way through the crevice floor and the air smelled cellar-damp and fungal. She collapsed on a boulder and leaned against the wall of the canyon. It was cool and hard at her back.

"We'll be okay in here," Dallas said, coughing and breathing heavily. "It widens out a few yards upstream. Nobody's gonna join us without coming down that exact same trail, without kicking more rocks loose and giving us plenty of notice. We have a good vantage point over the whole thing." He lowered his head into another rasping cough. "Excuse me," he said, turning away to spit. "So we'd hear him or his friends long before we'd see them." He looked at Christine, examining her eyes until she felt compelled to turn away.

Her normal pluckiness in the face of individual adversity, her ability to be the bravest person in the room when dealing with her own illness or similar personal events, had consistently failed her all this week. Not because she was less than brave, but because her actions had so dramatically affected others and she couldn't reverse them. This was brand new territory for her. It was impossible to courageously shoulder consequences when others—Dallas, Uwanda, Layne, even Rudd—were bearing the brunt of what she had set in motion, what she was continuing to foster.

Layne wordlessly moved next to her and looked back up,

seemed to be studying their route, spotting strategic vantage points on the trail down. He touched her on the neck, then put a hand on her shoulder and began gently massaging. She closed her eyes and easily envisioned the shape of his hands, was surprised to find that she had already memorized them.

She tried to smile at him, to thank him, but her lips were stiff and cracking. She straightened up and arched her back and inhaled deeply. Her eyes met Dallas's. He had been watching her.

"Maybe we lost him," she said in a bedraggled tone, part question, part wanting to believe, but mostly betraying the inner battle that she had been steadily losing.

Dallas paused for a long second. It was just a hairline fracture, but a moment too long to provide Christine any real assurance. "I'm sure we did," he said.

Billowy spring clouds had backed up in the late afternoon on their flowing journey from the Pacific to the Rockies, but Manos didn't have the time or inclination to appreciate the perfect white ceiling arched above. He lay prone on top of a giant boulder, a garage-size hunk of broken limestone, counting push-ups. Dressed in jeans, a T-shirt and Adidas high-top pumps, his perfectly rigid body levered up and down off the fulcrum of his toes. Two pistols, brushed blue-black metal with nonglare surfaces, were lying off to one side next to a black silken jacket. An embroidered yellow Chinese tiger glowered from the shiny fabric.

". . . ninety-eight, ninety-nine, a hundred," he counted quietly under his breath. He had cheated on some of the final push-ups, not going down all the way; nonetheless, on one hundred, he shoved himself into the air and clapped his hands, almost missed and barely caught himself, and then went down heavily onto his stomach and chest. Heaving for breath, he silently declared it a victory, his immaculately tanned face and arms still trembling and glistening with sweat. The T-shirt clung to him and the emerging wet spot spread up the small of his back.

In prison, in all the joints Manos had ever seen, most of the cons performed infinite push-ups and sit-ups in their cells and then went down and pumped iron in the weight rooms. They shrunk their shirts and walked the prison corridors with their arms bowed out. They also attended federally funded college classes aimed at improving thought and literacy and made efficient use of the prison law library. All this so they could sue everyone's ass off while they were in the slammer and then thump all the rest when they got out.

As he recovered his wind, he slid forward on his stomach, keeping low, carefully edging his way to the front of the boulder. Resting his chin on his hands, he moved cautiously the final inches until his eyes cleared the stone's rim. Then he peeped down into a deep chasm, which was like suddenly peering over the side of a thirty-story building. It took a second to adjust to the twinge of vertigo. He cupped his hands into a visor against his forehead and allowed his eyes to grow accustomed to the diminished light below. They were still down there, the two men sitting together, the woman still asleep on the sandy bottom nearby. He shook his head, still amazed to find them in such a place, to see that they had run to some subterranean canyon, something out of a goddamn Tarzan movie.

The old cowboy held his rifle across his lap. He was easiest to spot because of the hat. The woman stirred, rolled onto her other side and lay still again. Good. Sleep on, sweetheart, rest up.

The Docksteader broad had been a big, lumpy barn with a lot more fight in her than he'd expected. And strong, surprisingly strong. He had three gouges in a row across his cheek and a cut on the back of his neck to prove it. She wasn't going easy, so he'd ended the debate with a bullet and got on with his search. Lots of paper—legal stuff, notes, articles—but nothing by Rudd.

A pair of small gray birds with black and white stripes chased each other and skittered through the pinions and sagebrush, touched down quickly on his boulder, then flitted away to continue their mating dance. Oh, the joys of the great out-of-doors, Manos thought. He'd gone camping once, way back when he was a kid with one of his many "Daddies." He'd hated the mosquitoes, the hard black crust on the hot dogs, the cold, musty-smelling earth they'd tried to sleep on. He hated that particular daddy, and in retrospect, didn't have much use for his mother either. It was for certain that he never went camping again.

Manos drew back from the edge and rolled onto his back. He had located the Land Cruiser around noon. He'd had to follow these characters patiently, swearing vengeance when he finally figured out that they were dragging something to cover their tire tracks. He'd stayed with them, though, examining the road carefully at all turns, almost getting the Jag stuck a couple of times. It was a piece of pure luck that finally helped him spot the Cruiser: a sudden reflection, the sun glancing off its windshield at just the right moment. Once he found their vehicle, it was easy to locate the trail they had taken down into the canyon. After searching the Land Cruiser and finding nothing, he'd decided to wait them out. He wasn't fool enough to go straight at them down in there. They'd see him, or hear him coming. He speculated that they were going to try to make it out of there in the dark, but in the meantime, they were trapped in their own little hideout.

He wished again that he had the cowboy's rifle and scope, or his own, deadly accurate at this distance. But he would have to make do with what he had: the snub-nosed .38, accurate to about forty feet, and his high-tech Heckler and Koch pistol. The latter was better, but still not a distance piece. He wasn't going to try lobbing a shot in on them and hoping it would hit. Besides, he wanted to make sure and get the cowboy, guessing that he was the most dangerous when armed.

Manos moved to the middle of the rock and sat up. He was thirsty. This was one dusty crust of hell out here and he didn't have any water. Cross-legged, twisting his torso, he stretched his back and began a few simple yoga exercises. Like so much of his work, it all came down to a waiting game. He knew where they were; they didn't know where he was. Why hadn't they run to the law when he shot at them? Why were they holed up down here? Because they had Rudd's book with them, that's why. It was stolen property; it was worth risking their lives for. And that's why it was worth his time. And he didn't mind waiting. Prisons teach different things to different people, but all cons learn how to wait.

Back in one of those other lives that seemed so distant now, back when Layne had practiced big-firm law in Salt Lake City, he and his entourage would approach "going to trial" the way generals approached going to war—staunch, starched and inspired. On the morning of, they would square their pinstriped shoulders as their wing tips echoed down the marbled halls of the old Federal Court Building, warriors representing mammoth corporations in pursuit of more wealth from the Western lands, more water from their strangled rivers. He was a *litigator*. His arena was the courtroom and he understood the rules of combat perfectly, and in that context, feared no one. From there, however, it was a long and tenuous drop to where he now sat, trapped in a desert hole in the ground, enmeshed in a predatory snarl with a dangerous and anonymous adversary who took what he wanted and would kill to get it. Layne felt by degrees outraged, helpless, and scared shitless.

It was late afternoon. Time passed agonizingly slow and Layne had grown anxious. Sitting next to him was a silent and dreamy Dallas. Christine, thankfully, had finally fallen asleep and was now obliviously perched on a berm of dry sand several yards away. Her back was to them, her head pillowed on the day pack, with Layne's sweatshirt covering her shoulders. She seemed small and far away, a harbor of mysterious thoughts and dreams that, for an instant, he yearned deeply to know. And hoped for the chance to. He wished he could sleep, but responsibility, residual adrenaline and frayed nerves rendered that impossible, so there was little to do but wait. When they had arrived midmorning, the sun was high on the canyon head-wall facing east. Now it was high on the opposite wall facing west. Other than that, absolutely nothing had changed in the passing hours; in fact, little had changed down here in a million years.

Layne had hiked dozens of slot canyons and this one was just garden variety, nothing special, not even any sign of the ancient Indian activity so prevalent in canyons throughout the southwest. A lateral seep spring wept from a fissure in the sandstone; a few scraggly ferns made a living off it, and a small pool of water, brackish and filled with tadpoles, gathered in the bottom. They had refreshed themselves in it, had even drunk the water in spite of its rank appearance, Dallas and Layne both assuring Christine that if the tadpoles could live with it, so could they. A nominal overflow from the pool trickled past them, carving a shallow rut.

Layne watched as Dallas began rolling the umpteenth cigarette of the afternoon, dallying and extending whatever small pleasure he found in the ritual. They should get out of here as soon as possible, Layne had decided. He wanted to make a run back toward Las Vegas the second it was dark, maybe even before. His fondest wish was to get that damn manuscript into the hands of the press and Attencio, to make sure that it hit the headlines. This had to be Rudd's only copy and someone, or some group, was willing to kill for it. Everything had spun so far out of control that he was now determined to stop it at the earliest possible moment. If Christine had been awake, he'd strongly argue that they start hiking out this very instant.

Instead, he continued observing Dallas. "I've seen chimneys smoke less," he said.

"That's why I buy it by the bag," Dallas replied, the faint traces of a crinkled smile playing at the edges of his eyes. "You get my age, there's not much to lose."

"Shit, gimme a break. You're not that old."

"Well, I'd think you'd give me this much," Dallas said, suddenly coughing down between his knees, suppressing it, glancing toward Christine, trying, it appeared, not to awaken her. "Lungs are the least of my problems."

Layne shook his head and gazed at the sliver of water passing before them, finding something almost hypnotic in its small pulse over the sand.

"Besides," Dallas continued, "I always looked at cigarettes as a form of *in-surance*."

"Okay, I'll bite," Layne said, playing the manly game, responding without looking. "What kind of in-surance?"

"Insurance that something definite, something hard-core and real will kill me," Dallas said, striking a wooden match off the leg seam of his Levi's. "My biggest fear is someday being haul-bagged off the ranch, ending up in a rest home droolin' and pissin' on myself."

"Well, you may have wasted your money then, because the tobacco industry will have to get in line for that job." Layne's retort came a bit too quickly, a little too glibly, and he regretted it.

Dallas glanced at him, then broke into a soft chuckle, looking Christine's way again. "Seems so," he said softly. "But whatever ends up killing me is not my big concern. There's beginnings and endings, and living on that broke-down ranch all my life, I've seen plenty of each." He lowered his voice even further. "Still, quick endings are the way. I would never let an animal suffer, or a man for that matter; in the larger scheme, we're all part of the same herd."

"Hey, I wasn't serious," Layne said. "We're just sitting here passing time, just bullshitting."

"That's right. So don't worry about it." Dallas stood up gingerly and hoisted his rifle. He motioned Layne to follow him. "Let's check downstream, have a look at that trail out."

Layne picked up the pistol belt and, almost as an afterthought, the briefcase, before following Dallas. Christine was still sleeping soundly with her back to them. It was only two or three hundred feet to the point where they had dropped into the canyon, but it seemed longer because they had to wind their way through a twisting corridor of rock, climb over a couple of boulders, and in one particular spot even turn sideways for a few feet where the gray stone walls gathered close and narrow. Earlier, when they had first arrived in the bottom, Dallas and Layne had taken a quick look downstream, below the trailhead. They were quickly stopped by a precipitous drop of at least a hundred feet and could rest assured that, except for the bats and swallows, there was indeed only one way in or out of this canyon.

They stood shoulder to shoulder surveying the tongue of cliff and rubble that led back up toward the rim where they had parked the car. Things couldn't have looked more calm and deserted. A lone turkey buzzard drifted soundlessly high in the canyon, turned, and was gone.

"I don't think that trail is a good idea in the dark," Layne finally said.

"I was thinking the same thing," Dallas replied. "But how about we let Christine sleep just a little longer?"

Layne nodded and placed the pistol belt on a waist-high rock. He tossed the briefcase down next to it. "You know," Layne said, "I haven't even opened that thing since I first read through it with Christine that day up on the ridge behind your ranch. We just scanned parts, read here and there, but I haven't looked at it since."

Dallas sat down on another boulder and leaned against the rock wall, still gazing back up their descent trail. "I haven't either," he said absently, as though it didn't really matter or hadn't occurred to him.

Layne took a seat across from Dallas. "None of us has," Layne said. "That's kind of odd, all things considered, isn't it? I mean, look at where we are, what we've been through," he pointed at the briefcase, "all for that. And that poor Docksteader woman." Layne dropped his eyes. A wave of regret passed through him with such force that he felt nauseous.

"It's terrible," Dallas said, grimacing, "that was a terrible thing. I don't want to dwell on that book of Rudd's; I just want to expose it and that damn test site. We already know what Rudd intended it to be. Others will have to decide whether it holds up in court. Or in the public opinion."

"Well," Layne said, frustration beginning to mount and come through in his voice, "I just hope they get the chance. Seems that some of those *others* have a slightly different agenda for this damn thing." Layne gave the briefcase a shove across the top of the rock, creating an echoing thud as it bumped into the wall.

Dallas took his hat off and rubbed his forehead. He looked up at Layne. "You'll never know just how sorry I am that you got drug into all of this. I certainly never intended it to go this far."

Layne wanted to change the subject, tried to wave him off. "Aw, don't mind me. I'm a big boy. I take responsibility for my own decisions." But he wasn't convinced, wasn't sure how his life got so tipped over, how he got in so far. It had been one step at a time, and he felt foolish that each step always seemed to lead in the wrong direction. He generally prided himself on being a logical fellow, even though a number of his old lawyer buddies from Salt Lake City might dispute that since he had highjacked his life and taken it to southern Utah.

Layne shook his head. "I don't blame you for a minute. Dallas."

"Well, I'd sure understand if you did."

"I'm looking forward at this point, just interested in solving the problem," Layne said. "And right now, or before sunset, I say we get the hell out of here. Once this thing is published in the press, then we just have to hope it's no longer worth killing for."

Layne heard how selfish he sounded. Dallas's troubles weren't over, not by a long shot, even if they got clear of Rudd's book without being tied to it. Dallas still faced a murder charge.

"I'm sorry," he said. "I didn't mean . . ."

"Don't sweat it," Dallas replied. "I know what you meant." He gave Layne a half-smile, taking him off the hook. "And I couldn't agree more. I want you and Chrissy to get free of this. I'm the one who messed things up here."

"Well, anyway, let's take one thing at a time." Layne looked down at his watch. "No one's playing the blame game. You've only done what you felt you needed to do."

Dallas had a handful of pebbles and was aimlessly tossing them one by one a short ways up the scree slope, then watching them roll back down. "You know, counselor, as long as we're just passing time here, there is something that I find kind of curious."

"Yeah?" Layne answered slowly, drawing the word out into a question, his mind immediately coming to attention. He was tired and scared and in no way ready for a heart-to-heart. It certainly was his right, but Layne hoped Dallas wasn't going to delve into the whole Christine thing, ask about his intentions and whatnot.

"You've never really asked me what happened that night," Dallas said without emotion. "You started to in the jail that first day, and you've had plenty of chances since, but you never brought it up again."

"Christine told me the story," Layne answered abruptly and with some relief.

"Christine wasn't there," Dallas replied. "Oh, she was there for a few minutes, but I was there for two, maybe three hours."

Layne hesitated, looking at the ground. "I . . . I'm your lawyer," he said, as if that explained why this conversation gave him pause. Fundamentally, the system was designed to reward winners and punish losers. So what does a litigator, particularly a criminal lawyer, want? The truth? Or a story he can sell to the jury?

"I just presumed that the known facts speak for themselves," Layne said. What he didn't say was that he knew Dallas was protecting Christine and would do so at all costs. Further, he wasn't quite ready down here in this hole in the ground to gear up for all . . . that. To interview his client. Or to satisfy some macabre impulse of his own to see if Dallas really did cut Rudd's throat in cold blood to safeguard his niece. Right now, he preferred to concentrate on one giant mess at a time.

"So what you're telling me is that you don't *really* wanna know everything." A hint of taunting had entered Dallas's voice.

"I want to know."

Both men's heads snapped around in unison. It was Christine. She was standing there in the shadows of the narrow canyon.

She stepped forward. "If you're anxious to tell somebody, how about telling me?"

Dallas's face visibly tightened. "I . . . guess the counselor here was right. The facts speak plain enough for themselves."

"You're up," Layne intruded cheerily. "How was your sleep?" Then he busily gathered his things up off the rock. He felt for Dallas, and they didn't need this right now. It was just over an hour until dark. "Time to go," he said, trying to sound both firm and light.

Christine and Dallas both eyed him narrowly, then seemed to shrug and began preparations for the walk back out.

The trek was uneventful, scrambling uphill in the loose rock and sand was much easier and safer than the precipitous steps down. The physical release of movement seemed to relieve everyone. Dallas and Christine didn't pursue the conversation, though Layne sensed that Christine was not placated and that Dallas would now be forced to talk about that night with her sooner than later.

As they reached the top and crested out onto the desert, Layne handed Christine the briefcase, then unholstered Dallas's old Colt pistol. The gun felt cool and strange in his hand. He had hunted as a kid, as a Boy Scout, but lost interest by college. If the need arose, however, he had no doubt that pulling the trigger on their pursuer would be easy. His aim he was less sure about.

They paused, motionless, scanning the area. Layne and Dallas separated and crept forward, crouching and alert, looking about for any sign of intrusion or danger. Layne moved from juniper to juniper, motioning Christine to stay with him, taking cover where they could. Keeping tabs on Dallas, who traveled parallel and to his left, he continued slowly and in this stealthy way. At the same time, he was struck by how weird this was. Never in his life had he done something like this for real. No wars, no clashes with the law, just a regular life. Now he felt like a kid again, running with the neighbor kids and choosing up sides, playing cops and robbers, cowboys and Indians, as they darted behind the fences, dodged from tree to tree.

Gradually, however, they began to relax. Nothing in the least looked out of place. A refreshing breeze brought a pleasant change from the dead air in the canyon bottom and a few chickadees, excited by the last hour of light, twittered and jumped from branch to branch. The sun was dropping fast now, as if magnetized by the western horizon.

Layne finally saw the shape of the Land Cruiser off in the trees and realized for the first time how safe and welcoming a motor vehicle could be. No disturbances, no signs of danger. He motioned Christine to stay behind, put a hand on her shoulder urging her down even further. He edged toward the Land Cruiser with Dallas ahead of him now. As they approached, Dallas held up his hand, indicating that he wanted Layne to hold it there, to wait and see.

Dallas continued toward the car. As he got to the front of the Cruiser, he bent over and then went down on one knee, examining the ground in front of the car. Quickly, he jumped up with his rifle pointed, turning in all directions, searching, and then Layne heard the shots. They were muffled, really didn't sound like gun shots, but Layne knew that's exactly what they were. Dallas turned, looked back at Christine and Layne with an odd expression—tentative and unprepared—as he slowly sank to the ground. Layne heard an abbreviated scream and spun around. That's when he saw the guy, the one with the black Jag, standing right next to Christine, the barrel of a large, high-tech-looking pistol pressed against the side of her head.

The look of death—vacant and twisted. It was a look most people rarely glimpsed, and in fact, Christine had never actually seen it before now. She had attended her share of funerals, seen good women lose their battle with cancer. She had gazed with real sorrow at the deceased in their calm reposes, lying in their lustrous satin-lined coffins, makeup favorably applied. But she had never witnessed a murder or even been the first to arrive at a violent highway crash where bodies were twisted and broken, dead or dying.

Christine sat with her hands bound behind her back, her ankles strapped together with lengths of red nylon, the same tubular webbing that Dallas had used to drag that tree behind Layne's vehicle when they drove in here this morning. Layne was about ten feet away, hog-tied in the same nylon, tape over his mouth. Christine looked at him, saw that he was trying to console her with his eyes.

She watched as their assailant, Manos—"You can call me Manos, that's my name," he said by way of introduction—now stood casually at the hood of Layne's car and thumbed through Rudd's manuscript, one page at a time, exactly as he had been doing for the last ten minutes, occasionally shaking his head or laughing. It was still light enough to read outside, but wouldn't be for long. The sun had just dipped in the west and a maze of dayglow colors—orange, rose, pale blue, and white—bloomed on the horizon.

Dallas's body was only a few feet away, his face almost squarely down in the dirt, his hands and arms crumpled beneath his torso. He hadn't moved since he went down under the impact of that sudden barrage of bullets fired directly into him. The blood had poured from the upper part of his body, deep red at first and absorbing into the sand, now drying into a tarry black. He looked so uncomfortable lying there in that contorted position. Crying quietly, only the first fragments of her grief being exposed, Christine wanted more than anything to go to him and straighten him out, get his face up, and somehow put him at ease.

"No wonder them dumb bastards from the Federal Building

wanted this." Manos grinned down at her from his reading. "Could be just a *little* embarrassing. I'm sure someone will pay to get their hands on it."

Christine lowered her eyes as he resumed turning the pages. A common thug, she thought; he'd kill just for your shoes.

Christine had watched in shock as Dallas fell to the ground. Layne was told that if he moved even an inch, she would be the next one dead. Layne had hesitated and then tossed the gun aside. After that, this Manos guy gathered them both near the front of the Cruiser, then knelt and checked for Dallas's pulse. Pulling out a long, ominous looking knife with a gleaming blade and carelessly waving it around, he sliced the heavy, one-inch nylon like it was fresh pasta. He had aggressively wrapped Layne's mouth shut with duct tape, taking what seemed like an unnecessary number of turns all the way around his head.

As he did so, he spoke to Christine. "Like I said, call me Manos, Ms. Parker. We can engage in stimulating conversation, and no doubt will. On the other hand, Mister Harting here won't be calling me anything. Or saying anything. Because if he does," he said, bandying the knife around again, "suffice it to say that I've talked to enough hack lawyers to last me the rest of my life."

Everything had happened with intense speed, and yet it had been the longest moment of Christine's life. Dallas shot, gone so suddenly, and then she and Layne were immediately under this monster's control. She sat in silence.

Christine knew that they were going to die, that this asshole could not risk any witnesses surviving. She felt her body and her mind slipping further into shock. It was impossible to tell what Layne must be going through, eyes wide and rolling as he finally ceased the futile struggle against his bonds. Christine couldn't take any more of this, but every time she thought it couldn't get worse, it did. Hell—this was what hell was. Dallas was dead. Uwanda was dead. This guy was going to kill Layne, who, after all, had just been their lawyer. These were the unreconcilable facts, crazy and cruel.

Finally, Manos finished his reading. He placed the manuscript, first taking care to arrange it neatly, back in the briefcase and snapped it shut. He patted its top and left it sitting on the hood of the Land Cruiser. "Well, nice little prize we have here. A fellow should be able to make something of this, I should think. Of course, you dopey do-gooders were just going . . ." He went on speaking, but it all floated away from Christine as her internal voices took over.

Please, don't let this be happening. Don't let Dallas be dead. Why was she here? Why wasn't someone coming to rescue them? Don't kill Layne, don't kill anybody. Oh God, please.

". . . almost got you into the car," he said. "I think you bought my act." He was looking at her strangely, head canted to the side. "Are you listening to me, baby?"

She tried to focus on him, then glanced desperately over at Layne.

"Don't look at him for help," Manos said, a more menacing tone now in his voice. "He's just a spectator at this party."

Christine turned away from Layne, did as she was told. She had no idea why, other than to avoid further provocation.

"The Docksteader broad, now there was a piece of work," he continued.

Christine listened with the heavy, almost nauseated sensation of being drugged. He was saying something about Uwanda? Christine fought for clarity. Why was he talking about her?

"Fat broad. Definitely not my type," he said. "She tried to bite me. I'd a killed her ugly ass just for that. No big, ugly broad bites me."

Christine shook her head. "What . . . ?" she half-slurred. "Why are you saying . . . these things?" She wasn't surprised to hear that he'd killed Uwanda, but what was he doing now?

"I'm just telling you," he said, as he came closer to her, "that I don't like ugly women." He reached down and, with the same knife that he seemed to produce at will, cut her ankle ties, then went behind her and freed her hands. "Get up," he said. He wore the sleek black gun in a shoulder holster.

Standing was difficult. Christine was tired and sore and numb in parts. The blood rushed away from her head in the act of rising, but she quickly stabilized and her head began to clear. She unconsciously rubbed her wrists where they had been tied. The movements, the stirring of her limbs and changing positions, helped her to concentrate.

"Nice," he said, looking her up and down. "Tight little thing, aren't you?"

Christine reflexively took a step back.

"Now, don't you be moving away from me. What's the matter?" he asked, smiling. He advanced one step and watched to see what she would do, then took another step forward, closing the gap between them. "Come on now, baby. You don't want to *fuel* my rage, as they say."

It felt as if his teeth were right in her face. She brought her knee up toward his groin with all the force that she could muster. Her action, firm and aggressive, provided her with the second biggest surprise of the moment. The first was that he completely anticipated it. Turning his leg inward and deflecting her blow, he caught her behind the knee with his hand and dumped her unceremoniously flat on her back in the dirt. Before she could even think about it, he was on top of her, his hand squarely on her crotch, squeezing and jerking his fingers upward, hard into the seam of her pants.

"I like a lady with fight," he said, bunching his fingers and ramming them again hard against her vagina. Then he was off her and standing up. "Get up," he said. "There are other ways to do this. We don't have to roll around like pigs in the dirt."

Christine slowly gathered herself. The fear was overwhelming her, making her feel wild and almost weightless. She had no idea why she'd tried to knee him. It had come without thought or planning, just pure reaction, but it freed something. It showed her another way of resolution here, that she didn't have to be frozen and helpless, that whatever happened, she could go down fighting. Or perhaps it signaled that she didn't care enough anymore.

"Here's the game," he said, as if he could read her mind. He retracted the pistol from its holster, walked over to Layne, and discharged a round into the dirt within a foot of Layne's head. Dirt and pebbles sprayed convulsively. "You get to play too, lawyer boy, you get to watch.

"It's called free bondage," he instructed, leading her to the front of the Land Cruiser. "Stand here, in front of the bumper. That's right. Make yourself comfortable." He holstered the gun. "Here's the deal. No matter what I do, you remain still. If you raise a hand to hit me, I shoot your boyfriend in the hand. If you raise a foot to kick me, I shoot his foot." He watched her closely. "Now pay attention, if I tell you to . . . let's say do this or that with your mouth . . . and you screw it up? Then I shoot lawyer boy here in the mouth. Nod if you understand exactly how it works." He put his hand up to her mouth and ran a finger inside her lips as if he were examining a horse. "Open your mouth, that's it. Wider. Good. This is a little no-bite training for what's to come."

Christine stood there with tears streaming down her cheeks, but she kept her hands absolutely still at her sides, his fingers tasting of cologne, sweat, and dirt. She understood what he meant and she understood that he meant it. Biting him was out of the question now, no matter what he put in her . . . She was sobbing, aware of that fact only by the strange, breathy sound she was emitting.

Then he removed his fingers from her mouth. The knife was back out and before she could assimilate its arc through the air, he had raggedly cut her blouse up the middle, across the shoulders, and down the sleeves until there was only tattered cloth left hanging at her waist and wrists. She got the distinct feeling that he had done this before.

"Not the frilly bras I normally like," he said, lips pursed. "But everything else is nice." Then he languidly brought the knife forward again, set it against her stomach, rubbing the blade back and forth in a mock sharpening motion, working it higher onto her chest. Christine kept her head up, eyes forward. With a brief motion so quick and expert that she couldn't have anticipated it, he cut her bra apart, right in the front. The cups sprung apart. Her whole breast was bare while her falsie, her prosthesis, her funny-looking foam piece, twirled from the bra and fell spinning to the ground.

His smirk vanished. "What . . . the fuck?" he stammered, hurriedly stepping back, half-stumbling over a sagebrush, suddenly awkward and out of control.

His eyes, riveted on her chest, caused her to look down at herself. Everything was just as the doctors had left it.

"Jesus Christ, lady," he half yelled, "who the hell—"

She heard a voice and it took her a moment to recognize it as her own. "You goddamn asshole," she said through her tears, which seemed only to quicken and sharpen her words. She took a step toward him. "What the hell do you think this is?"

"You, you bitch, you . . .," he spat the words at her and scrambled back another step.

"Don't you dare . . .," she screamed, risking another step toward him. "Don't you dare say another word, treat me like . . ."

He pulled the gun from the holster and she stopped. His arm was straight out and rigid as he advanced toward her, the gun pointed right between her eyes, only a couple of feet away. "End of fun and games," he said. "Party's over, lady. That is . . . disgusting."

All Christine could see in that moment was the tiny black hole in the end of the black barrel and all she could hear was an explosion.

As far as Christine knew, the only women who ever fainted were two things—Southern or in the movies—but she learned otherwise. When her eyes first opened, a watery figure was bending over her and she struggled for focus, convinced somehow that she must be in the final, painless stages of dying. She began to regain her senses, however, and could see that it was Layne, covering her chest with a sweatshirt and cradling her head in his hands. Slowly, she began to understand that some time had passed. She attempted to sit up and then became aware of someone else. She heard the soft Texas drawl and saw Mack Sayles, the FBI man, bending over Manos.

"Go ahead and get a shirt on there," he said over his

shoulder toward her and Layne.

"Yes sir. Looks like a fatal shot," he continued saying to Manos's prone body. "Be a shame to have to waste the money on a trial for this. Then you got your appeals, all that time on death row, then you got to listen to your press interviews, scum-celebrities I call 'em, maybe they even write a book. Gawd damn, aren't you all just as tired as I am of all that . . . media nonsense?" He stood up and brushed his hands together. "I'm quite sure he's dead. I did pretty good in marksmanship back at the academy. But we'll give him a few more minutes of free-bleeding to cinch that fact."

Christine was being helped to her feet by Layne. He pulled the sweatshirt over her head and removed pieces of shredded blouse from her waistband. He pulled her to his chest and did his best to console her. She let him comfort her for a moment and then, tentatively, she moved toward Dallas and knelt beside him, Layne following. Her tears had stopped, mostly out of exhaustion. She reached her hand out and rubbed the back of Dallas's head and began trying to turn him. Layne gently assisted.

Mack Sayles seemed to busy himself with other things for a few minutes, but it soon became apparent that he was getting anxious. Christine remained kneeling next to Dallas's body as Layne finally went over to the FBI man. What now? she wondered. Would they be going from nylon bonds to steel handcuffs? Would this never end?

"Sorry as I can be," Mack was saying to Layne.

"Well . . .," Layne seemed to be struggling for thought and speech, "it's us that owes you . . . our lives. Thank you."

"Glad I made it in time. My buddy, Gordo, that's our resident nerd back at the office, figured a way to hone in on the tadpole, in spite of the low battery."

Layne had a puzzled look on his face.

"That's what I put under your car to follow you." Mack scratched something on the side of his neck and looked down. "This guy is a bad one," he said. "Or was a bad one. He won't be bothering anyone now."

Christine could hear them talking and she was relieved that

Manos was dead, that by some miracle, she and Layne had survived. But Dallas . . . She remained at his side as sorrow increasingly overtook her, a sorrow unlike any she had ever felt before, a feeling with terrible weight and substance that might ride there the rest of her life.

"I have to tell you, Mr. Harting—"

"Layne, please call me Layne."

"Sure, Layne," Mack said with no trace of sarcasm. "Look, the support team is due to arrive—you know, the black helicopters and all that—sometime soon." He motioned toward Christine.

She could tell that he wanted her to join them. She stood and walked over beside Layne, listened carefully, and became even more disheartened by what Mack Sayles was saying.

"It's going to get very busy and confusing around here and . . . well, there'll be a lot of young polyester cowboys descending on this place. It'll probably just add more stress to what's already happened." It was almost dark and Mack Sayles peered at them through the twilight.

"But," he said brightly, "we *could* take your statements at a more convenient time." Then with a shrug, "I think I have a pretty good idea about what went on here."

Sayles's eyes seemed to purposefully drift over to the hood of the Land Cruiser and settle on Layne's briefcase. Christine and Layne's eyes followed his gaze until all three of them were looking at the briefcase. An uncomfortable silence ensued.

"And, if you want to motor on out of here, I don't think we need," Mack paused, "any more trouble to come from . . . this thing." He continued to stare at the briefcase.

Christine could feel the temperature rising in her, a sudden anger sweeping from her core—a willingness to carry this all the way to the end. Earlier in the day, even moments ago, she would have surrendered that damn manuscript in a heartbeat just to be rid of it and move on. But all the facts had changed now.

"If you think you can take that," she said to Mack Sayles, "and just push it back under the rug, cover it—"

"Whoa," Mack interrupted her forcefully. "What I'm saying here is . . . and you folks ought to pay strict attention now, is that . . . let's start over." Mack clasped his hands together.

"I'll take care of Mr. Parker here, we'll transport him into St. George, notify you so you can come claim him. Trust me, you two have had enough." Mack smiled directly at her. "Now, and furthermore, I have a real hunch that Parker disposed of Rudd's manuscript by sending it to the press or to some judge or something like that. Are my sources incorrect?"

Christine and Layne were both paying strict attention.

"Well, then," he said, shaking his head at them, "unless someone contradicts me in the matter, that's what I think and that's what my report will reflect."

Christine looked at Layne and back at Mack. Was he telling them what she thought? Could she walk away from Dallas's body like this, not accompany it . . . somewhere? What would Dallas want her to do?

Layne moved to her side, but didn't attempt to make the decision for her. He had a lot to lose in this as well, she quickly realized, if more agents showed up here and found them in possession of that manuscript.

"You're right, Mr. Sayles. Thank—"

"Mack," he interrupted her.

She nodded, tired of speaking.

"Ms. Parker?" he said.

She gazed at him in the receding light, saw a kindly man.

"Your uncle?" He hesitated. "He was a good man. I wish I'd known him better, and in a better time. A damn good man."

Christine struggled. She would not break down again. "Thank you, Mr. . . . Mack," she said, "thank you very much."

"Yeah," he said, "you kids make sure he didn't die in vain. That's all you can do now. If he hadn't mailed that thing off, or whatever, it would just go into some dusty box for another fifty years, never see the light of day. Hell, you know, I'm a citizen just like you. Just like him."

Christine couldn't help herself. In the last moments of the day, as it turned the corner into night, she put her arms around the FBI, around Mack Sayles, and gave him a soft kiss on the cheek. "Thank you, Mack," she whispered, "you have no idea how much that means to me."

"Hell, almighty. You'll embarrass an old man like that." But he was grinning widely. "Well, you got to get going now. Just keep heading east on this track, it'll take you right to the back door of Mesquite and then to the freeway. Just for your information, it probably won't even be me that conducts the follow-up interview."

Layne began to escort Christine to the passenger side of the Land Cruiser in a gentle effort to get moving. She climbed in. He then walked back around to the hood of the car.

Mack was just standing there. "I was scheduled for retirement in a couple of months," he said, "but I decided to take it early. Like next week. So I probably won't be seeing you again."

Christine watched Layne through the windshield as he paused next to the fender, resting his forearm just inches from Rudd's book, seemingly afraid to touch it or even acknowledge it. She couldn't blame him. All the trouble. What if this was just another . . .

"Don't forget your briefcase there, Layne. It is April. You probably got your tax returns in there, all ready to file. Hate to have to come back after you for something like that." He was still smiling, first at Layne and then at Christine, then shooing them away with the back of his hand. Layne snatched the briefcase off the hood and got behind the wheel.

Christine could still hear Mack Sayles's voice through the open window as the Cruiser came to life and Layne settled it into reverse. "And my wife just called me on the cell phone not an hour ago. My little hen won the futurity today, you believe that? First one home from five hundred miles out, twenty thousand dollars. It was such a nice . . . ," until the sound of the engine slowly backing up through the sagebrush finally drowned him out.

DynaFlow

"WHY CAN'T I DRIVE?"

It was just a question, but Uwanda knew that it would prompt the same tidal wave of responses from her mother as it always did.

Vera Docksteader, both hands on the steering wheel of their two-tone—lime and spring green—1952 Buick DynaFlow, glanced over at her daughter, gave her a sympathetic smile, and launched into the excuses that had become as familiar and well worn as an old robe. "As soon as we get . . . It's just too . . . I promise, I'll make the time . . ."

If Antimony, Utah, had been a wide spot in the road, then Mount Dutton, where Uwanda and her mother were now headed, was a blink of the eye, but a family named Zimmer lived there, with a sick boy, and that's why they were going. Right now, though, it was just the two of them on a rutted dirt road stretching toward the horizon without another car or house or even a fence anywhere in sight. Just miles of sage and the big, blank, gray skies of November wrapping all around.

Uwanda found that her mother's aimless conversations, like these roads they traveled, could stretch on forever. Vera, in fact, was still going on about it: "Next week, honey. I promise we'll get you down to St. George to take your driver's test."

Uwanda smirked slightly and stared out the side window, her mood flattening like the dull light of this late afternoon. They could go all over southern Utah to visit other people, but they couldn't take an afternoon out for her. She had been hearing that promise for the past weeks since she'd turned sixteen, celebrating her birthday with a few girlfriends and a slumber party, the highlight being when they put Jackie Conrad's size 32A bra in the freezer and presented it to her the next morning, frozen. Uwanda didn't know if Jackie was ever going to talk to any of them again.

"What's the matter?" her mother smiled kindly, her wiry gray halo of hair half-managed with a couple of bobby pins on one side. "I'm not going fast enough for you?" She made a show of straightening up in her seat and then accelerated. The car responded, though it was almost nine years old now and felt more like a lead bathtub than the powerful family car it once had been. Her father had bought it as a surprise for them during better times. Vera had always wanted a family car so that they wouldn't have to pile out of a truck like a bunch of hillbillies at church or other important functions, but Nate had maintained that anything other than a truck was foolhardy and unreliable. Vera frequently pointed out that it was too bad he hadn't lived to see just how sturdy and dependable his sweet surprise, the Buick DynaFlow, had been.

Uwanda sat there brooding about when or if she'd ever get her driver's license. Her mother had good intentions, of course. It was just that she made so many promises to all sorts of people—often people they didn't know. Even the backseat of the DynaFlow was full of her promises: blankets, boxed canned goods, discount bakery items, plastic graveside wreaths. And stacks of flyers, of course. Vera didn't go anywhere without a hefty supply of those. She absolutely had to spread the word, let people know of the dangers, get people to stand up.

And what did Uwanda and her mother get in return? Purple fingertips—ink off the old mimeograph machine set up in their basement to spit those flyers out night and day, the machine's heavy, rotating wheel sending out a dull "chnk, chnk" that Uwanda was sure she heard even in her sleep.

"Not true," her mother constantly countered. "There's a lot of gratitude from these people, Uwanda. Just look a little harder. And if nothing else, remember . . . we're doing this for your father."

There was always that line, said quietly, almost as an afterthought. Why didn't her mom just heat up the waffle iron and squeeze Uwanda's grubby little heart into it?

Maybe more than anybody else, Uwanda had been totally unprepared when her father, Nate, had died four years ago. Never played another practical joke, never complained again about taxes. Just crumpled over, alone in one of his now empty fields, looking over his bankruptcy papers instead of a thousand head of healthy sheep.

It took two months after the funeral for Vera to completely cry herself out, and then she arrived at some cold, rocky place that truly scared Uwanda. Her mother would stand outside at the clothesline with a basket of wet laundry at her feet, for instance, and she'd talk to the clothes. Uwanda wasn't close enough to hear what Vera was saying, but she could see her mother's hands slicing the air, her head shaking at the clean sheets as they flapped and danced in the wind.

It was more than just the reams of legal documents from bankruptcy court and the required insurance forms that were making Vera angry, though they were bad enough. Court appearances, signatures, notaries—the lawyers, the banks, and the insurance company wanted her, as the sole representative of the estate, to jump through a hundred hoops, and the day she finally received the life insurance check from Sheepman's Mutual written for the sum of ten thousand dollars, she unceremoniously deposited it in the bank. "It'll have to last awhile," she told Uwanda. The land and house were gone, the equipment sold, and they were now renters in a forty-two-dollar-a-month shabby, white clapboard in Cedar City.

Vera was angry at the sheep, too. She admitted that it wasn't entirely rational, but she connected the Docksteaders' bad luck, their devastating financial losses of the previous year and even Nate's death, to these dumb, woolly creatures. He had been wrung dry and worn out last spring burying sheep carcasses and a little bit of himself with each load of dirt. He had tried to keep the ranch intact, worked twice his normal hours, and then in his little spare time, had attempted to get some answers about the fallout they'd encountered on the Nevada winter range and compensation from the government to save the ranch. And if Vera was mad at the sheep, there weren't words to describe how she felt about the Atomic Energy Commission and anyone connected with the Nevada Test Site, which blithely persisted in producing maps, bulletins, and distorted figures backing their denials.

"How stupid do they think we are?" Vera asked that question repeatedly to her family, her friends and neighbors. She sounded like a scratchy record to Uwanda. Some days, her mother stayed in her robe all day long, and some nights she did nothing more than open a can of tomato soup for their dinner, then sit there at the table, listless and far away. First her father and now her mother. Uwanda wondered how much more a twelve-year-old heart could take.

Then in August, a week after school had started, the Mormon elders had come visiting the Docksteaders. Bishop Rayfield, Brothers Barns and Skidmore. Uwanda didn't know the name of the fourth man.

It was late, already dark outside. Vera watched from the window as the men got out of their car. She told Uwanda to answer the door, while she ran to the bathroom to wash the Pond's Cold Cream from her face.

"Sister Docksteader," said the bishop, "is this a bad time for a home visit?"

"Oh . . . no," Vera said. "No, please come in."

"Are you sure?" The bishop presented his palms to her. "Myself, the other elders, we can come back some other time."

"Come in, Bishop Rayfield."

The four men filed quietly through the door and spread themselves around the living room in an uncoordinated circle of cheap aftershaves. They wore ties and dark suits and gave Vera best regards from their wives at home. Bishop Rayfield took his glasses off and slowly cleaned them with a big, dingy white handkerchief, his small sunken eyes squinting in the lamplight.

Brother Skidmore clasped his hands in front of his belt and kept clearing his throat. Vera brought two kitchen chairs into the living room.

From the kitchen table where she returned to her homework, Uwanda watched the entire visitation, head down and peering from the tops of her eyes. She could hear them expressing their well-intentioned concern for the family—did they have enough to eat, money for fuel this winter—while quoting an occasional verse from the Book of Mormon. Then Uwanda heard Bishop Rayfield say something that she never forgot.

"Sister Docksteader. The elders are concerned. In testimonial on Fast Sunday, you made some statements to the congregation . . . about your husband's sad passing." The Bishop paused and glanced into the kitchen. Uwanda quickly looked down, hoping he hadn't noticed her staring.

"Your misfortune has grieved us all, Sister Docksteader. But we feel . . . well, that your statements regarding Brother Docksteader's death, and your other losses are perhaps . . . inappropriate."

Vera kept her eyes on the floor. "There was no need for Nate to have died," she said weakly. "Fallout killed the sheep, wiped out our ranch, killed . . ." She looked up, fidgeted, then cast her eyes back down and went quiet.

"It's such a complicated issue, Sister Docksteader. Just as we must have faith in our church, we must have faith in our country." Bishop Rayfield continued on and Uwanda's mother didn't say another word. When they asked her if she wanted to receive their blessing, she just sat there, choking on her grief or her embarrassment or . . . Uwanda didn't really know. Nor did Vera protest when they gently guided her to the center of the room and sat her down on a kitchen chair.

With stern faces, the four men gathered round, standing over her, reminding her of her obligations: family, church, country.

"You're tired," one told her.

"We'll get some of the sisters to come by and help with the house," said another. Jackets off, in their wrinkled white shirts and thinning hair slicked back with Vitalis, the patriarchy gathered closer around.

Vera fell into silent weeping, simply staring and twisting at the folds of her dress covering her knees. Uwanda squirmed at the kitchen table and tried to concentrate on her math book, though fractions seemed to have no place in the world at that moment.

Then the elders reached out and laid their hands upon Vera's head, stacked up, Uwanda thought, like so many pink pancakes, until Brother Skidmore finally moved his down to her mother's shoulders. They prayed for her and blessed her. "Sister Docksteader . . ." They must have repeated her name ten or twenty times, mumbling over one another, as if they were imploring Vera as much as they were God. Finally, having exhausted themselves, they said good night and shuffled out to their car.

Vera never spoke directly about the incident, but she and Uwanda began missing church occasionally and then frequently, Vera making vague excuses—she felt like she might be getting a cold, it looked like it might rain. Within a few months, their Sundays no longer belonged to the Mormon Church, but rather to the Buick, which was loaded up so that they could go visit the sore and afflicted. Vera said no God that she knew would want it any other way.

Just as water seeks its own level, Vera needed to be with people who understood, who were carrying around the same sadness, shock, and outrage as she. People, like the Zimmers, who might want to be comforted, just as she had craved such comfort.

The Buick's heater fan had a small ding and made a steady ticking noise, but it kept the vast interior of the car warm and comforting. Vera reached forward and turned on the headlights.

Nothing would ever be the same again for the Zimmers. Their seven-year-old was sick—dying, the doctors told them. Acute leukemia. He had been such a normal kid, out running with his puppy and dutifully feeding his four rabbits, but then came the nosebleeds, the fact that he just wouldn't eat. As ranchers on the high, cool plateau of central Utah, the Zimmers didn't have the money for doctors, let alone specialists, but they drove to Salt Lake anyway, borrowed money for the transfusions and medication, which only helped their son temporarily. He was bedridden now, just a pale whisper beneath the cotton quilts and blankets. His family—exhausted, heartbroken—had finally brought him home to die.

"I don't want to see him. Okay?" Uwanda said. She would help. She would be her mother's companion. She would tote and carry, tell these people how sorry she was. She would cook and clean and babysit, but she didn't want to sit in a room with the dying.

Vera scowled over at Uwanda and shook her head. "Okay," she said, "but I just hope everyone doesn't feel that way when you get ready to . . ." Vera quietly turned on the windshield wipers. The darkening sky had doubled down, turned miserable, and was spitting a cold, wet slosh that was somewhere between rain and snow.

Not being here with her mother had never been an option for Uwanda. When Vera had first taken to the road—wanting to help, needing to change things—Uwanda had been in the sixth grade, too young to sit home alone, her mother said. Uwanda hadn't possessed the artillery to fight her then, and now she didn't have the heart to use it.

"The important thing is just that we see the Zimmers," said her mother, "let them know that somebody cares. Listen to them." Vera shook her head. "I can't imagine how hard it would be to lose a child. Like that. Senselessly. For no good reason whatsoever."

And so it had gone for Uwanda and her mother over the last four years. Word got around. It came to the point that Vera would even receive occasional anonymous calls from someone she thought must surely be a sympathetic AEC monitor. "Injuries reported, up here, and over there." Click.

Then off they'd go, up to the tiny mining town of Tempiute, Nevada, to see postmistress Anne Bangeter and two young girls, Thesis Dweard and Sue Ann Jones, each reporting burns, severe headaches, nausea, and vomiting, each finally succumbing to cancer. Or over to Kanab, Utah, to visit Marjorie Lewallen, who was lying in bed with her tongue so swollen she couldn't speak, could barely breathe. To Lemuel Braithwaite's out on the Paria where he ran his cattle, where he looked up as one of the clouds passed over and was burned so badly on the face and eyes and even up under his hat that they considered skin grafts, but he went blind and died first. Or off to Lilly Pender's in Veyo, Utah; she had walked bare-legged through their alfalfa fields at ten in the morning after an atomic test and sustained burns and permanent scarring on her extremities, and by the next year had taken to bed, her bones so brittle she couldn't risk the stairs. And over to St. George, to console Nancy Young, who was to be married next month, who was combing her elegant, raven black hair when it began coming out in clumps, leaving her bald within a week.

All of these were sturdy, rural people. Self-reliant. They didn't jump on bandwagons, but the statistics became too odd and alarming. Among the tiny communities of Koosharem, Sevier, and Antimony, there were seven children with confirmed cases of leukemia. Four of them already dead. At first, nobody, including some of the country doctors, had ever heard of leukemia out here, and certainly nobody wanted to believe that their government could in some way be causing such sickness.

"Why don't you wipe the windows for me, honey?" Vera was straining now to see through the fogged-up windshield. The car was warm as toast, but their breath still condensed on the glass. She had slowed the Buick to around twenty miles an hour so that it felt like they were only creeping through the soggy twilight. A strong wind was blowing from the north, making the sleet come at them at an angle.

Uwanda reached over and rubbed a clear circle for her mother to see out. "Mom," she said hesitantly, "this doesn't look like it's going to let up."

"Well, then, neither are we," Vera said. "The Zimmers are

waiting for us. And I'm sure they don't get visitors that often out here." It seemed to Uwanda that her mother had developed an unrealistic blind faith in their old Buick.

"We're not party poopers, are we?" Vera asked.

"Huh!" Uwanda made a face. "It's not exactly a party we're going to."

"No, you're right," Vera said, a discernible sadness entering her voice like drifting smoke.

Vera's hands and heart went out to all the people unfairly hurt by these atomic tests, but Uwanda knew that it was really the sick children who got to her. They were bone-thin, without color, just wasting away. And it wasn't only leukemia. There were all different kinds of cancer. Worse yet, sicknesses that the doctors couldn't even identify: bones deteriorating, organs shutting down. Then there were the newborn children and their deformities. A little boy down in Colorado City with a gaping hole in his face. Two more in the same town with serious spinal oddities. North, in Parowan, a brother and sister born two years apart, both of them with huge, misshapen heads. On one block in Cedar City, four retarded children. And there were plenty who didn't even get born—miscarriages that Uwanda, of course, didn't see but she heard the descriptions. Not remotely human babies, but things that looked like, in the words of one doctor, a tangle of roots, an odd bunch of grapes.

There was a box full of pinwheels in the backseat of the DynaFlow and they were specifically for the children's graves. Vera said there was nothing sadder than those plain little unadorned headstones scattered across the lonely, windswept graveyards.

The temperature was falling, and the snow was in earnest now. A layer of slush had turned the dirt road slick and the back end of the Buick was slipping sideways occasionally. There was a low, dull sound as Vera geared the car down into second.

"You be my extra set of eyes," she told Uwanda.

The driver's handbook wasn't really specific, Uwanda thought, but it stressed the term "sensible and prudent," which in her estimation this was not. "How much farther?" she asked.

"Not far," her mother answered, but then she would have replied the same had they been headed for China.

Byron Zimmer was a tall, thin man who had caught a glimpse of their headlights and come out to stand on his porch, totally amazed that these two had actually dared the road in this weather. He took a quick inventory of them as they hurried to the porch and then smiled. "We sure do appreciate you comin'." He might have been a younger man, but he didn't look it to Uwanda, the weariness and grief of his household having settled around his eyes and mouth, bowing his shoulders. "Didn't think you'd make it tonight. No way."

"It's the Buick," Uwanda's mother told him. "No bravery on our part," she laughed. She put her arm around her daughter and the two followed Mr. Zimmer into the house.

Later, maybe it was people like Mr. Zimmer who started the talk, after they had buried his boy, of course, and he had a chance to work himself partway back to normal. The talk was always of this green Buick, and of this woman and her daughter who showed up at every mining camp, on any ranch, down the most desolate parts of the Arizona Strip. Every time someone got sick. Every time someone was buried. As stories go, are told and retold, it was the Buick, the DynaFlow, right until Vera's death from pneumonia in 1969, that kept moving on: it had 350,000 miles on it, never needed gas, topped Skinner's Pass in a blizzard, carried Joel Picket off Boulder Mountain and down Hell's Backbone after a runaway log crushed both legs and his pelvis. Or the time it got caught in a gully-washer on the East Fork of the Virgin near Orderville, floated down to Glendale, and kept on floating clear to Mt. Carmel Junction where, with the engine still running, it put out again.

Mushroom clouds, the spirits of dead children, green Buicks. That's what Vera Docksteader always knew they would do: float, until they put out again.

Epilogue

TIME CAN BE RIGID AND UNFORGIVING, STRETCHING FROM here to infinity. For Christine, that's the way it felt at first, all those hours of making arrangements and long distance telephone calls, then meeting her grief-stricken parents and siblings as they stormed St. George, and finally holding herself steady through the short, private service for Dallas. Days passed, however, then a week, then two, and slowly Christine could feel the change: time curving, bending, softening. Her family had gone home and now everything and everyone seemed to be drifting back to a state of normalcy, not the same as it was before, of course. With all that they had been through and with Dallas gone now, the world simply could never be the same place again. Nevertheless, there were more and more lapses during which food and sunlight, music and sweeping the floor took on undeniable pleasure for Christine. And there was Layne, of course, through it all, quiet and supportive, insisting that she come to Saraville, stay with him, get through the tail end of this nightmare.

Now, one month later, she could see that he had been leading her here to this twilight unfolding around his grassy backyard, leading her gently to. . . a celebration. There could be no other word for it. And it was definitely time, Christine thought as she sat firmly in the middle of all the noise and activity. Faye's kids had teamed with some neighbors for a game of baseball in Layne's horse pasture, and good old Roy,

Faye's husband, was umpiring and keeping the peace and trying to help the little ones get a hit. There was the sweet smell of burning hickory chips from the barbecue and the cool, damp luxury of grass under Christine's bare feet.

The back screen door banged shut and Trevor came bustling out and set down some mismatched wine glasses. He looked over at Christine in animated disapproval. "Obviously, your friend here doesn't own a full set of anything."

Christine raised an eyebrow, gently rocking in her lawn chair. "Trust me, he does where it counts." She smiled wickedly at Layne, who just shook his head and took another sip of beer.

Then she surprised everyone, most of all herself, by saying, "If anyone here is missing a full set . . ." She stopped and smiled benignly, content to let them finish her point.

"There's nothing missing," Layne said, without missing a beat, "not where it matters."

Trevor was less prepared and stared at Christine in a rare loss for words as Faye walked up to him, looped her arm over his shoulder and said, "Hey, those glasses are better than what you'll find at my house. Dead pacifiers and Mickey Mouse sippy cups."

Christine had discussed her breast cancer openly with Faye, refusing to be ashamed or embarrassed. Perhaps a St. George women's group lay in her future; perhaps she would try helping others the way her old friend Gwynn had helped her. The way Uwanda had tried to help them all.

Over by the fence, a tiny lion roared, fell to the grass and somersaulted, then stood and bowed for the makeshift audience on the lawn. Christine clapped loudly, though for the life of her she couldn't tell if the child she was looking at was a girl or boy: short floppy blond hair, Osh Kosh overalls, a big semi-toothless smile. Layne put his fingers to his mouth and whistled loud enough for the next county to hear. Faye rolled her eyes and walked over to her offspring. "Okay. Enough. You go on and play with the others."

The others. There were six Barlows—seven if you counted their father, Roy. Add the neighbor kids, whose names Christine didn't yet know, and you had the makings of a small riot out in the pasture. There had already been one child injured with a bat, several disputed calls, and a hearty round of name-calling. Peacemaker and burly coach Roy was out there waving his arms, attempting to keep the game in progress.

Layne's whistle must have brought Limbo and Rawley up from the river, because they suddenly appeared, ran into the middle of the ball game and shook, scattering kids and spraying water on everyone at home plate.

Faye sat tiredly in a lawn chair next to Christine's. "I swear, if I had it to do all over again, I might opt for a nunnery in India."

Christine patted Faye's pudgy arm. "Not me," she said. "I'll take this normal backyard routine any day of the week."

"You haven't been here long enough," Faye said. "After I turn you into my ace babysitter, you'll be begging for my supply of Valium." She glanced over at Layne, then back at Christine. "Oh, but I forgot. You two have your own special forms of entertainment." She giggled at herself.

"You guys," Trevor shook his head, walking back up the steps and into the house, "are all a bit wacko tonight."

Layne smiled and raised his beer bottle. "If this is wacky, sign me up."

Faye leaned farther toward Christine. "Welcome to the neighborhood, honey."

Though Christine had known Faye for only a month, a firm alliance had already formed between them. From the outside, they appeared to have little in common, but they had met each other during the same pocket of grief, each losing a family member within the same week. Perhaps that was the initial bond between them, but Christine also found myriad qualities in Faye that she thoroughly enjoyed: humor, a blunt intelligence, a willingness not to take herself or anybody else too seriously. Life-sustaining qualities, Christine thought. And the more she watched and listened to Faye, the stronger the resemblance to Uwanda grew. Of course, Faye would have denied being much like her cousin, but there was a definite genetic similarity—not just in the size of their bodies, but also in the size of their hearts.

"Who needs Valium when you've got wine?" Trevor said, letting the screen door slam behind him, lifting a bottle with a glossy label and showily presenting it all around. "Royal Oaks Cabernet, 1992." He began to uncork it.

Christine didn't need Valium; she just needed Layne. For the first couple of weeks, her pain and loss had been so deep that she had found herself unable to speak at times. Somehow, Layne understood these symptoms, had ushered her into his school house, given her a tour, showed her how to light his old gas stove so she could make a pot of tea. To avoid the strain of making any big decisions about their romance, both of them behaved as though this living arrangement were merely convenient and temporary. Layne cleared spots in the closet and bathroom cabinet for her things and allowed her plenty of other space to deal with her grief.

The one thing she didn't fully understand was how she could be hurting so much for Dallas, and for what had happened to Uwanda, and still be so . . . ravenous. It was a strange confluence of feelings, and yet, they didn't exclude each other. What Christine did understand was that she was fully in love, and though that fact might have scared her at some other point in her life, she embraced it calmly now, accepted it like the weather—large and simply unavoidable.

"I hope the vintage meets with your approval," Trevor said in his best wine steward's voice. He glanced up. "Well, I guess it won't meet with yours, will it, Faye? Still subscribing to the local idiosyncrasies?" The cork came out of the bottle with a short pop.

Faye put a hand on her hip and gave him the raspberry. "Oh, and aren't *you* just the fine one to talk about idiosyncrasy." She bent forward in her chair to get a closer look. "Oh, pour me a dot of that and hush up. I mean, after all, it is just old grape juice."

Out in the pasture, Roy had taken over the pitching, was lofting big soft throws that even the smallest batters could occasionally knock.

"Roy's great with those kids." Layne nodded at the game. "He's a good guy."

Faye squinted toward the pasture. "Yeah, just as long as you feed him right and don't expect much in the way of conversation." The others laughed. "No, no," she waved her hand, "Roy's my boy. We're seventeen years together. Now doing eighteen to life . . . more if you count the afterlife," she said, shooting a mocking look at Trevor.

Layne turned around from where he had gone to check the barbecue, a stream of smoke over his left shoulder. "Right now, the score's ten to zip, favor of the ladies." He pointed a spatula at Trevor, "Never seen you quite this far back on your heels, pal."

Trevor, passing out the wine, gave Layne an injured look. "I've been saving this bottle of wine for a special occasion. Some thanks I get."

One of the myriad Barlow kids approached them dejectedly. Faye quickly slid her wine glass down and behind her.

"Mom, Sam says I'm no good. He doesn't want me to be on his team anymore." The boy tossed his mitt onto the grass to display his point.

"Piddle!" Faye said. "Sam's not running the game out there. Besides, it's a school night. Time for baths. Tell your dad I said so."

The boy wandered back to the game even more dejectedly, and not long after, the gang began to zigzag noisily through the field toward the Barlow back door, Rawley and Limbo chasing first one kid and then another. In a few minutes, they were gone, serenity and purplish air settling over the pasture.

Christine watched as Layne left the chicken to smolder on the barbecue and rejoined the circle. Trevor was sitting down now. "Thanks for the nice bottle of wine, Trevor," she said, raising her glass in a spontaneous toast. But words suddenly failed her. She held her glass suspended for a long moment, looking over at Layne to see if he was still in the rescue business, then quietly took a sip of wine.

To Christine's mind, it was Joseph Attencio who had come up with the right words: "The price of justice was simply too high." Three weeks ago, he had stood up in the St. George Pioneer Hall amidst Uwanda's packed funeral and slowly delivered her eulogy. He started to speak, then stopped to gather himself and began again. *Reflection, truth, dedication: these are the elements that comprise a well-lived life.* Of course, Uwanda never would have approved of a funeral, per se. Her husband Van had been a trooper and with Faye's help they put together a service with no mention of God or other patriarchs. Music was provided by two old hippies, the Hafen Brothers on accordion and fiddle, playing slow and soothing melodies that still had some life to them. Uwanda's daughter Shelby seemed to have the most difficulty coping, and according to Faye, had started wearing Uwanda's old Birkenstocks, was practically inseparable from them.

After the funeral, Christine, Layne and Attencio had huddled outside under a vine-covered arbor, and in his deep, weary voice, Attencio assured them that the privilege of confidentiality was fully intact, and no one was ever going to know about their part with the manuscript. Not from him.

"FBI's already questioned us once," Layne said, under the shady alcove. "We were able to play dumb," he winced skyward, "and lay it all on Dallas." Christine kept her eyes riveted on the ground.

Attencio nodded. "You can expect another interview or two, but you just stay with your line. There's no fire to find more bad guys."

Since then, he had kept them updated via the telephone. It looked as if the downwinders were finally going to be vindicated; the judge had granted plaintiff's motion for an extended continuance and declared that he was taking the case under advisement until everything could be sorted out. In the meantime, representatives from the attorney general's office in Washington, D. C. were summoned and personally directed by the court to begin a full-scale investigation of Chief Deputy Jillian Fetch and her friend R. C. Hiney for obstruction of justice and for engaging this Manos character. Most recently, just two days ago and after ample scrutiny by the court, Rudd's manuscript had been ruled admissible and the government's immunity waived on the basis of demonstrable fraud and deceit.

"Looks like the government finally got caught with its pants down," Attencio had uncharacteristically put it, calling from Las Vegas yesterday, "and you can bet they don't like a public viewing of their bare behind. I can almost hear Uwanda whooping and hollering somewhere up there in protester's heaven."

Christine kept telling herself that at least Uwanda and Dallas would have been happy with the unfolding of each new event. It was some small consolation. Other than that, she spent her time sitting on Layne's porch or feeding his horses or meandering around the healing green of his yard while eavesdropping on the Barlow children as they bounced on their backyard trampoline and pondered what had happened to their mother's cousin, Uwanda.

"She croaked, stupid. She's dead. She's worm meat."

"Nuh uh. The angels took her and she's in heaven."

"In heaven you don't have to do dishes or clean your room or nothin'."

"They drain your blood, do-do. Then they pump you back up with air or jello or something. Sometimes you explode."

Christine wavered between laughter and nausea during these conversations, but the innocent bantering quickly pared her thoughts to their core. Uncle Dallas—he was dead. He was gone. They'd had a wake for him. Christine's family from Phoenix and a few other friends, sat around the old stained table out at the ranch, told each other their stories, hugged and cried and laughed. Dallas's body had already been cremated, according to his instructions, his ashes handed back in a garish urn provided by the mortuary. Bolstered with bourbon during the wake, Layne said he couldn't stand looking at that "horrible vase" any longer and transferred the remains into one of the pouches of Dallas's old leather saddlebags. And that's where they now sat, in Layne's house, draped over the back of a chair waiting for her.

A couple of days after the wake, Layne produced Dallas's will. It was over a year old and Layne had been the lawyer, but never once hinted about it to Christine until the appropriate moment. Dallas left all his personal possessions to her, and the ranch to the three Parker children with Christine as executor. A neighbor was being paid to oversee things out at Motoqua, but soon Christine and her siblings would have to make some decisions. She had already decided that she would never sell Wasco and the young mare that Dallas had found so promising. Beyond that, they'd just have to see.

Layne was back at the barbecue turning the chicken one more time. "Almost ready, folks." Somebody made a wisecrack and everyone laughed. Christine looked wistfully around and thought that Dallas would have gotten a real kick out of Faye and Trevor. She knew that's the way life would be now, to some greater or lesser extent—her measuring the world with Dallas's yardstick.

Her thoughts drifted farther away from the group and into tomorrow. The day would undoubtedly have the outward appearance of any other day—sunshine, soft wind, a lazy sense of time carried in the shadows—but tomorrow would be different. Up at dawn, she would gather Dallas's saddlebags and drive out to Motoqua. More than once, Layne had offered to come along with her, but she had demurred. This was hers to do alone. She had no idea exactly what she would do, how she would spread his ashes or even where. All of that would happen spontaneously when the time came; all of the sweetness and memories bound with that place would guide her, something would speak to her. She hoped it would be Dallas. She had so many questions for him and wanted to tell him the things she had not said that last day. And if Dallas's voice didn't arrive, there would be the gentle tapping of the screen door in the wind, the murmur of the cottonwood leaves, and her own voice, softening, repeating the things Dallas had already taught her, including the fragile, elusive words needed to find her own forgiveness.

Afterword

AFTER MORE THAN FORTY YEARS OF DENIALS, THE UNITED States government finally acknowledged the damage done to civilians downwind of the Nevada Test Site. Congress created the Radiation Exposure Compensation Act together with other acts and amendments in the 1990s. Albeit an imperfect solution with rigid standards, it was supposed to be something of a vindication for victims.

As of 2001, however, the Act offers little consolation to those meant to benefit from it. Loss of official records, nearly impossible criteria for qualification, and lack of funding by Congress have relegated the R.E.C.A. to little more than headlines and publicity for a few politicians. Without funding behind the Act, Congress has been issuing I.O.U.s to sick downwinders, many of whom will never live to collect their compensation—or as many victims refer to it—"con-pensation."

The fight to gain full disclosure of governmental activities knowingly harmful to innocent citizens continues. The Clinton Administration, through the office of then Energy Secretary Hazel O'Leary, began the lengthy process of declassifying certain materials from the Cold War era. This declassification is yielding much new and incriminating information. For example: The AEC consistently concealed off-site fallout levels from the Nevada Test Site which it knew to be dangerous. The AEC concealed more than twenty percent of the nuclear tests at the Nevada Test Site. The military purposefully exposed soldiers to unacceptable levels of radiation during testing in Nevada; Oak Ridge, Tennessee; and Dugway, Utah, while assuring them there was no harm. Radioactive releases in large quantities were carried out, deliberately and secretly, by the military and the AEC at Hanford, Oak Ridge, Los Alamos and Dugway, to study fallout on the general population. The AEC and other agencies, employing doctors sworn to their Hippocratic oath, knowingly conducted over eight hundred radiation tests on humans (mental patients, unwed pregnant girls, prisoners, indigents, African-Americans, and others) in the 1940s and 1950s. Energy Secretary O'Leary finally declared of the declassified materials, "I looked at the history of the Energy Department with the downwinders. It doesn't occur to me that is the posture I want to be in."

But not everyone, even at this late date, would agree. The Nevada Test Site has now been given the new subtitle, "An Environmental Research Park," where anyone with a minimal security clearance can sign up for a day tour. There you load onto a bus and a friendly guide, perhaps a retired patriot in a red baseball cap, will show you the new facilities—a low-level radioactive waste storage site, a chemical release test area available to private industry. Then the guide will tell you, secretly and hopefully, that preparations for more atomic testing, probably underground, are ongoing, that money is being spent daily to keep all the mechanisms in place. During the course of the tour, the guide will also take you through the remnants of their windswept atomic museum: Yucca Flat, Frenchman's Flat, Doomtown, a bank vault, a parking garage, motel row. Somewhere, later in this day, the guide will wax nostalgic and talk about the good old days at the test site, will even offer you and the others on the bus a chance at a pop quiz: What is the biggest single source of radiation? You might wonder if it's Yucca Flat or the tires on the bus. Then he will beam and tell you, "It's the sun." And you might recall a time when the AEC actually proposed that their standard unit of measurement for fallout be designated in "sunshine units." Back in the fifties, back in that time of incredible innocence, the AEC told all of us, particularly in Utah, "There is no danger; it's just like the sun."

And then you are left to ponder the extent to which the past informs the future and what lessons, given who we are, any of this finally has to offer.

The authors at their home in Boulder, Utah

Dianne Nelson Oberhansly was born on a homestead nine miles from the Nevada Border near Motoqua, Utah. She won the 1992 Flannery O'Connor Award for her collection of short stories, *A Brief History of Male Nudes in America.* Curtis Oberhansly is an inactive Utah lawyer and an active Utah outdoorsman. They live in Salt Lake City and Boulder, Utah.